FIGHTING JACOB - DISCREET

SHANDI BOYES

Edited by
MOUNTAINS WANTED PUBLISHING

Illustrated by
SSB DESIGNS

COPYRIGHT

Play List

"I can't fall in love without you." — **Zara Larsson.**

"I hate u, I love u." — **Gnash & Olivia O'Brien.**

"This Town." — **Niall Horan.**

"Be Alright." — **Dean Lewis.**

"I'm so tired." — **Lauv, Troye Sivan.**

"I won't Give Up." — **Jason Mraz.**

ALSO BY SHANDI BOYES

Perception Series

Saving Noah (Noah & Emily)

Fighting Jacob (Jacob & Lola)

Taming Nick (Nick & Jenni)

Redeeming Slater (Slater and Kylie)

Saving Emily (Noah & Emily - Novella)

Wrapped Up with Rise Up (Perception Novella - should be read after the
Bound Series)

Enigma

Enigma (Isaac & Isabelle #1)

Unraveling an Enigma (Isaac & Isabelle #2)

Enigma The Mystery Unmasked (Isaac & Isabelle #3)

Enigma: The Final Chapter (Isaac & Isabelle #4)

Beneath The Secrets (Hugo & Ava #1)

Beneath The Sheets (Hugo & Ava #2)

Spy Thy Neighbor (Hunter & Paige)

The Opposite Effect (Brax & Clara)

I Married a Mob Boss (Rico & Blaire)

Second Shot (Hawke & Gemma)

The Way We Are (Ryan & Savannah #1)

The Way We Were (Ryan & Savannah #2)

Sugar and Spice (Cormack & Harlow)

Lady In Waiting (Regan & Alex #1)

Man in Queue (Regan & Alex #2)

Couple on Hold(Regan & Alex #3)

Enigma: The Wedding (Isaac and Isabelle)

Silent Vigilante (Brandon and Melody #1)

Hushed Guardian (Brandon & Melody #2)

Quiet Protector (Brandon & Melody #3)

Enigma: An Isaac Retelling

Twisted Lies (Jae & JR)

Bound Series

Chains (Marcus & Cleo #1)

Links(Marcus & Cleo #2)

Bound(Marcus & Cleo #3)

Restrain(Marcus & Cleo #4)

The Misfits (Dexter & Megan)

Russian Mob Chronicles

Nikolai: A Mafia Prince Romance (Nikolai & Justine #1)

Nikolai: Taking Back What's Mine (Nikolai & Justine #2)

Nikolai: What's Left of Me(Nikolai & Justine #3)

Nikolai: Mine to Protect(Nikolai & Justine #4)

Asher: My Russian Revenge (Asher & Zariah)

Nikolai: Through the Devil's Eyes(Nikolai & Justine #5)

Trey (Trey & K)

K: A Trey Sequel

<u>**The Italian Cartel**</u>

Dimitri

Roxanne

Reign

Mafia Ties (Novella)

Maddox

Demi

Rocco

Clover

Smith

<u>**RomCom Standalones**</u>

Just Playin' (Elvis & Willow)

<u>Ain't Happenin'</u> (Lorenzo & Skylar)

<u>The Drop Zone</u> (Colby & Jamie)

Very Unlikely (Brand New Couple)

False Start (Cash & McKayla)

<u>**Short Stories**</u>

Christmas Trio (Wesley, Andrew & Mallory -- short story)

Falling For A Stranger (Short Story)

<u>**One Night Only**</u>

Hotshot Boss (Octavia & Jack)

Hotshot Neighbour (Jess & Caleb)

<u>**The Bobrov Bratva**</u>

Wicked Intentions (Katie & Ghost)

Sinful Intentions (Alek & Ana)

Devious Intentions (Yev & ??)

WANT TO STAY IN TOUCH?

Facebook: facebook.com/authorshandi

Instagram: instagram.com/authorshandi

Email: authorshandi@gmail.com

Reader's Group: bit.ly/ShandiBookBabes

Website: authorshandi.com

Newsletter: https://www.subscribepage.com/AuthorShandi

CHAPTER ONE

JACOB

I'm sitting in my Dodge Charger at a T intersection, waiting for the light to turn green when a pair of stunning legs catches my eye. I can't see much of the hot mess cursing at the bus schedule tacked to a pole near the bus stop, but her scarcely concealed thighs are sparking enough interest out of me to offer a stranger a ride home. Her legs are intensely hot, and I've always been a legs man—especially when there's a possibility of them being curled around my head.

"Do you need a lift?"

When she peers past the pole, a grin curls on my lips. She's a fucking stunner. Curly caramel hair, a straight, although slightly curved-at-the-tip nose, and lips that have my cock notching up as high as my pulse. Add those features to the mischievous glint in her eyes, and I'm confident she isn't standing at a bus stop this late at night for virtuous reasons.

After cocking her brow, the sassy blonde drags her teeth over her bottom lip. Her hot pink lipstick is the same color as her halter-neck top. It's sparkly and glossy, as dazzling as the stars filling the almost midnight sky.

When she notices my perusal of her body, her hellion insides shine, freeing me to say, "I don't bite... *much*."

With a wink that exposes she heard my mumbled comment, her eyes stray back to the bus schedule. If she's looking for a way out of a conversation, she's shit out of luck. The last bus left nearly ten minutes ago. How do I know this? I've been a Ravenshoe local all my life. Before I got my license, I knew the bus schedule as intimately as the back of my hand.

I glance into my rearview mirror when a honk bellows through the somewhat quiet night. The old geezer sitting behind me is unimpressed I've ignored the traffic lights' switch to green. I noticed its change, but I'm not going anywhere until the blonde bombshell answers my question. A wink isn't a yes, but it isn't a straight-up "no" either. Furthermore, there's plenty of space for him to go around; he just needs to stop sniffing my keister to figure it out.

When he honks again, my foot gets friendly with my accelerator. I smirk when my revs startle him enough to stop riding my ass. He reverses before skidding past me like he's outrunning cooties.

Grinning in victory, my gaze floats back to the hot mess at my side. Her eyes are bouncing between me and the tire marks the car behind me left on the road surface. I assume my lack of respect will have her backing away with her hands held in the air, so you can imagine my surprise when she mumbles, "All right," before rounding my hood and slipping into the passenger seat.

She mumbles an address in a town I've only heard of once before fixing her seat belt into place. I take a few moments to relish her floral scent before my foot becomes chummy with the gas pedal. As I weave between the traffic of my hometown, from the corner of my eye, I stalk my new companion. Her pupils are the size of dinner plates, but the seductive curl of her lips reveals she loves the adrenaline she's getting from my speed.

Her smile has me pushing my car to its absolute limit. I go way over the designated speed limit, making the cars surrounding us blur like her off-the-scales sexiness is blurring my mind. Most blonde bombshells have the standard blue-eyes combination. This girl throws those statistics out of the park. Her eyes are a light brown, as gleaming as the exposed skin high on her thighs. Her sexiness slams into you, meaning she won't just leave you breathless; you'll have drool pooling in the corner of your lips as well.

When an upcoming traffic light turns red, we grind to a halt. With a slanted head and my interest unconcealed , I introduce myself. "Jacob. Nice to meet you...?"

Her nose crinkles at my pathetic attempt to ignite a conversation, but she plays along. "Lola."

Why am I not surprised her name is as seductive as her face? Probably because everything about this girl is dynamite. Her voice... if I wouldn't have her looking at me like a creep, I'd tug on my dick, begging for it to calm down. I offered her a ride home, not a ride on my cock.

I'm known for getting a little friendly too quickly with the oppo-site sex, but this is different. For one, Lola isn't fawning over me, begging for my attention. If I hadn't caught the occasional glance my way beneath thick lashes, I'd be worried she didn't like what she sees. Two, she gives off a vibe she isn't to be messed with.

That makes me even more interested.

I love girls with sassy tongues and strong backbones. They usually have that whip-smart edginess that keeps things interesting. The thrill of the chase is always exciting, but once it fizzles, so does my interest. I don't see that being an issue with Lola.

When the light switches to green, I stop scanning Lola's too-hot-to-handle body to return my eyes to her face. She shoots me a flirty look, making me aware she saw my scan of her body, but she's not bothered by it.

One point for Jacob!

I plant my foot on the gas pedal but don't floor it like I did earlier. I need a few more minutes to ensure I'm picking up the right signals from Lola. I'm not a pro at understanding the signs women regularly throw out, but I've learned a few tricks in my almost twenty-two years on this planet. Such as, she isn't biting her lower lip because she is nervous—she's teasing me, knowing I'd give anything to replace her teeth with my own, and the faint press of her thighs isn't solely due to the healthy rumble of my engine. She feels the chemistry brewing between us just like I do.

After taking a left down a familiar street, my eyes stray from the road to Lola. "What were you doing in Ravenshoe this late at night? You're not here for the clubs because those aren't dancing shoes." I quickly drop my eyes to her sexy-ass shoes before returning them to the road. "And you're not drunk because you don't have the slightest gleam in your eyes." *Except for the one that exposes your hellion insides.* "So why are you here so late on a Saturday night? You weren't on a date, were ya?"

Please say no. Please say no.

"If I was, would your offer of a ride home become null and void?"

"Not at all." My eyes stray from the road to her. "I'd simply ask for his name, so I could tell him how much of an idiot he is. If you were my date, I'd never let you out of my sight, much less my car."

Lola laughs. "I love that you think he had a choice." Her laughter dies down when she realizes I'm not following what she's saying. "He didn't let me out of his car, Jacob. I let myself out."

"You let yourself out?"

She nods. "Yep. He wanted something I wasn't willing to give him, so I left. Plain and simple."

My grip on the steering wheel tightens when I hear something she didn't mean to express. "He didn't hurt you, did he?"

Her livid eyes slide my way, softening when she sees nothing but genuine concern reflecting in my wide gaze. "No, he didn't."

"Good. I'm glad." I flex and unflex my fingers, fanning the sweat coating my palms. "You should still be careful, though. It isn't safe out here this late at night."

"Unsafe for whom? Me or you?" She tilts her torso my way, allowing the moon to dance in her eyes. "If anyone is in danger in this car, it isn't me. Don't you know I'm the Big Bad Wolf? I gobble up men like I'm a gym junkie, and they're my only source of protein."

"Gobble up men like you're a gym junkie and they're your only source of protein...*wow*." My chuckles make her squirm in her seat. I can't help but laugh. I fuckin' love that saying. "Then why did you dive out of your date's car? Was he vegan?"

Lola's laugh doesn't make me squirm, but my god does it have my dick aching. "I would have preferred him to be vegan rather than a mommy's boy."

"Eww. One of them?"

Her nose twitches like a rabbit. "Yep. I hadn't even sliced through my steak, and he was already planning for me to meet his momma."

"Maybe he was smitten?"

She gives me a look, one I don't know how to decipher since we just met. "What about any of this says, take me home to visit Mommy?"

She flashes her eyes at me. They're beautiful, mischievous, and reveal she's untouchable. She doesn't give a fuck what I think about her. She isn't changing who she is for anyone. I've heard of women like her before, but I've never seen them, much less sat across from one. I thought they were a myth, a fucking legend; I had no clue I'd stumbled onto one while running from its opposite.

I'm not out late for no reason, either. I was on a date. A painful, *wish it would have ended three hours earlier* date. Daphne didn't just have daddy issues; she had a whole heap of fucked-up baggage I wasn't willing to dig through to see if she had more than a pretty face. Some people take years to show their true selves. Lola isn't one of those people—guaranteed. We just met, but I'm confident I'm on to something sweet.

"I'd take you home to visit my momma." Her eyeroll stops halfway when I add on, "If I had one."

"You don't have a mom? Everyone has a mom."

Some of her sass fizzles when I explain, "I *had* a mom. She passed when I was three."

"Oh...sorry."

Although her apology is genuine, it isn't required.

"Don't apologize. You have nothing to be sorry about." I give her a frisky wink, lightening the mood before my eyes drift back to the road. It's lucky traffic is light tonight, or we may have been in a wreck by now since I can't take my eyes off her. "So, am I in with a chance now?"

Lola's golden brow cocks high on her face. "I should let you into my panties because you have a dead momma?"

"What? No... unless that's a possibility?" She socks me in the arm, proving my earlier worries about her safety weren't necessary. "I was actually referring to a date." No matter how hard I try and iron out the hope in my voice, it doesn't happen. "You can devour your steak without worrying about me inviting my mom for dessert. So what do you say? Wanna grab a bite to eat with me?"

She smiles, making me hopeful my greatest wish is about to come true. If only the gleam in her eyes wasn't saying the opposite. "I appreciate your offer, but I'm not a dating type of girl."

"Weren't you just on a date?" Confusion rings in my tone.

"No, I said I jumped out of my *date's* car. That's different."

"How?" Anyone would swear she told me she gave someone a lobotomy with a spoon for how high my voice is.

While raking her teeth over her lower lip, she deliberates on whether to tell me the truth. I'm assuming she's gone the honesty route when she murmurs, "Some people think a date is where the guy turns up with a bunch of flowers and a bottle of wine before taking you out for a candlelit dinner. My ideal *date*..." — she expresses this "date" with a husky purr – "is when two consenting people come together for a night of raunchy sex with no strings attached. My *date* wanted to date. Since I didn't, we parted ways."

"Hold on, let me get this straight." I pause to make sure I have the facts in my head right before articulating them out loud. "You told your date that you wanted to have raunchy, no-strings-attached sex with him, and he turned you down?" When she nods, I gasp. "Is he a fucking imbecile?"

Lola takes my questions as a compliment, believing I'm joking. I'm not. I'm dead fucking serious. She's beautiful. Just one glance at her face has my dick turning to stone. She can hold a conversation and doesn't appear to have any weird neuroses, so why the fuck didn't he accept her offer?

When I ask her that, she shrugs. "Maybe he doesn't like sex. I don't have sexual guilt. I love sex, and I'm not ashamed to admit it, but not everyone is like me. More often than not, my big mouth gets me in trouble."

I thank god for my baggy pants when the looseness in the crotch saves me from making a fool out of myself. Her straightforward attitude is refreshing, but my cock isn't getting the memo that just because she likes sex doesn't mean she'll have it with me. He could be responding to the crackling of energy teeming between us, but I don't want to get ahead of myself. As I said earlier, I often jump the gun when it comes to relationships, so anything I can do to avoid it this time around, I will—such as continuing with our conversation even if I'm swimming way out of my depth.

"That's a real shame you can't admit to loving sex. What year is it? I thought all that chauvinistic shit died in the eighties?"

"Ha! I wish." Lola tilts my way before crossing one killer high heel over the other. "It only grew worse as the misandrists' numbers climbed, except now, they're not just hating on men, they hate strong-willed women as well."

I wait for a semi to roar past my window before asking, "Misandrists?"

Her teeth rake her lips in a sexy-as-fuck way. "Manhaters. Pretty much the woman who made you believe that outfit is sexy." She wiggles her fingers over my khaki pants and long-sleeve shirt.

"You think man-haters are responsible for my choice in clothing?"

"Yep!" The "p" pops from her mouth. "Don't get me wrong, you give off a real playful vibe, but I had to dig through all of that to find it..." She once again waves her hand over my outfit. "You're lucky you stumbled upon me when you did, or your night might have been occupied with a lady who has severe attachment issues, or even worse, one who wants to call you Daddy."

I vomit a little in my mouth. That's precisely the woman I was sprinting from tonight.

Although she hit the nail on the head, I play it cool. If I show my hand to a woman like Lola too quickly, I'll be out of the game by the first round. "If my outfit is *sooo* concerning, why did you get in my car?"

She smiles a slick grin. "As I said earlier, I'm not the one in danger here."

"And I am?" My voice is as high as my brow.

She rakes her eyes down my body, only stopping when she reaches the crotch of my pants she so vehemently despises. "Uh-huh. Because if I acted on a single thought currently rolling through my head, you'd not only race back to the date you were fleeing when you noticed me at the bus stop; you'd cry into her bosoms while her mommy fixed the naughty wolf's bite."

"You don't think I can handle you?" I'm fucking confident I can't, but I want to hear it directly from the source.

Her eyes return to my face. "I don't *think* anything, Jacob. I *know* you can't handle me."

My dick becomes chummy with the seam in my pants from her purring my name. It was throaty and filled with a need as desperate as the fire burning in her eyes for me to prove her wrong.

"I've got more tricks up my sleeve than you're giving me credit for."

"Is that so?" Fuck me; her voice could only be hotter if it were lava spilling out of a volcano. "Is that why they're three sizes too big, so you can hide your tricks up there?"

"Maybe?" I swish my tongue around my mouth, loosening up my next set of words. I could never be accused of being overly cocky, but I'm done denying the tension brimming between us. Stranger or not, it's too fucking intense to ignore. "Or maybe I like throwing out challenges. No one likes predictability, Lola." I express her name as huskily as she did mine. "Once you're predictable, no one is interested anymore—not even khaki-wearing nobodies who'd give their left nut to stumble upon a girl like you just once in their lifetime."

I see her response in her eyes, hear it hissing on her tongue, but our arrival at Bronte's Peak steals her words. Bronte's Peak is a popular hookup location halfway between Lola's hometown of Erkinsvale and my stomping ground of Ravenshoe. People only come here for one reason—to fuck.

I'll shut this down faster than a married man sidestepping a paternity test if I've read Lola wrong. But if I haven't, and our electricity is as strong on her side of the car, I'll show her all the tricks I'm hiding, and then some.

The rise and fall of Lola's chest increases when I glide my car to a spot at the very end of the lot. I'm not seeking a secluded location. It's just too packed for me to park closer to the exit. I shut down my engine, push my seat back until it almost becomes one with my back seat, then angle my torso to Lola. She's eyeing me through lowered lids, her breaths as shallow as mine, her hope just as high.

When I jerk up my chin, commanding her to my side of the car, a grin that will forever highlight my dreams stretches across her face. "You can't be accused of corruption when the victim comes to you."

The tension crackling between us intensifies when I tilt nearer to her. "Does a victim also drive himself to the crime scene?"

Her smile grows. "Not usually, but there's a first time for everything."

"True. Tonight's the first—"

"Time you've brought a girl to Bronte's Peak? Why am I not surprised? You seem *very* innocent."

"That wasn't what I was going to say." I bring my mouth even closer to hers before angling my head to the side so we share the same air. "I was going to say, it's the first time I've let another man feed my date before stealing her for dessert."

"Who said I'm dessert? There's not an ounce of sweetness in me, Jacob..."

Her words trail off when our lips brush for the briefest second. It creates an immense amount of friction between us, as blistering as the heated breath she expels when I sink back into my seat.

After taking in the way she licks her lip, hoping for another taste of my mouth, I drop my eyes to the minute portion of air between her knees and the dashboard. The only way I'll squeeze into that tight space is by time-traveling back to when I was a toddler—and even then, it would be a tight fit. If she wants this to go further than an innocent peck, she needs to make it a possibility.

Perceiving things the same as me, Lola huffs before climbing over the middle console to straddle my lap. Some people may see her forwardness as off-putting. I'm anything but ordinary. I fuckin' love it.

She must be pretty damn uncomfortable wedged between me and my steering wheel, but her sexy voice does not indicate this. "When I destroy you, remember it was *you* who chose to walk this path, Jacob, not me."

She waits for me to nod before sealing her mouth over mine. Gone is the flirty stranger who spoke her mind without a second thought, replaced by a tigress who knows what she wants and isn't afraid to get it.

My heart beeps in my neck when her tongue traces the seam of my lips before delving it between them. When she purrs a cock-twitching moan, I get in on the action. I bite down on her lip before dragging my tongue along the roof of her mouth.

Hot. Fucking. Damn. She tastes as scrumptious as she looks.

We kiss for several minutes, the heat fueling our exchange undeniable. The windows fog, my pants pitch a tent, and Lola's panties dampen so much, I'm confident my crotch will wear her wet spot for hours to come.

By the time she pulls back, I'm praying she doesn't have any rules about not fucking on the first date. Although this isn't technically a date, I'm more than happy to pretend it is. I'll promise to take her to the most expensive steakhouse in town once we're done if it keeps this going.

Lola's minty breath fans my lips when she purrs, "I guess it's true."

"What's true?" I give her ass a frisky squeeze while pretending cum isn't sitting at the crest of my cock, begging to be released. I may have never sampled a mouth as delicious as hers, but that doesn't mean I'm free to make an idiot out of myself. I told her I had tricks. Premature ejaculation is not a trick I want to showcase.

"Guys with big hands..." Her micro skirt rides up high on her thighs when she grinds down on my cock. "Have big dicks."

I don't know whether to groan or laugh, so I do both. "I'm glad you approve."

It's true, I do have the world's biggest hands, but I'd look pretty stupid being a giant with the hands of a boy. I guess the same rules apply to my cock?

My cock hardens even more when the flare of her skirt rides up high enough I catch the quickest glimpse of her panties. They're skimpy and made of lace, a combination designed to bring men to their knees. We just met, so I know she didn't wear these for me, but that doesn't mean I can't appreciate them.

Wanting to test the waters, I push her skirt up a little higher, wondering if she'll stop me. She doesn't. As she inches back to peer at me with wide, lust-filled eyes, she wiggles her hips, turning her micro-skirt into a belt. Like things could get any more scandalous, she snakes her hand between the minute gap between us to stroke my cock through my pants. "Car sex isn't about slow sensual lovemaking, Jacob. It's for quick, hard fucking—"

"And a prelude of escapades to come?"

Her lips furl at my assumption there's going to be a second time, but when I tug my pants down my thighs, her words get stuck in the back of her throat. Jack and Rose might have had romantics believing car sex is a romantic rendezvous with lots of slow kissing and teasing touches, but everyday Americans know real life isn't a movie production. Car sex is uncomfortable as it comes, but oh so fucking worth it.

Does that mean Lola risks leaving our meeting unsatisfied? Not a fucking chance in hell. It just means I can't take my time with her—yet. There'll be no laying her out and sampling her body for hours on end. We'll fuck hard and fast, then, at a better time and place, I'll take my time with her.

As I drag my cock through her wet folds, Lola cracks open her purse, pulls out a three-strip of condoms, rips one open with her teeth, then raises herself onto her knees.

"Jesus..." I swear her whole body shudders when she drinks in my cock for the first time, making him bigger and meaner than he's ever been. "You've got to have something better than this, right?" She waves the standard regular-size condom you pick up at every drugstore before lowering her eyes back to my cock. "This isn't going to fit, and I can't touch *that*..." Her eyes widen as she takes in my dick. "...without *this*..." She wiggles the rubber ring in her hand "...so I hope you started your date as well-prepared as me."

I nudge my head to the glove compartment. "I've got my bases covered."

Faster than I can snap my fingers, Lola snags a Magnum Trojan condom from the box of ten in my glove compartment, returns to her kneeling position, rips open the foil with her teeth, then glides the snuggly fitting condom down my shaft. If she ended things right now, I'd still die a happy man. I've never seen a more erotic sight in my life than a sexy little hellion prepping me to get down and dirty.

Her eagerness to get things started is unearthed when the headlights of a vehicle at the top of the lot shine into my car. It's not a late-night visitor who's finished and heading home. It's the high beams of a patrol vehicle.

"If you want this, Jacob, you better hurry the hell up."

She doesn't have to tell me twice. With my hand weaved through her hair, her panties slipped to the side, and my eyes locked on the two officers approaching the first line of unsuspecting motorists, I slam home.

"Fuck!" Lola's teeth munch on her bottom lip as her head flops back. When her pussy throbs around me, protesting my sudden penetration, I freeze, hating that I've hurt her.

Lola takes advantage of my frozen state to ride my cock. She slides up and down my shaft, the lubricant included in the condom packaging aiding in her endeavor. She's wet, but you need more than natural lubrication to take all of me. Yeah, yeah, I know it makes me sound cocky, but it's also the truth.

As the police officers approach vehicles three and four down a long line of many, I use my grip on Lola's hip and hair as leverage to guide her up and down my cock. We rock as one, our natural rhythm found extremely quick for two strangers.

I nearly come just as fast when Lola brings her lips to my ear. "Just the thought of gagging on your cock makes me want to suck it so bad."

I'm an inferno right now—hot all over. We fuck like wild animals, the thrusts of my hips enough to mess Lola's hair with the lining on my car's roof. I drive home on repeat, ramping up her moans with every pump. Her screams encourage me to go harder, more violently.

I shove down my pants even further, then spread my knees are far as they can go in the tight confines. Once I've got her glorious ass between my thighs, I raise mine off the seat and jackknife my hips up on repeat. My balls slap her ass with every frantic grind as her screams turn ear-piercing.

"Jesus... Fucking... Christ."

When the tingles racing through her body are felt all the way to my balls, I bury myself into her as far as I can, then rock my hips up in slow, dedicated thrusts. When my pelvis grinds against her clit, she screams so loudly, I know she's on the cusp of orgasm.

"Come on, Lola. Bring it home." I'd rather have my ass hauled off to jail for public indecency than have her leave unsatisfied. "Scream my name for the world to hear."

Her head falls forward with a moan as the shudders coating her skin with goosebumps spread to her nape. "I'm close... so fucking close."

I add a swivel to my hips, praying it will give her the final push. I don't even care if I don't come, but I sure as hell don't want her heat dismounting my cock until she does.

It appears my wish is about to come true when she digs her nails into my shoulders. Her breathing turns wild as her pussy tightens around me; then, not long after that, she shatters like glass.

When I slow the speed of my pumps to guide her through her blinding climax, her lusty eyes drop to mine. "Don't stop. Please, whatever you do, don't stop. Real girls power through the craziness. It's better this way."

I return to my previous pace before she came. I thrust into her on repeat, pounding into her with everything I have until her screams grow so loud, I have to stifle them with my hand. She's making such a ruckus, the fog on my windows won't be the only reason the police officers skip the dozen cars between us. It's her vocal announcement of what we're doing.

How good I feel.

How wet she is.

And the best yet, "Oh, God, I'm coming—again!"

Her confirmation arrives a mere three seconds before a baton taps on the window next to my head. Mercifully, it also occurs two seconds after cum rockets out of my cock.

CHAPTER TWO

JACOB

With a misdemeanor citation sitting over the box of Magnum condoms in my glove compartment, I restarted our drive to Lola's house almost forty minutes ago. We've made the trip in silence. I wouldn't say it's necessarily uncomfortable. Lola just needs some time to recoup from her two mind-blowing orgasms. I could spark a conversation, but since I'm still riding the same high, my mouth refuses to cooperate with the prompts of my brain.

Tonight was—fuck, I don't have words to describe it. I knew from the moment my eyes landed on Lola that she was different from the other girls I've dated. I just had no clue how different. Most have a three-date rule before granting me access to their cookie jar. Lola awarded me an all-inclusive backstage pass within twenty minutes of meeting her.

I'll admit, I'm shocked my boldness worked, but as Lola said earlier, we're consenting adults who enjoy sex. Despite the citation in my glove compartment, our car romp didn't harm anyone. It was too fucking good to spark controversy, and I can't wait for round two.

I realize how easy things were handed to me tonight when, within two seconds of entering the driveway of a small but modern brick house in the middle of the burbs, Lola throws open her door, dives out of my car, then charges down the sidewalk. "Thanks for the ride."

What the fuck?

I throw off my seatbelt so fast, it hits my window before ricocheting back. While rubbing the new bump on my forehead, I peel out of my car and chase her down. My calves scream with every step I take, their earlier cramped conditions not forgotten, but nothing slows me down.

"Do you wanna grab that bite to eat next weekend? I guarantee you'll make it all the way through your steak this time. Scouts honor." I cross my heart in an entirely wrong manner. "You might even get dessert this time around—*real* dessert."

Lola freezes just outside her front door, her shoulders rising and falling as she inhales big, nerve-penetrating breaths. Several long seconds pass before she pivots to face me. Gone is the big badass she's portrayed all night, replaced with someone who looks a little petrified. "I had a great time, Jacob, but our fuck didn't change my stance on dating."

"Then we'll go on a *date* instead." I nearly have her, until I stupidly add on, "We'll just grab a beer beforehand—"

"I don't drink beer." Her tone is sassy, but the flare brightening her eyes moments ago is still present. "I also don't do..." she waves her hand between us, "...this."

"This? What's *this*..." I mimic her hand gesture.

She steps closer to me, her nostrils flaring when she detects the smell of sex wafting off my skin. "You want to date."

"*Pfft.* No, I don't. I just don't want you to make me look like a dawg. After what we just did, the least I can do is buy you a beer—"

"I don't drink beer." This confirmation comes with a stomp of her foot. I'm pleased to say it's a wobbly stomp that reveals her body is just as achy as mine. It's a good ache, but an ache nonetheless.

"Wine then? A cocktail? I'll even order you a cock-sucking cowboy if you'll agree to go out with me...*as a friend.*" I add on the last three words in a hurry when her smile switches to a frown. I had her at the cock-sucking cowboy part before I stupidly added the "dating" reference. "Come on, Lola, what's the worst that could happen? You end up stranded at the bus stop after letting yourself out of my car?" That brings back the smile I'm dying to see. "You're the Big Bad Wolf, remember? You gobble up men like a gym junkie with a lack of protein, saving us from women who think this is sexy."

When I drag my hand down my outfit, her eyes follow it. Now I've got her. Her pointed-up nose reflects more than family genes, but she knows what's hiding beneath my baggy shorts and long-sleeve combination, and she's more than eager to test it out for the second time.

After she finishes her avid assessment of my body, she bridges the gap between us. The seductive swing of her hips gains the attention of my cock, not to mention smelling my skin on hers. When she stops in front of me, a grin tugs on my mouth. She has to crank her neck back to peer into my eyes. She's average height for a girl, but she's got nothing on my six-foot-five frame.

I struggle not to fist pump the air when she says, "Pick me up Friday night at eight."

"Yes, ma'am."

After a final smirk, smitten at my reply, she spins on her heels and saunters to her front door. Once she's safely inside, I jump into my car so I can tap out my excitement on the steering wheel. My happiness should waver when Lola yells, "And it's not a date!" before slamming her front door shut, but it doesn't. Not in the slightest.

The way she purred my name when I was inside her proved she was right—she'll be more than I'll ever be able to handle, but that doesn't mean I won't give it my best shot. She's piqued my interest to a never-before-reached level. That alone deserves further exploration.

CHAPTER THREE

JACOB

"Can you drive yourself to Mavs tonight?"

Noah stops shoveling cocoa puffs into his mouth like he's never been fed to peer up at me. Because he never drives after consuming alcohol, my request frustrates him. A majority of his pay at Mavericks is in the form of unlimited beer, but I wouldn't be asking if it wasn't necessary, and Noah knows that.

That's why he agrees to my request with only the slightest bit of curiosity. "Yeah, no worries. Why?"

I waggle my brows. "I have a date."

"Another one?"

When he slips off his chair to wash his now empty bowl in the sink, I bump him in the shoulder. "Don't be jealous." He's always snarky about my love life because he doesn't have one. "I can't help that I'm popular."

"Jealous? Yeah, sure, whatever you say, Jake." After ruffling my hair, he leaves the kitchen. He's halfway through the dining room when he shouts, "I'll ask Marcus for a ride."

Air whistles between my teeth when I laugh. I should have known he'd find a way to drink. He isn't an alcoholic by any means, but after all the shit he's been through, I can't blame him for taking advantage of the unlimited beer his gig comes with.

Noah is the lead singer of the band Rise Up. I've been asked numerous times by their rapidly growing fan base why I'm not part of his group. My replies never alter. One, I can't play an instrument to save my life. Two, I'm tone-deaf. And three, I have my own dreams I want to pursue. I don't need to ride my best friend's coattails to achieve them. Music is Noah's passion. Fighting is mine.

Not that anyone knows that.

Noah has been my best friend since the sixth grade. When my dad spotted him walking home from school in the pouring rain, he offered him a ride. I had seen Noah around, but we hung with different crowds. Back then, Noah wouldn't have weighed fifty pounds wringing wet. He was nothing but skin and bones. Noticing that, my dad drove straight to our house, where he gave Noah the pastries and tarts he had baked the day before.

Ever since then, Noah has been a part of our family. I've always respected my dad, but it grew tenfold when he offered Noah the spare room in our house when his little brother was killed in a traffic accident. He never said why it was vital for Noah to move in with us, but as I grew older, I realized if he hadn't done what he did, Noah most likely wouldn't be with us today. Don't get me wrong, my dad was, and still is, a hard ass. He disciplines me and my brother Patrick when we step out of line, but he stepped up to the plate when Noah needed a male role model.

The line I gave Lola earlier this week wasn't a ploy to get into her panties. My mom did die when I was three, so I know what it's like to grow up without a female influence. I can only imagine what it was like for Noah not having either a male or female role model. His dad was a drunk long before he was incarcerated, and his mom was rarely in the picture. When his eldest brother killed himself, he was truly alone in the world.

As much as this kills me to admit, I don't remember my mom. The only memories I have of her are from the family photos my dad has of her around our home. Even eighteen years after her death, my dad still loves her. I don't know if he dates, but if he does, he's very discreet about it.

My eyes lift when Noah re-enters the kitchen. He switched his boxers for a pair of jeans and threw some products into his hair. "Who's the lucky girl?"

I smirk before murmuring, "Lola." Even her name rolling off my tongue is sexy.

"Nice." He pops two slices of bread into the toaster, revealing why he's no longer the skinned rabbit he once was. "Where are you taking her?"

My lips twist. I haven't worked that part out yet. Lola said it wasn't a date, so I doubt she'd appreciate me taking her to a steakhouse as I had planned, but I've been in her panties, so I've got to do more than drive her straight back to Bronte's Peak like my wicked head is begging. I'd also like to avoid another citation. I'm not technically working right now, so I don't have money to pay fines more expensive than a fancy hotel for the night.

There's an idea—is booking a hotel considered a date or a *date?*

I stop deliberating when the heat of a gaze captures my attention. Noah is gawking at me with his brows furrowed. "Is it the same girl responsible for your floral scent the other night?"

When I nod, he inches back from the refrigerator. "Let me get this right." He takes a breather so I can hear him through his breathless chuckles. "You fucked a girl, then you asked her out. She accepted your cock, but she won't go on a *date* with you?" Her air quotes the word "date." "What the fuck did you do wrong?" His eyes lock with mine. They're brimming with humor. "You didn't blow in your pants, did you?"

"Whatever." After flipping him the bird, I stalk out of the kitchen.

He chases me down. "Jake...come on... I was joking." When he catches up to me, he places his hand on my shoulder. "I wasn't making fun of you. I was just..." He stops talking when he fails to come up with an excuse. He knows I'm notorious for disastrous dates, so he's stumped about why I'm so frustrated.

"Lola is unlike anyone I've ever met."

Hearing something I didn't mean to divulge, the humor in Noah's eyes shifts to understanding. "All right, then why don't you bring her to Mavs? It's not a 'date' type of place."

I give his suggestion some consideration. I did offer to buy Lola a drink, and Mavericks sells drinks, so Noah's idea could work.

"All right. Sounds good."

"Good." He slaps my shoulder again twice, his smile returning. "Then I can see why she has your panties all twisted up."

CHAPTER FOUR

LOLA

"Does this outfit say, 'I love your cock, but I don't wanna be your girlfriend?'"

My younger sister Emily's head pops up from the hideous pink bedspread she's sprawled on. Her brows stitch as she stares at me, dumbfounded. I love teasing her. She's so timid and shy, I swear she blushes on cue. We share the same DNA, but I've often wondered if one of us is adopted. We're total opposites. She has dark, tanned skin; mine is beige and pasty. She thinks studying is fun; I prefer to party. But the most profound proof is that she's a prude, and I am not.

"Ah... I think you look nice?"

Smiling at the unease in her tone, I flop onto her bed. "Nice wasn't the look I was going for."

Warmth blooms across my chest when she giggles. She has the cutest little laugh. Sometimes she even snorts when she giggles too hard—not that she'd ever admit it.

"Who's the lucky guy?"

I roll over to join her in staring at the popcorn ceiling in her room. "A guy I met last week. When he offered me a ride home, we ended up at Bronte's Peak. Oh my god, Em, the size of his co–"

She slaps her hand over my mouth before I can finish my story. "I get the picture."

When she frees my mouth from her hand, I spread mine apart to indicate the length of Jacob's cock. She acts unaffected, but her throat working hard to swallow gives away her true response. She's as mortified as I was when my dive out of my *date's* car left me stranded in Ravenshoe until six in the morning.

Ten minutes—*ten goddamn friggin' minutes*—was all it took for me to be on the cusp of homelessness. Thank goodness Jacob arrived when he did, or who knows what tricks I would have needed to dust off to stay warm?

Calm down, I'm joking.

I didn't sleep with Jacob as payment for a ride. I did it because, for the first time in a long time, I acted on the crazy thoughts in my head instead of shutting them down. Jacob was a breath of fresh air, the bundle of naughtiness you don't realize you need until they unkink your knots.

I was also dying to see if he was as sexy out of his hideous khaki pants and long-sleeve shirt as he was in them. He was—if not better! My god—his body is a machine. I just wished he showcased it in all its glory. Don't get me wrong, the sex was good—*actually, it was amazing*—but I'm sticking with my initial assumption: Jacob is too sweet for me.

He seems like a guy who wants to get married, have 2.5 kids, and make slow, sensual love to his wife every Tuesday night, whereas I'm a girl who'd rather stay single, keep anyone under the age of twelve as far away from me as possible, and fuck as often as the urge arrives. Call me what you like. I am who I am, and I'm not changing for anyone.

Despite my beliefs, not even our dead silent forty-minute drive from Bronte's Peak could conjure up a way to let Jacob down gently. Jacob is gorgeous, and his stamina could give mine a run for its money, but little things he said and did during our rendezvous flashed up clinger warnings.

The last thing I want is a relationship. They don't end well for me, so I don't go out with men who want more than a friendship between the sheets. So why do I keep giving in to Jacob? He must have a magic wand—and no, I don't mean the one between his legs.

Although peeved I caved to his suggestion of a friends-only date, excitement is still heating my veins. Not even a saint would feign disinterest in bedding a man as well-endowed as Jacob. I'm far from saintly, but our sweaty car romp has highlighted my dreams every night this week. It's been a nice change from the nightmares I usually have.

After shaking my head, freeing them from the silly thoughts in there, I drop my eyes to Emily. "You have to go to Bronte's Peak one day, Em. The fun you could have there. . ." My words trail off when she stiffens. We're not the closest of siblings, but I still know her well enough to know when she's keeping stuff from me. "You've been there before, haven't you?"

When she shakes her head, I *tsk* her. She's the worst liar.

"What base did you get to?" When her eyes open even wider, my jaw falls to the floor. "*Emily Faye McIntosh!*"

I'm stunned beyond words. My timid, innocent sister isn't the virginal preacher I thought she was. Someone pinch me because I must be dreaming. I tickle her ribs, smitten to have found traces of the same blood in our veins. "You little hussy."

"I'm not a hussy."

My tickling onslaught stops when regret fills her eyes. "I know that. It wasn't what I meant. I'm just shocked." My tone is sincerer than earlier. "I hope your V-card was stamped by someone worthwhile."

Her eyes shoot back to the ceiling as a disappointed sigh spills from her lips. "I thought so at the time. He turned out to be nothing but a frog."

My heart clenches when tears well in her eyes. We may be opposites, but she's my baby sister, so I'll always love and admire her. "Don't let him get to you, Em. No matter how foolish you feel, it's nothing on how foolish he'll feel when he realizes he had perfection in his grasp but gave it away for something worthless."

This is the reason I am the way I am. I used to let things bother me too. Not anymore. By not allowing anyone to become attached, I won't end up disappointed. I wouldn't recommend that Emily follow my footsteps, but she needs to stop worrying about what people think about her and be the person *she* wants to be. It's the only way she'll be guaranteed to make it out of her teens intact.

Emily nods when I murmur, "It takes an ugly storm to create a rainbow."

"And more than one froggy kiss to find a prince."

I laugh. "That's right, although you better limit the number of frogs you kiss. I don't see Prince Charming being a fan of cold sores."

We lie shoulder to shoulder for several minutes before time gets away from me. The massive dong of a grandfather clock is indication enough, much less the excitement buzzing in my stomach.

"I better go finish prepping for my non-date."

When I lean over to hug Emily, she returns my embrace. "Have fun."

Her lips furl when I saucily wink. "You know I will."

Hoping to keep tension out of the air, I remove myself from her bed in an unladylike fashion. When I land on the floor with a thud, Emily giggles. I'm glad I've made her smile before heading out for the night. I wouldn't have had any fun if she was still upset. I've been called many names in my short twenty-one years, but I hope never to add "shitty sister" to the list.

As I pace out of Emily's room, I struggle to figure out who she gave her virginity to. She wouldn't hand it over to anyone, so it would have been someone she thought was special.

Several minutes later, I'm still at a loss. As far as I'm aware, Emily hasn't dated in over two years, so I'm suspicious the guy responsible for the broken look in her eyes can also be blamed for her lack of dating. I guess there's only one way to find out. I'll have to pay more attention to my little sister's love life. Unlike Emily, I'm not a fan of snooping, but if it's the only way to stay informed, I'll take it in stride.

———

THIRTY MINUTES LATER, I finish applying a final coat of mascara to my lashes. I have no clue why I'm putting in so much effort. I told Jacob it wasn't a date, yet I'm the one getting glammed up to the nines. I'm all for putting your best foot forward; I just hope it doesn't give Jacob the wrong idea. I like him—*enough to know he doesn't deserve to be lumped with someone like me.*

At precisely eight PM, Jacob knocks on the front door. I stand behind it for a few seconds, praying he didn't bring the cliché flowers and bottle of wine most suitors arrive with. Don't get me wrong, it's a gesture normal girls would swoon over. I'm anything but ordinary. The fact I let Jacob in my panties before taking me out for dinner is a clear sign of this.

After a big exhale, I pull open the door, sighing when I discover Jacob's empty hands. His dark-washed jeans and long-sleeve button-down shirt give him a sexy yet casual look, and his smirk does wicked things to my insides—so much so, I balance on my tippy toes to greet him with a kiss before realizing that isn't how friends greet each other.

When I inch back, Jacob's eyes drop to mine. They're blazing with an equal amount of lust and mischievousness. "You ready?"

I wink, hoping it will break out the cheeky side he seems to have a hard time unleashing without a little bit of goading. "Sure am."

After closing the door, I shadow him to his car. When he opens my door for me, I almost comment that we're in the twenty-first century, so I'm more than capable of opening my own door, but I hold in my bitchy remark when I see his gentle smile. He's not a bad guy; he's just picked the wrong girl to find attractive.

He closes my door then jogs around his car to slip into the driver's seat. Just as it did last week, the deep rumble of his engine vibrates right through me, activating a handful of sensory buttons not many guys know about. Mix its hearty purr with the yummy scent of Jacob's aftershave, and a panty disaster is bound to happen.

Jacob latches his belt before his eyes drift to me. "I thought we might watch a gig at Mavericks bar, if you want?"

His nervous stumble over his last three words makes me smile. "Sure, sounds great."

Some girlfriends mentioned a band of hotties who perform at Mavs every Friday night. I've not yet seen them play, but from their description, they sound like a band I'd appreciate.

APPROXIMATELY FORTY-FIVE MINUTES LATER, we pull into the lot of an establishment that looks like it was built in the sixties...and hasn't been touched since. Rise Up must be the only thing attracting people to this shit hole, because there's no way they're here for the decor.

A vein in my neck twangs when Jacob parks in the manager's spot at the back of the dimly lit lot. "You're the manager of Mavs?"

"No." His laugh works me over better than the vibration of his engine. "Ollie lives a block over, so he lets me use his spot."

When he cranks open his door, I mimic his movements, stealing his chance to open my door for me. "I would have gotten that for you."

I roll my eyes. "I know. That's the point."

He eyes me curiously before smiling a scrumptious grin. "You're unlike any other girl I've ever dated."

"I know," I reply again. "That's *also* the point."

He throws his head back and laughs. He has a wonderful chuckle. It makes me all warm and fuzzy... *What? Jesus, Lola! Get a grip.*

Needing distance before I once again act on the stupid thoughts in my head, I make a beeline for the back door of Mavs. Smoke smacks me in the face when I break through the warped wooden door. It's coming from a group of partygoers at the back of the thrumming space washing down their beer with a hit of nicotine. The number of people under twenty-five is shocking. For how rundown Mavs is, I thought it would be full of dirty old geezers escaping their nagging wives for a night. I was wrong—*very wrong.*

When we reach the bar that stretches across one wall, Jacob locks his baby blues on me. "What would you like to drink?"

With my painted lips twisted, I scan the vast selection of alcohol-laden glass shelves behind the bar. Nothing tickles my fancy as much as Jacob's watchful glance, so I blurt out the first thing that pops into my head. "A beer?"

Suspicion crosses Jacob's face. "I thought you didn't like beer?"

"I don't, but I don't go on dates either, yet here I am, entertaining you with my wit."

Smiling like I just gave him next week's lotto numbers, Jacob orders two beers from an elderly lady working behind the counter. They must know each other because they banter back and forth while she collects his order. For an older woman, she has a rocking body. Her white jeans showcase her long, lean legs, and her red shirt reveals gravity hasn't taken hold of her rack just yet. She's got style, even while glowering at me.

After handing me a beer, Jacob pivots on his heels and exits stage left. "I'll be back in a minute."

I watch him approach a group of good-looking men at the side of the dance floor with my mouth gaping, mortified I've been ditched —*for men!*

I stop giving him the stink-eye when a deep voice on my right says, "Hey, Maggie, can I grab a beer?"

When I turn my eyes, my vision is rewarded with a tall, gorgeous man wearing grungy jeans and a white V-neck shirt. The veins in his arms pop when he leans over the counter to greet the barmaid with a peck on the cheek, which also exposes his drool-worthy ass. He's not as built as Jacob, but even a nun would ogle all he has going on.

Recalling Jacob's ditch and run, I step closer to the mysterious stranger. Let's see how quick Jacob returns when he thinks he has competition. "Hi." I add a seductive grin to my greeting.

He isn't the type I usually go for. My tastes lean more toward blond-haired, blue-eyed men, so he's a little too dark and mysterious for me, but there's something more than bitterness encouraging my attempt to ignite a conversation. I just have no clue what it is.

The dark-haired hottie takes a swig from his beer before bracing his back on the bar. "Hey. First time here?"

I quirk my brow. "That obvious?" He laughs but remains quiet. "Do you come here often?"

His lips lift against the rim of his beer before he takes another large gulp. After scrubbing his hand along his wet lips, he murmurs, "You could say that."

His smile reveals he has dimples—a past favorite of my little sister's.

As my heart rate climbs, I thrust out my hand in offering. "Lola."

He wipes his condensation-covered hand down his thigh before accepting my offer. "Nice to meet you, Lola; I'm Noah."

CHAPTER FIVE

JACOB

As Slater's eyes roam over Lola's body, he rocks on his heels. "She sure is fine."

I'm too busy scrutinizing Lola's exchange with Noah to take in the tiny denim shorts and spaghetti-strapped top she's wearing. I shouldn't have ditched her like I did, but when I noticed Noah approaching, I wanted to see if she fussed over him like every other female around here does any time he's in the vicinity. She saw him immediately, but their conversation has lacked the fluttering lashes and puckered lips I usually witness.

I didn't think she would, but Lola passed my test with flying colors.

After they finish shaking hands, I stroll back toward them. Lola doesn't register my approach. She's too busy staring at Noah, but it's not the same heated look she gave me beneath lowered lashes last week. She actually looks a little constipated.

After jerking up his chin in greeting, Noah shifts his focus back to Lola. "It was nice meeting you, Lola. Might see you around sometime?"

Lola twists on the spot. "Hopefully."

When Noah meanders past me, he gives me a curious stare. I don't have time to evaluate what it means when Lola asks, "How do you two know each other?"

"He's my brother." When her brows stitch, I chuckle. "Not literally. He's my brother from another mother."

"Oh... okay."

We take a swig of our beers in sync. My body welcomes the bitter, cold concoction. Lola's response isn't as embracing; her nose screws up as her throat fights the urge to gag. Once she forces the malty liquid into her stomach with numerous swallows, she returns her watering eyes to me. "Does Noah have a girlfriend?"

I spit malted liquid all over the bar top, shocked. After witnessing their exchange, that's the last thing I expected her to ask. No sparks were flying between them whatsoever—*none!* So why the fuck does she care if he's single?

The beer I'm choking on finishes sliding down my throat when Lola mutters, "Not for me." She stares me straight in the eyes. "*I* don't date, but even if I did, he's not my type."

She doesn't need to say that I am her type. I can see it in her eyes. She digs me.

"Noah doesn't date either."

Don't get the wrong idea. He has no problems with the ladies. His list of admirers grows exponentially after each gig, but, excluding me, I've never seen anyone permanent in his life. Hookups aren't permanent, but dating is. That's why I'm praying Lola didn't see our exchange last week as a one-off hookup. We created magic—magic that deserves to be explored time and time again.

I eye Lola with suspicion when she murmurs, "I bet his stance on dating will buckle when he meets my baby sister."

While swigging on my beer, I shift on my feet to face Noah. For the first time in a long time, he seems content, so I doubt he'd appreciate anyone fucking with his personal life. Furthermore, he never lets anyone in, so whatever scheme Lola is cooking up, she's wasting her time. Noah is convinced he's a bad omen. For that alone, he keeps everyone at arm's length.

Once my beer runs out, I order another round of drinks for Lola and me. I request a beer for me and a fancy milky drink for Lola. She hasn't complained about her beer, but her screwed-up nose tells me everything I need to know. She's not a fan of frothy beverages.

Since Maggie is run off her feet, it takes her a good ten minutes to fill my order. "Sorry, Cindy quit this morning, leaving us short a barmaid. If you know anyone looking for work—"

"I'm looking for a job," Lola pipes up from behind my shoulder, her mouth circled with hope.

Maggie sizes her up before returning her eyes to me. She remains tight-lipped, but she doesn't need to speak to seek my thoughts on whether Lola would be a good fit for Mavs. Her motherly eyes ask on her behalf.

I nod. Not only will Lola be a great addition to the Mavericks family, but I'll also be able to see her more regularly. It's as if fate is aligning in my favor for once.

Taking my pledge at face value, Maggie swings her eyes back to Lola. "Can you start next week?"

When Lola nods, Maggie hands her a business card with her mobile number scribbled on the back before moving down the bar to serve other patrons. Once she's out of eyesight, Lola throws her arms around my neck. "Thank you so much! If you hadn't backed me up, I doubt she would have offered me the job!"

When her tippy-toe stance gains her more than a few admiring glances at her delectable backside, I swivel her around until her back is flush with the bar before returning her embrace. "It'll be my pleasure."

OVER THE NEXT HOUR, we enjoy Rise Up's set. We drink, chat, and Lola often gets up to dance. Since I'm not a fan of busting a move, I watch from the bar... until her seductive moves have a pack of ravenous sharks circling her.

I don't dance, but there are no laws stopping me from standing next to Lola while she shakes her ass like she's on a stage lined with dollar bills. If my stern glare doesn't give her admirers a clear sign to fuck off, my stern finger point won't be denied.

When I reach Lola, she twirls around me, her sweaty scent flooding my brain with memories of last weekend. "I thought you didn't dance."

"I don't. Just figured it would be safer in here than out there with the 'call me daddy' girls."

"She's here?" Lola's wide eyes glide to the left, then to the right. "Which one is she?"

Don't ask me to swear on the Bible, but I'm reasonably sure she sounds jealous—that or she felt how hard her scent made me when she ground her backside against my crotch.

Playing along with my ruse, I ask, "Should I point them out individually, or just nudge my head in their direction?"

"There's more than one?!"

Oh, yeah, she's jealous alright.

When Noah spots me in the middle of the dance floor like a massive turd that refuses to flush, he smiles so wide, he nearly misses the intro of the song he's performing. Serves him right. If he minded his own business, he wouldn't fuck up.

I stop giving Noah the finger when Lola says, "How about we make things interesting for them?"

I twist my lips, acting only partly interested. "What do you have in mind?"

Please, God, let it be one of the naughty thoughts in my mind. I don't care which one. I'll take any you're willing to give me.

My prayers are answered when Lola balances on her tippy toes to sling her arms around my neck. We're already squashed close together because of the number of Rise Up fans in the space, but this isn't about a lack of leg room. It's more than that. Her eyes are holding the same gleam they held last week, the shimmer that says she'll be my greatest reward, but only after being my biggest pain in the ass.

When she angles her head to the side to better align our lips, I lick mine in preparation for our kiss. She inches closer and closer until her cherry lip gloss overtakes the scent of the cocktails she's been downing, but instead of kissing me as I'm praying she will, she shouts, "What do you mean you don't want us to be exclusive anymore?! I thought I was your snugglebutt!" She pushes away from me, her dramatics gaining her more than a handful of spectators. "I only agreed to call you Daddy because you said you loved me. Clearly, that was a mistake. You'll have to find someone else to tuck you in at night and mend up your boo-boos. I'm done."

I swear on my mother's grave, her last sentence gains the attention of women from all walks of life. Some gawks are in sympathy, but more than a dozen are from a range of crazies. There are the straight-up kooky ones who don't attempt to hide their wackiness, the ones who seem normal until you get them alone, and the ones who'll hide the fact they were raised in a mental asylum until they've popped out three of your kids.

"She was joking."

When the freaks hover in close with a promise to heal my broken heart on their faces, I push off my feet to chase down Lola, who's halfway out of Mavericks by now. "What the fuck?! You threw me to the wolves. I was seconds from getting mauled."

"Serves you right." She cocks her hips before spreading her hands across them. "Next time you'll think twice before responding to jealousy."

"Responding to jealousy...? Whatever!" I make a *brrrr* noise with my lips like she's one of the airheads I left inside.

She peers at me over the roof of my car. "So you weren't jealous? You just joined me on the dance floor to dance?"

"Uh-huh. What other reason would I go onto a dance floor?"

She taps her glossy lips. "Oh, I don't know. Maybe because you were... *jealous!*"

I unlock the door and slide into the driver's seat without bothering to open her door for her—tell me one jealous person who does that?

I wait and wait and wait for Lola to join me in my car. When she doesn't, I peer out the passenger side window. She's no longer standing beside it. She's storming back toward Mavericks' back entrance.

Dust kicks up around my feet when I clamber out of my car. "Where are you going?"

She pivots around to face me, flashing her mischievous grin that got me into all sorts of trouble last week. "Figured since you weren't jealous, I may as well go dance some more. Who knows, I might get lucky."

Like a meteor crashing to earth, I finally realize what's happening. Lola wasn't the only one placed under the microscope tonight. I'm under there as well, being scrutinized by a woman determined for me to know we aren't on a date. The fact she told me that exact thing over half a dozen times tonight already makes it clear, but I'll play along with her little game because I'd rather spend the night with her as a friend than with any of the freaks eyeing me earlier. I like Lola, even without her cookie jar in my sights.

Lola's brows draw together when my taillights blink, announcing I've locked my car. "What are you doing?"

"I thought we were going to dance?"

The fake anger on her face switches to confusion. "We?"

"Well, you." I fill the gap between us with three big strides. "I'm going to sit back and enjoy the show."

She could misconstrue my comment as meaning the risqué performance she puts on when she dances, but she's smarter than that. "What show?"

I smile, loving that she took my bait hook, line, and sinker. "You just announced in a room full of men that you like calling your suitors 'Daddy,' and that you're newly single. This could only be more interesting if you stuck a big sign on your chest that said, 'Freak Between the Sheets.'"

She stops me from entering Mavs by placing herself between me and the door. "Maybe we should head out?"

"I thought you didn't care what people thought about you—?"

"I don't. It's just late, and Rise Up is about to finish their set, so why hang around here? There are a lot more interesting places we could go."

"Like...?" *Please say Bronte's Peak. Please say Bronte's Peak.*

"Umm..." Her eyes stray around the dingy parking lot like the answer is directly in front of her. It is, but it isn't what she was expecting. "...There."

I glance down to where she's pointing. A flyer for a dance club in Hopeton is floating across the dusty ground. "You want to go to A+?"

"Yeah. Why not? It looks like fun."

"Alright." It isn't how I wanted us to get sweaty, but I'm always up for trying something new—such us pretending I don't want to date her when I do.

CHAPTER SIX

JACOB

"That was crazy. I swear, I've never danced so much in my life." Lola peers at me with bright, glistening eyes and a sweat-drenched face. "Thanks for taking me out. It was a lot of fun."

"You're welcome. Hopefully we can do it again soon?"

I slide into the driver's seat of my car before she can voice the rejection I see in her eyes. When she slips into the passenger seat, her phone dings with a text halfway through latching her belt. As I pull out of the lot at the back of A+, she snags her phone out of her purse.

When her brows furrow, I try to keep the mood light. "It's not Maggie texting you your shifts, is it? She's a bit of a night owl who forgets most of the world is sleeping at three in the morning."

Her eyes stray to mine, her mood different from the girl who shred thousands of calories shaking her tuckus like no one was watching. "No. It's from an unknown number."

"One of those *we have three hundred million dollars from a deceased relative you've never heard of* messages?"

"I wish. It's nothing but strings of gibberish." She swivels her phone to show me the screen.

"Maybe it's code for something?"

"Or maybe someone is on crack." With a shrug, she stores her phone away before kicking off her shoes and tilting toward me. "Talking about braindead idiots, I just realized I have to turn down Maggie's offer."

"Why?" Confusion dangles on my vocal cords. She was so excited when Maggie asked if she could start next week, so I'm a little lost as to why she's backing out now.

Apprehension crosses her features before she whispers in a huff, "I don't have a license, so I have no way of getting to Ravenshoe for my shifts."

"You don't have your license? Why not?"

She folds her arms in front of her chest, raising her fantastic tits higher on her chest. I've yet to see them unconcealed, and it's fucking killing me. "I failed three times—not because I'm incompetent. I know how to drive. My instructors were just female."

A chuckle rumbles up my chest. I'm an ass for laughing, but I can't help it. Women as gorgeous as Lola are accustomed to getting what they want—especially when it comes to men—but often other women see them as bitches. Although someone disliking her personality could be the reason she failed, I don't see that being the *only* reason.

"I'll drive you to your shifts..." My words taper when Lola's eyes narrow into tiny slits. "Then I'll teach you how to drive, so you can drive yourself to work."

"I know how to drive... I just can't work out the stick thingy."

I laugh. "That could be the cause of your troubles. You're probably yanking on it too hard. Sometimes you have to be gentle."

She peers at me with a smug grin on her face. "Are we still talking about the gearstick?"

My shoulder touches my ear. "I don't know. Are we?"

After rolling her eyes, she shifts them back to the scenery whizzing by her window. I think it's the end of our conversation, but her faint whisper proves I still have much to learn about this woman. "If I agree to your offer, what will you get out of our deal?"

You, I mutter to myself, but knowing that will most likely piss her off, I keep that snippet of information to myself. She's reminded me plenty of times tonight that we're not on a date, so acting as if we are won't be well-received. Instead, I waggle my brows, making light of the situation.

"You can be designated driver the next time we go clubbing. You may want to increase your lift ratios, though. My ass is heavy when it's laden with alcohol."

She accepts my jest better than anticipated, simply smiling before returning her eyes front and center. Ten minutes later, we pull into the driveway of her family home. I freeze with my belt halfway across my torso when Lola hits me with a firm finger point. "Uh-uh! *Friends* don't walk their *friends* to the door."

She steals my chance to retaliate by pressing her lips to mine, giving up that cherry lip gloss I've been dying to taste all night. It's only the briefest peck, but it fills me with hope. I don't know about you, but I certainly don't kiss my friends goodbye on the lips. That may have more to do with the fact they're male, but still, it's the truth.

When Lola inches back, I run my tongue over my lips, ensuring I get every smidge of lip gloss she left there before digging my phone out of my pocket. "We should exchange digits... so you can text me your shifts, then I'll know what time to pick you up." I only add on the last part because she was seconds from once again reminding me that we're not on a date, so number swapping is a no-go zone.

My brow arches when she inputs her number by copying it off a card stored in her purse. "I recently got a new number, so I don't know it by heart yet."

I guess that's why she was freaked about an unknown number messaging her at three in the morning?

After storing her number in my contacts, she hands me back my phone, almost leans in for another kiss before remembering that isn't something friends do, throws open her door, then bolts down the sidewalk like her backside is on fire. Once she enters the safety of her home, I drop my eyes to the screen of my phone.

I try not to look too deeply into the two x's at the end of her name.

I miserably fail. I knew she digs me!

THE NEXT MORNING, Noah's head pops up from the bowl of cereal he's devouring when I enter the kitchen. "What're your plans this weekend, Jake?"

I grab the orange juice from the fridge. "I'm gonna head to the gym for a few hours; wanna come?"

"*Hours?*" He looks seconds from barfing. "No thanks."

I laugh at the disgust crossing his face. I've dragged him to the gym a handful of times the past twelve months, but his limit is an hour—max. I like to go much longer than that. I'm not a gym junkie by any means; I just grew an obsession with fighting after I was approached by a trainer a little over four months ago. . .

"Can you fight?"

Peering up from my large Taco Bell meal, I'm met with the curious eye of a dark-skinned man wearing mirrored glasses and a wonky smile. I glance over my shoulder, unsure if he's talking to me or someone behind me.

As my eyes return front and center, I witness him pulling out the chair across from me, spinning it around, then straddling it backward. "Can you fight?" He talks at me as if I'm slow, which I find amusing.

"I haven't needed to. Because of my size, no one is game to take a swing at me."

The stranger chuckles while pulling off his sunglasses so he can look me in the eyes. "Hank." He nudges his head to the back entrance of the food court I'm dining in. "I own a gym in this complex. I also train fighters. Would that be something you'd be interested in pursuing?"

I take a moment to consider his question. I've been studying busi-ness via correspondence, but my efforts have severely lacked the past few months, so a changeup couldn't hurt.

"I could be interested."

Grinning as brightly as a sky of stars, Hank's hand delves into his trousers to pull out a wallet. After securing a tattered business card from inside, he hands it to me. "Come to the gym. I'll put you through some drills. They'll soon tell us if you have what it takes."

Not speaking another word, he stands then stalks away. I wait for him to be out of eyesight before dropping my eyes to his card. "Hank's Gym," I read off the card. Nothing original there.

When a sweet voice above asks, "Is this seat taken?" I shove his card into my pants pocket.

A pretty blonde in a light blue sundress is standing above me, raking her teeth over her lower lip. She has bright blue eyes that pop off her face and an enticing body. I noticed her when I entered the food court ten minutes ago, but figured it'd be best to finish my lunch before going on the chase.

Clearly, she has other plans for us.

"It is now."

I kick out the chair Hank just vacated with my foot before gesturing for her to sit, liking that she came to me instead of waiting to be chased. As I said earlier, a changeup rarely hurts anyone.

BY THE TIME *I enter my room later that night, I've completely forgotten about my run-in with Hank. If his card hadn't fallen out of my pants while I was stripping for a shower, I wouldn't have given our conversation a second thought. Now I'm giving it a third and fourth once-over.*

I've never considered professional fighting as a career, but there's no harm giving it a shot. I'll try anything once. It's not like I'll be beating the shit out of some random for no reason. It's a professional sport with referees and shit. It's above board and legal, unlike some activities I undertook in my teen years.

I'll try it. If I hate it, I won't do it again. Plain and simple.

MY STOMACH LAUNCHES *into my throat when I enter Hank's gym early the next morning. There's a funky smell in the air. It's not a stinky armpit smell you'd expect after a hard workout. It's an indescribable scent that fucking reeks.*

"It's about time you showed up."

When my eyes drift to the voice, I spot Hank skipping rope near a ratty, old punching bag chained to the ceiling. For a guy in his late fifties, if not sixties, his body is ripped. His black afro is clipped close to his scalp, and his torso and arms are covered with tattoos.

After slinging the jump rope around his neck, he grabs a towel from a worn-out bag on his left. "You can't work out in cargo pants. Go change into gym clothes, then meet me in the ring."

Once I'm dressed in black gym shorts and a long-sleeve shirt, I make my way to the boxing ring at the back of the deserted space. Compared to the gym I lift weights at, the equipment here is badly outdated. It doesn't look used, just old.

When I stop next to the ring, I stare down at the ropes, unsure how I'm supposed to get into the ring since they go all the way around. With a shrug, I pull them down before stepping over them. Hank laughs loudly. "You're supposed to go through them, not over them, but whatever works, man." He strolls toward me with a pair of red boxing gloves in his hands. "Lose the shirt."

I hesitate. I'm no longer the little fat kid who got bullied at school, but I'm self-conscious enough about my body that I'm not a fan of wandering around shirtless.

Noticing my hesitation, Hank gives me a look, one that reveals I either remove my shirt, or he'll remove it for me.

"Fuck it." I yank it off before hanging it on the ropes.

My biceps flex when Hank pulls my hands in front of me to slip on the gloves he's holding. "I knew you'd be ripped, so why hide under baggy clothes?"

I don't answer him. I'm not being ignorant; I just don't know how to explain my annoying neurosis. I've always worn layers of clothes. It's just the way I am.

Once my gloves are in place, Hank inches back before raising a set of protective pads in front of his face. When he instructs me to hit them, I do, albeit hesitantly. Hank is buff for his age, but he isn't overly tall or wide. I don't want to knock him on his ass.

Hank mocks the lack of oomph in my swing with a chuckle. "What's your weak spot?"

When he bounces around the mat, I follow him. "I don't have one."

"Bullshit! Everyone has a weak spot."

I take a step back when he swings his pad at my head, but I'm too slow to avoid colliding with it. He smacks me upside the head with the pad before stinging my left cheek with a non-playful slap.

My next set of whacks to his pads connect harder than my first few. I'm usually pretty laidback... until you piss me off.

"Do you have a girlfriend?"

While shaking my head, I continue following Hank around the mat, jabbing left and right combinations as instructed.

"Daddy issues?"

I once again shake my head.

"Mommy issues?"

I glare at him over the gloves protecting my face. "My mom is dead."

He murmurs an apology before attempting to wipe the arrogant expression off my face with a sneaky left hook. I block his hit this time around, his smile telling me I did the right thing.

"Okay, so no weak spots. Then why are you such a pansy? Hit me!"

He just found my weak spot.

There's nothing I hate more in the world than being called a pansy. My brother Patrick calls me a pansy all the time. How was I to know when you're being called a fat cow by schoolyard bullies in kindergarten that you aren't supposed to cry?

Patrick told our dad I cried, but instead of comforting me as all good dads should, he gave me a lecture on how boys aren't allowed to cry—ever! I haven't cried since that day, but my brother never lets me forget the one time I did.

As my anger rises, so does the power behind my swings. I pummel Hank's pads over and over again until the occasional fist slips to regions of his body not protected by thick padding. Hank doesn't seem to mind. He smiles before using his pads like gloves. He gives as good as he's getting... until a right hook steals more than the wind from his lungs. It sends blood dribbling down his chin as well.

Regret hits like a ton of bricks when he gargles water before spitting it into a bucket. It's vibrant red. "It's safe to say we found your weak spot."

"Shit, Hank, I'm sorry—"

He cuts off my apology with a swipe of his hand through the air. "Don't apologize; your giant ass is going to make me rich!"

I chuckle when he jumps into the air with more agility than a man his age should have...

For the next four weeks, we trained sun up to sundown seven days a week in preparation of my heavyweight fighting debut. Another three months have passed since then, and I still haven't competed. I'm not scared. I'm just... *scared?* Not of losing. I just hate failing.

I'm done with that now, though. It's time to put some serious thought into my career. I'm not getting any younger, so I need to seize the moment, or whatever other shit my dad said to me last week.

I also have a new motivator. I offered to drive Lola to and from her shifts without putting any thought into the ridiculously high gas prices lately. I'm studying, which means I don't have an income, so being Lola's chauffeur is an expense I can't afford—but refuse to give up. I get Lola alone for eighty miles every shift. That's worth more than any prize money I'll make during my fighting career.

CHAPTER SEVEN

LOLA

Butterflies take flight in my stomach when I send Jacob a text saying I'm due at Mavericks at 7 PM. He offered to drive me, but I still feel guilty, like I'm using him for a ride. I don't have another viable option. A taxi would gobble up my pay before it hits my bank account, and my mom's double shifts at the hospital mean she can't pick me up at whatever ungodly hour my shift finishes. My dad could drive me since he's unemployed, but with him rarely around, I haven't had the chance to ask. Instead, I reached out to the one man who offered assistance without any stipulations attached.

God, am I making a mistake? I don't want Jacob to get the wrong idea. I like him; I just don't trust myself around him. It's like granting me a bite of my favorite cake, then telling me I can't have any more. That's worse than torture.

Forever a gentleman, Jacob replies to my text promptly.

Jacob: *I'll be there at six xx*

And there's the cause of my worry. Two little symbols that can mean so much more when viewed by the wrong eyes. Stupid kisses. Stupid driving instructors who failed me because they were snooty cows. *Stupid heart that got so severely broken, it's lost its trust in everyone.*

After trudging into my bedroom, I search my closet for the full-length jeans Maggie instructed me to wear. When my hunt comes up empty, I put on white denim shorts instead. This outfit is sexier anyway, so it'll help patrons be more generous with their tips. A win for all involved—Maggie included.

Not long after I've finished applying my makeup, a car horn sounds outside. When I peer out the lace curtain, I spot Jacob's car in the driveway and smile. He's learning quickly, which means my body should soon understand that we're *only* friends.

I dart into my room to grab my purse before racing outside, bypassing Emily's room on my way. "I'll see you tonight."

Her head pops up from the giant textbook she's reading. "Okay. Good luck."

Waving, I dash outside, my pace remarkably fast considering the height of my stilettos. My strides half when I notice Jacob's entranced stare as I saunter past. I add an extra swing to my hips, loving the zeal in his eyes before realizing prancing like Bambi isn't something friends do for other friends either.

Ugh! Why does this have to be so damn hard?

"Hey, Jake." As I slip into the passenger seat, I drink in how his light blue long-sleeve polo shirt makes his eyes pop off his ruggedly handsome face.

His grin makes me wonder if he also noticed my prolonged gawk. "Hey. You ready?"

"Yep!"

I cringe when my girly voice bounces around his car. My nerves can't be helped. Even though Mavs is a piece-of-shit pub, I'm still excited to have secured a job. I've been looking for ages, but since I don't have a college degree, my applications were constantly over-looked. I could have gone to college on student loans, but with my mom already working double shifts to pay for our tiny house in one of the most expensive counties in the state, I didn't want to burden her with more financial worries.

If I had brains like Emily, I could have applied for a scholarship. Unfortunately, I spent more time worrying about how I looked instead of hitting the books during my senior year, leaving my grades less than stellar. So, as much as Mavs is only a stepping stone, a job is a job, and I'm stoked to finally secure one.

When the first ten minutes of our trip occurs in silence, I attempt to spark a conversation. "How was your week?" Talking won't settle the nerves in my stomach, but it's got to better than humming like an idiot.

Jacob scratches his brow before he shrugs. "It wasn't bad. You?"

"Could've been better." I wait for him to ask what went wrong. It's the longest two minutes of my life.

"What's going on with you? You're..." *Freaking me out. Making me wonder if I slid into the wrong car.* "...quiet."

His eyes stray from the road to me. "I'm always quiet when I think. I'm not good at multi-tasking."

"Oh...then who did I fuck at Bronte's Peak? He had the hair-pulling, clit-flicking, animal fucking down pat."

"Jesus fucking Christ, Lola." He tugs on his dick, making my body green with envy. "You can't say shit like that to me."

"Why not? I was wondering earlier if I got in the wrong car. Now I'm certain. You don't have a twin, do you? If so, do you have any rules about not fucking the same girl?"

His growl is as cute as fuck. "I have a brother; he's not my twin, and I'd cut his dick off with a saw if it got within an inch of you."

"Alright. Calm down, Big Boy." I playfully wink, loving the return of the Jacob I've been toying with the past two weeks. "If you're merely thinking, why not do it out loud? Maybe I can help ease whatever is going on in that big head of yours."

"You wanna talk? Fuck—maybe I should cut my dick off. It'll make my transition into womanhood easier."

I slap his bicep. Stupid mistake. It whips up the smell I'm struggling to ignore—his scrumptious aftershave. "I don't necessarily want to talk. I just need to do something to settle the nerves in my stomach." Stealing his chance to reply to my pathetic statement, I say, "So, come on, out with it. What has you sitting there like an army sergeant with a GI Joe stuck up his butt?"

"Eddie Murphy?"

"What?" *Why does he have Eddie Murphy on his mind?*

"*Delirious* by Eddie Murphy. 'And GI Joe got stuck; GI Joe got stuck in the water.'"

I laugh loudly while pretending to clamp my hand around a gigantic air turd. "And then a big brown shark came."

We laugh for several long, fascinating minutes. It clears the nerves from my belly by pushing them down several inches. Jacob's laugh is as delicious as his face.

"I can't believe you watched that. I thought I was the only one who loved classic standup."

I wipe away laughter-induced tears before angling to face him. "I watched it years ago but had a recent refresher when it was put on Netflix. It's hilarious—my favorite standup routine of all time. It's the realness behind it that makes it so funny."

"True." Jacob's nod says more than his words. Just like me, he's an everyday American. He wasn't raised with a silver spoon in his mouth and a trust fund worth millions. He's just an everyday guy. That makes me like him even more.

Disturbed by my inner monologue, I return my eyes and my torso front and center. Not long later, we pull into Mavs' parking lot. Unlike last week, Jacob doesn't attempt to open my door for me. He just lingers at the side, waiting for me to gather my things before shadowing me inside.

"Go show them who the Big Bad Wolf is." He nudges me toward the bar before heading to his friends, who are seated near the stage. Stupid butterflies are fluttering in my stomach, and my palms are slicked with sweat, but I have a big, beaming smile on my face.

Well, I did, until Maggie's eyes arrow in on my denim shorts.

"I don't own any full-length jeans."

Maggie's brow cocks. "Uh-huh... and?"

"And... I'll buy a pair with my first paycheck?" It sucks admitting I don't have the money to buy a pair now, but since it's the truth, I run with it.

Maggie exhales a big breath like she heard my wordless confession. "Alright. Go through those doors." She points to a set of double doors behind the bar. "There's a pile of shirts on shelves as you enter. Find your size, get changed, then meet me back here."

Happy to escape the tension in the air, I make a beeline for the door. After several yanks and a couple of pushes, I finally break through the heavily weighted door. For future reference, it's a push door.

My nose screws up at the moldy smell lingering in the air when I enter the dingy space. I locate the shirts right where Maggie said they'd be. The shelves are rusty but perfectly adequate to hold shirts. After snagging the smallest size I can find, I fling off my tank top to replace it with my very first uniform.

It's halfway slipped over my head when a male voice breaks through the silence surrounding me. "Oh shit, sorry."

After fixing my shirt, I pivot to face the voice. A man with a shiny head is sheltering his hands with his eyes. If that isn't confirmation enough he wasn't sneaking a peek at my boobs through their lace bra, his gaze is fixated on the wall on his right. He's so uneager to look, my ego gets unexpectedly bitch-slapped.

"It's safe now."

He lowers his hands before running his eyes over my shirt. The snug fit showcases my puppies in a flattering light, adding to the sexiness of my tiny shorts.

"Hi, I'm Ollie."

When he offers me his hand to shake, I take in his features more diligently. His face has a substantial set of wrinkles, and the few strands of hair left on his head are gray. If I had to guess his age, I'd say he's at least mid-sixties. His Maverick shirt is similar to mine; it just hugs his midsection instead of his chest.

"Lola. Tonight is my first shift."

Ollie nods like my newness explains everything. "There are bathrooms over there." He points to a door with "Restroom" written across the front.

"Thanks." I roll my eyes. It took me five seconds to switch my shirt, so why go all the way to the bathroom to do it? "What do you do here?" He doesn't have the height or build of the bouncers I've seen, so I would guess he's the cook.

"I'm the owner."

My mouth dries when my jaw gapes. I am usually much better with first impressions, especially when it's the opposite sex. Warily smiling, Ollie dips his chin in farewell before entering an office concealed by a shelf of shirts—the same shirts I stripped in front of. *Goddammit!*

After stashing my purse in an empty locker, I dart back out to the bar. The first person I spot when exiting is Jacob. His eyes bulge out of his head when they land on my tight red shirt. "Jesus, Lola. Are you trying to kill me?" When he adjusts his crotch, I flash him a flirty grin. "Cock tease."

"Don't ever forget it." Loving the boost of confidence his appreciative glare has given me, I strut to Maggie, who's unstacking glasses from a dishwasher concealed by the wooden bar top. "How can I help?"

When she peers up from the dishwasher, disbelief masks her face. "You could go and get dressed?"

I air slap her while giggling. My laughter halts when her eyes narrow so much, they're close to closing, but I'm saved by a deep voice on my right. "Be nice, Maggie."

Noah gives me a sneaky wink, revealing he has my back, although I doubt even he could save me from Maggie's death stare. She's a lot sterner than I expected.

Hoping to prove I belong here, I serve Noah as I would any other customer. "What can I get you?"

His plump lips turn upwards. "A beer would be great."

"Beer. Great. Coming right up." After clapping my sweaty hands together, I scan my side of the wood and leather bar, seeking the coolers. There's beer on tap, but since I have no clue how to pull a beer, Noah will have to drink from a bottle tonight.

Several painstaking seconds later, Noah points toward the only section of the bar I haven't searched. I mouth a quick *thank you* before bobbing down to retrieve a bottle of Bud Light. I crack off the cap on the countertop before setting it down in front of him. "That'll be…" I stop talking, having no clue how much Mavs charges per bottle.

Laughing at my stunned expressed, Noah snatches his beer off the counter before making his way back to his bandmates.

"The band's drinks are on the house." Maggie moves to stand next to me. My quick thinking proved I'm here to work, but her shoulders are still taut. "You've met Noah. The blond on his left is Nick. The dark-skinned cutie on his right is Marcus, and the one with the dreadlocks is Slater. They form Rise Up. They're supplied with unlimited beer every Friday night."

"Okay. Great." I scan the members of Rise Up into my memory bank for future reference. It's not a hard task. They're all gorgeous. Not quite as handsome as Jacob, but they're pretty darn close.

While wiping down the already spotless counter, Maggie says, "Tonight, you'll serve premixed beverages. Then, over your next couple of shifts, I'll teach you how to mix drinks."

Her sentence barely finishes leaving her mouth when we're hit by six thirsty patrons.

FOR THE NEXT FOUR HOURS, I'm run off my feet. They're aching; blisters are forming on my heels, and my muscles are screaming in pain. Anyone would swear I endured a marathon instead of a four-hour shift at a rundown bar. I'm exhausted. I had no clue a shit hole like Mavs was so popular. We're only slowing down now since Rise Up has finished their set.

"You did well." Maggie's praise isn't needed, but it's nice to hear. She doesn't seem the type to give unnecessary compliments, so it's even more reason to pat myself on the back. "You're right to head off. I'll text you some extra shifts tomorrow."

I hold back my squeal until I'm in the backroom, then, after gathering my purse, I hobble to the table Jacob and Rise Up have used the entire night. Unfortunately, they're not alone. There are several heavy-breasted females seated with them.

Jacob doesn't pay them any attention when I stop to stand next to him. "How'd you go?"

"Good." Despite my aching feet, I smile. "Maggie is texting me some extra shifts."

The pretty brunette seated next to Jacob glares at me, wrongly believing I'm her competition. I'm not, but there's no need to get snarky. We women should fix each other's crowns instead of destroying them over a man.

I realize how two-faced I am when the unnamed brunette claws Jacob's thigh. He's as unprepared for her friendliness as I am for the emotions attacking me. I've never been jealous, but if I were asked to place my hand on the Bible and swear I'm not seconds from scratching the brunette's eyes out, I wouldn't be able to do it.

I'm not afraid my hand will be scorched from being placed on a religious artifact.

I just hate lying.

CHAPTER EIGHT

JACOB

I swivel my barstool, facing my back to the brunette who just tried to stake her claim in front of a woman she'll never win against. Two weeks ago, I would have jumped to the numerous pleas in her eyes. Tonight...not a chance in hell. There's only one girl I've got in my sights. It's the one pretending she isn't annoyed by the many daggers she's been hit with tonight. Not just from girls jealous of all the attention she gets—but from Maggie as well.

Maggie can be a little stern, but it's her way of keeping those she cares about on the straight and narrow. I've overheard many stories about her younger years. She had—and still does have—a wild side, so I'm confident any conflict of interest between her and Lola is simply a clash of personalities. They're too similar to get along.

Noticing Lola seems a little flat on her feet, I ask, "Are you ready to head out?"

"Yes." She gives me a look, one I don't know her well enough to read. "My feet are killing me."

I cringe when she removes her black stiletto with a hiss. There's a massive blister on the back of her ankle. "Remind me to wear more suitable shoes next time."

Nodding, my eyes drift to Noah. "You ready?"

I get hit with the same deadly glare Lola got when she arrived at our table. It isn't coming from Noah. It's from the blonde who's been vying for his attention all night. She's more pissed than Noah was when I forgot to tell him I couldn't drive him home tonight until he already had a few beers under his belt.

With Nick and Marcus having plans, and Slater's only mode of transport his motorbike, Noah either leaves with us or rides bitch on the back of Slater's bike. There's no way he'll do that, so he jumps to his feet. "Yep. I'm good to go."

He downs the remainder of his beer, then slips on his leather jacket. Much to the blonde's dismay, he leaves her side without so much of a goodbye. She shouldn't be shocked. He's not known for affectionate behavior.

OUR DRIVE to Lola's house is made in silence. Neither Lola or Noah have murmured a peep. Their behavior is so out of character, I feel like I've been zapped to an alternative universe—even more so when my arrival at Lola's house coincides with her inviting me inside.

I eye her curiously, confused as fuck. She's adamant we'll never be a couple, yet she's inviting me into her home.

What the fuck?

Earlier tonight, I sat in my car, honking like an ass to assure I maintained the "friends zone" she wants. I was itching to pick her up at her door as my dad taught me to, but since that isn't something a friend does for a friend, I kept my ass planted in my seat. It was a fucking hard feat—especially when I saw her teeny tiny shorts.

I like Lola, so I'm more than eager to be her friend, but we've fucked. That's not something I can merely forget. Three lifetimes would pass before I'd forget how scrumptious her lips taste, much less how good her heat felt wrapped around my cock.

While licking my lips, hoping to find a morsel of her cherry lip gloss on my mouth, I shift my eyes to Noah to seek his opinion on Lola's offer. He nods, giving me the go-ahead. He's good like this. He's not a fan of dating, but he isn't a cockblocker either.

As we enter Lola's cozy living room, the vibe shifts from playful to teasing. A current always bristles between Lola and me, but it's stronger now that we're in her private domain.

After gesturing for me to sit on a hideous floral armchair, Lola plants her backside on the arm of my chair. There are another five spots she could take up, but she'd rather share a seat with me.

I like that—I like that a lot.

Wanting to gauge her true response, I place a hand on her thigh. Is she messing with me, or does she want to *mess* with me? When she doesn't flinch against my touch, I ask, "Are you drunk?" quiet enough Noah won't hear me. "Did you fall over and hit your head? You do realize I'm not my brother, right?"

Giggling, she slaps my chest. "Seriously, Jacob."

I eye her as if to say, *yeah, I'm serious*. I'm as confused as fuck right now. "Is this because I called you a cock tease? I don't regret it, but if this is the outcome, please let me know so I can say it as often as possible."

"Maybe...?" My cock flexes against my zipper when she straddles my lap. "Or maybe I just want you to kiss me. Can we do that without fifty questions? Or shall we divulge our entire medical history first—?"

I cut off her question by slicing my tongue across her lips. If she wants me to kiss her, she doesn't need to ask me twice. This girl has lips so sinful, they should belong to the devil.

After a few minutes making out, Lola flips our embrace on its head for the second time tonight. She pulls back with a huff, her mood the complete opposite of mine. I'm seconds from mauling her like a hungry lion, whereas she's giving me silent marching orders. With a nudge of her head to her front door, she breathes out, "Thanks for the lift."

I snarl at her, declaring I don't appreciate the severe case of blue balls she just handed me before glancing at Noah over her shoulder. "We better head out. You ready?"

My disappointment about leaving is evident in my tone, but Noah misses it because he's eager to stop watching us suck face. "Sure am." He shifts on his feet to face Lola, his brows joining when he notices her in my lap. "Is it okay if I hit the can before we leave?"

Lola flashes me a beaming grin before cranking her head back to Noah. "Sure, it's down the hall on the left."

I balk when her instructions conclude with her mouth returning to mine. Her rapid shifts in personality have me wondering if she has some kind of mental disorder.

When Noah enters the hallway, Lola un-suctions herself from my lips, then stands. After tugging down her shorts from the height they gained to straddle my lap, she drags her finger over her kiss-swollen lips. Her eyes are dazzling with lust, but there's something more than desire brightening them. I just wish I knew her well enough to know what it is.

"What are you up to?"

When she twirls to face me with a mammoth smile planted on her face, I tug on my dick, begging for him to calm down. She doesn't miss the grab of my crotch, but she's got other matters on her mind right now.

"I told Noah the bathroom is on the left."

I remain quiet, waiting for her to elaborate. When she leaves me hanging, I say, "So...?"

"The bathroom is on the right; my sister's room is on the left." She rubs her hands together, feigning an innocence she'll never pull off. "Now watch the sparks fly."

Although pissed she used me as a ploy to get Noah and her sister to meet, I'm not overly angry. The hunger I've been craving the past week was just fulfilled. Now I need to work out how to get her matchmaking to fix the rock behind my zipper.

NOAH IS SO quiet the first half of our drive home, I grow worried he's discovered Lola's ploy to force him and her sister to meet—even more so when he asks, "What do you know about Lola's sister, Emily?"

The unease in his voice settles my nerves. I've never heard him use this tone before. He seems generally interested in my reply, like everything he's ever worked for is precariously balanced on my answer.

With my brows arched and my smile genuine, my eyes drift from the road to him. When he notices my goading look, his jaw tightens. "Get fucked."

He plays it cool for the remainder of our trip, only speaking once I pull into the driveway of our home. "Could you ask Lola for Emily's number?"

I step into the role I was born to play by shaking my head. "Nope, not happening."

"Why not?" His short reply can't hide the quiver in his jaw.

"Because you don't date, and Lola said Emily is a dating type of girl."

When I clamber out of my seat, Noah mimics my moves. He slams his door shut before sprinting up the path to catch up with me. His eagerness exposes how interested he is. "I didn't say I wanted to date her; I just wouldn't mind getting to know her a little better."

His cool, calm demeanor isn't fooling anyone. Sweat is beading on his temples, and his pupils are massive. He's more than eager. He's shitting bricks.

Happy for him to sweat it out a little longer, I murmur, "I don't know... it's risky. She seems like a *real* nice girl." When his nostrils flare like he's seconds from decking me, I put him out of his misery. "Alright, I'll ask Lola for her number."

He drops his eyes to my jean pocket, encouraging me to hurry the fuck up.

"Jesus, calm down; no need to get your panties in a twist." Laughing, I yank my cell from my pocket and text Lola.

Me*: Noah wants Emily's number*

She must be waiting by her phone because her reply is quick.

Lola*: I friggin knew it! It's 555 315 4558*

Me: *See ya on Tuesday?*

Lola: *Yep!*

Noah stores Emily's number in his phone when I recite it to him.

Now that I've done him a favor, it's time for him to help me out. "Do you have any plans next week?"

He places his phone in his pocket before raising his wide eyes to me. "Nope, why?"

"Remember that prank we've done a couple of times? Lola needs driving lessons, so I thought I'd conduct them at the State Forest, you know, for safety and all." I waggle my brows, hoping he'll get the drift without me needing to spell it out for him.

He catches on rather quickly. "Name the time and the place. Just don't do it on a Friday."

After slapping my shoulder, he climbs the stairs of our home. I enjoy the cool night for a couple of seconds longer, praying my ruse will work its magic on Lola, because I can't stop thinking about the one and *only* time we've slept together.

CHAPTER NINE

After Hank finishes taping my knuckles, he steps back. "You're good to go."

I jump up from my seat to warm up my muscles for my debut fight. Tonight's event is being held in a rundown gym on the outskirts of town. Hank said I have to start at the bottom rung before working my way up. Once I get a few wins under my belt, the locations and prize money should improve—I hope.

I haven't told anyone about my match tonight. I don't know why. I think it's because fighting is the only thing I do for myself, so I'm not willing to share my passion just yet. That or I'm afraid of getting my ass kicked in front of my friends. With how hard nerves pummel me during my confession, I'd say it is the latter.

Tonight, my competitor is a local fighter who goes by the name "The Terminator." He's been fighting the past year professionally. Hank isn't concerned about my lack of experience. He wouldn't have put me in the octagon if he didn't believe I was ready.

When a middle-aged man announces it's time for my fight, I yank my long-sleeve shirt over my head before shadowing Hank into the hub of the old gym. The tangy scent of blood filters into my nose when we break through the corridor. A cage sits in the middle of the abandoned space with numerous black steel chairs lining its edges. The early fight time means people are just starting to flow into the cobweb-filled area.

When I enter the cage, butterflies tap dance in my stomach. Out of all the careers in the world, I picked one that requires my fists. Picking up on my uneasiness, Hank tries to settle it from the sidelines. "You've got this, Jacob."

His reply ends just as my opponent enters the cage. He's as built as me but a head shorter. His red shorts are so skin-tight, I'm not convinced they aren't underwear, and he's wearing brand name shoes. A chuckle rumbles in my chest, amused by his outfit selection. Upon hearing my laughter, Hank's eyes slit as he motions for me to quit chuckling. I give it my best shot, but nothing works. I'm fighting a fucking tool.

My humor is set aside when my opponent glares at me. He's not here for a good time. He wants to kick my ass.

Let's see if he can.

After tapping gloves, the ref steps back, indicating it's time to fight. The Terminator bounces around on the mat, prancing like the women in skimpy bikinis did before he arrived. I watch him closely as he throws jabs into the air. Sweat is beading on my brow, but my stance is firm. I just need him to make the first move, then I won't feel bad when I knock him out.

With me paying attention to his top half, I'm left blinded when he swoops for my legs. He wraps his hands around my ankles and yanks, making me plummet onto the mat with a winding *oomph*.

When he straddles my waist, I protect my face like Hank has taught me the past four months. He throws a left and right combination against my arms, but none of his swings hit my face. Adrenaline-thick blood races through my veins, making me hot with anger. Feeding off the rage, I curl my legs around his torso and pull back with force. The Terminator's back bends harshly before he gives in to the strain.

I move in to execute my revenge when he flops onto his back. I straddle his hips like he did mine before unleashing a triple set of hits to his unprotected face. When a jab to my ribs leaves me breathless, I roll off him.

Ignoring my winded composure, I scramble to my feet, hoping to bring our match back onto solid ground. I fight better when I'm on my feet.

The Terminator follows suit, but his footing isn't as steady as mine. He has a massive gash above his right brow, and his nose is bleeding. I protect my face before tucking my elbows close to my side. I've never been a dancer, so unlike my opponent, my stance remains stable.

It's for the best. Within seconds, The Terminator's prance around the cage reveals his shortfall. Every time he swings his left hand, he leaves his left side open for infiltration. He does counter-weight his movements with his right.

With the grin of a madman and my guard up, I step closer to him. When his left fist becomes friendly with my right ribcage, I punish him with a quick one-two combination to his exposed face.

Cracking drifts through my ears a mere second before The Terminator's body flops onto the mat. As the ref rushes to him, I move to the outer wall of the cage to await his verdict. After checking my opponent's pulse, he declares the fight over by technical knockout.

I get a decent amount of leverage when I leap into the air. "Hell yeah!"

My heart thrashes against my ribs as adrenaline surges through my veins. The feeling of victory is euphoric. Now I understand why fighters become addicted. The rush is unlike anything I've ever experienced. I just won my debut fight by a knockout in under four minutes. Fuck—you can't get better than this—except perhaps my car romp with Lola.

After settling down my pompousness, I make my way to my

opponent. When the ref notices my approach, he dives for me. "No, no, no, the fight is over!"

I shrug him off me. "I know that." *I'm not a fucking idiot.*

When I stop in front of The Terminator, his weary eyes lift to mine. He glares at the hand I'm holding out in offering, unsure what the hell I'm doing. The constant hum that's been filtering through the gym all night softens when I aid The Terminator to his feet.

"Good fight." I tap my gloves on the hand dangling at his side.

"Maybe for you."

With his brows as low as his frown, his manager assists him out of the cage. Hank arrives at my side not long later. He gives me a ribbing, saying I'm supposed to portray arrogance in the cage, or I won't be seen as a serious fighter.

"You don't help your opponent off the ground after knocking them out, Jacob."

"Why not? The fight's over, so why do I need to continue acting like an ass?"

With a deep sigh and a shake of his head, Hank exits the cage.

I follow after him, grinning like a dog with a meaty bone.

THE NEXT MORNING, I'm a little worse for wear. The Terminator was a worthy opponent. He has my ribs and torso screaming in pain, but the feeling of victory makes the ache worthwhile. Besides, none of his jabs landed on my face, so no one will know I was in a fight last night.

Because of my win, I'm automatically scheduled for a match next week. Fight nights are on Saturdays, so I'll maintain my current schedule: gym Monday to Friday, Mavs each Friday night, and Saturdays will now be dedicated to fight night.

I'll also squeeze Lola in as often as she'll have me—*if she'll have me.*

WITH SUNDAY SPENT RECUPERATING, I arrive bright and early Monday morning to Hank's gym to prep for my next fight. Yep, that's how addictive it is.

Hank spots me the instant I walk in. That's not hard, considering there's rarely anyone here but me. "You need to come up with a fight name."

I take a few seconds to settle my queasy stomach from the stench smacking into me before shifting on my feet to face Hank. My senses have adjusted to the smell the past few months, but I still get queasy.

"A fight name?"

Hank jerks up his chin. "Yeah, like a nickname; they won't just call you Jacob."

Unappreciative of the mirth in his tone, I flip him the bird. He laughs it off before he continues working the bag like he was when I entered. As I sit down to tie on a pair of gloves, I try to think of a name. Is it just me, or does it seem pretentious to give yourself a nickname?

Once I'm ready for my three-hour morning session, I join Hank near the boxing bags. "I'll let you pick my name. Just don't pick anything stupid."

When he grins, I realize I just made my second fatal mistake. My first was playing along with Lola's ruse of pretending we're *only* friends.

CHAPTER TEN

JACOB

I arrive at Lola's house at the designated time we scheduled last week. My heart skips a beat when she darts toward my car with a broad smile stretched across her face. We've been "friends" the past four weeks, but this is the first time she's greeted me with so much jubilation. Don't get me wrong, she's still a cock tease, but her stance on us dating hasn't changed. She's adamant she isn't the girl for me. I'm not yet convinced.

Her scent whips up when she plops into the passenger seat before leaning over to plant her lips on mine. Always willing to test the waters, I swipe my tongue against her glossy mouth. I expect her to pull back like she generally does, so you can imagine my surprise when her lips part at the request of my lashing tongue. She doesn't lead our kiss like she did at Bronte's Peak. She lets go of the reins, trusting I've got this.

I do. I'll take care of her real good.

When she opens her mouth, groaning into mine, I kiss her so hard, I'm certain it won't be another four weeks before she begs me to kiss her again. We kiss and kiss and kiss until she either pulls back for air or suffocates. As she peers at me with needy, shocked eyes, she murmurs, "Em is coming with us. Is that okay?"

"Yeah." I'd agree to anything if it gets her lips on mine again. "I'd do anything for you."

My plan works to perfection. After smiling at my approval, she kisses me with so much passion, my dick aches. I'm not a player like Nick, but the past four weeks is cutting it close to setting a new record of abstinence for me. If I don't get some cookie sampling soon, I'm going to burst.

Just as Lola's tongue wrangles mine into submission, a car door slamming shut booms into my ears. Eager to discover who has Noah's panties twisted up, I pull back and crank my neck to the side. I understand Noah's interest when my eyes land on Emily. She's as beautiful as Lola; she just seems a little more down to earth.

I try to ease the panic flaring in her eyes with a friendly smile. "Hey, Em, you ready for this?"

I wonder if she is as timid as first thought when she screws up her nose and sticks out her tongue. "As ready as I'll ever be."

Pretending I can't feel Lola watching with meddling eyes, I fire up my ignition and pull out of their driveway.

Phase one is set. I sure as hell hope Lola is ready for phase two.

LOLA DOESN'T NEED as much training as predicted. She's so comfortable behind the wheel, I'm beginning to wonder if she was failed because her instructors didn't like her ballsy attitude.

With our lesson going longer than anticipated, I completely forget Noah is waiting for us under the railway bridge until Nick's truck pulls in behind us. He flicks on his high beams, scaring the shit out of Lola and Emily.

I flip up the rearview mirror to stop his lights from impeding Lola's vision before my eyes drift to hers. "Keep your attention on the road. They're no concern of yours."

When she nods, I glance over my shoulder. Curiosity crosses Emily's face when I wave my arms in the air like I'm landing a jumbo jet. With her hand shielding her eyes, she follows the direction of my gaze. The vein in my neck beeps out a tune when she notices two figures in Nick's truck. I don't know if she can see them. I'm fucking hope she can't, or I'm in deep shit.

Since no cars are surrounding us, Emily indicates to Nick that he's safe to pass. He thanks her by bringing his bull bar to within an inch of my bumper.

"Arrogant assholes," she mutters before flipping them the bird.

Realizing Noah has no clue I'm not driving, I devise a way of getting us off the road before we're forced off. "Pull in there." I point to a closed gas station coming up on our right.

With Lola's anxiety as high as mine, she yanks the steering wheel at a speed too fast to be safe. When my tires slip off the asphalt, they fishtail in the gravel. Panicked, Lola slams on the brakes.

That's the final nail in our coffin.

With Lola and Emily's squeals in my ear, my car spins out of control. In no time at all, we're concealed by a massive dust cloud. My lungs kick up a stink about the filthy air as Lola shuts her eyes, surrendering to her fate.

As quickly as our nightmare began, it ends. My car jolts three times before coming to a complete stop. By some miracle, we're still upright. I have no fucking clue how. I was confident we were cartwheeling. Lola did incredibly well to maintain control of the car. That would have been difficult for an experienced driver, much less someone learning how to drive.

Although grateful she did well, I'm too dumbstruck not to react. "Oh my fucking god." I whack the dashboard with my fists. "How could they not realize it wasn't me in the driver's seat?!"

Lola would be five-foot-five at the most, so it should have been pretty fucking obvious I wasn't driving. When my outburst startles Lola, I leave my car so I can get ahold of my anger. I didn't mean to scare her, and if anyone is deserving of my wrath, it's Noah, not her.

After a few big breaths, I tap on the driver's side window, startling Lola for the second time. "Holy shit, Jacob, you scared the crap out of me."

"Sorry. I thought perhaps you'd like to swap places so I can drive?"

I try to suppress my smile when she asks if my house is close by because she needs a drink, but the faintest grin creeps across my lips. I hate scaring her, but I'm desperate for some alone time with her.

During our drive to my home, my mind wanders. I recall how badly Lola flinched when my fist indented the dashboard, and how she seems more rattled by my anger than our near-death spin in a dusty parking lot.

Certain I'm misreading things, I lean across to grasp Lola's hand in mine. A second wave of frustration crashes into me when she pulls her hand out of my reach. The happy, carefree Lola I was making out with earlier tonight has vanished, leaving nothing but a woman who looks frightened.

By the time I arrive home, my anger is at an all-time high. Although Lola's dismissal isn't Noah's fault, his earlier antics smack back into me when I spot him leaning on the front door of my home wearing nothing but a pair of boxer shorts and an arrogant smirk.

"Can you give me a minute to talk to Noah in private before joining us?"

"Sure," Lola is quick to reply, which frustrates me even more. It's as if she can't wait to see the back of me.

After giving Emily a pleading look to have a word with her sister on my behalf, I make my way to Noah. "You could have killed them!"

The veins in my neck pop with every syllable I speak, but it does little to subdue the murderous gleam in Noah's dark gaze. He's as worked up as me.

"That's all part of the game; isn't it, Jacob?" His voice is as high as mine, his anger just as palpable. "Get them so rushed up on excitement, they'll come back here for more heart-pumping entertainment?"

I balk, stunned by his response. "Get them excited? You scared them both to death."

When my eyes drift to my car, a spasm hits my jaw. Even from this distance, Lola's eyes are darker than usual. I just can't tell if it is because she's scared or turned on. The expressions that cross a woman's face in ecstasy can look like other emotions.

With a growl, I return my eyes to Noah. "You fucked up. That shit you pulled wasn't the plan."

"*I* fucked up? It was *your* plan. This is what *you* wanted!"

I shake my head so furiously, sweat flings off my temples. "This wasn't what I wanted."

"Then why did you bring them here, Jake? Why didn't you take them home?" The furious beat of Noah's heart puts an edge in his voice. "Because you still want to have fun, don't you? You want to ride the rush. That's why you play these games all the time, because you need to get as much attention as you can before things get boring, and they leave you for their next big rush."

Hating that he's using my neurosis against me, I spit out, "Fuck you, Noah. You're only pissed because you're worried Emily would rather hang with someone like me than slum it with you!"

The instant the words escape my lips, I want to reel them back in. I'm peeved as fuck, but that was a below-the-belt hit.

"Noah... Man... Shit. I'm sorry."

His chance to reply is lost when someone unexpectedly places their hand on my shoulder. I'm so riddled with remorse, I yank away from her, scaring Lola for the second time tonight. She steps back, her eyes widening. My size can be intimidating at first, but once you get to know me, you realize I'd never hurt a fly, so why does she keep flinching? I fuckin' hate it.

When Noah storms into the house, I drop my eyes to Lola. "Why do you keep flinching?"

I keep my tone low, hoping I don't frighten her again. It has the opposite effect. Her cheeks redden with anger as her arms fold in front of her chest. "I don't *flinch* at you." Her hair whips my chest when she pivots on her heels. "But I do think you should take us home."

With my heart shut down and my suspicions at an all-time high, I do precisely that.

Our drive back to Erkinsvale is made in silence. Nothing is mentioned about the driving lesson, the prank, or Noah and I almost having a fistfight, but more concerning than anything is the fact I've made Lola flinch twice in one night.

When I pull into the driveway of Lola's house, Emily squeezes my shoulder. "Thanks, Jacob." Her eyes reveal she's feeling the tension in the air too.

Before Lola can follow her sister, I seize her wrist. I'm barely grabbing her, so she could leave if she wants, but I really hope she'll stay.

When a few seconds pass without contest, I say, "I'll never hurt you, Lola."

She sinks into her seat with a sigh as her eyes seek mine. "I know that."

My heart constricts when I notice how much moisture her eyes are holding. They're so crammed with tears, I'm confident she's seconds from crying. My hands rattle when I drag my thumbs across her cheeks that are dangerously close to feeling the wetness of her tears. "Who did this to you?"

"No one, Jake, just drop it. This isn't your fight." Her words are so soft, if I hadn't seen her lips move, I may have never known she spoke.

After pressing her lips to the edge of my mouth, she throws open her door and races into her home. I sit in my car for several long minutes, struggling to work out what to do. Should I demand she tell me what happened or walk away? I want to help her, but if I push her, I'll most likely lose her.

With that in mind, I reverse my car out of her driveway and head home.

Every mile I travel fills me with even more anger, so it's no surprise Noah and I rehash our argument when I arrive home. We stumble over the same shit we argued about earlier, only stopping when I disclose that Lola was driving the car when we veered off the road.

"Are you kidding me, Jacob?" He storms toward me, his anger unmissable. "Why the fuck would you let her drive knowing we were there waiting for you?"

When he fists my shirt, I take a step back. I'm seconds from retaliating, but Hank has my skills on a very short leash. If I use them outside the cage, he's done training me. For that alone, I keep my hands fisted at my side.

"I forgot you were waiting—"

"You forgot! How the hell could you forget?!" He sucks in a deep, ragged breath. "We could have killed them, Jake." He stumbles back, his eyes watering. "Then I would have had another death on my hands."

He looks physically ill as he backs away with a raging chest and clenched fists. He's as worked up as me, but instead of taking it out on the person he believes responsible, he goes outside to unleash his fury on a tree trunk. He pummels it without remorse, knowing violence will never end violence, but having no other way to rid himself of his guilt. We all cope in our own ways. Mine is seeking attention from the opposite sex. Noah's is the brutality he was raised with.

After collapsing onto his knees from exhaustion, Noah turns his eyes to me. They're the darkest I've ever seen them. When he takes off down the driveway, I snatch up my keys from the hallway table and go after him.

My quick strides out the screen door falter when Patrick blocks my exit. "He won't do anything stupid; he just needs some time."

He can say that because he wasn't there when I threw Noah into the shower every morning to sober him up after his brother killed himself.

When I attempt to skirt past Patrick, he steps back into my path, causing my jaw to tick. "You need to stop babying him. He fuckin' hates it. Give him a day or two to sort his head out, *then* you can deal with him."

I nearly tell him to go row up a creek, but a set of wise eyes stops me. My dad is standing at the side of the porch, his expression revealing he agrees with Patrick.

CHAPTER ELEVEN

LOLA

"*There's no fuckin' chance I'm taking you out looking like that. Go get changed!*"

Callum, my boyfriend of nine months, forcefully walks me into our bedroom. When his older brother's abrupt chuckle vibrates through my chest, his grip on my arm tightens so much I grimace. I've noticed the past few months that anytime Curtis is over, Callum is more aggressive than usual.

"Ouch, you're hurting me." I search my arm for a bruise when he shoves me into our room. I don't have one—yet.

As Callum's hands rake his spiky blond hair, his nostrils flare. "Are you trying to embarrass me in front of my brother?"

When I shake my head, his squinted gaze drops to my outfit. I'm wearing a pair of denim shorts and a black fitted shirt—a favorite outfit of mine he's seen me in many times the past year. These shorts aren't even my raunchiest pair, so I have no clue why he's so agitated.

"Get changed!"

When I fail to jump at the command in his voice, he rids my closet and drawers of every article of clothing I own. They fly across the room like cannonballs shot from a cannon. Half land on the bed, but the other half don't even make it more than a foot from my drawers.

Once he finds a Callum-approved outfit, he shoves it into my chest. "Now, Lola. I won't ask you again."

"No." I dump the clothes onto my bed before folding my arms under my chest. "I'm not changing so you can impress your moronic asshole of a brother—"

My words fall short when fiery heat creeps across my cheek. I'm only just getting over the shock that he slapped me when he rears his hand back for the second time. This hit is even more painful than his first. Although shocked I'm being hit, I don't register the pain. I'm too stunned to do anything but glare at Callum.

His face is as hard as a stone, not the least bit concerned he turned a verbal altercation physical. "Get. Changed. Now."

Afraid of what he'll do if I don't comply, I slip out of the shorts, replacing them with the pants he shoved into my chest before placing a long-sleeve shirt over the one I'm already wearing. It's not cold outside; it's actually quite warm, but the icy cold glare Callum is giving me makes it seem as if it's the middle of winter.

His anger remains even with me doing as asked. "Now get your ass into the car and keep your fucking mouth shut."

Who is the person standing in front of me? He isn't the Callum I met twelve months ago. He's not even half the man he used to be.

CALLUM, Curtis, and I have dinner at a pizza and wings bar in their hometown of Ravenshoe. I sit quietly, watching them banter and chat as if my face isn't harboring a new red welt. They eat their pizza and guzzle down beer while enjoying each other's company.

Curtis is a few years older than Callum, but when they sit side by side, they almost look like twins. Their blond locks hang loosely on their heads, and their blue eyes are practically identical, except

Curtis's have a ring of black surrounding his irises. I always joked that was his dark side being exposed. Now I'm confident it is.

My eyes float up from my plate when a waiter's apron brushes my arm. "Are you finished?"

I offer him a hesitant smile before nodding. I've hardly touched the meal Callum ordered for me. I can't trust my stomach to keep anything down. I'm still gobsmacked. Callum can be cruel with words, and he's occasionally shoved me, but tonight was the first time he's physically assaulted me.

When the waiter moves away from our table, my pulse quickens. Callum is glaring at me. I smile at him, hoping to appease his anger. He doesn't smile back. He just throws some bills onto the table before demanding I get my ass back in his car.

Our trip home is as quiet as our one to the restaurant, and the silence does little to settle my flipping stomach. If anything, it makes it worse. Callum's jaw is ticking so profusely, I hear every grind it does.

When he shadows me into our house, his stomps overtake the ringing of my pulse in my ears. He bands his arms around my waist to yank me back. His cock is thick and braced against my ass, but he's not cuddling up to me for that. He's mad.

"I can't even take you out for pizza without you flirting with another man."

I ram my elbow into his ribs when his hand slithers under my shirt to grope my breast. When he stumbles back, I pivot around. I'm prepared to protect myself, but nothing could prepare me for what happens next.

The man standing before me isn't the man I fell in love with. He's a monster.

"What happened to you?"

"Me?!" He storms toward me with his fists raised and his eyes black. "What the fuck happened to you?!"

I wake up screaming. Sweat is coating every inch of me, and I'm on the verge of crying. It takes several scans of my room to remember

I'm safe and alone, and even then, I still shake without control. That night was over twelve months ago, yet it still haunts my dreams.

That was the first and *only* time Callum laid his hands on me. When he fell asleep, I fled his house and never returned. My friend Natalie took me in until my bruises faded enough I could hide them with a good concealer, then I scampered home with my tail between my legs.

To this very day, my family is none the wiser as to what happened to me. They'd support me, but I'm too embarrassed to admit someone like Callum got the better of me. I'm stronger than that, and I refuse to be made a victim. That's why I'll never change who I am for anyone. I don't want approval on what I can or cannot wear any more than I want to update someone on what I'm doing and whom I'm doing it with. If that means I'm portrayed as the predator instead of the prey, so be it. I'm not out to impress anyone. I just want to live my life how I want to live it. Is that asking too much?

My chances of doing that are less likely when I check the time on my phone. It's a little after two in the morning, and I have twelve unread messages from Jacob. They all follow a similar tune: he's sorry if he scared me, and he promises not to do it again.

I like Jacob, but his messages prove we need distance. He's becoming attached, which will only end badly. I could continue our friendship if denying him wasn't above my skillset. Just the way I fell for his trick last night proves this without a doubt. One swipe of his tongue and I was incapable of denying the pleas of my body for a second longer. I've done it the previous four weeks. It was pure hell. I don't have the strength to continue doing it, so it leaves me only one choice. I have to cut contact with him.

He'll hate me for it, but over time, he'll realize it's the nicest thing I ever did for him.

CHAPTER TWELVE

JACOB

Noah stops strumming his guitar when he notices me standing outside his bedroom door. This isn't his room at my home; it's the place responsible for his backside having an indent in a chair around my family's dining room table the past four years.

"Is it safe to come in?"

When he gestures that I can enter, I take two steps into his room before stopping. There's nowhere else for me to go. Noah's childhood bedroom is as sparse as they come. His mattress doesn't have a frame; his clothes don't have any drawers, and the only other décor he has is a bunch of magazines stacked in the corner. Other than that, his room is empty.

Feeling my hesitation, Noah jumps up from the mattress to offer me his hand to shake. It's been two weeks since I last saw him. That's the longest we've gone without speaking. When Patrick said to give him some time, I expected it to be a few hours, maybe a day or two, so I was surprised when weeks passed without word from him.

The first few days, I was pissed he didn't man up and talk to me, but since Lola was also skirting my calls and texts, I let it slip by without too much notice. By the second week, I was furious. I didn't understand why he was shunning me from his life as Lola had. We've always been there for one another. We're brothers from different mothers. As thick as thieves. We never let anything come between us.

It was only after talking to my dad did I realize I wasn't the only one deserving of an apology. *I* asked Noah to participate in the prank that night. *I* forgot he was there waiting for me. So technically, *I'm* to blame for our fight. So, with my tail between my legs, I'll apologize and hope he'll forgive me.

I use his offer of a shake to drag him in for a man hug. He hates any mollycoddling, but I'm not stirring him today. I've genuinely missed him. "You know you don't have to stay here, man; my house is your house."

"Yeah, I know. I just had to sort my shit out."

Hating the worry in his voice, I bump him with my shoulder. "This is the longest you've been away. Dad keeps asking why the fridge is full."

He throws a couple of jabs into my mid-section. "Maybe if you switched your steroid-loaded shakes for real food, your dad wouldn't have noticed I was gone."

I arch my brow, hiding the fact a few of his hits connect with bruises I collected last night. I had another fight last night, my sixth professional one. Since everyone lost contact with me at the same time, I threw myself headfirst into my fighting goals. Did it make the sting of their rejection any easier to swallow? No, it didn't. But it did increase my love for the sport.

I've won every bout, and although last night's fight went a few rounds longer than I would have liked, at the end of the day, a win is a win. The prize money has grown more impressive with each fight too. Last night, I pocketed nearly a thousand dollars for my efforts.

Unsure why I've gone off-script, Noah brings me back to earth. "I'll pop over and see the old man this week."

I don't know why he's pretending to visit my dad. My home is his home. I was hoping he would have realized that by now.

After we go a couple of rounds of impromptu boxing in his room, my thirst gets the better of me. "Wanna grab a beer?"

Noah looks up at me with wide, dilated eyes. "Sure."

I dodge his hair ruffle before nudging my head to his duffle bag. The grin I'm wearing doubles when he collects both his guitar and his bag. That means he heard the words I didn't speak, the ones where I'm welcoming him back home with open arms.

WHEN WE ENTER Mavs ten minutes later, my heart whacks out a funky tune. Lola is working. This is the first time I've seen her in two weeks. After exhaling my nerves with a big breath, I shadow Noah to the bar.

"Hey, Lola." Noah adds a smile to his greeting before placing an order for two beers.

When Lola sets them down on the glistening bar top, she drifts her eyes to me. "Hey."

I dip my head in greeting before guzzling down a mouthful of my beer. I'm dying to talk to her, but I'm still pissed she cut ties with me. I also don't trust myself not to drop to my knees and beg for her scraps. I've never had my prank backfire so badly before. You can be assured I won't be doing it again anytime soon—if ever.

My eyes stop floating around the bar when Noah asks Lola if she passed her driving test. She shakes her head. "Not yet. Maggie is scheduling me on day shifts so I can catch the bus."

It's the fight of my life to only mumble my curse word instead of screaming it from the rooftops. I'm pissed—fucking ropeable. Not only am I not good enough to talk to anymore, but she also pissed all over my offer of a ride. That's fucked.

Needing to leave before I say something I'll regret, I make my way to one of the many empty tables around the dance floor. I'd leave entirely if I weren't such a sucker for punishment. I know there's more to Lola's pullback than she's letting on. It didn't occur after her near-teary confession for no reason. If she's embarrassed, she doesn't need to be. I see past the shield she wears to protect herself—why do you think I fell for her so quickly?

After ordering another round, Noah joins me at a table near the pool tables. "What's the deal with you two?"

He opens a second bottle of beer before sliding it to my side of the table. I guzzle it down as quickly as I did the first, praying it will douse the fire roaring in my gut. Once it's sitting as low as my heart rate, I shrug. "I have no fucking clue. She confuses the fuck out of me." I keep my reply simple, not wanting to divulge any of Lola's private life without her permission.

OVER THE NEXT TWENTY MINUTES, Noah keeps the beer coming hard and fast. He stopped drinking as soon as he noticed I planned to have more than my usual two. When I set down my fourth empty bottle, his dark eyes lift to mine. "Shall we play a game of pool, or do you wanna head straight to the boxing ring?"

"You don't have to mend my broken heart. We never 'dated.'" I air quote my last word. "Rack up the balls; kicking your ass may be the most entertaining thing I do this week."

BY THE TIME we play two rounds of pool, I'm smashed from guzzling down too many beers in quick succession. "You done, Jakey-boy, or do you have a couple of rounds left in you?" Noah's tone is smug, loving that he whipped my ass our last two games. I don't think I sank a single ball.

"Best out of five."

As I rack up the balls, a sweet voice trickles through my ears. "Interested in a game of doubles?"

My mouth dries up as I absorb the owner of the heavenly voice.

Her face is as appetizing as her body. Large breasts stuffed into a teeny tiny shirt, curvy hips, and long, lean legs. Her brown eyes hold a gleam as wicked as the casual, man-eating smirk she's wearing, and her hair is blonde and straight. I'd give her brunette friend a quick once over if her sights weren't locked on Noah, but her batting lashes tell me everything I need to know. She isn't here for me.

My eyes drift back to the blonde when she asks, "What do you say? Best out of the three?"

When I glance at Noah to gauge his response, he curls his arm around the brunette's shoulders. "She's my partner."

Her childish giggle would be nauseating if I weren't so drunk. I offer my hand to the heavy-breasted girl. "I guess that means we're partners. I'm Jacob."

"Lucky me," she purrs while accepting my handshake. "Stephanie."

While playing pool with Stephanie and her friend Shell, Lola shoots daggers at me. I know this because I'm stalking her as adeptly as she's stalking me. I shouldn't love her annoyance, but I do. It's nice to see the shoe on the other foot for a change. The whole time we've known each other, it's always me getting smacked with jealousy.

When I lean over Stephanie's shoulder to show her how to aim correctly, Lola shoots out from behind the bar and darts my way. "Can I talk to you?"

My eyes bulge out of my head when she cocks her hip. She's wearing the teeniest tiniest pair of shorts I've ever seen, and I'm 100% jealous of her shirt. It's closer to her skin than my hands have been the past month.

After locking the image of her long, sexy legs into my memory bank for future use, I return my eyes to her face. "Why can't we talk here?"

The beer I've been guzzling makes my words come out snappier than I intended, and they have Lola's anger ramping up. She glares at me, warning me I'm seconds from having my nuts extracted from my body. I consider my options for a few seconds. If it gets her hands on any part of my body, I'm willing to suffer.

After a short deliberation, I nudge my head to the hallway where the restrooms are. I'm still contemplating disembowelment; I'd just rather it be done without witnesses.

I promise Stephanie I'll be back in a minute before following Lola. I barely get two steps into the lemon-scented space when she pounces on me. Unfortunately, it's a verbal altercation instead of a physical one.

"Do you think this is a good idea?"

I hold my hands out in front of my body, as if to say, *you don't want me, so I may as well have fun with a girl who does.*

My ego takes a hit it never saw coming when she adds on, "You know Noah is interested in Emily, so why are you encouraging him to hook up with a random bar skank?"

I take a step back, shocked. I thought she was angry about me getting friendly with Stephanie. How fucking stupid am I? She's not worried about me hooking up with any random. She's concerned about who Noah might go home with.

"Who Noah fucks is no concern of yours."

I skirt by her, my steps slowing when she retaliates, "You're only doing this because you're angry at me. Don't sacrifice their chance of happiness because things didn't work out for us the way you hoped." She stares me straight in the eyes, the moisture brimming in hers foreign. "I thought you cared about Noah—"

"I do."

"Then start acting like it!"

With that, she spins on her heels and returns to her station behind the bar. I take a few moments to expel my frustration with a long, unintelligible rant on how she is the most frustratingly beautiful and opinionated woman I've ever met. I tug on my hair; I scrub my tired eyes, and I mouth a million curse words to God before making my way back to the main area of Mavericks. I don't look toward the bar, but I don't need to see Lola to know her eyes are on me. I can feel them.

Shell stops sucking Noah's face when I stand next to them. "You ready to head out?"

"Now?" Noah peers at me, dumbfounded.

"Yep." I turn to face the set of eyes I feel burning a hole in my temples. "I'm sorry, but I have to go. Maybe we can catch up another time?"

Hearing the words I didn't express to save face, Stephanie huffs before storming off in the direction of the washroom. Reluctant to leave Noah's side, it takes Shell a few seconds to follow after her. She looks as pissed about Stephanie's dramatics as Noah is about mine.

I'm pissed Lola is more concerned about Noah's bed companions than mine, but that doesn't mean I don't agree with her. Noah deserves to have someone like Emily in his life. If that means I have to miss out on a little action for one night, then that's what I'll do for my friend.

Furthermore, Noah may hate me for the cockblock, but I doubt it would be worse than how much I'd hate myself if I let Lola's lack of interest persuaded me to take Stephanie home. Stephanie is a nice girl, but she's neither stubborn nor opinionated, so she's not the right girl for me.

AN HOUR LATER, sprawled on my bed, chugging down yet another beer, my phone dings with a text message.

Lola: *Thank you.*

In my drunken haze, I reply.

Me: *You owe me.*

Lola: *I know...*

I stare down at my cell, unsure if I should reply or not. I want to leave her alone like she clearly wants, but I'm dying to know why she hasn't reached out to me the past two weeks.

Fuck it—I'm already in the shit, so what's the worst that could happen?

Me: *What did I do?*

I swear, the moon circles the earth ten times before she replies.

Lola: *It wasn't you.*

I groan.

Me: *Please don't give me that bullshit excuse. It's not you; it's me.*

Lola: *Lol, I wasn't! I meant it wasn't you who made me this way.*

Her reply has my suspicion piqued about the baggage she's carrying. Doesn't scare me away, though. Not in the slightest.

Me: *Then why did you cut ties with me?*

I wait patiently for her to reply. It's a long-ass thirty seconds.

Lola: *I want to be your friend, Jacob, but you want more.*

My fingers fly over the screen of my phone.

Me: *I'd rather be your friend than not have you in my life at all.*

I glare at my phone, praying for it to ding. Lola takes it one step further by calling me instead.

"Are you sure this is what you want?" she questions, not waiting for me to issue a greeting. "I can't give you anything more than my friendship."

"It's better than not having you in my life at all."

Nothing but honesty rings in my tone. I like Lola. She has spunk and charisma, and I enjoy spending time with her, even when we're not doing anything sexual.

"Then let's be friends."

With my drunk head hearing her giggled statement differently than she intended, I growl down the line, "Is this a friends with benefits deal?"

Her laughter tightens the front of my pants. "Maybe..."

That's good enough for me... *for now*.

CHAPTER THIRTEEN

LOLA

"What the fuck are you wearing?"

I swing my hips harder, working my disastrous getup like I'm a model on the catwalk. My attempts to act seductive only make Jacob laugh even harder.

"Shut up." I slap his chest, praying it will shut his mouth. His laugh... *my god*. Enough to moisten the panties of a saint. I love his hearty chuckle. It's one of his best assets...amongst many other wonderful things.

Six weeks ago, when I told Jacob I didn't want Noah hooking up with a bar skank, it was a ploy to cover my jealousy. Seeing him flirt with another girl directly in front of me irritated the shit out of me. What he does in his free time doesn't bother me, but I'd prefer him being discreet. Not that I'd ever tell him that. The fact he made me jealous already has me at a disadvantage, so I'd never up the ante for him.

Our "friendship" has been going great the past six weeks. Only three times have we overstepped the line we drew in the sand. It's not my fault I succumbed to the chemistry bristling between us. I've been in a sexual rut, and since it's Jacob's fault, it's only fair he fixes the problem.

A majority of my days are spent at Mavs. When I'm not there, I'm with Jacob. Being friends with him is the equivalent of strapping a big neon sign to my chest, warning guys to back the fuck up. If Jacob is around, they refuse to approach me. Our harmless flirting may have tiptoed over the rules we negotiated weeks ago, but we're adults who understand the "friends with benefits" situation we have going. We're not hurting anyone, so why does it matter if those around us don't understand our arrangement?

Jacob watches me round the hood of his car and slip into the passenger seat before asking, "Seriously—what the fuck are you wearing?"

"I thought this might help me pass." I shrug. "No harm in trying, right?"

This morning, I have my fourth driving test. Although I'm confident in the skills Jacob has taught me the past two months, despite what people say, I know my last three fails were because the female driving instructors didn't appreciate my miniskirts and midriff tops as much as the male instructors did. Today, I decided to mix things up. By dressing conservatively, I'm hoping they'll judge my driving skills instead of my so-called "slutty" reputation.

Grinning, Jacob climbs into the driver's seat of his car. As he latches his belt, his eyes stray to me once more. He laughs again, even louder this time.

"Alright, now you're just being an asshole." I fold my arms under my chest, pretending to be mad. I'm not, but his laugh is making me want to do naughty things I swore we wouldn't do again.

"I'm sorry, Lola." Breathy chuckles punctuate his words. "But you just extinguished any wet dreams I might have had about you this week."

My mouth pops open as my heart beats double-time. One, he just admitted I star in his dreams. And two, he insinuated he doesn't find me attractive.

Ouch, take that ego!

"What's wrong with what I'm wearing?" I keep my breaths at a pussy cat purr while climbing over the console to straddle his lap. "Do you have something against naughty librarians who spank bad boys in the book stacks?"

Air hisses from his mouth when my endeavor to wrap my legs around his chunky hips causes the split in my skirt to ride up high. Add that scandalous bit of skin to the unbuttoning of my blouse to give him a sneak peek of the lace bra hiding beneath, and we've got a reaction no amount of laughing could deny. He's heavy underneath me, the pulse in his cock enough to detonate every one of my hot buttons.

"Jacob..."

His lips steal the rest of my plea. With my hair fisted in his big manly hand, he tilts my head back before slipping his tongue between my parted lips. He devours me with long, sensual licks and teasing bites while I respond to the tingles dancing in my core by grinding down on him. It's 10 AM on a Saturday, yet we're acting as if we're parked anywhere but in my parents' driveway.

I'm seconds from whipping his cock out of his pants when a car honk interrupts us. Considering our location, that means it can only be one of two people interrupting us.

With wide eyes and swollen lips, I peer past Jacob's shoulder. As suspected, my dad's rusty blue truck is parked behind us. Even from a distance, I can see his snarl.

Eek! Busted!

When Jacob's eyes flick up to the rearview mirror, the pulse in his neck thrums like the one feeding his cock. "We better get going." His usually smooth voice is extra scratchy. "Don't want you to be late for your test."

After pouting like a child, I plop back into the passenger seat. Although I'm on the verge of climax, I should probably pick a better location than the driveway of my parents' house in the middle of the day.

Sorry, Dad!

I should also pick a different companion to get down and dirty with. My relationship with Jacob is *supposed* to be platonic, yet here I am, on the verge of orgasm after doing nothing more than the grind up every thirteen-year-old boy expects during seven minutes in heaven. I need to resurrect the barriers before one of us gets hurt. And for the first time ever, I'm afraid that person may be me.

CHAPTER FOURTEEN

JACOB

With Lola spending a majority of our trip to the DMV in silence, I reflect back on how our morning started. I shouldn't have laughed when she strutted toward me looking as if she'd just finished filing my tax return, but I couldn't help it. I've become accustomed to seeing her in teeny shorts and tank tops that struggle to contain her generous rack. Today she's donning a black knee-length skirt, a white floral blouse, and a red knitted cardigan I swear I saw in my grandma's closet last winter. If her outfit wasn't bad enough, her wild locks have been wrangled into a low ponytail, and her makeup is basically non-existent.

It's lucky she can rock the granny look, but I was happy pretending she couldn't if it risked bringing out the hellion I've grown to love the past two months. My skate across thin ice paid off. Lola hated my tease, so much so, she retaliated in a way only she could. She proved without a doubt she's the sexpot deserving of the title "Cock Tease."

It's a pity her dad interrupted us. I didn't think I'd leave his driveway still breathing. I probably wouldn't have if Lola did take up my campaign.

When I pull into an empty spot at the back of the lot, Lola's eyes finally lock with mine. They're clouded with regret, and she has a deep groove between her brows. I try to pretend I don't know what's she's sorry about. "What's up? Nervous?" When she shakes her head, I *honk* her nose before clambering out of my car. "Good. Cause you have *nothing* to worry about."

My assurance has a double meaning. Every time we overstep the boundaries we discussed six weeks ago, she apologizes for leading me on. Every time she apologizes, I reply with the same thing: "You've got nothing to be sorry about."

I won't have her apologizing for making out with me. I love hanging out with her, even when we're following the rules. Besides, the handful of times we've gotten carried away, I instigated them, so there's no way she owes me an apology. If anything, I should be expressing regret for not being able to keep my hands to myself when she's in my vicinity.

When Lola's confused eyes meet mine, I give her a frisky wink. "Come on, let's get this done, then you can terrify more people than just me when you get behind the wheel."

Giggling, she throws open her door and steps onto the sidewalk. I learned early on that she isn't a fan of guys opening her door, ordering her food, or telling her what to do. Stick to those three little rules, you'll get along with her like a house on fire. Ignore them...enjoy your last days on earth.

After guiding her through the glass door at our local DMV, Lola goes to the counter to check in, while I head for the plastic chairs lining the foyer. Even in the hideous outfit she's wearing, she attracts numerous pairs of male eyes. I put up my blinkers, acting like the jealousy bug isn't stinging me. I should take up acting because my ruse is outstanding. It probably helps that Lola only has eyes for me as she makes her way across the room to join me in the waiting area.

Just as she's about to sit next to me, her name is called. A disgruntled moan rolls up her chest when her eyes lock on the person calling her name. This time around, she got a male instructor.

"You'll be fine." My words are barely heard through my chuckle.

After unclenching her fists, she struts to the male instructor with her hips swinging and her bosoms bouncing, working her disastrous getup as if it's the latest fashion craze. I'll give it to her, she's got the assets to pull it off.

FOR THE FIRST half an hour of Lola's test, I scroll my Facebook feed. Once that becomes brain-draining, I flip through the outdated magazines in the lobby. I'm through my fifth car magazine when my cell vibrates in my pocket. When I yank it out, I notice it's a call from Hank.

As I press my phone to my ear, I walk outside. "Hey, Hank."

"How's *Jake the Giant* this morning?"

With a huff, I roll my eyes. Hank was as original with my fighting name as he was with his business. As much as I loathe the name he picked, I'm now known as "Jake the Giant" in the fighting circuit.

It's lucky my stats are impressive enough no one ribs me about the childish name he gave me. I've remained undefeated the last ten rounds, which means I'm the twelfth-ranked fighter in my division. With a better ranking comes a better purse, but the caliber of my opponents has always increased. I don't mind. I like a challenge, hence my relationship with Lola.

I push my phone closer to my ear when Hank discloses, "There's been a change to your fight tonight. Rampant is out. They want you to fight The Constrictor."

"Who is The Constrictor?" I haven't heard of him in our local fight scene.

"He's from the West Coast, undefeated, and has been the past year."

"A year?"

Alarm resonates in my tone. I've only been fighting in the minors the last couple of months, so why are they matching me with a professional who's been undefeated for a year?

"You can win this, Jake, you just need to remember what you've been taught."

Hank is a great coach, but my intuition is warning me to be cautious. "Alright. It's too late to change anything, so we may as well run with it."

"You've got this, Jacob."

Hank disconnects our call, not giving me a chance to reply. He's done the same thing numerous times the past six months.

While shoving my cell back into my pocket, I stride toward the waiting room. I'm just about to break through the double glass doors when Lola throws herself into my arms. "I did it!" Her screech pierces my eardrums. "I passed!"

CHAPTER FIFTEEN

LOLA

When Jacob's excitement gets the better of him, he spins me around and around and around. My stomach automatically puts up a protest to his twirls.

"Please stop, or I'll puke."

His spins halt as quickly as they started. Through scrunched brows, he sets me back on my feet before his eyes roam my face. He looks genuinely concerned, like he too is seconds from barfing.

"You alright?"

Smiling a grin as mischievous as his handsome face, he nods, snatches my newly printed license from my hand, then hotfoots it toward the parking lot. I'm on his heels in under a second, but his long strides mean I have to sprint to catch up with him

I didn't think things through when I decided to dress like my mother. I forgot my horrendous lack of fashion would be displayed on my license for the next four years. My picture is hideous. The lady who snapped it didn't wait for me to be ready, and when I begged her to take another one, the old cow refused. To say I don't want my license circulated through social media would be an understatement. I'll die if it gets out.

I appear seconds from having my worst nightmare come true when I witness Jacob snapping a picture of my license with his phone.

"If you post that, I'll hurt you *real* bad."

He props his hip on the driver's side door of his car before his fingers fly over the screen of his phone, not the least bit intimidated by my threat. When I try to snatch his phone out of his hand, he yanks it out of my reach. Considering he's a giant, none of my springy jumps gets me close to his outstretched arm.

An arrogant smirk crosses Jacob's face when I give up with a huff. "What are you willing to give me for it?"

I smash my hand against his lips when he makes gaga kissy faces. His laugh at my denial of a kiss makes a brilliant idea pop in my head. Stepping closer to him, I crowd him between his car and me before dropping my hand to his crotch. His eyes widen when I grip his package in a hold soft enough he won't sustain permanent damage, but firm enough to reveal I'm not joking.

"Delete it." I add a squeeze between words.

Sweat beads on his temples as his eyes drop to mine. "Gentle."

"You should have thought about that before trying to embarrass me on social media."

"I wasn't going to post it. I was just gonna..." Sweat glides down his pale cheeks when I expose his lie with a tight squeeze. "Lol—"

"Delete it."

Nodding, he abandons the post he was halfway through uploading to Instagram.

"Now, the photo in your album."

It's amazing how quickly men follow the rules when their junk is on the line.

"There. Done. See?" He swivels his phone around to show me. It's open on his album, and although there's a handful of photos of me on display, they're ones I approve of, so I don't make him delete them.

"Good."

I snatch my license back with my other hand before releasing his crotch. He exhales a big breath as his hand darts down to check that everything is in its rightful spot. While he gives himself an in-depth feel up, I saunter to the passenger side of his car. Victory is heating my blood, euphoric that little old me took down someone as big as Jacob.

Confident his cock is still in working order, the cheeky glint Jacob's eyes forever holds returns stronger than ever. "If you wanna grope me, just ask. I'll never turn you down."

A smile curves my lips high. With how horny I am, I might take him up on his offer.

TWENTY MINUTES LATER, with his tease still in the forefront of my mind, I swivel to face Jacob. "Do you want to go out tonight?" I usually work Saturday nights, but my constant nagging about a lack of social life finally paid off. Maggie reluctantly gave me the night off, stipulating it's a one-time-only deal. "We can celebrate me *finally* getting my license."

The jest in my tone switches to disappointment when Jacob murmurs, "I can't. I... ah...I have plans."

"Oh..." I shouldn't be disappointed, but I am.

"Not *that* type of plans. I just have something important I have to do," he clarifies, making me realize I'd expressed my disappointment out loud.

"It's fine. You don't have to explain it to me. You're free to do whatever..." –Or *whomever*— "... you want."

I'm not surprised he has plans. I've witnessed numerous girls approach him and the members of Rise Up every time I work at Mavs. Even if I'm practically sitting on top of him, it doesn't stop their approach. They don't care if he may be taken, they still prowl for his scraps.

My eyes stray from my family home to Jacob when he asks, "See you next week?"

He sounds apprehensive, like me having a license will end our contact. It won't. I like hanging out with him. I just need to keep up those barriers he keeps knocking down; then we'll both come out of this "friendship" unscathed.

"Yep. I'll give you a call later in the week."

When I press a kiss to his lips, his tongue doesn't wrangle me into submission. He keeps our exchange friendly, reminding me that is precisely what we are: *friends*.

Once I slip out of my seat, I make my way to the front door, not once looking back. I'm about to glide down the hallway when my mom steps out, scaring the living daylights out of me. "Jesus, Mom, you scared me."

I stop clutching my chest when she asks how my driving test went. In true Lola fashion, I slump my shoulders and pout my lip.

"Don't worry, darling, I'm sure you'll pass next time."

Before she can wrap me up in a condolence hug, I yank my license out of my pocket, ensuring my thumb hides my hideous photo. "I passed."

After collecting her heart from the ground, my mom hugs me. "Well done. I knew you'd do it."

Her arms slacken when I murmur, "Can I borrow your car?"

I wasn't sure I'd pass, so I didn't consider not having any wheels.

With a giggle, my mom nods.

"Yay!"

I SPEND the rest of the afternoon prepping for a night out on the town. I haven't been out in weeks, so I'm more than excited to let go of the reins. It took me a few months to feel like myself again after what happened to Callum, so I've got a lot of good times to make up for.

With Emily taking forever in the shower, I rap my knuckles against the bathroom door. "Can I brush my teeth?"

"Yeah, sorry, come in."

When I enter the steam-filled space, my jaw drops. Emily's long, dark locks are no more. They've been cut to sit just below her shoulders, and honeycomb highlights frame her face, giving her an alluring yet mature look.

I twirl my finger in the air, motioning for her to turn around so I can get the whole picture. When she does as instructed, my mouth gapes more. Her highlighter-yellow dress fits her like a glove, and her pumps make her legs look like they stretch for miles. She looks incredible.

"We could be twins!" I slap her arm while laughing. "I just need to get you out of the sun and kink your hair."

Our personalities are on the opposite end of the spectrum, but as she stands before me now, we look very similar. If it weren't for her tanned skin and stick-straight locks, I'd begin to wonder if I was looking in the mirror.

When my gaze floats up from Emily's altitude-daring shoes, I catch her angry scowl. She's unimpressed with my taunt. I can't blame her. I hated when our mother dressed us like twins when we weren't, so I don't know why I made that reference.

"I'm joking. You look wonderful."

Rolling my eyes, I snag my toothbrush out of its holder then exit the bathroom. With Emily hogging the only bathroom we have, I'll brush my teeth in the kitchen sink.

Just as I spit the last of my toothpaste into the sink, my phone dings with a text message.

Jacob: *When you asked me out earlier today, was it a date?*

I can hear his nerves even over a text. Happy to keep him on tenterhooks, I reply:

Me: *Hmmm, I don't know... Maybe?*

His message comes through at a lightning pace.

Jacob: *Seriously?*

Me: *... I am horny.*

My honesty usually gets me in trouble, and I don't see tonight being any different.

Jacob: *Jesus, Lola, you can't say shit like that to me.*

Me: *Why not?*

He usually loves my honesty.

Jacob: *Because I'm not alone, and you're giving me a hard-on!*

My laughter bounces around my small kitchen as excitement surges through my womb.

Me: *Sorry... Do you want me to take care of it?*

Jacob: *Fuck, yes!*

My head shouts, "no," but my body ignores its panic.

Me: *Where are you?*

I glare at my phone, impatiently waiting for him to reply. It takes him a lot longer to respond this time around.

Jacob: *Can I meet you later?*

That's not the reply I expected, but I'm too horny to care right now.

Me: *Okay...*

Jacob: *Mavs at 11 PM?*

I must be getting old because I was planning to be in bed by then.

Me: *Alright, but don't keep me waiting, Jacob.*

Jacob: *I'll be there with bells on.*

His reply makes me smile.

Me: *Okay, I look forward to it!*

Jacob: *Me too xx*

I ARRIVE at Mavericks at ten PM, eager for my hook up with Jacob. I'm not desperate, but when you've been with someone as well-endowed as Jacob, a girl can't help but get a little excited.

"Hey, Maggie," I greet her when I see her at the end of the bar, wiping it down with her trusty red dishcloth.

Mavericks pulls in a decent crowd every Saturday night, but it's not as packed as the nights Rise Up performs. The band scheduled tonight is called Wanting Wombats. They're talented but lack the sex appeal Rise Up has. That might have more to do with them having the most ridiculous band name I've ever heard than their actual attractiveness.

"I thought I gave you the night off?" Maggie continues pulling beers for customers as we chat. Her work ethic is strong—nearly as sharp as her evil glare.

"You did; I'm meeting Jacob here."

I shrink to one half my size when Maggie's eyes snap to mine. "Are you two dating?"

"Nooo." I shoo away her mothering with a wave of my hand. "We're just friends." *Friends who like fucking each other,* but I keep that to myself.

Maggie has more of a clue than I gave her credit for. "Friends? Or... *friends?*"

Wanting to avoid any further interrogation, I ask, "Can I grab a lemon vodka?"

She stares at me for several long seconds before murmuring, "You know where everything is."

When she returns to serving other patrons, I dart around the bar to help myself to a drink. Maggie's eyes remain slit, but nothing can hold back her grin when I stick my tongue out at her. She acts like she doesn't like me, but she's warming to me. *Slowly.*

I SPEND the next hour listening to Wanting Wombats while impatiently waiting for Jacob to arrive. I've been offered drinks and invited to play pool, but since I gave Jacob my word I'd meet him here at eleven PM, I refuse all advances.

I WISH I weren't a woman of my word when another hour ticks by without word from Jacob. It's now past midnight, and I'm beyond pissed he stood me up. I know he said he had plans, but he shouldn't have made any with me if he didn't know how long his first "hook-up" would run.

"Can I buy you a drink?"

When I spin to face the mannish, accented voice, dizziness clusters in my head. I may be a little tipsy from the number of drinks I downed trying to cool the anger burning in my gut.

Flynn, the lead singer of Wanting Wombats, smiles before adding a head nudge to his offer. He's gesturing to the empty drink in my hand. "Looks like you could use a refill."

Flynn is cute, but he isn't the type I usually go for. His long brown hair hangs halfway down his back, and his face is so youthful, if I hadn't carded him weeks ago, I would have never believed he was twenty-five. He isn't as big as Jacob, but his athletic build is nicely displayed since he's wearing nothing but tight black leather pants. His guns are blazing, his abs stacked, and he has the sexiest Australian accent I've ever heard.

Come to think of it, he has a lot of attributes that myself and my stinging ego can appreciate. He has the eye of every woman in the room, yet he's talking to me. His attention is soothing the burn Jacob's rejection caused, and it has me thinking recklessly—recklessly enough to ask, "Do you want a drink, or shall we just get out of here?"

Hearing the intention in my question, Flynn drags his teeth over the piercing in his bottom lip before nudging his head to the door. "Let's go."

Pretending warning alarms aren't sounding in my head, I exit Mavs with my arms wrapped around his heavily tattooed torso.

CHAPTER SIXTEEN

JACOB

"Why did you do that, Hank?! I told you not to do that."

Hank crouches down in front of the padded bench my ass is sitting in. I just finished my fight—an unjust and rigged fight.

"I warned you to stay off the cage walls, Jacob, and where did you end up?" His angry voice echoes around the locker room. "On the fucking cage." He aggressively tugs on the tape on my hands. "I wasn't going to watch you get killed just so you can remain undefeated."

"I wouldn't give a fuck about being defeated if he didn't cheat! He *cheated*, Hank, making not only a fool out of himself but this organization as a whole!"

The instant my opponent dismissed my gesture of tapping our gloves at the start of the match, I knew he was going to fight dirty. Then, when he kneed me in the groin before executing an illegal punch to the back of my head, I realized it would be the dirtiest fight I had ever participated in.

Both tactics are illegal in the cage, but even with Hank protesting to the ref, no points were deducted from The Constrictor's tally, and the fight continued as if nothing had happened.

By the time the second round started, I was so furious about the ref's bias, I punished my opponent with a grueling left and right combination. It felt good watching him kiss the mat like the pathetic loser he was.

For the third round, we met toe to toe, chest to chest, eyes to eyes for an old-fashioned brawl in a back alley, neither willing to back down even when the bell rang. If it weren't for the ref dragging us apart, we'd still be fighting.

With exhaustion kicking in, the fourth round saw him bringing out his dirtiest tricks. While grappling on the ground, he gouged my eye with his thumb. When I stumbled back to protest to the ref, I ended up on the cage wall. I couldn't see a fucking thing, so I had no clue The Constrictor was coming for me until he unleashed a barrel of punches and kicks to my already exhausted body. That's when Hank threw in the towel, announcing my defeat against my wishes.

After removing the tape from my hands, Hank raises his nearly black eyes to mine. "Let me look at your eye." He lifts the ice brick from my right eye before completing a thorough inspection. "Your cornea doesn't look scratched, but we'll get it checked by an ophthalmologist."

"It'll be fine. Don't worry about it."

My tone is gruff. I'm not angry at Hank. I'm pissed shit like this still happens in professional sports. Losing sucks, but you won't get through life if you don't learn losses are a part of it.

"You'll get an opportunity to right the wrong that happened tonight, Jake, but not until I'm assured it'll be a fair fight."

After dumping the defrosted ice pack on the bench, I stand to get dressed. My muscles are stiff from sitting the last hour while doctors did a medical workup on me before clearing me to leave. Other than three broken ribs and a range of bruises, I'm uninjured. I just need to get my head in the right mind frame now.

"Do you want me to drive you home?" Hank questions from his station at the side of the locker room.

I shake my head. "No. I'm good. I have a date." That instantly picks me up. I still can't believe Lola has finally agreed to go on a date with me. It's been a long time coming. "What's the time?"

Hank's eyes drop to the silver watch circling his wrist. "11:45 PM."

"Fuck!"

Because my fight went longer than my previous bouts, and the medics wouldn't release me until they gave me a full check-up, I'm late for my date.

"I have to go. I'll see you bright and early Monday."

I snatch my gym bag off the floor, then hotfoot to the parking lot. My body screams with every step I take, but I keep moving. There's no way I'll stand Lola up. I'll lose the chance of a second date if I don't turn up to the first one.

En route to Mavs, my phone pings with a text message. As I pull up to a red light, I dig it out of my pocket to discover the message is from Lola.

Lola: *Maybe next time?*

I throw my phone into the console, pissed that the *one* time Lola agrees to go out with me is the *one* time my fight runs over. When the traffic light turns green, I hesitate on which way to go. Should I continue to Mavericks, which is one block over, or head home?

After a short deliberation, I head to Mavericks. I'm so close, I may as well keep going. If I'm lucky, Lola may still be there waiting for me.

Mavs' parking lot is deserted, revealing the band scheduled tonight has finished their set. Fans flock out Mavs' doors the instant the talent leaves. The scent of smoke and stale beer filters through my nose when I break through the double wood doors. My shoulders slump when my scan of the nearly deserted place fails to unearth Lola. She must have left before sending her text.

Spotting Maggie behind the bar, I stride toward her. "Hey, Maggie, have you seen Lola?"

When her eyes pop up from the glasses she's stacking, she sucks in a quick, sharp breath. "Jacob..." She stops to settle the crackle in her voice. "What happened?"

With a wave of my hand, I brush off her concern. "It's nothing. I'm fine."

I glance over her shoulder, wondering if Lola is in the back room Maggie reserves for employees only.

"Jacob...?" Maggie's stern tone demands my attention. When she gets it, she peers at me with worry etched on her features.

"I'm fine." My assurance does little to ease her hesitation, but I don't have time to settle it entirely. "Have you seen Lola?"

Her eyes stop absorbing the bruises on my face to lock with mine. "She left ten minutes ago."

So she could still be close?

I thank Maggie for her assistance before yanking my phone out of my pocket, dialing Lola's number, then squashing it to my ear.

Lola's voicemail answers a few seconds later. "Hey, you've reached Lola; you know what to do."

"Hey, it's Jake. . Ah, Jacob. Sorry I'm late. Maggie said you just left, so I thought I'd try and catch you before you head home. Call me."

I hang up before sending her a message.

Me: *Sorry I'm late. I'm waiting for you at Mavs.*

When I place my phone on the bar, I notice Maggie has set two bottles of beer in front of me. One is open, while the other remains closed.

"One is for you; the other for your eye," she advises when she notices my curious gawk.

I jerk my chin up in thanks before taking a swig out of the open beer and placing the unopened bottle on my swollen eye.

Malted liquid suspends halfway to my stomach when Maggie murmurs, "Jake the Giant." Noticing I've almost finished my beer in one gulp, she sets down a second one. "You're Jake the Giant, aren't you?"

"How'd you find out?"

Her brows furrow so tightly, a V pops between them. "I've worked at this bar for twenty-five years; I know everything."

She's not being modest. Drunk people are horrible secret keepers. I've never met one who can keep their mouths shut.

"When patrons mentioned a new fighter, I was stunned. His description sounded a lot like you, but I brushed it off, certain you're more of a lover than a fighter."

"I am."

"Then why professional fighting? You could be anything you want to be, so why pick such a violent sport?"

I shrug, genuinely unsure how to answer her. I don't want to lie because she's always treated me like a son, but she also deserves more than a halfhearted shrug. "Fighting is just for me. It's my thing."

It sounds selfish, but when I'm sparring with Hank or fighting in the cage, the focus is on me. It might only be an hour or two each day, but it's better than nothing.

"I'm glad you're doing something for yourself, Jacob. I just wish you picked something less brutal."

"It's not always this bad." I pull the bottle away from my bruised eye. "My opponent just..." *–cheated, fought dirty, was an a-fucking-hole* "...caught me off guard."

Maggie sighs, not believing me but also having no reason to distrust me. "Does Lola know?" My head stops mid-shake when she murmurs, "You can't tell her." She's so quiet I can barely hear her.

"Why?"

Realizing she's said too much, she moves down the bar to clear away visible spots on the countertop. Refusing to bow out of a fight for the second time tonight, I follow her retreat.

"Why, Maggie?"

I'm taken aback when I raise her head via her chin and notice the moisture in her eyes. Maggie doesn't cry. She's as tough as nails.

"It's not my story to tell." She dumps her dishcloth under the counter before propping her elbows on the bar. "But I will say one thing... Lola is *not* the girl for you."

"You don't know that."

She gives me a look as if to say, *yes, I do,* before she serves patrons who've not yet gotten the hint to leave. I watch her in silence for several long minutes. I'm pissed but also shocked. Maggie is firm, but she's never straight up told me who I can and cannot date, and sometimes, I wish she would. It would have saved a shitload of heartache.

OVER THE NEXT HOUR, any time Maggie catches my eye, she musters up a fake grin, but not a word seeps from her lips. That's also not like her. I'd keep stalking her from afar, but my focus shifts when Lola finally returns my text.

Lola: *I just got your message. I'm sorry, Jacob.*

I don't know why she needs to be sorry. I was the one who didn't show up on time.

Me: *Next time?*

Lola: *Maybe.... Night, Jacob*

Me: *Night xx*

As I drag my hand across my tired eyes, I shove my phone into my pocket. "I'm out. We'll restart our non-conversation tomorrow."

Maggie mumbles a hesitant goodbye before she starts packing down the bar for the night.

WHEN I ARRIVE HOME, I wash down some pain medication with a beer. I was hoping to have an early night, but what Maggie said won't stop running through my head. Why would it matter if Lola found out I'm a fighter? And why was she adamant that we aren't a good fit? She hasn't seen how well we get along when we're away from prying eyes. We couldn't be more perfect for one another.

After a few more hours and a handful more beers, Noah strolls into the living room, smiling a big beaming grin. He's the most care-free I've ever seen him.

"Where have you been all night?" I scare the shit out of him since he didn't notice me sitting in the pitch-black room.

After flicking on the lamp, he turns to face me. "What the fuck?" He lifts my chin to inspect a face I can no longer feel. The pain medication has kicked in nicely. "Who did this, Jake?"

"No one important. It's not as bad as it looks."

"Not as bad as it looks? Fuck, Jacob! You look like you've had the living shit beaten out of you."

I appreciate his worry, but it's not needed. "You think I look bad? You should see the other guy."

I'm not the only one sporting bruises. The Constrictor left the arena just as gingerly as me. I'm reasonably sure I broke his nose—in two places.

When I attempt to stand, I almost lose my footing. I should have adhered to the warning label on my pain medication. They didn't recommend mixing medication and alcohol. *My bad.*

"I'm going to take a shower."

As I hit the hallway, I recall Maggie's warning. Abruptly, I spin around, which smacks me with another bout of dizziness. "Please don't tell Lola you saw me like this."

Noah's nostrils flare, and his fists clench, so the last thing I'm expecting him to say is, "Alright, I won't tell Lola." I exhale a relieved breath. It's quickly drawn back in when he adds, "On one condition." He holds his index finger in the air. "If this happens again, I'll not only tell Lola; I'll hunt down the fucker who did this to you and break his fuckin' neck."

Once again, his concern isn't warranted, because the next time I meet The Constrictor, he'll have no fucking clue what's about to hit him.

CHAPTER SEVENTEEN

LOLA

Upon noticing my hungover stagger into the kitchen, my mom rests a newspaper next to her half-consumed mug of coffee. "Good morning."

I cringe at her chipper voice. My head is thumping too much to handle her level of happiness this early in the morning. "Morning."

"Coffee?"

After jerking up my chin, I slump into the barstool that's usually tucked under the breakfast bar. Considering it was my first night out in months, I got home at a decent hour last night. I just didn't stop tossing and turning until nearly 6 AM. Jacob was on my mind—all night. Considering he stood me up, he should have been the last person keeping me awake.

I'm resurrected from the dead when my mom places a strong brew of coffee in front of me. The heavenly rich scent awakens my senses, then, as caffeine trickles through my veins, its magical powers do wonders for the rest of me. By the time I've finished my first cup and preparing for my second, I'm back to my usual self.

I freeze with my mug halfway to the kitchen counter when my mom asks, "Is the person waiting outside a friend of yours?" She tries to keep things casual by popping two slices of bread in the toaster, but the vein in her neck gives away her true response. Her interests are as piqued as mine.

After shaking my head, I hold out my mug for a refill. My mom follows along nicely. "Perhaps he's a friend of Emily's?"

My brow curves high as my mom fills my mug. "*He?*"

When a pink hue creeps across my mom's cheeks, my mouth forms an O. After slipping off my stool, I skedaddle into the living room at a speed too fast for a hungover person to move. Yanking back the lace curtain, I spot a rusty red truck at the side of our driveway. When I adjust my vision, my pulse quickens. I've only bumped into him a handful of times, but his inky hair, chiseled jaw, and grungy leather jacket are hard to miss. Noah came to visit. That can only mean one thing. My ploy worked.

My mom's gaze seeks mine when I skip back into the kitchen, her eyes questioning if I know our mysterious visitor without a word escaping her lips.

"He's a *friend* of Emily's." I overemphasize the word "friend."

I smile at her flabbergasted expression before grabbing an apple out of the fruit bowl and making my way to Emily's room. She's lounging in her bed, scrolling through messages on her outdated phone. After huffing, she dumps her phone on her bedside table before dragging her floral bedspread up until it's stuffed under her chin.

"How long are you going to keep him waiting, Em?" Emily cranks her neck to peer at me with wide, dazzling eyes. "He's been out there since I woke up." I hide the fact I just woke up by taking a large bite of my apple. Its crunch sounds down the hall.

After taking a few seconds to read the mischievousness in my eyes, Emily's mouth pops open. She dives out of her bed and races to the living room, nearly bowling me over in the process. I laugh, loving her enthusiasm.

Faster than I can snap my fingers, she returns to her room to get dressed. "When did this happen?"

She yanks down a pair of jeans and one of her hideous vintage rock shirts before facing me. "Last night."

Once she's thrown on her clothes haphazardly, she yanks a brush through her long locks. I'm tempted to tell her to put in more effort, but then I realize she is who she is, so why am I trying to change her? If Noah doesn't like her as she stands before him now, he isn't the man for my little sis.

Emily brushes her teeth, dabs vanilla oil onto her neck and wrists, then sprints out the front door.

"Have fun!" I doubt she heard me. She's running too fast.

When I return to the kitchen, my mom pretends she wasn't sneaking a peek out the kitchen window. "Should I be worried? He's been out there since 7 AM."

I shake my head. "No, he's a good guy. He'll treat her right."

Noah is a friend of Jacob's, and Jacob is the kindest and gentlest guy I've ever met. I trust his judgment, so if he has no issues with Noah dating Emily, then I have no issues either.

"Stop worrying. Emily is a smart cookie." I band my arms around my mom's shoulders before guiding her to the breakfast bar. "What would you like to eat? My treat."

"You're *buying* me breakfast?"

Her shock is expected. Even with working at Mavs the past six weeks, I'm more broke than a two-dime hooker.

"No...but I can make you something."

She looks more worried now than she did when Emily bolted to Noah's truck.

AFTER HAVING breakfast with my mom, which consists of burnt toast and watery eggs, I wander into Mavs for my shift. The first person I spot upon entering is Maggie.

"Do you ever leave this place?"

She stops restocking the beer fridge to glance up at me. With a smirk, she shakes her head.

"No rest for the wicked, eh?"

When she shakes her head for the second time, I dash into the back room to store my cell and purse before jogging back out to assist her in replenishing the fridges. We work side by side for over twenty minutes without a word being spoken between us.

As we break down the empty cartons so I can take them to the compactor out back, I let her know that I got my license, so she can schedule me for any shifts she sees fit.

"Good."

She removes the stack of cardboard from under my arm before ditching them under the counter. I stare at her with my mouth hanging open. If I had done that, she'd kill me for messing up her beloved zone.

"Is everything okay?" The concern in my voice can't be missed.

Maggie stops cleaning the countertop with her infamous red cloth to face me. Her eyes are thin—nearly as stretched as my patience. I hate tiptoeing around things. If I've pissed you off, just tell me. It always works out easier that way.

"I saw you leave with Flynn last night." Maggie spreads her hands across her cocked hips. "You were here to meet Jacob but left with Flynn."

"It wasn't what it looked like—"

"It wasn't?" When I shake my head, she asks, "Then what *did* it look like? You walked out of here wrapped in another man's arms." I thought she was a hard ass when she was my supervisor; she's worse when her protective mother instincts have kicked in. "Just as I was beginning to respect you, you do something stupid. I know what happened to you, and I'm sorry for what you went through, but I will *not* stand by and watch you destroy Jacob. He deserves more than you're offering him."

"I agree—"

"Then I suggest you think long and hard about what you want

from your life. If you don't want to be *still* working here when you're a senior citizen, stop the games and start acting like the adult you are."

After glaring at me for several uncomfortable seconds, she storms into her office at the back of the bar. I stand frozen, numbed by her outburst. For one, I didn't think anyone knew what happened between Callum and me; and two, if Maggie knows I went home with Flynn, does that mean Jacob does?

Before I can configure a response, a customer arrives at my side to place an order. He's closely followed by a handful of regulars who spend more time at Mavs than with their families. In between pulling beers and mixing concoctions too potent for the early hour, I barely get a chance to look further into Maggie's outburst, but I do get a small amount of reprieve.

If Maggie's history is anything to go by, some of her anger about things in her own life may have been projected onto me instead. It's easier to blame others when your life doesn't work out the way you planned.

***

FOR THE REST of the afternoon, Maggie and I work side by side. She doesn't speak a word to me until my shift is over. "New schedules are on the noticeboard. There are changes you need to take note of."

"Okay. Thanks."

I collect my purse and phone from my locker before scanning the noticeboard. It takes me several minutes to go through the schedules since nearly six weeks' worth are pinned up. My teeth crunch when I check Maggie's schedule against the calendar in my phone. She hasn't scheduled me for one Friday night for the next six weeks. Friday nights are the busiest night of the week. Half my pay comes from the tips I get each Friday.

With my purse shoved under my arm and my anger sky high, I

storm back into the main area of Mavs. "You haven't scheduled me on a Friday night for the next six weeks."

I thought Maggie would babble out an apology before fixing her error. She does no such thing. "I know."

"The weekends are the biggest nights to earn tips. I won't earn enough to live only working weeknights."

"You should have thought about that before messing with one of my boys."

I take a step back, stunned. She can't be serious, can she? She can't punish me because I left with Flynn last night. What I do in my private life is none of her business. When I tell her that, she just twists her lips and shrugs.

"And here I was thinking you were different than the rest, that you didn't like me because you saw a lot of yourself in me." I shake my head, nearly sending tears streaking down my cheeks, which only angers me more. "How wrong was I? You're just as judgmental as every other person in this town." With that, I bolt for the exit.

I'm halfway there when Maggie shouts, "Do I take your storm out as your resignation?"

"Hell no! You can't get rid of me that easily. I'll be here first thing Monday morning for my shift."

It could be my pulse raging in my ears, but I swear I hear Maggie murmur, "Good," just as I burst into the parking lot at the back of Mavs.

I'm so worked up by our disagreement, I do something I never thought I would.

I rely on someone.

Well, I would have if Jacob had answered his phone instead of getting his voicemail. "Sorry I missed your call; leave a message after the beep."

"Hey, it's Lola. Call me."

CHAPTER EIGHTEEN

JACOB

I flop my legs off my bed with a groan before peering at the clock on my bedside table. I bite out a curse word when I notice it's a little after 3 PM. I slept for ten solid hours, yet my muscles are still aching. And don't even get me started on my thumping head. I'm never mixing pain medication with alcohol ever again.

My bare feet trudge across the carpet when my burning throat becomes too intense to ignore. When I enter the kitchen, I spot my dad sitting at the breakfast bar, reading a classic hardcover book. I freeze. With how badly my body is bruised, there's no way I can hide my injuries from him.

After inhaling a shaky breath, I move to the fridge to grab a carton of orange juice. I'm too thirsty for extra theatrics. I've filled my cup halfway by the time my dad notices my arrival.

"Good *afternoon*, Jacob." He emphasizes the afternoon part of his comment. He's an early riser, often waking before the sun, so my very late sleep-in would be shocking for him. "Do you know where Noah went this morning? He was up before the sparrows."

"No fucking clue."

I curse for a second time—inwardly this time. I just cussed in front of my father. He's not a fan of curse words.

When my colorful language reaches his ears, he sighs before peering at me over his book. His pupils widen when his narrowed gaze lands on my face. After placing a bookmark in between the pages, he sets it next to his plate of cut strawberries and almond shards, his snack of choice.

"Do I want to know?" His voice is both stern and concerned.

I scratch my brow as my throat struggles through its dryness. "Probably not."

"Anything illegal?"

I wait for him to prop his hip on the counter next to me before shaking my head. "No."

He folds his arms in front of his chest while sucking in a big breath. "You know I'm here if you need someone to talk to, don't you, Jake?"

"I know."

He's a hard ass, but that's what makes him a great dad. Patrick and I kept out of trouble when we were younger because he was so stern, we were too scared to push his buttons, but that doesn't mean he hasn't always been there for us.

"Alright. As long as you're aware."

He ruffles my hair before exiting the kitchen. I wouldn't pay much attention to his slumped shoulders if he didn't leave his snack of choice behind.

"Dad?"

He stops halfway out of the kitchen to peer back at me.

"Have you got a minute to talk?"

AN HOUR LATER—*NO, I'm not joking*—I head back to my room. My heart isn't as heavy, but my shoulders are a little more weighed down. Dad and I haven't talked like that in months, but no matter how much I tried to tell him about my fighting career, I couldn't bring myself to do it. People say I'm more a lover than a fighter; the same can be said for my dad. He did raise me, so it's only fair I got some of his traits.

My pace quickens when I hear my cell phone ringing. I grab it up just before it goes to voicemail. "Hey, Hank," I greet upon noticing his name flashing across the screen.

"Jacob, how are you feeling today?" His voice is still holding the concern it held after my fight last night.

"Yeah, good. I'll be back at the gym bright and early tomorrow, ready to train."

"That's good, Jake, *real* good. I'll see you in the morning."

He once again disconnects my call before I can say goodbye. When I drag my phone from my ear, I notice I have a voicemail.

Aren't I popular today? Not as popular as my opponent was last night, though. He had the full entourage with him, and the way the crowd surged for him when he made his way to the cage proved he wasn't a low-ranked fighter.

I stop grumbling about being played when Lola's seductive voice shrills down the line. "Hey, it's Lola. Call me."

I do precisely that without a second to spare.

"Hey, that was quick. I just left a message." Her voice is distant like she's using speakerphone, but I can't miss the uneasiness in her tone.

"Yeah. I was talking to my dad. Are you okay? You sound a little low."

Air whistles down the line. "I'm good. Just a tough day at work."

"Is Maggie giving you a hard time?"

She sighs. "Yeah... but I kind of deserve it."

"Why? What did you do this time?"

My tease has the effect I'm aiming for when she laughs. It isn't her usual full-hearted laugh, but it's better than nothing. "What I always do—I fucked up."

A small stretch of silence crosses between us. It worries me more than what she said. Silence isn't Lola's forte. If she isn't loud and obnoxious, someone is close to dying.

I'm about to ask her who I need to kill when she murmurs, "I'm sorry about last night."

I don't know why she keeps apologizing. I'm the one who failed to show up at the designated time.

"Quit apologizing; if anyone should be sorry, it should be me."

My brows furl when she asks, "You have no idea, do you?"

"About what?"

She exhales quickly before pushing out, "Nothing... I've got to go."

When she disconnects our call, I stare down at my phone, confused as fuck. I don't know why I'm shocked. Women in general are complicated, let alone ones as high-strung as Lola.

I'm still staring at my phone when Noah strides into my room. He's smiling like he won a hotdog eating contest, and his eyes have a twinkle I've never seen before.

"Hey, how you feeling?" His jerked-up chin asks more questions than his mouth verbalizes, such as, *are you going tell me who beat your ass yet?* But there's too much going on with him to keep the focus on me.

"I'm good. You?"

"I'm fucking great."

When he waggles his brows, I feel like he slaps me with a wet fish. Who the fuck is this guy standing in front of me? I've never seen him so carefree and happy...

My inner monologue trails off when reality dawns. *No. Fucking. Way!*

"Who has your panties in a twist?"

He rubs his hands together as he rocks heel to toe. "Emily."

I cock a brow. "Emily... *Emily?* As in Lola's sister, Emily?"

I didn't know they had contact since the car prank we pulled months ago.

"Yep." The "p" pops from his mouth. "You should see this girl, Jake. She's so fucking beautiful, yet she has no clue."

"I've seen her, remember?"

I laugh when he rolls his eyes. "Whatever."

"Is that where you took off to this morning? Dad was interrogating me about your movements earlier."

He nervously shifts from foot to foot. "Uh, yeah." He's embarrassed we spotted his eagerness. "We spent the day at Stoney Creek Falls. She jumped off the waterfall with me."

"No shit?"

I didn't think Emily would have the brass to jump off the boulder at Stoney Creek. Maybe she's more like her sister than I thought.

"Anyway, I'm going to take a shower—"

"To work out the kink?" I interrupt with a laugh.

When he ignores me, I realize that's precisely what he's going to do. *Welcome to McIntosh blue balls territory, Noah. It's neither pretty nor nice.*

Once he reaches my door, he glances over his shoulder at me. "Will you ever tell me what happened last night?"

My lips twist as I scratch my brow. "Yeah, one day."

His eyes narrow as he shakes his head. "Don't ever play poker, Jacob. You'll lose more than your shirt."

CHAPTER NINETEEN

LOLA

"Guys are such pigs."

I shake off my funk as I exit the men's bathroom at Mavs. I've just finished cleaning the urinals as part of my continued punishment from Maggie. After our disagreement weeks ago, she's given me every shit chore she can find. Because I really need this job and have yet to find a replacement, I have no choice but to put up with her unjust treatment. She isn't being fair because she doesn't know the agreement Jacob and I have. Associating with another man isn't cheating when you're not in a relationship.

When I round the corner to head back to the main bar area, I crash into a well-formed chest. "Sorry."

I attempt to maneuver past the person, but a deep voice halts my steps. "I knew I'd eventually bump into you."

With my heart beeping in my neck, I raise my eyes. After clearing ripped jeans, a fitted blue shirt, and a tattooed neck, I come face to face with Callum Parker—my ex-boyfriend.

"Callum." I muster up a smile, pretending I'm not scared. I am, but I'd rather he not know that. "How are you?"

His heavy-lidded gaze lowers to my tight red Mavericks shirt before drifting past my white denim jeans. My endeavor to keep our conversation in warm waters is lost when he sneers, "Still dressing slutty, I see."

"You're unbelievable."

I attempt to skirt past him again, over our exchange within a second of it starting. Before I even get two steps away from him, his hand shoots out to seize my wrist. "I wasn't done talking to you yet."

His hold is so firm, I nearly call out for help. The only reason I don't is that I remember only Maggie and me are working this afternoon. Even Maggie's unjust treatment won't let me put her at risk. She doesn't deserve Callum's wrath any more than I do.

"Let me go." My voice is surprisingly calm for how fast my heart is racing. "If I don't return to the bar soon, they'll come looking for me."

He digs his fingers into my wrist so hard, I whimper. His hold is going to bruise me—*again.* "Do you really think the old biddy behind the bar will save you?"

My eyes bounce between his when he traps me between him and the paint-peeling wall. He isn't the height or the width of Jacob, but he's undeniably taller than my five-foot-five frame.

"What do you want, Callum?"

He pushes in closer, stealing my ability to scan the area for help. I've got nothing in front of me but a pair of angry, glossed-over eyes. "I want *you...*" With the hand not grasping my wrist, he grips my face so firmly, moisture burns my eyes. "...in my bed, where you belong."

The last of the air in my lungs leaves in a grunt when he narrows his filthy mouth toward mine. I yank my head to the side, struggling with all my might to break away from his hold. Unfortunately, he's too strong. I can't get away.

With my body pinned to the wall by his, his tongue lashes my lips, requesting that I accept his kiss, but I keep my mouth shut tight. I'll even go as far as biting off his slimy tongue if he forces it into my mouth. That's how much he disgusts me.

Realizing I'll never give him what he wants, Callum inches back.

The tick in his jaw is more profound now, and I can hear his teeth grinding together. He's as unhinged as he was the night he assaulted me.

I'm about to ask him to leave before he makes another mistake he can't take back, but I lose the chance when his hand gripping my face drops to my neck. Panic surges through me when he clutches my throat as fiercely as he did my face. He squeezes me tight, stealing the air from my lungs as swiftly as he once swept me off my feet.

I claw at him, giving it everything I have to pry him away from my neck. Nothing weakens his tight hold. The more I fight, the more he chokes me.

"Callum, please." I can barely talk through the pain, but I'm hoping my pleading eyes will take up my plight. If he doesn't release me soon, he will kill me.

"*Please?* Please what? Please forgive me for running out on you in the middle of the night without saying goodbye?" When his grip firms even more, tears flow down my cheeks. "Please forgive me for wasting nine fucking months of my life I'll never get back? What is your *please* for, Lola? You walked out without an explanation, without a fucking reason. You just left!"

I don't say anything. I can't. I can't breathe, much less talk.

"Don't I deserve better than that? I gave you nine months of my life—nine fucking months!" The veins in his neck bulge with every word he spits in my face. My pulse is fading under his touch, my head growing woozy. I'm seconds from passing out—literally moments from death.

Just as I think I'll never suck in air again, Callum loosens his grip. I want to say my begging eyes finally subdued him, but that isn't the case. There's someone in the corridor with us. I can't see them, but I can feel the anger radiating out of them.

"Get off her right now!"

Fear thickens my blood when I recognize the voice. It's Maggie. She has a baseball bat suspended mid-air and the eyes of a murderer.

"It's okay, Maggie. I can handle this. You don't need to get involved." My scratchy voice reveals how close to the grave I am. If Maggie was ten seconds later, I would be dead.

Maggie either ignores my assurance or she didn't hear it. "This is your last warning: let her go."

When Callum fails to comply again, she slices her bat through the air, smacking his arm like her bat is an ax, and his arm is a chunk of wood she's splitting. Her hit is so impressive, it dislodges Callum's hand from my neck with a roar.

"You fucking bitch!"

The threat in Callum's tone does little to deter Maggie. She raises her bat once more, ready to swing again if needed. I try to get between them when Callum prowls toward her, but he shoves me against the wall, rattling out the last snippet of air in my lungs with a brutal push.

Despite Callum smirking evilly at her, Maggie strengthens her stance, not once backing down. "This bat isn't the only weapon I'm carrying," she warns, her tone deadly serious. "If you don't leave my bar this instant, I won't hesitate to show you the way out with a bullet."

When her other hand slips around her back, Callum's prowling steps halt. He takes his time to authenticate her threat. It's a painfully long ten seconds. Not even I'm sure if her threat is idle or not.

Once Callum reaches his conclusion, his eyes drift to mine. They reflect nothing but hate and disgust. They mirror mine to a T. "This isn't over," he whispers, hoping I'll be the only one who hears them. If the quiver in Maggie's top lip is anything to go by, he failed his mission for the second time today.

After raising his hands in the air, faking innocence, he skirts past Maggie. I keep my eyes locked on him until he disappears from my view—then, I collapse onto the floor.

CHAPTER TWENTY

JACOB

"You gave her a heart attack."

"Me?" I slide into the passenger seat of Noah's truck as he slips behind the wheel. "You got her all flustered."

An amused mask slips over Noah's face. *"Here, let me help you, young man."* I grin at his impersonation of the waitress's voice. *"Oh, so hard, young man."*

Chuckling, he fires up his engine then pulls away from the curb, sending a plume of smoke into the air. His truck is a gas guzzler, but its sentimental value far exceeds its dollar worth. This is the truck he was rebuilding with his brother before his demons got the better of him.

We drove into town this morning to pick up parts required to make Noah's truck's exterior as shiny as her core. He finished rebuilding the motor over a month ago, so this week, we'll refurbish the interior. Since it was after midday when we arrived in town, we stopped at a café to grab a bite to eat. While the waitress filled my cup with coffee, she made gaga kissy faces at Noah. He got in on the act by giving her a playful wink. She was near eighty, so what's the worst that could happen... ?

Scorching hot coffee landing in my crotch instead of my cup, that's what.

In haste, I jumped out of the booth, shifting the scalding beverage from my cock to my thigh. Mortified she burned my cock on a stake, the waitress grabbed a wad of napkins off our table to soak up the coffee. To say I was embarrassed a lady older than my grandma was patting my dick like he was as good boy would be a major understatement. I was horrified.

Noah wasn't mortified, though. He was far from it. He was so close to breaking, he was biting his fist to stifle his laughter.

No amount of gnawing held back his laughter when the waitress said, "Oh, so hard, young man."

Noah lost it, which meant every pair of eyes in the café turned to gawk at me. With cheeks the color of Noah's chortling face, I snatched the napkins out of the waitress's hand, then sank low into my seat.

I got a free lunch out of the catastrophe. I would have preferred to pay.

"She was talking about my thigh muscle."

Noah's laughter gets a second wind. "Sure she was, Jake. Whatever you say."

I'm about to retort, but my ringing cell phone stops me. After yanking it out of my pocket, I glance down at the screen. I don't recognize the number, but it does have a local area code. With a shrug, I swipe my finger across the screen then press my phone to my ear.

"Hello."

"Hi, Jacob, it's Maggie."

My brows stitch. "Oh, hey, Maggie."

Noah's eyes stray from the road to me, just as surprised about Maggie's call as I am. I have her cell number stored in my phone in case of emergencies, but I've never had any reason to use it.

Maggie exhales a big breath before asking, "I was wondering if you could do me a favor?"

Her unease upsets my stomach. She's usually so confident. "Sure. Anything."

She always lends an ear when I'm frustrated about shit she has no interest in, so the least I can do is help her back when she needs me.

When Maggie remains quiet, I ask, "Are you alright?"

Hearing the panic in my tone, Noah pulls his truck to the side of the road. After shutting down his engine, his eyes wordlessly seek information.

I shrug, as lost as he is. I hold my finger in the air when Maggie slowly breathes out, "I'm okay, but Lola is a little rattled."

"Lola? What happened?" The pounding of my heart is audible in my questions.

"It's not my place to say." She breathes out slowly as if worried she's making a mistake. "She doesn't know I'm calling, but I don't want her to go home alone. I'd take her, but I can't find anyone to cover my shift, so could you drive her home for me?"

"Yeah, I can do that." Even though I sound calm, I'm anything but. "We're in town, so I'll be there in around five minutes."

"Thanks, Jacob."

I suck in some big breaths while lowering my phone from my ear. My gut is so knotted, I feel seconds from bringing up the meal Noah and I just shared. That skittish, scared Maggie I was just talking to isn't the Maggie I know. Usually, nothing rattles her.

"Is everything alright?"

My eyes drift from my phone to Noah. "I don't know. Maggie asked me to drive Lola home. She said she is too rattled to drive. Can you take me to Mavs, then follow me back to Lola's house?"

"Yeah, no worries." He fires up his truck, executes a U-turn, then heads back into town. We don't talk the entire time. The silence adds to the havoc somersaulting in my gut. Something's not right; I just don't have a fucking clue what's wrong.

When I break through Mavericks' double doors, I scan the nearly deserted surroundings. Including Maggie, who is standing behind the bar, there are only a handful of people milling around.

I make my way to Maggie. When she catches my approach, she wearily smiles.

"Where's Lola?"

My long strides are sliced to half their length when I notice Maggie's usually sparkling eyes are full of moisture. She appears seconds from crying, but her focus remains on Lola. "She's in the storeroom."

Glancing back to Noah, I gesture my head toward Maggie. I'm torn. I hate leaving Maggie while she's upset, but I don't want to leave Lola if she's just as devastated.

The weight on my shoulders eases when Noah nods, wordlessly advising he'll take care of Maggie while I handle Lola. I wait for him to round the bar before heading for the storeroom out back. The urgency of the situation is unearthed when Maggie fails to object to us trespassing on her domain. Usually, no one but staff is allowed behind the bar—that includes the storerooms.

"Lola," I call out when I enter the dark and dingy room.

I hear sniffling a mere second before I spot Lola crouched in the very corner of the nearly black space. Her arms are wrapped around her knees, and she's sobbing hard.

Ignoring the heavy pit burrowing in my chest, I squat down in front of her. "Hey, you okay?"

She flinches when I touch her, but that's quickly pushed aside for relief when she realizes who I am. "*Jacob...*"

When she bounds off the ground to throw her arms around my neck, her quick movement sends me sprawling onto my ass. She doesn't hurt me; my heart is too busy breaking from the pain etched on her face to register any pain.

I pull her close to my chest before bracing my back on the shelves she was cowered against. I'm confident she'll hear my raging heart, but I don't give a shit. I'm both angry and panicked as to what has her so upset. Just like the Maggie I was talking to earlier, this isn't the Lola I know. She'd never cry so hard she'd soak my shirt in under a minute.

As I comfort her the best I can, my brain struggles to work out what happened. During the day, only regulars drink at Mavs, so I doubt any of them would have upset her. Furthermore, I've witnessed firsthand how quickly Lola defuses drunken idiots who get a little handsy with her. She whips them into shape in a snap, so once again, I don't see that being an issue.

So if a customer isn't to blame for her tears, who is?

Realizing I have the answer sitting in my lap, I raise Lola's tear-stained face to mine by her chin. She's trembling so much, her shudders rattle my hand. The cheeky spark in her eyes has been tainted. Now instead of being shiny and unique, they're haunted and bleak.

I'm about to ask who did this to her, but her request for help stops me. "Can you please take me home?"

Nodding, I remove the last of her tears from her cheeks with my thumbs before standing to my feet, taking her with me. You have no idea how hard it is for me to set her down. The only reason I do is because she's quick to slip her hand into mine when we lose contact.

We walk into the main bar area, hand in hand, only breaking contact when Lola notices Maggie peering at us. With a sob, she makes a beeline for Maggie, startling her when she throws her arms around her neck like she did me. Maggie returns Lola's embrace with just as much admiration and respect, her chin dipping when Lola whispers, "Thank you."

OUR DRIVE to Erkinsvale is so quiet, every shallow breath Lola takes adds additional cracks to my already fractured heart. It's killing me that she's hurt but doesn't trust me enough to tell me what's going on. I'm on the verge of falling to my knees and begging her to open up to me, but since we're in the confines of her mom's car, I can't. My knees are nearly around my ears, so there's no way they'll reach the ground.

Instead, I interlock our fingers. Her pulse is raging so fast, you'd swear I was gripping her heart instead of her hand. Its thump is so convincing, I glance down at our hands to make sure I'm not. Air traps halfway to my lungs when I notice more than overworked veins. There's a large mark covering a majority of her wrist.

"What the fuck is that?" My voice shakes with both fear and anger. If that's what I think it is, someone gripped her so tightly, they bruised her.

Lola pulls her arm back to her side of the car before yanking down the sweater she's wearing over her Mavs shirt. It does little to ease my agitation. The bruise is too large to be hidden by the knitted material. It's there for the world to see—*for me to see.*

I raise my eyes to her face. "Is that why you're upset? Because someone hurt you?"

My surging anger is evident in my voice. I'm not angry at Lola; I'm fucking pissed someone placed their hands on her so roughly, they marked her skin.

Working my jaw side to side, I struggle to swallow my anger. My endeavors do me no good when Lola whispers, "I don't want you in the middle of this. It isn't your fight."

"In the middle of what?" I steer Lola's mom's car into the driveway of her family home before tilting to face her. "And this is *my* fight, Lola. You're my girl."

New tears drop down her cheeks. "No, I'm not. That's what no one understands."

When she throws open her door and hotfoots it down the concrete path, I drag in some calming breaths before taking off after her. Noah watches my trek with concern slashed across his face, but I don't have time to update him. My conversation with Lola can't wait. I'm so twisted up in knots, if she doesn't start giving me some answers, I'm seconds from going on a rampage. I'm not a violent man, but I'm so close to detonation right now, I'm sure it won't be too much longer before I am.

CHAPTER TWENTY-ONE

LOLA

I feel Jacob's presence before I see him. His brooding, temperamental persona would be well-received under different circumstances, but since it's a mere hour after I cried so hard, his shirt still shows the wetness of my tears. I'm so tired and upset, I want to crawl into bed and pretend this day never happened.

I would if I could ignore the pleading look Jacob gives me as he gathers my uninjured hand in his. "Please let me in. Let me help you."

I try not to nuzzle into his hand when he cups my jaw, but his comfort is impossible for me to deny. I want him to take away the pain, to remind me of who I was before Callum pinned me to the wall by my throat. I want him to look at me like he did only yesterday.

"*Please, Lola.*"

The pain in his eyes is all the proof needed of why I should never date. I don't want to be saved. I can take care of myself. I also don't want to drag him into my complicated life.

But perhaps I should? Then maybe he'll realize why I'm not the girl for him.

With my heart as locked down as my head, I ask, "Can I get changed first?"

He nods, unsure why I need to change clothes. Clearly, he can't smell the same disgusting scent my flaring nostrils are sucking in. Callum's aftershave is embedded in my shirt. That's why my stomach won't quit churning. I can taste him in my mouth and smell him on my skin.

Jacob stays glued to my side when I replace my Mavs shirt and sweater with a tank top and a long-sleeve shirt. I dump my offensive clothing into a bin under my desk before sitting on my bed. The mattress squeaks when Jacob fills the spot next to me. His physique is intimidating in general, but as he presents now, it's almost over-whelming. I'm not scared of him; I'm just afraid about what I'm about to do.

"Promise me you won't tell anyone what I'm about to tell you." Jacob stops nodding when I add, "No, Jacob, I need more than a gesture. I need you to promise."

A nod won't assure me my family won't find out about what happened to me. It's bad enough Jacob saw me cry, so I refuse to add more witnesses to my disastrous life.

Jacob licks his dry lips before breathing out, "I promise." His usually smooth timbre is raspy and low.

My lips twitch, but not a syllable escapes them. I'm hesitant to share my story; I've never shared it before, and it's more daunting than I care to admit. Sensing my unease, Jacob curls his hand over mine that's fisted in my lap. He gives it a gentle squeeze, reminding me that he's nothing like the other men I've dated. I can trust him with my secret. I'm just praying he'll handle what I'm about to tell him with the respect he's given me since the night we met.

I clear my throat before I speak words I never want repeated. "I thought my ex was a great guy. His personality was similar to yours. He was cheeky and lovable." My words start to rattle. "But as the months went on, his personality changed. He began isolating us from our friends and was often withdrawn and moody. His moods..." I shrug as if it will explain how different they were. When it doesn't, I use words. "They shifted like the tide: beautiful highs and devastating lows."

While exhaling a deep breath, I pretend I can't see the veins in Jacob's neck throbbing. "To start with, he taunted me and called me names. Then one night, he took it further."

Jacob's grip on my hand tightens. Not enough to hurt me, but enough to convince me he knows what's coming next.

"His brother was over. Any time he visited, Callum's behavior was more erratic than normal." Like ripping off a Band-Aid, I blurt out my confession in one quick sentence: "I don't know what made him snap, but it was only once."

Jacob scrubs his hand along the scruff on his chin, hiding the twinge inflicting his jaw. "What do you mean, he snapped?"

Tears burn my eyes. I've never said the words out loud before because if I don't admit it happened, doesn't that mean it never did?

"Lola—"

"He hit me."

Butterflies jitter in my stomach when Jacob lurches off my bed to pace. Because my room is so small, he only takes three steps before he turns around and goes back the other way. Although he's handling my confession better than I expected, his response still reveals why I chose to keep it a secret. He'll look at me differently now. He won't see the strong, opinionated Lola he used to know. He'll forever see a victim.

My eyes float up from my feet when Jacob asks, "Was it him who made you upset today?"

The haunted, shallow look in his eyes makes me want to say no, but my heart forces me to nod instead.

One little bob, and the mask on Jacob's face switches from sympathetic to furious in an instant. "Where does he live?"

I leap from my bed as fast as he did seconds ago. "You promised you wouldn't tell anyone."

"I'm not telling anyone; he already knows what he fucking did!"

His roar has me recoiling, but not enough to stop me from saying, "I don't need you to defend me; I handled it. It was once, then I fled and never returned. Today was the first time I've seen him in months."

My knees wobble when I move to stand in front of him. He'll never hurt me. Just like I know I can convince him I'm not a damsel in need of saving. "Stay with me."

I cup his cheeks like he always does mine before seeking his gaze. When I get his sad, tormented eyes, I wordlessly beg him to stay with me, to comfort me, to choose me above anything else. Above anger, above jealousy, above revenge. I want him to stay.

My pleas seem to be getting through to him when he whispers, "I can't let him get away with this."

He seems torn, like he wants to comfort me, but he feels wrong doing it. I try to settle his uneasiness. "Stay with me, Jacob. I need you."

After balancing on my tippy toes, I seal my lips over his. His lips remain hard-lined for barely a second before he parts them to accept my kiss. Warmth blooms across my chest when our tongues duel in a loving embrace. We've never kissed with such open hearts before. It's a kiss unlike any I've ever had, leaving me to wonder just how deeply he's embedded himself under my skin.

With my heart now racing more from excitement than fear, I'm disappointed when Jacob inches back. It's not all bad. The torment his eyes held before we kissed has softened, replaced with the gentle eyes I'm growing to adore more every day.

As he stares down at me in admiration, he removes the blobs of moisture our kiss didn't dry.

The sincerity in his eyes has me acting carelessly. "Stay with me."

I curl my hand around his before taking a step back, allowing my actions to speak on my behalf. I want him. Now... *and possibly forever.*

I'm relieved when he fills the gap I'd placed between us. He doesn't need to speak for me to know his decision. His eyes reveal everything. He's choosing me over everything and everyone. He's staying.

When he drags his index finger down my cheek and along my jaw, my head lolls to the side. I love when he touches me like this, gently and slowly like he's savoring every inch of me.

Fisting his shirt, I tug him in the final inch. I need him more than my lungs need oxygen. I want him so bad, I'm not ashamed to admit it. "Please..." I stop myself before I beg. I'm desperate for him, but I'll never let him know that.

Mercifully, he doesn't need to hear my pleas to know of their existence. As his lips follow the journey his finger took, moans purr from my throat like a kitty. He bites and nibbles on my jaw before dragging his stubble down my neck.

My opposite ear is close to touching my shoulder when he suddenly jackknifes back. "What the fuck?"

His deep exhale blasts my cheeks with air when he pulls my hair away from my neck. When his eyes return to my face, my throat works hard to swallow. The fury settled behind them is unnerving.

"He's fucking dead," he growls through gritted teeth. "I'm going to kill him!"

Nothing but the smell of his aftershave is left in his wake when he darts out of my room. I stand in silence for several moments, my mind a jumbled mess of confusion. He went from staring at me lovingly to storming out of my room in under thirty seconds.

My neck—he was staring at something on my neck.

With my heart in my throat, I rush to the full-length mirror in my room. I gasp out a sharp breath when I pull my hair back like Jacob did mere seconds ago. My springy locks were concealing the bruises Callum's fingers made when he choked me. They're purple and angry—as violent as Jacob's eyes when he made his threat.

On quivering legs, I run out of my house to catch up to him. By the time I make it outside, he's climbing in the passenger seat of Noah's truck.

"Jacob, don't do this. He isn't worth it!"

When his gaze shifts to me, my attempt to change his mind is abandoned. He's too far gone. The loving eyes I was staring at mere minutes ago have been replaced with a pair I no longer recognize.

CHAPTER TWENTY-TWO

JACOB

As Noah reverses out of Lola's driveway, I peer into her light brown eyes, praying they'll quell the anger tearing me up inside. I want to stay and offer her comfort, but what kind of man would I be if I stood by and watched the woman I've fallen in love with be attacked and not do anything about it? Callum can't get away with this. I refuse to let him put his hands on my girl and not do anything. He needs to be taught a lesson, and I'm the perfect man to teach him one.

No longer capable of harboring my anger, I throw my fists into Noah's dashboard. She doesn't deserve my beat down, but I need to hit something, and it's the closest thing, so it will do—for now.

"What do you want to do, Jake?"

Noah's eyes shift from the road to me when I yank my phone out of my pocket. "I'm going to fucking kill him, that's what I'm going to do."

After scrolling to my recent calls list, I hit the number of the last call I received. Maggie answers a few seconds later. "Mavericks, this is—"

"Where does he live?"

Maggie knows every local in Ravenshoe, so if anyone knows Callum's whereabouts, it will be her.

"Jacob, this isn't a good idea—"

"Where does he fucking live?!"

Noah socks me in the arm, warning me to calm down before adding a stern finger point to his threat. Confident I've got things under control, he holds out his hand palm side up, soundlessly requesting my phone. I don't want to give it to him, but with my anger making me lash out, I hand it to him.

"Maggie, it's Noah... No, I haven't talked to him yet... I know... Maggie... I'll make sure. Bye." He disconnects the call before tossing my phone back to my side of the cab. "He lives in Hopeton."

After checking it's clear, he executes a U-turn and heads in the opposite direction before his eyes stray to mine. "How much did Lola tell you?"

"That he assaulted her once, then she ran, and today was the first time she has seen him in months." My words are ground out through clenched teeth.

"What about what happened today?"

My fists ball so firmly, my clipped nails dig into my palm. "She didn't say, but she has a bruise on her wrist... and her fucking neck." Anger steam rolls back into me. "The mark on her neck isn't little. He had to clutch her pretty hard to inflict that much damage."

"From what I got out of Maggie, that sounds about right." Noah tightens his grip on the steering wheel. His anger is just as intense as mine, his blood pressure just as high. "Maggie went to check on Lola when she took longer cleaning the bathrooms than usual. She found Callum pinning her to the wall by her throat." His breathy chuckle confuses me until he discloses, "Maggie hit him with her baseball bat, then threatened to shoot him if he didn't leave."

I'm glad Maggie protected Lola, but now I feel horrible for swearing at her. I'll be sure to apologize the instant I'm done dealing with Callum.

"She's not one hundred percent convinced, but she thinks he was on something. His eyes were all fucked up." He waits for a truck to roar past us before locking his eyes with mine. "Be careful, alright?"

After jerking up my chin, I drop my eyes to my busted knuckles. I haven't reached Callum yet, and I'm already sporting bruises. I'm not usually an aggressive person, but this isn't something I can ignore. Callum didn't hit Lola once; he hurt her twice. I may not have been there to protect her the first time, but I can *and will* now.

Around twenty minutes later, Noah pulls his truck to the curb of an old brick house on the outskirts of town. The lawn is unkept, not seeing a lawnmower the past year, and the shutters are hanging off their hinges. It looks more suitable for a horror movie set than a family home.

I jump out of the passenger door and stride toward the rundown house. Blood is still surging through my veins, my anger not dampening the slightest during our drive. As I take the front three stairs of the porch, Noah pleads, "Don't kill him; just rough him up a little."

I'm about to knock on a broken screen door when a blond-haired, blue-eyed man walks down the litter-filled hallway. His hair is greasy, and his clothes are stained, but if you peel away the mess covering him, I can see how he might attract a girl like Lola. He's got all the attributes of a bad boy. It's just a pity women don't realize the bad boys in romance books don't rate as highly in real life.

After opening the screen door separating us, the man props his shoulder on a paint-peeled door. "Aww, isn't this sweet? She sent her bitch to fight her battles."

"Are you Callum?"

He smirks an arrogant grin. "If I am?"

"Then I'm about to teach you a lesson on what happens when you put your hands on a woman—*my woman.*" Grabbing a fistful of his shirt, I drag him to within an inch of my face. "Are you Callum?"

"Maybe...?"

His smirk grows so wide, his yellow teeth glisten in the afternoon sun. His pompous attitude has my anger reaching breaking point.

The fact he thinks he can assault Lola as if it's a fucking game causes me to snap.

Without a thought crossing my mind, I head-butt him right in the nose. He sprawls back, his ass hitting the wooden porch with an almighty thump since his hands are too busy protecting his nose from another hit.

Sensing my slip in composure, Noah pushes off his truck and heads my way.

"Wait." I hold my finger in the air, requesting a minute.

His eyes reveal his unease, but since I've yet to place a hand on Callum, he maintains his security officer stance halfway down the cracked path.

Callum exhales a ragged breath when my boot lands in his rib. He coughs up blood as his lungs fight to replenish the air they just lost. Grabbing the scruff of his shirt, I drag him back onto his feet. Because I want him to experience the fear Lola went through, I push him backward until his back splays against the outside wall of his house, then I curl my hand around his throat. I place enough pressure on his neck to make his eyes pop open but not enough to kill him —*unfortunately*.

I shouldn't relish the way his body shakes when it grows panicked he's not getting enough air, but I do. He should be grateful Lola is still on the forefront of my mind, or I'd continue our little game for a few more hours. Alas, my girl needs me more than I need revenge.

My lips brush Callum's ear when I warn, "If I *ever* see you near Lola again, I'll come back and finish this. Do you understand?"

He can't nod with how hard I'm gripping his neck, but he manages—somewhat.

It's just as hard for me to release him from my hold. I'd rather strangle him until he passes out, but Noah isn't the only one waiting for me. So is Lola. With that in mind, I let him go, pivot, and leave.

I freeze halfway down the path when he spits out, "She'll always come running back for this." When I turn around, I witness him grabbing his crotch. "She can't get enough of it."

Seeing my anger twisting up from my stomach to my throat, Noah tries to calm me down. "Let it go, Jake. He's not worth it."

He's right. He isn't worth it. Besides, the more time I waste dealing with him, the less time I'll have to comfort Lola.

I nudge my head to Noah's truck, signaling it's time for us to leave. "I've wasted enough time on this piece of shit."

"You can't make a ho into a housewife." Callum's weaselly laugh hackles my spikes. "Believe me, I tried. Couldn't even beat her into submission."

That's all it takes for my anger to boil over. I charge for Callum, the pulse thumping in my ears almost drowning out Noah's roar, "Do you have a fucking death wish?!"

One hit, and Callum is out cold, but I don't stop. I beat the living shit out of him, only dispelling half the anger cutting me in two when images of him hitting Lola flash before my eyes. He beat her, and now I'm beating him, but he won't come out on top like Lola did. She kept her pride because she's so fucking strong. Callum isn't. He's a weasel of a man who didn't deserve a woman half as perfect as Lola.

I can't see anything through the fury blinding me. It's all a blur of fists and blood and Noah begging me to stop. Not even police sirens hollering in the distance slow me down. I want him to pay.

I want him dead.

"Jacob!" It takes everything Noah has to drag me off Callum, and even then, some part of my body is still whacking into him. "Enough. You taught him a lesson; now we have to go."

Like a lightbulb switching on, I snap back to reality when my eyes absorb the blood on my hands. There's enough to make me wonder if Callum is still alive.

I'm not the only one suspicious. Noah is checking him for a pulse, but he stops when a police officer draws a gun on him. "Put your hands in the air."

Noah's wide eyes flick to mine before he raises his hands as requested. After holstering his gun, the officer rushes for him. He handcuffs him before pushing him forward, making him land on his stomach a mere inch from a lifeless Callum.

In a dazed state, I move to assist him. He wasn't doing anything wrong, so why is he being cuffed? My stumbled movements gain me the attention of the police officer. His pupils widen as he redraws his gun. "Stay where you are." He directs his gun at my chest, his hands shaking.

He's young. If I had to guess, I'd say he's a first-year rookie. He's also nervous about my size. That isn't unusual; most people are threatened by my height, much less the span of my shoulders.

When I hold my hands out in front of my body, signaling I'm not going anywhere, a deep voice at my side murmurs, "Jacob?"

Only moving my eyes out of fear the nervous officer will shoot me if I move my body, I spot Ryan—friend and detective—standing on the bottom step of Callum's porch.

"Hey."

I inconspicuously nudge my head to the nervous officer, praying he'll instruct him to lower his weapon, or at the very least, have him remove his finger from the trigger before he shoots me.

CHAPTER TWENTY-THREE

LOLA

Tears sting my eyes when I peer through the one-way mirror at the Ravenshoe PD. Jacob is cuffed to a steel table. His usual happy-go-lucky exterior is nowhere to be found, replaced with a man who looks lost and confused. This is why I tried to stay away from him. If I had kept my distance, he wouldn't be sitting in an interrogation room facing charges.

"Lola?"

Turning toward the voice, I'm met with a handsome man with short inky hair and blue eyes. His tailored dark suit showcases a muscular physique I could appreciate if I weren't panicked out of my mind.

"Yes, I'm Lola."

He waves for me to step forward. "Could you follow me?"

Nodding, I shadow him down the bustling corridor, my gaze only straying back to Jacob for the quickest second. His low-hanging head tells me everything I need to know. He feels as defeated as me.

When I enter a small interview room on the heels of the detective, the suspicions running rife through my veins the past two hours are proven accurate. Maggie is sitting behind a rectangular table.

She's not cuffed like Jacob, but her shoulders are sagging just as low. She smiles a weary grin when she spots me, but she keeps her eyes on the tabletop, unable to maintain eye contact.

"Why am I here, Maggie?"

With Maggie refusing to acknowledge my presence, the detective takes up her slack. He takes a seat in a chair opposite Maggie before gesturing for me to sit beside her.

"Lola, my name is Ryan. I'm a detective at Ravenshoe's Police Department. I was the one who called you earlier and asked you to come in." When I nod, he continues, "I'm hoping you can provide me with a statement about an incident that occurred earlier today at Mavericks Bar." He checks his paperwork. "At approximately 1 PM."

Ryan's gaze drifts up from his paperwork when I mutter, "You said you wouldn't tell anyone."

My words aren't for him, but I'm too angry to keep it on the down-low. After Callum attacked me, Maggie swore she wouldn't tell anyone.

My anger gets a second wind when reality hits me like a freight train. She's the reason Jacob turned up to Mavs in the middle of the afternoon, isn't she? He doesn't usually show up until well past six.

"You called Jacob, didn't you?"

Maggie keeps her gaze fixed on the wooden tabletop while nodding. "Yes."

I hate the tears sliding down her cheeks, but not as much as I hate being lied to. "You promised."

"I know I did, but Jacob needs our help. He's in a lot of trouble." She peers at me with remorse-filled eyes, revealing the burden I'm carrying on my shoulders is just as heavy on hers. "He needs your help."

I understand what she's saying, and I know it's the right thing, but I don't want anyone to find out the secrets I've been hiding. Look what happened when I told Jacob. I don't want to drag more people into the mess.

I try to walk away. I try to tell myself that Jacob is an adult who should have considered the repercussion of his actions before jumping the gun, but no matter how many times I tell myself this isn't my fault, it is.

My gaze turns to Ryan. "What do you need me to do?"

"Maggie informed us that Callum Parker assaulted you earlier today at Mavericks and that his attack may have contributed to Jacob's frame of mind when he attacked Callum. Is that correct?"

"Yes." Who knew one little word would be so hard to deliver?

I add proof to my verbal confirmation by tugging up the sleeve of my sweater. Air expels from Ryan's nose when he takes in the purple, almost black mark circling my wrist, then his jaw spasms when I show him the bruises on my neck.

After standing to his feet, he gathers the papers off the desk. "I'll have you make a statement advising what happened today, then I'll start the process of having Callum charged."

"What?" I question, my voice panicked.

Ryan lowers his concerned gaze to mine. "What Callum did is illegal. We'll charge him with assault and battery, then file a restraining order so he can't come within five hundred feet of you." He drags his paperwork to his chest. "I'll have a female officer take photographic evidence of your assault, then I'll take your statement..."

His words trail off when I shake my head. "I'm not pressing charges."

If I have Callum charged, it will only be a matter of time before everyone knows what happened. Gossip in small towns like ours spreads like wildfire, and I refuse to be portrayed as a victim the rest of my life. It's bad enough I'll see it every time Jacob looks at me; I don't want to see it from strangers as well.

Maggie grabs ahold of my hand. Her hold isn't painful. It's more panicked than anything. "You can't let him get away with this."

"He didn't get away with it. Jacob took care of it."

"There's a legal way to handle this." This statement isn't coming from Maggie. It's from Ryan. He's peering at me with concern, hating that I'm letting Callum get off scot-free. I hate it as well, but when forced to pick between being a martyr or remaining quiet, I'll always choose silence.

"Will pressing charges help Jacob?"

Ryan hesitates before he shakes his head.

"Then we're done here."

My steps to the door slow when Ryan says, "An official statement could still help Jacob. Will you at least do that?"

"Just a statement?" I double-check. I don't want to be blindsided for the second time today.

"Yes. It will only be used as evidence to assist in Jacob's case."

My heart drums out a lively tune as I nod. "Okay. I can do that."

FOR THE NEXT HOUR, I draft a statement on what occurred earlier today at Mavericks under the pretext it will only be used in Jacob's case. Ryan is hoping to use my statement as evidence as to why Jacob attacked Callum with just cause. If the DA accepts our statement, Jacob's charges may be downgraded to assault and battery instead of attempted murder.

Just hearing how serious Jacob's charges are cracked my heart. Jacob is the kindest, gentlest guy I've ever met. He's a gentle giant who's now facing years in prison because of me. He must regret the day he offered a stranger a ride home.

I sign the bottom of my statement and date it before raising my eyes to Ryan. "Is that it?"

He nods. "Yes. Thank you." He guides me to the door and down the hall. "If you change your mind about charging Callum, my number is on here. Use it any time, day or night." When he hands me his business card, I accept it, even knowing I have no intention of using it. "Even without pressing charges, the restraining order is still valid. If Callum comes near you, call me."

I nod before walking out the large double glass doors of Ravenshoe PD. Just as I'm about to gallop down the stairs, I hear Maggie shouting my name. She's leaning against the wall, smoking a cigarette, the shudder of her hands visible from a distance. I had no clue she smoked. If her screwed-up expression when she puffs down the last half of her cigarette is anything to go by, neither did her lungs.

After stubbing out her smoke, she strolls my way. Her eyes are full of tears, and her lips are twitching. "I'm sorry I broke my promise. I just didn't know any other way to help Jacob."

"It's fine; don't worry about it." I'm accustomed to people not keeping their promises, so what's another name on an already long list?

The composure I'm struggling to maintain nearly raptures when Maggie mutters, "He loves you, Lola. That's why he responded like he did."

I bite the inside of my cheek, warning my voice it better not crack. "I know." *That's why I have to stay far away from him.* "Can you find someone to cover my shifts?"

Maggie steps back, her brow inching up in concern. "For how long?"

I give her a tight smile before starting my gallop down the stairs again. "Forever."

I race down the cracked sidewalk, not once looking back on what will be my old life.

CHAPTER TWENTY-FOUR

JACOB

My eyes float up from the cuff circling my wrists when a door creaks. Ryan is heading my way. His shoulders are still slumped, but they're not as low as earlier.

"Did Noah get out okay?"

He sits on a hard steel chair across from me before jerking up his chin. "Yeah, the neighbor who called in the disturbance issued a statement saying he was a bystander. He left around an hour ago, saying he'll be back as soon as he gets you a lawyer."

He spreads his knees to the width of his shoulders before leaning forward to undo my cuffs. When they're removed, I rotate my wrists in a circular motion to loosen them. The officer who brought me in tightened them to the point they pinched my skin.

After dumping my cuffs in a briefcase balancing on the desk separating us, Ryan returns his eyes to me. "Are you sure you don't want me to call someone? Your dad or brother?"

"Nah, I'm good." The longer I keep this secret, the better for all involved.

I'm still struggling to understand why I reacted so poorly today. It's pretty scary realizing you can kill someone with your bare hands.

If Noah hadn't dragged me off Callum, I'm confident that would have been the result, so not only am I grateful Noah avoided charges, I'll forever be in his debt for pulling me off him.

Noticing the low hang of my brow, Ryan says, "Don't beat yourself up, Jacob. Most guys would have responded the same way."

This is why I like Ryan. He looks past what others believe to form his own opinion.

Our heads shift to the door in sync when a tap sounds into the room. The officer who cuffed me to the table is standing outside, requesting to speak with Ryan. They chat for a few minutes, but I don't hear anything they're saying because my thoughts are elsewhere. Mainly with Lola, but a small part wonders how I'll explain what happened to my dad and Hank. Hank said if I ever used my skills outside the cage, I'd be booted from his training schedule. I don't want that. I love fighting... nearly as much as I love Lola.

I lock my eyes with Ryan when he returns to his seat. "Lola and Maggie issued statements on what happened today."

"Does that mean Callum has been charged?"

Ryan's jaw ticks as he shakes his head.

"Why not?"

"Because Lola won't press charges." He breathes his words out slowly like they're as hard for him to deliver as they are for me to hear.

"Why? He hurt her. Did you see the marks on her neck?" I shoot out of my chair, needing to pace out the anger boiling my blood. "If Maggie didn't intervene, he would have killed her."

The door of the interrogation room flies open as fast as I rocketed from my chair. If Ryan didn't dive out his chair to position himself between the officer who cuffed me and myself, I'd be kissing the pavement right now. That's how much hate is in the officer's eyes. He thinks I'm the criminal instead of the man who nearly choked a woman to death.

What the fuck is wrong with him?

With his fists clenched at his side and his veins pulsating, Ryan steps closer to the unnamed officer. "I've got this."

Their intense showdown lasts for several heart-thrashing seconds before the officer finally relents. After a last sneer directed at me, he exits the room as quickly as he entered it. I stare at his retreating frame in shock, stunned about how badly he's misjudged me. I might have just beat a man nearly to death, but I had a legitimate reason to hurt him.

While scrubbing a hand across his chin, Ryan pivots around to face me. "Please sit down before I'm forced to cuff you again."

His threat holds no steam, but I stride back to the table and slump onto the black steel chair I've been seated at the past four hours. I've caused him enough issues tonight. I don't want to add more shit to his plate.

It's the fight of my life to remain seated when he discloses, "Lola supplied a statement to assist your case, but she won't press charges against Callum."

"So I'm pretty much fucked? Is that what you're saying?"

He stares straight into my eyes but says nothing. His silence is all I need to know my fate. I'm going to jail for defending my girl. Would I change anything if I knew this would be the outcome? Not at all. I'd do it all again tomorrow if given a chance. Callum got what he deserved. I just wish Lola would add to his punishment instead of bowing out of the fight.

***

APPROXIMATELY TWO HOURS LATER, a guy dressed to impress enters my holding room. His swanky suit and hundred dollar haircut assures me he's not my lawyer—neither Noah or I could afford such costly representation—but if he's not here to defend me, why is he here?

He unbuttons his suit before holding out his hand in offering. "Jacob, I'm assuming?"

"Yep." I stand from my seat to accept his handshake. Once I'm extended to my full height, a smirk furls his lips.

"It's nice to meet you; I'm Isaac."

When he sits, I mimic his movements. "Are you my lawyer?"

He seems too young to be a lawyer, but maybe an intern was all Noah could afford. When you're swimming at the bottom of the pond, you take what you can get.

"No." He chuckles, amused by my reply. I don't know why. "But I do have a proposition for you. You need a lawyer, and from what I've heard from Nick, you can't afford one."

"Nick...?" I leave my question for him to fill in.

He follows along nicely. "Holt. My brother."

"Oh." *Ohhh.*

Isaac's smirk reveals he caught my extra "oh." Nick and I are friends, but we don't really get along, if that makes any sense? He's a bandmate of Noah's, but we don't see eye to eye. Probably because he's such a short little fucker.

My inward chuckles cease when Isaac says, "If you agree to work for me, my lawyer will get your charges quashed."

"You want me to work for you?" Curiosity echoes in my tone. From what Noah told me, Isaac owns a dance club in Ravenshoe. When Isaac lifts his chin, I ask, "Doing what? I don't dance."

His chuckle bounces around my holding room. "I've got my bases covered at my clubs. I want you to be my fighter."

His reply piques my interest, but not enough for me to forget who I am. "Sorry, can't. I'm already fighting—"

"Not anymore, you aren't," he interrupts, his tone mocking. "The instant you were charged with battery, you lost the right to fight in a professional capacity."

"What?" I'm too dumbstruck to form more than one-word sentences.

Isaac pulls out paperwork from a satchel he's carrying before handing it to me. Each page is filled with examples of cases where fighters were prosecuted on assault charges. In every case, they were given a lifetime ban from fighting.

"What would you prefer, time behind bars or fighting for me?"

I peer up from the papers I'm scrutinizing. "Is neither an option?"

With an arrogant smirk, Isaac shakes his head.

"I don't want to go to jail." *Who will protect Lola if I'm locked away?*

Isaac hands me a pen. "Then I suggest you accept my offer. Sign a contract stating you'll fight exclusively for me, and I'll ensure you don't do any time."

ISAAC IS a man of his word. Within an hour of me agreeing to be his fighter, I'm walking out of the police station on bail. While driving me home, he advises his lawyer will work on a plea to ensure I'll avoid jail. I'll most likely have a conviction on my criminal record and be placed on probation, but I'll be a free man.

I doubt that would be the case if Isaac hadn't agreed to compensate Callum. It seriously pisses me the off that Callum can put his hands on a woman, then get a payout. It doesn't make any sense. Where's the justice? I would have put a stop to it if Isaac didn't say it was the only way I'd avoid time behind bars.

"I'll contact you as soon as I know anything."

Nodding, I slid out of Isaac's top of the line BMW. He's so swanky, he doesn't even drive himself around. He has a fancy-schmancy driver, although he's not wearing a chauffeur's hat.

"Thanks for your help."

Isaac smirks. "The pleasure will be all mine."

I wait for his taillights to disappear down the driveway before entering my home. The first person I spot is Noah sitting in the living room. When his eyes lock with mine, he leaps off the sofa and spans the distance between us. I'm shocked when he slings his arms around my shoulders to give me a brief man hug. He's not a touchy-feely type.

"Does Dad know?" I ask while returning his embrace.

"No. I didn't think you'd want me to tell him."

His answer coincides with my dad sauntering into the room. He has a book in one hand and a glass of lemonade in the other. Feeling our stare, he stops reading to peer at us. "Jacob, Noah."

After a final glare warning us to behave, he continues his trek to his favorite recliner in the corner of the room. He places his drink on a side table before returning his eyes to us, still frozen in the middle of the living room.

"What are you two up to?"

"Nothing."

Our mirrored reply increases his suspicion. His eyes slit as his lips purse. He appears two seconds away from giving us one of his infamous hour-long lectures.

"I'm going to take a shower, but...uh...Noah wants your advice on something. He's just started dating someone, and he's not sure if he's treating her right."

Ignoring Noah's ticking jaw that warns I'm about to be murdered, I bolt for the hallway, leaving him defenseless against an old romantic who loves teaching men how to treat a lady right.

I'M DRYING my shaggy hair with a towel when Noah enters my room. He's clearly pissed, but there's a bit of amusement behind his dark eyes. "Thanks for that, asshole. Now my ears are bleeding."

"Sorry." I try my hardest not to laugh but miserably fail. "Did he give you any good advice?"

Noah gags. "Only to wrap it before I tap it."

When I throw my head back and laugh, he tries to maintain his serious expression. It doesn't last long. Within seconds, he's laughing right along with me. "It wasn't fucking funny at the time. I wasn't sure if I'd ever have sex again."

We laugh for several more minutes before the humor on his face recedes for anxiousness. "What happened today, Jake? I've never seen you snap like that before."

I run my hand down my face as I flop onto my bed. "Have you ever asked my dad how he met my mom?"

Noah cocks his brow as if to say *do I look like a sucker for punishment?*

"You should ask him one day. It's an interesting story." I roll over to face the ceiling before giving him a recap of the events. "My mom moved into my dad's neighborhood when he was fifteen. He claims she was the most beautiful, carefree girl he had ever laid eyes on. What he didn't know was that she was raised by an abusive, alcoholic father."

Noah sucks in a sharp breath, the similarities between his childhood and my mom's too similar for him to ignore.

"When my dad arrived at her house uninvited one afternoon, he discovered firsthand the abuse she had endured since she was little. He reacted the same way I did today. He beat my grandad to within an inch of his life." I smile. I'm not proud of the violence I showed today, but I am proud I stood up for Lola.

"Because my mom didn't want my dad prosecuted, they fled in the darkness of the night and never returned. I've met my dad's parents a handful of times, but I've never met my grandparents on my mom's side. I don't think they even know I exist, which suits me just fine."

"Wow." Air whistles between Noah's teeth. "I'm not surprised; your dad is a good man. I just hope you're not getting any ideas about running away." He's joking, but there's also a touch of worry in his deep tone.

"I don't see that happening anytime soon." When he peers down at me with furrowed brows, I add on, "Lola won't press charges against Callum, much less run away with me."

She's also not answering any of my calls, but I keep that snippet of information to myself.

I don't express my words, but Noah still hears them. "She'll come around. *Eventually.*"

He sounds as unsure as I feel.

CHAPTER TWENTY-FIVE

LOLA

"I just want five minutes of your time." I brace my back on my partially cracked open front door, certain the boot holding open the frail wood doesn't belong to who I think it does. Why would Curtis turn up now? I haven't seen him since the day I fled his little brother's house.

Bile works up from my stomach to my throat when reality dawns: he knows about my connection with Jacob.

His next comment proves my theory without a doubt. "Come on, Lola. Don't make a mountain out of a molehill—*again*."

"What happened wasn't my fault—"

"I didn't say it was."

He's lying. I can't see his face, but I don't need to. I heard the untruth in his words. Curtis is a pathological liar, a manipulator, and a person I'd give anything to see the back of—even more so since I'm home alone.

When our standoff lasts another five minutes with no signs of ending, I suck in a deep breath, push off the door, then spin around. Because Curtis' boot is wedged in it, my move away from the door coincides with its opening, revealing him and his brooding six-foot-two frame. He's dressed like the last time I saw him: designer jeans and shirt, but it's rolled up at the cuffs, exposing the tattoos snaking up his thick biceps. An idiot could accuse him of being handsome if he weren't such an asshole.

I cross my arms in front of my chest to hide the shake of my hands. "Your five minutes has started, so get talking."

He lurches for me like a child jumping out of the closet to scare a sibling. "Boo!"

He scares the shit out of me—on the inside. I won't give him the satisfaction of knowing he intimidates me. I'm sick to death of the Parker brothers and their self-entitlement issues. Curtis hated me on sight. And for what? Because I wanted his brother to have a better life than the miserable one they had as children?

"What do you want, Curtis?" My pitch is low and jam-packed with anger. I'm tired and hormonal, and five seconds from slamming my door in his face.

"A little less attitude wouldn't go astray."

I curse a million times in my head when his hand moving for my face causes me to flinch. I shouldn't be so hard on myself. Old habits die hard.

"I won't hit you."

Once again, he's lying. Don't ask me how I know; I just do.

He brushes my hair away from my neckline so he can drink in my week-old bruises. "I didn't realize Callum took my taunts so seriously."

When his hand lowers from my neck, I move my hair back into place, ensuring my bruises are concealed. Long-sleeve shirts, foundation, and the length of my hair mean no one is any wiser about what happened last week at Mavs.

"Now that you have proof of what Callum is capable of, you're free to leave."

I unlatch my front door and take a step back, only stopping when Curtis says, "Do you know Callum is addicted to crack? Supposedly he has been for over a year. That means he began using when he was with you."

I didn't know, but the change in his personality, his irritability, and isolating us from our friends now makes sense. Callum dabbled in recreational drugs when we first began dating, but that was only occasional ecstasy or sometimes he smoked a joint, and it was only when we went out. It wasn't everyday use.

"Did you encourage him to take drugs?"

The viciousness in Curtis's tone reveals he won't believe me no matter what I say, but I can't help but reply, "No, Curtis, I didn't. Callum is a big boy. He's capable of making his own decisions."

I'm referring to more than just Callum's drug usage. Just like his decision to hit me months ago was his choice, so was last week's incident, so why is his brother fighting his battles?

"Yes, he's an adult, but then women like you throw wrenches into the works, making usually sane men insane. Take your boyfriend, Jacob, as an example."

My eyes snap to his as my heart thuds against my ribs.

He smiles, loving my stunned response. "You didn't think I knew about him?" He leans in close to my face. "I've known for months. He was doing well until he started dating you. I guess you have an adverse effect on the men you mess with."

With an arrogant smirk, he saunters to his truck parked at the end of my driveway. Just before he climbs inside, he turns his evil eyes back to me. "Tell your boyfriend his day is coming."

Detesting the threat in his tone, I slam my door shut before securing the lock into place. Our run-in has my hands shaking as much as my thighs. It takes me several tries to get the lock into place, and even then, I double, triple-check it. The rumble of Curtis's engine tells me I'm safe, but I don't feel it. I'm trembling all over, which only increases my irritation. I'm furious at myself that he has me fumbling like an idiot. I'm stronger than this—I'm also not a victim!

Anger is still bubbling in my veins when I hear my cell phone shrilling from my room. I know who is calling me without needing to look at the screen. It will be Jacob... *again!* He hasn't quit calling since he arrived at my house last week, begging for a chance to speak to me just as Curtis did. I didn't give in to him, though. I maintained my stance like I wish I had just now.

When my phone rings again a mere second after sending his call to voicemail, my anger gets the better of me. I snatch up my phone, swipe my finger across the screen, then squash it to my ear.

Jacob is so relieved I've answered his call, he doesn't wait for me to greet him. "Lola... *finally*. I've been calling you for days."

"I'm well aware of that. What do you want?"

He takes my angry, rude tone in stride. "I wanted to make sure you're okay."

His genuine concern halts my bitch façade. "I'm fine." My tone isn't as harsh as seconds ago.

"Okay. Good." He breathes out before continuing, "I also wanted to apologize for how I reacted when you told me what happened."

"It's too late for apologies. What is done is done, but maybe next time, consider the consequences of your actions before banging your chest like an ape. I didn't need saving, Jacob. I'm more than capable of taking care of myself."

The shake of my words makes a liar out of me. I don't mean to act cowardly, but my blood pressure is too high for it not to affect my voice.

I hear him scrub at the stubble on his chin—the stubble that used to tickle my chin when he kissed me. "I wasn't trying to save you, Lola... I just snapped."

"No, you didn't just snap; you acted like an imbecile." As I am now. I'm not weak, so why am I acting as if I am? "I have to go—"

"Please don't shut me out of your life again."

His somber tone nearly breaks me. It would have if I didn't believe this was best for us both. "I'm sorry, but our arrangement isn't working for me anymore. It's time for us to move on."

Before he can talk me out of my decision, I disconnect our call and shut down my phone. With the dam in my eyes close to breaking, I clench my fists into a white-knuckle hold before screaming out my frustration at the top of my lungs. I'm hollering so loudly, I'm certain the neighbors will call in a disturbance, but if I don't do something, I'll break—then everything I worked so hard for the last year will be wasted.

I hate what I just did to Jacob—he didn't deserve all of my anger, but Maggie was right. I need to stop the games and start acting like an adult. I can't do that *and* continue leading Jacob astray. He deserves better, and so do I.

That's why first thing tomorrow morning, I'll hand in an official resignation to Maggie, then I can go back to the life I had before Jacob entered it. Back to one where I'm not responsible for other people's actions. I'll miss Jacob, but like I've already said, walking away is the nicest thing I'll ever do for him.

CHAPTER TWENTY-SIX

JACOB

Six months later...

"Have you got ants in your pants?"

Emily stops squirming in my passenger seat to peer at me. "I'm nervous."

"You'll be fine."

I'm tempted to twang her protruded lower lip, but since Noah isn't here for me to rile up, I save my tease for a more appropriate time. We're in the process of moving Emily into her dorm room at Parkwood State College. Noah initially planned to help us, but his band has a huge meeting with a record label interested in signing them, so I'm picking up his slack—slack we wouldn't have if Noah canceled his meeting as planned.

He hates backing out of any agreements he makes. If I hadn't convinced him we're more than capable of moving a handful of boxes unsupervised, he would have postponed his meeting with Destiny Records. That's how much his word means to him.

That and the fact he hates leaving me alone with Emily.

I'd never touch a hair on her head, but I have too much fun teasing him to ever let him know that. He has a bit of a jealous streak when it comes to Emily. I can't blame him. I've seen the way heads turn when she enters a room, but I see her more like a sister than anything else. I want to say sister-in-law, but Lola made sure that's not an option.

I haven't seen Lola since my arrest. She was pissed I thought she needed to be saved. That wasn't what I was doing. I was teaching Callum a lesson. Did it work? Who knows? But he'll think twice before he lays hands on a woman again.

Lola no longer works at Mavericks. From what I heard, she got a job at a bar in her hometown. I could investigate her life more thoroughly, but in all honesty, I'm not sure I want to. I begged her for forgiveness. I left her hundreds of voicemails and even more text messages. She didn't return a single call — not one.

At the start, I understood her anger. I took up a fight she didn't want me involved in, but within weeks, that understanding waned. I became furious she had projected all her anger onto me. I flushed my fighting career down the toilet for her, and for what? Nothing but resentment and anger.

Although I was peeved about how things turned out, my fighting career with Isaac smoothed the rocky waters. It doesn't matter whether I win or lose in his fighting circle. I turn up, fight, then get paid. I'm not saying I don't fight to win; my track record is solid. In the past six months, I've maintained my undefeated title.

Size doesn't matter in the circle I fight in. If you believe your fighter is good enough to fight another, you propose a fight to their "owner." If both sides agree, it's scheduled for a few weeks' time. The three-thousand-dollar-a-fight purse I negotiated with Isaac seems too good to be true, but I'll take everything offered. I don't see many business owners willing to hire a manager with a criminal record.

I don't know what I'll do once our agreement ends. I might take it a week at a time and see how it goes. I was given two years' probation for beating Callum, so I have plenty of time to work out what I want to do between now and then.

My mind clicks back to the present when we approach Emily's dorm. "Stairs or the elevator?"

Emily glares at me like I'm crazy for even suggesting we take the stairs. "The elevator." She balances the one puny box she's lugging onto her hip. "This box weighs a ton."

She's such a lightweight. She wouldn't be if she occasionally came to the gym with Noah and me. After giving Noah a brief recap on how my parents met, I told him about my fighting career. Because Isaac had just become my "owner," I ghosted over that part of my confession.

Although shocked at my career choice, Noah said he'd support me. That's how I've managed to drag his ass to the gym a handful of times the past six months. I support him by watching his gigs, and he supports me by sparring with me.

Hank took an instant liking to Noah. They often go a few rounds in the ring while I skip rope for an hour. If Hank's plan to make my fighting stance not as solid weren't working, I'd strangle him with the rope he has me skipping a minimum of two hours a day. I doubt skipping will make me more agile, but since it's part of Hank's punishment for being charged with assault, I'll do it.

Hank was furious with me when he found out I'd been arrested. Weeks passed before he forgave me, and even then, he barely spoke a word to me. Mercifully, he's still my trainer; he just gets paid by Isaac instead of getting a cut of my profits.

During one of our sessions, I asked Noah not to tell Emily what happened to Lola. I don't like forcing him to keep secrets from her, but I promised Lola I wouldn't tell anyone. She may not want to associate with me, but I am a man of my word. Noah was hesitant, but he understood why I didn't want anyone to know, so he agreed to keep quiet on all aspects of it—my illegal fighting career too.

I'm snapped back to the present for the second time this afternoon when the elevator dings, announcing the car has arrived at the lobby. When a bunch of college girls pile out, I greet them with a friendly wink. "Ladies."

They return my friendliness with sultry smirks and batting lashes. Emily's response is nowhere near as sociable. "Really, Jacob, *ladies* is the best you can come up with?"

"What? It's hard to talk with my tongue hanging out my mouth. I might tag along when Noah comes to visit. Parkwood State looks like a place I could enjoy visiting."

I stop waggling my brows when Emily makes a barfing noise. "That's not funny."

I'd give her a stern finger point if my hands weren't loaded with boxes. Instead, I take a giant step away from her. "Yeah, it is."

She dry-heaves again, louder this time. Noah must have told her about my morbid dislike of hearing people get sick. I hate barf, vomit, spew, chunder, whatever you want to call it. It's disgusting, and just the thought of someone being sick makes my stomach churn.

Emily continues teasing me until the elevator arrives at her floor. I shadow her giggling ass into the room she'll call home for the next four years. When I enter her dingy space, flashbacks of Noah's childhood bedroom race to the forefront of my mind. There's only one notable difference: Emily's mattress is on a bed frame instead of the floor.

After dumping my boxes, I go collect some more from my car. "I'll be back."

Emily nods, acknowledging she heard me, but she remains standing in the middle of her room. Her nose is screwed up, and her brows are hanging low. She looks bewildered that this is it, her entire life in a handful of boxes. She's got more than most. Noah only had the clothes on his back and holey shoes when he accepted the spare room in my family home.

Needing to make up for the training session I'm missing to help Emily move, I take the stairs instead of the elevator. I only lug one box this time since it weighs a fucking ton.

As I take the last three flights of stairs, I read the description written on the box. *Sex toys and lingerie.*

I remind myself to read in my head when two girls in the stairwell giggle. Although they're giving me kissy gaga faces, I continue climbing the stairwell without exchanging digits. I'm too interested in figuring out how Emily has enough sex toys to fill this box to play nice. I'm not lying when I say it weighs almost as much as I bench press. I didn't think Emily was a sex toy type girl. Lola... she'd have enough to fill a truck.

When my curiosity gets the better of me, I lower the box onto the top step of Emily's floor. My eyes dart around the cold, empty stairwell to ensure no one is looking, then I take a peek inside the box, eager to find out what toys Noah has at his disposal.

I huff.

There's nothing remotely like a sex toy in this box. It's full of boring books.

After a roll of my eyes, I spot Noah exiting the elevator, the smug grin on his face illuminating a lightbulb in my head. I race a few paces in front of him and dart into Emily's room with only a second to spare.

"Where do you want this box?" I waggle my brows, ensuring she knows I read the box's inscription, but I don't give her any indication that I peered inside. "What the hell do you have in here? It weighs a ton."

I wait to detect Noah's presence before pretending to take a peek inside the box. He slaps down the box's flap and snatches it out of my grasp. "That's for me to know and you to never find out."

Point one to Jacob!

"Come on, man, don't be a tease."

My rile doesn't have the effect I'm aiming for. Noah has Emily in his sights, which is my cue to leave before my retinas are burned with images I do *not* want to see.

While Noah and Emily suck face, I head back to my car for the last of Emily's boxes. I'm just about to break through the fire exit doors when I catch sight of an attractive blonde sauntering down the hallway. She's attractive but in a natural way that's hard to explain; maybe it's the freckles adorning her nose. They give her a youthful appearance that would have some guys backtracking.

Upon noticing my gawk, her lips curve into a smirk. "I've seen you at Mavericks, haven't I?"

I nearly shake my head, confident I would have noticed someone as beautiful as her, but hold back when I remember how many months I've spent staring at Mavericks' doors, waiting for Lola to walk through them.

"You're always there when Rise Up plays. Are you their manager?"

"No," I chuckle. "They're friends of mine, though."

"Lucky friends." Not even a gay man could misconstrue her flirty tone. She's throwing out feelers, praying I'll catch one.

I do. "I'm Jacob." I offer her my hand to shake.

"Crystal." She accepts my handshake as her teeth rake her lower lip. "Any chance I'll see you at Mavericks Friday night?"

I try to hide my smug grin. You can be assured I'll never win an Emmy. "There's a very good chance—if that's what you want?"

I haven't missed a Rise Up show, but I'll pretend her invitation is the reason I'm showing up if it keeps her looking at me like she is. It's been a while since I've had someone eye me like this. I've only seen the gleam in her eyes once before. It was when Lola begged me to stay seconds before I left.

Crystal's lip is freed from her teeth when she smiles. "I'd like that very much."

"Then I guess it's settled. I'll see you at Mavericks on Friday."

My shot out of nowhere becomes a slam dunk when Crystal purrs, "I can't wait."

After flashing a smile, she moseys down the hall, and that's when my nerves kick in. Crystal is the type I usually go for, but I haven't been on a *date* in over six months. Noah jokes I ran out of dating privileges because I used them too frequently in my teen years, but I know the real reason I can't move on. I can't get a feisty, temperamental, infuriatingly beautiful, buxom brunette with the most dazzling light brown eyes out of my fucking head.

I miss Lola every day, but I can't force someone to be a part of my life. Especially someone as stubborn as she is, so as much as I wish circumstances were different, I have to pull my head out of the sand and start living again. I'm certain she's already moved on, so it's time for me to do the same.

After collecting the last two boxes from my car, I head back to Emily's room. She's still sucking face with Noah. "Get a room!" I tease them.

A smile etches onto my face when Noah gives me the finger. "These are the last two boxes, Em." I dump them on the bed they're making out on before shifting on my feet to face them. "How was your meeting, Noah?"

I forgot to ask him earlier. It's not entirely my fault. He had Emily on his radar, and there's no stopping him once he spots her.

"Good, *really* good. They enjoy the sound we're creating and want to experience it live. They're coming to watch our gig this Friday."

"They'll love you guys!"

I add to Emily's enthusiasm by slapping his shoulder. "That's great news, Noah. This is what you've been working for your whole life."

Realizing this is the perfect time to reignite my earlier tease, I wrap him up in a big bear hug. Noah isn't a touchy-feely type of guy, so I hang on to him until I feel his heart raging in his chest.

I'm certain he's seconds away from telling me to fuck off, so you can imagine my shock when he chuckles, "Alright there, big guy, don't start crying."

My arms drop to my side like atomic bombs. After too much beer last Christmas, Patrick told Noah about the *one* time I cried in primary school. Noah has used it against me ever since. *Asshole.*

Eager to return his scorn, I shove him away from me. "Whatever."

Before Emily has a clue about what's going to happen, I curl my arms around her and spin her around the room. "Emily loves my big hugs. Don't you, Em?"

After spinning her enough times I'm afraid her earlier fake vomiting will become real, I lower her back to her feet. Since I'm still in teasing mode, I ensure her body remains plastered to mine during descent. My rile pays dividends when Emily's cheeks bloom a mere second before Noah yanks her away from me.

"Get off her, Jacob!"

Another point for Jacob.

Emily almost makes it too easy for me to win. I shouldn't use Noah's jealousy against him, but could I really call him my best friend if I didn't? Furthermore, with all the hype his band is getting, it's my job to keep him grounded.

That's why I add extra sass to my smile when I wave goodbye while pacing into the hall. "Bye, Emily."

My heart beats triple time when Noah races over to slam her bedroom door in my face. "Fuck off!"

While pacing down the nearly empty hallway, I cup my hands over my mouth to replicate the murmur of a noisy crowd. "Game, set, and match, the winner is Jacob!"

CHAPTER TWENTY-SEVEN

LOLA

My heart races a million miles an hour as my nervous gaze floats over the dozen patrons wasting a glorious Sunday afternoon at Mavericks. Although there are more people than I was anticipating, I inwardly sigh when I fail to locate Maggie behind the bar.

After exhaling a big breath, I make a beeline for a table in the far back corner of the room. The fewer witnesses to my "date," the better. I'll never forgive myself if this gets out. I can't believe out of all the establishments in Ravenshoe he had to pick from, he chooses Mavericks. I haven't been here since the day I resigned. Nothing has changed. It still has the same homey feeling sought by lost souls at all hours of the day and night.

I've just slipped into my seat when Callum breaks through the large wooden entry doors. Now that he's clean, he looks like the Callum I used to know. His hair is shiny, minus the grease from the last time I saw him; his face is clear and void of blemishes, and his clothing looks new.

His endeavors to reach me were as extreme as Jacob's after the incident, and I ignored him as adeptly as I did Jacob. There was just one difference: Jacob gave up within weeks. Callum didn't. He continued messaging and calling every day until I finally caved...

"Please leave me alone," I plead into the phone.

I'm having enough trouble forgetting Jacob, let alone having images of him pop into my head every time Callum's name flashes across the screen of my phone.

"Please don't hang up." The sincerity in Callum's tone shocks me. I haven't heard him use manners in months. "I just want the chance to tell you how sorry I am."

Although I'm surprised by his change in demeanor, I'm still not eager to talk to him. "Apology accepted; now leave me alone."

I stop dragging my phone away from my ear when he rushes out, "I'm clean. I've been drug-free for the past six months."

"That's good; I'm glad."

Deep down inside, I know the Callum who attacked me wasn't the same Callum I fell in love with, but that doesn't mean I'll let him back into my life now that he's clean. There's too much water under the bridge for us to ever be friends. He's the reason I've been living the life of a recluse the past six months. I hate him for that...and for what he did to Jacob.

"Take care, Callum."

My thumb hovers over the disconnect button when Callum shouts a name I'll never forget.

I push my phone back to my ear so fast, I smack myself up the head. "What did you say about Jacob?"

Knowing he has me by the throat, Callum's tone changes in an instant. Back is the asshole I know all too well. "I can't tell you over the phone. Meet me in person, then you'll know everything."

"Nice try, Callum, but I wasn't born last week."

"You won't be so quick to say that when you hear what I've got to say."

The superiority in his tone pisses me off, but not enough to weaken my curiosity. "If that were true, you'd tell me now. You've never been good at keeping secrets."

"I can when it hurts people I care about."

"Hurt who? Me or Jacob?"

I don't give a shit about myself. I made my bed, and now I have to lie in it, but if this is in regards to the threat Curtis made against Jacob months ago, I want to know.

Worry brews in my gut when Callum breathes out, "Both."

"Then just tell me now—"

"No, if you want to know, you have to meet with me."

I fist my shirt, unsure what to do. I refuse to be in the same room with Callum, but I want to know what's going on so I can warn Jacob.

"I'll meet you somewhere public."

Callum breathes harshly down the line. "I won't hurt you again, Lola."

"In public or not at all. Those are my terms."

A sturdy length of silence stretches between us. It's as tension-filled as you'd expect.

"Okay," he finally gives in. "I'll text you a time and the place later today."

With that, he hangs up...

When he texted an hour later requesting that I meet him at Mavericks, I initially refused. Mavs is Jacob's home turf, so there's no way I could do that to him. I was halfway through punching out a refusal when I recalled Emily saying Jacob was helping her move in today. With traffic extra hectic from everyone preparing to return to school, the drive from her university to Mavericks was a solid two hours.

With that in mind, I changed my text, agreeing to meet Callum here.

I'm snapped back to the present when Callum swoops down to plant a kiss on my cheek. "Thanks for agreeing to meet me."

I'm about to tell him to keep his mitts to himself when a much more dangerous situation arises. Maggie is standing just behind Callum. Her eyes are slit, her fists balled.

"Get out of my bar!" She steps closer to Callum, locked and

loaded on her target. "And if I ever see you here again, I won't hesitate to bring out my bat...or my gun."

Callum jackknifes back, seeming confused about why Maggie is so angry. His eyes dance between hers before he slants his head to me. Only now does it dawn on me that he was high when he attacked me.

"I'm sorry, we'll leave now."

I slip off my barstool and make a beeline for the door, only to have Maggie snatch my wrist. "You can stay." Her squinted gaze strays back to Callum. "But he has five minutes to get the hell out of my bar!"

"What the fuck?"

With Callum's anger growing, I have no choice but to get him out of here before he detonates. After giving Maggie a look, one that says I'll always appreciate her help six months ago, I wiggle out of her hold before taking up my own on Callum's wrist. "Let's go. I'll explain it to you on the way out."

Just as we pace out the doors, Jacob's car pulls into an empty spot at the front.

Oh shit.

CHAPTER TWENTY-EIGHT

JACOB

As my shoes click the worn floors of Mavericks, I take in the patrons filling the space on a lazy Sunday afternoon. There are more people than I expected when I decided to wash away my crappy week with a beer or three.

When I stop at the bar, Maggie's eyes pop up from the sparkling counter she's scrubbing with her beloved red dishcloth. With how hard she's rubbing, I'm surprised she hasn't scoured off the varnish.

"Jacob...what are you doing here on a Sunday afternoon?"

I take a moment to decide if her high tone is shock or anger before answering, "Just finished helping Emily move, figured I could waste the calories on a couple of beers." I'm leaning toward shocked, even with sweat beading her neck.

She throws her cloth onto the counter. "Speaking of beer, can you help me bring up some cartons from the cold room?"

"Sure." When she races for the back exit of the bar, my brows furrow. "Now?"

She's so eager to get outside, I almost miss her head bob. I jog to catch up with her, equally alarmed and excited. I've never been granted access to this half of Mavs before, so I'm somewhat excited she needs my help. It gives me a chance to snoop.

When I enter the cold room, the first thing I notice is that it's half-empty. It's lucky Ollie schedules a delivery every Friday afternoon, or Noah's pay would be half the pittance it already is.

"Which boxes do you want?" When my question is met with silence, I spin around to face Maggie. Her attention is fixed on something outside. "Maggie?"

"Huh?" She joins me inside the cold room, her breaths visible in the frigid air.

I stare at her, struggling to work out why she's such a scatterbrain today before questioning again, "Which cartons of beer do you need?"

"Oh... umm. .. that one." She points to a single box stacked by itself. It looks like a Chinese-manufactured beer.

Scrunching my brows, I peer back at Maggie. "Just that one?"

She stops glancing outside to peer back at me. "Yep." Her shrug is as off-putting as the remorse in her eyes.

"Alright."

I collect the carton of beer she's requesting before attempting to leave the cold room. I say "attempt" because Maggie is blocking my exit. When I step to the left, she steps to the right, trapping me in the icebox that's close to turning my lips blue.

"Maggie...?" I want to say more, but I'm too stunned by the petrified look in her eyes. It's giving me more chills than the cold conditions surrounding me.

"I didn't need your help with the beer. I just needed you out of the bar before you saw them."

My throat works hard to swallow. "Saw who?" I already know whom she's referring to, I just want her to click all the pieces of the puzzle together for me.

"Lola..."

My breath hitches in my throat.

"And Callum."

My stomach slithers into my gut. I dump the beer back on the shelf and sprint out of the cold room, accidentally bumping into Maggie on my way past. With my heart pounding in my ears, I drag my eyes up and down the half-full parking lot before sprinting into the street. I can't see Lola anywhere.

I discover why when Maggie says, "They just left—"

"They?" *Lola couldn't possibly be that stupid, could she?* "Is Lola *with* Callum?" The way I murmur "with" leaves no doubt about what I'm asking. *Is Lola dating Callum?*

"They looked together." Maggie steps closer to me, her eyes revealing whose side she's on. "I refused to serve him. I told him he was never to step foot in my bar again."

I remain quiet for several long minutes. Just the thought of Callum being anywhere near Lola makes me fucking furious. He hurt her—more than once, so why will she speak to him and not me?

"Maybe they're just friends. Like Lola and you were friends," Maggie suggests.

Friends, yep, that was all we were, friends who slept with each other, but I still can't believe she'd take Callum back. He didn't just attack her once; he did it twice, and the second time it was in the middle of the fucking day. How could she trust being alone with him if he can do something like that in public?

"Does Noah know?" I question Maggie.

Lola's stupid decisions don't just affect me; they also affect Noah since he's dating her little sister.

"No, today was the first time I saw them together. Do you think I should tell him?"

I take a moment to contemplate her question. Noah's life is finally working out the way he had hoped, so I don't want to burden him with this, but Lola is Emily's sister, so he'd want to know what's happening so he can avoid the toxic people Callum could introduce to Emily's life.

"Leave it to me. Once I figure out *exactly* what's happening with

Lola and Callum, I'll talk to him." I cock my brow. "But can I get that beer now? 'Cause I'm *real* fucking thirsty."

I came to Mavericks to have a quiet afternoon. Instead, I'm dealing with shit that shouldn't be affecting me anymore. If only I could wash my hands of people who did me wrong as quickly as they do me. I loved Lola—*I still do*—so although she wants nothing to do with me, I'll still look out for her when I think she's making fucked-up decisions.

CHAPTER TWENTY-NINE

LOLA

Several eyes pop up from their meals when Callum and I enter Daisy's. Daisy's is a local burger and fries joint Callum and I frequented when we were dating. It's a public place, but since it's nearing 4 PM, it's not overly crowded, making it an ideal location for us to continue our meet up without spectators.

My blood pressure is still sky-high from our near run-in with Jacob. I was certain he'd bust me hiding in the hallway the bathrooms are in. He most likely would have if Maggie hadn't distracted him. I loathe the spineless woman I'm portraying, but I've stepped too far into the shitstorm to back out now. Once Callum tells me what he has to say, I'll go back to the old Lola, the one who doesn't back down no matter what.

When we take our seats, Daisy, the owner, heads over to take our order. "My goodness, I haven't seen you two in here for months. How is my favorite couple?"

Her eyes bounce between us as she flips open her notepad to jot down our order. She presses down her pencil so hard, the lead snaps when I mutter, "We're not together anymore."

With her eyes full of sympathy, they drift to Callum. "I'm sorry to hear that, sweetheart."

I roll my eyes, not stunned the blame for our failed relationship was placed on my shoulders. Strong, independent women are to blame for every bad event in the world, didn't you know?

When Daisy goes to gather our order of coffee and donuts, Callum glares at me. "Why did you tell her that?"

"Because it's the truth. We aren't together anymore."

Callum's fists clench so quickly, the dishware on our table rattles. His fast descent into anger is disturbing, but not enough for me to forget why we're here. "Enough stalling. I only agreed to meet because you said you had something important to tell me."

He waits for Daisy to fill our coffee cups before asking, "How well do you know Jacob?"

"Better than I knew you—"

"Quit the fuckin' attitude, Lola. I said I was sorry."

My eyes will get an intense workout this afternoon with how my times I'm rolling them. Just because he said he was sorry doesn't mean I've forgiven him. I'm not that forgiving.

While serving the donuts we ordered, Daisy smiles, but not even her bright grin can stifle the tension bouncing between Callum and me. It's so repulsive, the usually fragrant donuts smell like they've been dipped in arsenic.

Once Daisy is out of earshot, I return my focus to Callum. "I know Jacob. He's a good guy."

"So you know he's a street fighter?" He talks around the chunk of donut he pops into his mouth.

I laugh at the absurdity of him thinking Jacob is a violent person. "Jacob doesn't fight."

He must be mistaken. There's no way Jacob would compete in *anything* illegal, much less street fighting. The only time I've seen him angry was when he beat the living shit out of Callum, but he's too kind and gentle to participate in a bloodthirsty sport.

Loving my stunned expression, Callum smirks. "Yeah, that's what I thought. You don't know him at all, do you?"

"I know him. *You're* the mistaken one." The confidence in my tone can't be missed.

His tormented chuckle screeches through my ears. "I knew you'd say that." He digs his hand into his pocket to pull out his phone. "That's why I brought proof."

After tapping on the screen, he hands his phone to me. There's a video on the screen. Although the image is grainy since it's paused, there's no denying the physique of the man standing in the middle of the ring. It's Jacob. I'm so confident, I'd put money on it. We were only friends, but I know every inch of his body, having studied it in depth at every given opportunity.

Callum shoves another chunk of donut into his mouth before instructing me to hit play. When I do, the air in my lungs leaves in a hurry. The video only goes for forty-five seconds, but in that short period of time, it shows Jacob knocking out his opponent.

I watch the video another three times before returning Callum's phone. He licks powdered sugar off his lips while returning it to his pocket. Once he has everything in place, he locks his smug eyes with mine. "He wasn't who you thought he was, was he?"

Unable to speak through my dry, parched mouth, I shake my head.

CHAPTER THIRTY

JACOB

Several hours later than planned, I'm heading home from Mavericks. I hadn't intended to stay so long, but it took more beer to get me out of my funk than I thought. I could blame Lola, but what's the use? My decisions are mine to make, just as her decisions are hers.

My prolonged visit to Mavs wasn't all bad. I was talking to Flynn, the lead singer of the band that plays at Mavs each Saturday night. His group, Wanting Wombats, originated from Australia. They flew here nine months ago with the hope of making it big. He wasn't fazed when I said he'll need a better band name before that ever happens. The one they have is fucking hideous.

"It is what it is, mate," he said in his deep Australian accent.

I'll have to arrange a time to watch them one night when I'm not fighting because Flynn and his bandmates seem like a good group of guys.

When I stop at a red traffic light, a dark blue sedan pulls up next to me. The revs of his engine gain my attention, much less the illegal tint on his windows. It's so dark, I can't see any of the occupants inside. I don't need to see him to understand his request, though.

Street racing was huge in Ravenshoe a few years back. Its long straight roads were perfect for rev-heads wanting to disperse some testosterone.

With my veins still thick with adrenaline, I flatten my foot to the floor, accepting his challenge for a race. I've always loved the thrill of pushing my car to its absolute limit. It's why Noah and I traveled these streets many times during our youth. Noah never participated in drag races, but he was more than happy to support me.

As soon as the light turns green, I flatten my accelerator before completing a quick shift change into second gear. The blue sedan and I stay neck to neck as we speed through the desolate streets of Ravenshoe. When my gauge hits seven thousand RPMs, I shift gears again, my car surging in front of my rivals.

With victory within my grasp, I glance back at the blackened windows of my competitor. I've got a good twelve or so inches on him. He can't come back from this. I give him a playful wink before pushing my car to its absolute limit. She gives me everything she has, only stumbling when her ass end slides out.

What the fuck?

I glance over my shoulder, my heart rate picking up. My tires didn't lose traction because of the furious speed. My competitor rammed me.

My grip on my steering wheel tightens when his bull bar veers toward the back-quarter panel of my car for the second time. This time, he hits me with enough force, my tires aren't the only thing that loses traction with the road, my whole fucking car does.

As my car cartwheels down the street, I flatten my palms on the roof lining. My pride and joy crunching against the pavement is unlike anything I've heard before. It's nearly deafening, equally frightening and awe-inspiring. I didn't realize how tough she was until she became the only thing between me and death.

I don't know how many flips we do before I spot a telephone pole in the corner of my eye. I brace for impact, sure I'm seconds from death. My passenger side door impacting with the pole immediately halts my car's cartwheeling action. It whiplashes back before teetering on its side for several seconds.

I pop open my eyes, surprised I haven't been seriously injured. "Holy shit."

When I detect the scent of gasoline, I yank on my door handle. It refuses to budge. I'm trapped in a mangled wreckage that's leaking gas. This isn't good.

Using my fists, I smash through the glass of the driver's side window. Glass splinters my knuckles, but it could be ten times worse if the pole I've smashed into has an exposed wire. As I clamber out of my car, I notice the street is empty. The blue sedan I was racing is nowhere in sight.

Once I'm at a safe distance, I glance back at my car. Not one panel remains in its original condition. It's completely totaled. After scanning the street to ensure I'm alone, I grab my phone and dial a recently called number.

Noah answers a few rings later. "Hey, Jake."

"Hey, can I ask a favor?"

"Sure, what's up?"

I try to think of a better way to explain my situation. When I fail to come up with anything, I keep it simple. "Can you come pick me up... and bring the car trailer with you?"

I'm only six months into my two-year probation period, so the last thing I want is a street racing charge added to my record.

THE NEXT MORNING, my dad comes barreling into my room, scaring the living daylights out of me. "What the hell happened to your car!" He smacks me over the head with a rolled-up newspaper. "Get out of bed, young man; you have some explaining to do."

"Alright, alright, settle down!" I scamper out of bed, still half-asleep. When my dad's eyes snap to my crotch, I cover my half-masted cock with my hands. I don't know why he's shocked. I've slept naked since I was fifteen. This is his punishment for kicking me out of bed so early.

When I hear chuckling, I peer past my dad's shoulder. Noah is propped against my doorframe. His arms are crossed in front of his shirtless torso, and he's smirking like a smug fuck.

He's not so smug when my dad grumbles, "If I find out you and Noah are competing in illegal street racing again, you won't know what hit you."

I balk, but my ripple is barely felt through Noah's shock. He bolts down the hallway so fast, Mexico just recorded an earthquake. My plan to give him hell for his cowardly ways flies out the window when my dad devotes his attention back to me.

"Did you think I didn't know?"

My shrug sparks his agitation more than soothing it.

"I know a lot more than you think I do." He smacks me over the head with his newspaper another two times before spinning on his heels and exiting my room even faster than he entered it. "Get dressed so you can move your now *piece of shit* car out of my driveway!"

I stand frozen in place, staring at my doorway in shock. I had no clue he knew Noah and I participated in drag races years ago. Well, Noah didn't compete; he just sat in the passenger seat while I did.

I mosey to my drawers to grab a pair of boxer shorts when Noah snickers, "Is it safe to come in?"

"Yep."

He makes it two steps into my room before his hands shoot up to cover his eyes. "Fuckin' hell, Jacob! I asked if it was safe."

Loving his mortified tone, I swivel my hips in a circular motion. "Helicopter, helicopter, helicopter."

My cock stops swinging when Noah snags a football off my desk to peg it at my back. Air rustles between my lips when it smacks me in my right rib.

With my hands cupped around my mouth, I fake explosion noises. "Mayday, mayday, I've been hit."

Noah tries to maintain his prissy attitude, but his broad grin gives away his true feelings. With my attitude not at its best the past six months, he's loving the return of my playful personality... even if it arrives with my cock hanging out.

"What are you, five years old?"

When I nod, he shakes his head before bending down to pick up the football.

"If the singing gig doesn't work out for you, you could take up football again. Your right hook is still as hard as fuck." I strengthen my assurance by rubbing my aching ribs.

"Serves you right for swinging *that* thing around." He doesn't need to nudge his head at my crotch for me to understand his meaning.

After flashing him a cheeky grin, I put on my pants. Although Noah was quick to shut down my comment, I can see his mind ticking over. He tried out for quarterback when he was a junior. He was successful, but no amount of skill could force him to fall in love with a sport he wasn't passionate about. Noah's passion has, and always will be, music.

His placement on the team was fun while it lasted, though. During practice, when I was on the offensive line and Noah was the QB, I kept letting our opponents slip past me just to witness Noah getting slammed. It didn't take him long to catch on to what I was doing. If you look hard enough, I swear I still have an imprint of a football on my back from when my ruse finally caught up with me.

Even though football wasn't Noah's thing, he played half a season, then Michael died, and he stopped coming to practice altogether. Come to think of it, I haven't seen him touch a football since that day.

After putting my football back in its rightful place, Noah sits on my bed. "Your dad is pissed." He waits for me to nod before adding, "When did you tell him about us racing in our teen years?"

"I didn't. I have no fucking clue how he knows."

Noah eyes me curiously before notching his shoulder up. "Then I guess we better move your car before he returns to give us one of his famous lectures."

I shadow his chuckling ass out of my room.

IT FUCKING KILLS ME, but after going over my car with a fine-toothed comb, we tow it to the local wreckers. A car once worth thousands of dollars pockets me only five hundred dollars for scrap metal. It will have me thinking twice about street racing from here on out.

Huh?! Who am I kidding? Where's the fun in that?

On his way to rehearsal, Noah drops me off at Hank's so I can squeeze in a workout. I put in a solid three hours before hitting the showers. As I switch off the faucet, I hear my phone ringing. I shuffle across the tiled floor, trying not to slip ass over tit to answer my call before it goes to voicemail.

Just as I dig my phone out of my gym bag, it stops ringing. "Fucking typical," I murmur to myself.

As I dress, my phone dings, announcing I have a voicemail. Curious, I quickly throw on my shirt before seeing who it is.

"Hey, Jacob. It's Casey... Are you free tonight? Call me."

After lowering my phone from my ear, I stare at the screen, trying to figure out who the fuck Casey is. It's not a common name, but for the life of me, I can't recall her.

It takes me getting dressed, leaving Hank's, and waiting for Noah to pick me up before recognition dawns. I met a Casey a few weeks ago at Mavericks. She was a Rise Up fan. If I remember correctly, she has perky tits and striking blue eyes. To start with, she seemed a little shy... until I offered her a ride home. Then it was like unleashing a tiger. We didn't slide past second base, but she was more than eager. It was only me removing the bat from her hand before she got close to home plate that stopped us. I probably wouldn't have if our hookup were occurring anywhere but in my car. That place was sacred to me. I don't know why. It's clear Lola moved on months ago, so why the fuck am I sanctifying any place we hooked up?

With my blood still hot with annoyance, I return Casey's call. She answers on the very first ring, like she was waiting by the phone. "Hey, thanks for calling me back."

I play it cool, pretending I didn't forget who she was. "No worries."

"How are you?"

"Good. You?" I inwardly curse. This couldn't be any more awkward if I tried.

"I'm good... now." The need in her voice can't be missed. "Do you have any plans tonight?"

"I could—if you need me to?" Same crappy line. Same crappy result.

"I'd like that very much."

When Noah's truck pulls into Hank's gym, I clamber inside before covering the speaker of my phone. "Can I borrow your truck tonight?"

"Yeah, sure." He jackknifes back before arching a brow. "Hold on, what do you want it for?"

I waggle my brows. "I have a date."

My jest has the effect I'm aiming for when Noah looks seconds from being sick. "You better not have sex in my truck, Jacob. If I even smell a hint of it, I'll kick your fucking ass."

Pretending my heart isn't racing a million miles an hour, I drop my hand from my phone. "Can we meet at your place?"

CASEY WAS AS I REMEMBERED: long brown hair, the most striking blue eyes, and a piercing voice that will ring in my ears all night long. I'm still tugging on my ear when I pull into the driveway of my home.

As I shut down the engine, Noah sprints outside. "Do you ever answer your fucking phone?"

"I would have if I could hear anything over Casey's nasally squeal." I slap him in the chest, noticing how damp his shirt is. He's drenched head to toe, seconds from coronary failure. "What's going on?"

I stop seeking my dad when he says, "Em's cell keeps ringing out. After the fourth ring out, I went to check on her before I remembered someone took my fucking truck."

"I'm sure she's fine. Maybe she had an early night or something?" I say anything to pacify his worry. After all the loss he has endured, he's always panicked something bad will happen to Emily. "Maybe you wore her out, and she needs time to recover."

I give him a look, one that makes it seem like he's a stud. It does nothing to ease his agitation. His gaze remains as tormented as ever, his boots kicking up the gravel on the driveway. "I'll never forgive myself if something bad happens to her, Jake. Just the thought of her being hurt tears me apart."

"I know. You don't have to explain it to me."

I feel the same way about Lola. That's why it kills me knowing she's back with Callum.

"If she doesn't call you first thing in the morning, I'll drive you to Parkwood myself." I rib him with my elbow. "In your truck, since I don't have a car."

He finally cracks a smile. "Thanks, Jacob." He nudges his head to his still-hot motor. "Do I need to fumigate her first?"

The mirth in his tone furls my lips. "Nah. Not this time." I band my arm around his shoulders before noogying his head. "But I'll do my best to mix it up next week."

CHAPTER THIRTY-ONE

LOLA

As I head out of Pete's, my phone vibrates in my skirt pocket. I dig it out as I jump into the driver's seat of my Jeep. She's as old and as sassy as me, but she's mine, so I love her bad points as much as I adore her good ones.

When I glance down at the screen, my lips quirk. I don't recognize the number. With my suspicions piqued, I answer the call, curious who is calling me a little after midnight on a Friday night. "Hello?"

"Lola, it's Jacob."

I yank my phone away from my ear to recheck the number. It's still showing an unrecognized number, but not a thousand years could strip Jacob's deep timbre from my mind. *He must have gotten a new number?*

Just as I push my phone back to my ear, Jacob asks, "Lola...? Are you there?"

"Yeah, sorry, I'm here." My high tone exposes my confusion. We haven't had any contact in months, so why is he reaching out this late on a Friday night?

Oh.

"Are you drunk dialing me?"

His breathy chuckle does wicked things to my insides. "No. It's Emily."

Any playfulness heating my veins vanishes. "Emily? What happened?"

I jab my keys into the ignition to fire up my Jeep when he replies, "She's been admitted to Ravenshoe Private."

"I'll be there in thirty minutes."

Not worrying about my belt, I dump my phone on my passenger seat, throw my gearstick into reverse, then tear out of Pete's lot like a maniac. My forty-minute trip to Ravenshoe is a blur. I don't pay attention to street signage or the music playing on the radio; my focus remains on figuring out why Emily has been admitted to the hospital. We're not the closest, but that doesn't mean I don't love her, so to say I'm panicked would be an understatement. I'm petrified.

When I enter the multistory garage at the side of the hospital, I pull into the first available spot. I don't bother locking up. Making sure Emily is okay is more important than replaceable possessions. I'd give up everything I've worked for the past six months if it ensures she's safe.

When I dart through the double glass doors of the hospital, I spot Jacob waiting for me at the side. He moves for me as quickly as I race for him. Tears come close to toppling down my cheeks when my arms slinging around his neck coincides with him drawing me into his chest.

We stay huddled together for what seems like hours before the reason for our reunion smacks into me. "What happened to Emily?"

It takes Jacob a good thirty or forty seconds to set me down and drop his eyes to mine. "She was roofied at Mavs."

My eyes widen to the size of dinner plates. "What? Like a date rape drug... Oh god, please tell me she wasn't—"

"She wasn't," Jacob interrupts. "Noah got to her before anything bad happened."

With distress holding my words hostage, Jacob guides me down the long white hospital corridor with his hand on the small of my back. The putrid scent of disinfectant overtakes his scrumptious aftershave the further we travel. When we reach a room halfway down, he shifts on his feet to face me. "Noah is a bit agitated. Em's been out for an hour already. He's not handling it too well."

He waits for me to read the concern in his eyes before swinging open the door we're standing next to. Noah's eyes pop up when the door creaks. He looks as panicked as I feel. His eyes are the darkest I've seen, and a vein in his neck is working overtime.

After issuing him a hesitant smile, I make my way to Emily's bedside. Seeing she's safe firsthand is immensely satisfying, unknotting the rope that's been strangling my heart the past hour.

I press my lips to her temple before shifting my focus to Noah. He stiffens when I embrace him like I wish I could Emily, but his tough stance crumbles when I murmur, "She'll be okay. She's stronger than anyone realizes."

When his chin dips in agreement, I turn my eyes to Jacob. "Who called my mom?"

Suspicion is rife in my tone. My mom would be here if she knew Emily was admitted, so why isn't she? She works at this hospital, meaning she would have arrived within seconds of being informed.

My suspicions are answered in an unfavorable light when Jacob murmurs, "No one."

"What! Why?"

When Jacob requests to have a word in the hall, I glare at him before storming out. I'm peeved as fuck he didn't have the common courtesy to call the mother of the person lying unconscious in a hospital bed. Even if the person is a stranger, morals dictate that you contact their parents before anybody else—even their sister.

After taking on a strengthened stance, preparing for battle, I lock my narrowed eyes with Jacob. He's as worked up as me. His face is lined with anger, and his jaw is spasming.

"Why didn't you call my mom?"

"I tried to call your house, but for some reason, my number is blocked. Then when I tried your cell phone, I got the same message."

My brows scrunch. What the hell is he talking about? I don't have his number blocked.

"That's why I called you from a payphone."

The groove between his brow weakens when I murmur, "I didn't block your number. I don't even know how to do that."

"Maybe you should ask your *boyfriend*. I'm sure he'll show you."

My lips form into a snarl, suddenly understanding where his anger is coming from. He heard about my meeting with Callum on Sunday. Although I'm more than happy to remind him he has no right to tell me who I can and cannot see, I've got more urgent matters to handle right now.

After digging my phone out of my pocket, I raise my index finger, requesting a minute so I can call my mom. She's panicked when I tell her Emily was roofied, but my assurance that she's safe puts her mind at ease. After advising me she's minutes away, I disconnect our call, then pivot around to face Jacob. I've just dodged one wreck relatively unscathed, so I may as well dive headfirst into another to test my luck.

"Do you want to deal with this now or later?"

After a beat, Jacob says, "Now."

"Alright, then let's do this." Air snags in my throat when my eyes stray to the hard chairs lining the corridor. Noah's bandmates are heading our way, closely followed by Ryan, the detective who took my statement after Jacob was arrested. "Somewhere private."

After gathering Jacob's hand in mine, I guide him away from Emily's room. He doesn't utter a syllable as we stride down numerous hallways, through the hospital grounds, and into the parking garage, but his silence breaks the instant we enter my car.

"After what he did to you, how can you trust him?"

"I don't."

His ragged breath says more than his words ever will. He's disappointed in me. He's not the only one frustrated. I thought he knew better than to believe the rumors the old biddies in our hometowns bicker about every day.

"Don't believe every rumor you hear, Jacob. Sometimes they're nothing but made up stories."

"So you weren't at Mavericks with Callum Sunday afternoon?"

It's the fight of my life not to smack his snippy tone into next week, but I manage to hold back—barely. "You already know I was, but instead of asking me why, you've reached your own conclusion without any facts to back up your *assumption*."

I hate when my voice quivers at the end. Vicious rumors are nothing new to me. Usually, they roll straight off my back, but defending myself to Jacob isn't something I thought I'd ever have to do. It hurts more than I care to admit.

"It's a bit hard to ask you what's going on when you have my number blocked."

"Did you try to call me?" I bite back with just as much attitude. "Or did you just go out with... What was her name this week?" I tap my finger, pretending I don't remember the name that stabbed my heart a trillion times earlier this week. "Oh, that's right—*Casey*—just to get back at me?"

CHAPTER THIRTY-TWO

JACOB

My heart drops to my stomach when Lola spits out Casey's name, but it does little to leash my anger. Seeing Noah's reaction to Emily being roofied is already wreaking havoc with my emotions, so you can imagine how fucking close to the edge I got when every attempt I made to reach out to Lola was hindered by a blocked number. It's not the first time she's cut me out of her life, but blocking someone's number is the equivalent of unfriending them on Facebook. It's a clear sign you want nothing to do with them. It fucking gutted me knowing she could cut me out so quickly but keep Callum around.

"We're not here to talk about who I have or have not... *dated*—"

"*Dated?* Are we still calling it that?" Although Lola is asking a question, she doesn't wait for me to reply. "It's funny that we can't discuss your *dates*, but you're more than happy to throw out accusations as to whom I'm supposedly *fucking*."

Anger works up from my gut to my throat. "I don't give a fuck who you're sleeping with as long as it isn't Callum!"

Lola's glare warns me I'm seconds from being castrated, but it doesn't weaken my campaign in the slightest. Everything I'm saying should have been said months ago, so now that it's coming out, nothing will stop it from being articulated.

"My ass was hauled to jail where I was treated like scum for teaching a low-life piece of shit a lesson about what happens when you put your hands on a lady, and for what, Lola? For you to run back into *his* arms! He put his fucking hands around your throat. How can you forget that?! I thought you were smart, strong, and brave! Clearly, I'm not the only fucking idiot sitting in this car."

Regret hits me like a ton of bricks when tears drop down Lola's face. She's quick to wipe them away, but they're replaced with more before her hands are even halfway across her cheeks.

"Please don't cry—"

"I never asked you to defend me, Jacob! Not once. What you just said is the *exact* reason I tried to stay away. I didn't want you to get hurt."

"I know that." I drag a shaky hand over my head, finally understanding why Noah caves every time Emily cries. This hurts more than I can explain. I broke an unbreakable woman, and it's more painful than anything I've experienced. "What if it were Emily?"

Lola fights with all her might to settle her tears before peering up at me with big, watering eyes. She's confused, so I try and settle it. "What if it were Emily who was attacked by Callum instead of you? Would you want Noah to stand up for her?"

She contemplates my question for several heart-thrashing seconds before nodding.

"Exactly. That's my point. The way Noah defended Emily tonight was no different than the way I defended you when you were attacked. It's a natural instinct to protect the people you care about. I'll never regret standing up for you, Lola. I'm just disappointed I hurt you so much you won't even take my calls anymore."

"I did that for you." When her big, salty blobs come close to falling again, her eyes dart to the black sky. "The night I went to the police station to give my statement, I saw you. You were cuffed to the table, and your face was full of torment. All I could think of was that you would have never been in that situation if you hadn't met me."

I gather her hands in mine before silently coercing her eyes to me. When I get them, I say, "I wasn't worried about going to jail. I was panicked about leaving you." I wipe away the inky black substance sliding down her face with her tears. "I couldn't stop wondering who'd be there for you if he attacked you while I was behind bars. The thought of you going through that alone killed me, Lola. That's why you can't trust him. He attacked you in broad daylight, so what will he do if he gets you behind closed doors?"

"I'm not with Callum," she confesses. "I only agreed to meet him because he said he had vital information about you. That was the first time I've seen him since Mavericks."

"You're not with Callum?" I can see the honesty in her eyes, hear it in her words, but I still want confirmation.

My regular breathing pattern returns when she answers, "No, I'm not." She arches her brow in a way that makes me grateful I'm holding her hands. "Not that I need to answer to you about who I am or am not seeing. You're not the boss of me, Jacob. I don't answer to anyone."

There she is. The stubborn, hot-headed little temptress I fell head over heels in love with months ago is back full force. The wetness on her cheeks may fool a man into believing she isn't as strong as the woman she seemed to be when we met, but I'm confident the fire in her eyes will prove them wrong. My girl is strong—she has to be to put up with a man like me.

"Come here."

Lola folds her arms in front of her chest, feigning anger at my request. She shouldn't give up her day job. While staring at my lips, her tongue darts out to moisten hers. She only does that when she is preparing to kiss me. Yes, that's how in-depth I studied her when we were "friends."

When Lola arches a brow, goading me to make true on the threat in my eyes, I stumble into the danger zone without any fear. "Always so stubborn," I mumble over her lips before swiping my tongue across them.

She smiles against my mouth before accepting my kiss. I growl into her mouth; I've missed sampling her taste the past six months. Not even the saltiness of the tears clinging to her top lip can simmer the heat crackling between us. She tastes so fucking good, both naughty and nice.

When she climbs over the parking brake between our seats, my fingers weave through her hair. I hold her mouth hostage as I rock my hips up, ensuring she feels the effect she has on me. I'm hard as a rock, mere seconds from breaking the zipper in my pants.

Lola is just as turned on. With her skirt riding high on her thighs, the only thing separating my cock from her damp panties are my pants. Although I don't even see them being an issue too much longer. Lola's hand is skating down my abs, only stopping when she reaches the pesky fly keeping my erection contained.

As she slides down my zipper, her needy eyes lift to mine. "Fuck, I've missed you."

She has no idea how much I needed to hear that. Four little words and my entire world is righted again. I've been a bit lost without her the past six months—more than I care to admit. But I'm better now. Better than I was yesterday, but not as good as I'll be tomorrow, because she makes everything better.

"I've missed you too, baby."

Lola yanks back, her hand frozen halfway into my boxers.

"What?" I'm confused as to why her demeanor shifted so quickly. She's gone from looking like she's about to suck my dick until I'm exhausted of cum to biting off my cock so it can never be used again.

"Don't call me *baby*. I'm not a *baby,* so why call me one?"

And that, ladies and gentlemen, is the reason I fell for her so fast. She's so fucking strong, she can knock a guy my size onto his ass with nothing but words.

I rock my hips upward three times to ease the wrinkle between her brow. "Sorry..." I drag my lips down her cheek and along her jaw before coming to a stop at her ear. "I've missed you too, *Cock Tease.*"

Her hand finalizes its descent into my pants as she murmurs, "Don't ever forget it."

She slides her thumb over the crest of my cock, gathering the drop of moisture there before swiveling it around my head like her tongue usually does. I pretend the heated breaths hitting my neck as she works my shaft are the pants she makes when my dick is inside her. It's not hard considering her pumps are at the same frantic speed we go when fucking.

She lowers her hand to the base before returning it to the tip in fast, quick strokes. While she milks me, I free her gorgeous tits from the buttoned-up Pete's shirt she's wearing. I'm dying to see them again. It's been six months since I've seen a pair as perfect as hers.

Just as I get her last button undone, our hot and heavy make-out session is interrupted by someone tapping on the foggy glass of Lola's Jeep. When a security officer shines his flashlight through the condensation no amount of excuses will cover, Lola pulls her hand out of my boxers then plops back into her seat with a giggle.

"Here we go again."

Since the tap came from my side of the car, I manually roll down my window. I don't slide it down far — only an inch. I'd rather be arrested again than let a wannabe cop see Lola's tits.

A pair of worldly eyes peer at me through the crack. "Move along." He taps his baton on Lola's door. "If you're not gone in five minutes, I'll call the cops."

Stealing my chance to reply that we've been there, done that, he saunters back to his security golf cart parked one spot up. His swagger is cockier than his attitude.

As I roll back up the window, Lola's giggle echoes around the interior of her car. "Move along."

I grin at her impersonation of the security guard's accent. My smile doesn't linger for long. She's doing up the buttons I just finished unbuttoning.

"He has no clue how lucky he is to have survived forty-five seconds in your presence."

Only once her blouse is done up does normal function return to my brain. "What are you talking about? What forty-five seconds?"

I tempted to tell the guard he can screw his five-minute warning when Lola says, "From what I've seen, you're over and done with in forty-five seconds."

My brow cocks. "You sure as hell know I last longer than forty-five seconds."

With a giggle, she slaps my chest. "I didn't mean in the bedroom."

My ego is loving the stroke she's giving it nearly as much as I enjoyed her stroking my cock, but my deflated chest sinks when she murmurs, "I meant in the boxing ring."

CHAPTER THIRTY-THREE

LOLA

Jacob raises pads to his face before stepping closer to me. "Come on, stop being a girl; put some effort in."

"You weren't complaining about me being a girl last night."

His chuckle stops bouncing around the gym we're working out in when I throw a right hook into the protective pad sheltering his jaw. Ever since we rekindled our "friendship" weeks ago, he relentlessly nagged me to join him for a session at his favorite gym. He made out it was for a bit of fun, but I know the real reason he brought me here. He wants to teach me how to defend myself in case I have a run-in with Callum again.

His motives are sweet, but I wish he could have picked a location that didn't make my stomach revolt when we entered. I've smelled some funky things in my time, but nothing compares to the stench that hit me when we burst through Hank's Gym's doors. Jacob swears I'll get used to it. I'm not so sure. Some things are unforgettable.

Take Jacob's face when I let slip I knew he was fighting in an illegal circuit as an example. He was panicked out of his mind that I was mad. He had no reason to be worried. He might be the size of a truck, but he wouldn't hurt a fly. Not once since Callum revealed

Jacob's secret have I been concerned about my safety. In all honesty, his video turned me on. From the day we met, I was adamant Jacob was too nice for me, so finding out he isn't as squeaky clean as his boy-next-door looks convey add an additional thrill to our relationship.

From the videos I've watched on YouTube, it doesn't take a genius to realize Jacob isn't arrogant like his competitors, but there's an edge of confidence not even grainy footage could take away. Fighting might seem brutal to some, but Jacob loves it, so that's all that matters.

"If I agree to the bi-weekly training sessions you're suggesting, will you let me watch you fight this weekend?" My words are breathless. I had no clue how demanding boxing is until now. I won't need to go running for a month.

Jacob pulls the pads off his hands before handing me a half-empty bottle of water. "I don't know, Lola. I reaped the benefits after you watched me on YouTube, but knowing you're all hot and bothered in the stands watching me live might be too much of a distraction."

I don't know whether to kiss the spunk out of him or punch it. I go for the latter when he friskily winks. He's loving my response.

I'm about to back up my hit with a kiss when a mannish voice outside of the ring stops me. "Looks like you went and got yourself a weak spot?"

When I swing my eyes to the voice, I'm met with a middle-aged African American man with a bright, beaming smile. He's peering at Jacob with a mischievous glint in his eyes, forcing him to admit, "You could say that."

After Jacob pulls apart the ropes to assist him into the ring, he heads my way to offer up an introduction. "Hello, pretty lady, I'm Hank."

"Lola. It's a pleasure to meet you, Hank."

When I accept the hand Hank is holding out, instead of shaking it, he uses it to twirl me around. Most women would be peeved by his avid assessment of my body. I'm not most women. Furthermore, his gaze isn't intrusive. It's more inquisitive than anything.

"*Definitely* a weak spot." He gives Jacob a look as if he's pleased for him, and perhaps a little worried, before returning his focus to me. "Has my boy taught you anything, or has he just been fooling around in my ring?"

My lips curl high. "Fooling around. This is Jacob we're talking about."

Jacob's laughter picks up when Hank grumbles, "True," with a roll of his eyes. "Can I give her some pointers?"

After taking in my wide eyes and sweat-dotted forehead, Jacob nods. "Be my guest."

"First, your stance is all wrong. You need to spread your legs wider." Hank kicks my running shoes until he's satisfied I'm standing correctly. "Your feet should match the width of your shoulders, but you need a heel-toe stance."

He lifts my hands until they're right up close to my cheeks. "The most important rule when fighting is to protect your face. We don't want this pretty little face getting any marks on it, so keep your arms up high, and your elbows tucked in."

A squeak pops from my lips when he cozies up to me from behind. He's close enough I can feel his raging heart, but not close enough I feel uncomfortable. "Elbows in; chin down." After making his arms extensions of my limbs, he displays what he means with actions instead of words. He brings my elbows in close to my body before lowering my chin nearly to my breasts.

"Good girl. Now step closer to Jacob." When Jacob holds out his palms, Hank uses my fisted hands to strike them. "Left, right, left, right." He's puppeteering my movements, but it allows me to see how my stance was wrong when sparring with Jacob earlier.

My hands flop to my chest when Hank releases them from his grip. "Hands up; protect your face." His shouts mimic ones I heard while watching Jacob's fights on YouTube. "Elbows in and get on your toes. You don't want clumpy feet like Jacob."

Ignoring Jacob's snicker, I do as instructed.

"Now hit. Left, right, left right. Duck."

I bob down in just enough time to miss Jacob's loosely swung hand soaring above my head. We practiced this move for an hour this morning before Hank arrived.

"Good, now back up on your toes!"

OVER THE NEXT THIRTY MINUTES, Jacob, Hank and I try a number of boxing techniques. I won't lie; my cheeks are hurting from how hard I'm smiling. Boxing is hard, but I have a better understanding of why Jacob loves it. I'm a newbie, yet I loved every friggin' minute of our session.

After removing the last of the tape from my hands, Hank raises his eyes to me. "You did really good today, pretty lady. If you ever want a career in boxing, let me know."

My narrowed eyes stray to Jacob when he murmurs under his breath, "No fucking chance."

My glare has his throat working hard to swallow, but Hank acts oblivious to the tension brewing between us. With a laugh, he walks away, leaving Jacob defenseless to the ass-whooping I'm about to give him.

"Who died and made you my boss?"

"No one, but I don't need to be your boss to tell you there's no chance you'll ever accept Hank's offer."

The cheekiness in his reply swallows some of my sass. "Why not? I'd make a good fighter."

"You would, but this isn't the career for you. For one, you don't follow instructions—"

"I followed Hank's instructions today without so much of an argument!"

Jacob's grin picks up. "Yeah, why was that? I almost lost my nuts for opening your car door, but Hank can boss you around and not be in fear of his life! What the fuck?"

The jest in his tone makes me smile. "My relationship with Hank is different than ours. I *like* him."

I try to hide my smile when his jaw drops to the floor. "What are you saying? You like him more than me?"

When I nod, he snaps my backside with the towel he's holding. Its loud crack echoes around the deserted gym as quickly as it makes excitement rush to my womb.

With his arm slung back and his smile the biggest I've seen, Jacob says, "Tell me you like me more."

"Or what? You'll spank me until I relent?"

My knees curve inward when he nods. The Jacob standing before me now is the Jacob I get wet over while watching YouTube videos of him fighting. He's confident, yet cheeky, an unusual but highly craved combination.

When he arches his brow, warning I'm seconds away from getting my butt whipped, I murmur, "I like you...*nearly as much as I like Hank.*"

The last half of my sentence comes out in a flurry from my mad dash to the women's locker room. I think I've made it to freedom when I enter the domain that smells like sweaty socks, but Jacob is quick to prove me wrong. He bands his arm around my waist before tugging me back.

Any wishes to flee him fly out the window when I feel his cock hard and heavy against my back. I'm trapped by a lust haze in under a second. Nothing is on my mind but wondering how long it will take to spring his cock out of his gym pants and get it in my mouth.

"*Jacob...*"

My words trap in my throat when he drags his tongue along my neck. As he continues walking us into the women's locker room, my eyes stray to Hank's office. The blinds that were open only moments ago are now closed, and his door is shut. He's either accustomed to gym members shredding extra calories in his showers, or he felt the chemistry bristling between Jacob and me the past hour.

I can only hope it's the latter, and not because this is something Jacob often does. I'd ask how many women he's fondled in the showers, but when his lips are on mine, not even something as extreme as envy can steal my focus away from him.

CHAPTER THIRTY-FOUR

JACOB

Six months later...

When I enter the living room of my childhood home, Emily greets me with a hug. "Merry Christmas, Jacob."

I return her embrace. "Merry Christmas, Em."

Just as she pulls back, I spot Noah entering the living room from the other end. With my playfulness at an all-time high, I tug Emily back in for a second embrace before raising my eyes to Noah.

"_So hot,_" I mouth to his murderous glare.

He's not pissed about me hugging Emily. It's Christmas; even the Grinch hands out hugs on Christmas. He wants to kill me because I'm humping Emily's leg like a dog in heat.

After slapping my chest, Emily slips out of my embrace. Although she's dying of embarrassment, she places herself between Noah and me before Noah can act on any of the inane thoughts in his head. I'm not worried. He's my little bro; it's my job to rile him up.

I flash him a quick smirk before sealing my tease with a wink. "Merry Christmas, Noah."

He gives me a stern finger point. It's the same finger he uses every time I piss him off. "I'm going to kick your ass one day."

I chuckle. His threat holds no steam. You can't threaten someone you love.

After soothing Noah as only she can, Emily shifts on her feet to face me. Her cheeks are pinker now than they were when my crotch got friendly with her leg. For some ridiculous reason, she only has eyes for Noah—that's why using her against him is so much fun.

"Are you sure you don't want to come with us? My mom has gone overboard; we'll be eating leftovers for a week."

Her eyes say the words she refuses to say: *and you can see Lola.*

"Thanks for the offer, but I'm good. It's always been the old man, Patrick, and me for Christmas. I don't want to break tradition."

Furthermore, although I'd love nothing more than to see Lola today, I understand our arrangement, even if those around us don't comprehend it.

"Would you mind giving Lola something for me?"

Not waiting for them to reply, I rush into my room to grab an envelope off my bedside table before hot-footing it back to the living room. Emily's brows inch together when I hand it to her.

"It's her Christmas present," I explain to her confused expression.

When Emily shakes the envelope to make sure it isn't empty, Noah snatches it away with a chuckle. "Stop snooping."

The confusion on Emily's face jumps to his when he takes in the inscription on the envelope. "CT? Who's CT?"

"Just give it to Lola; she'll understand."

I band my arms around both their shoulders before forcefully walking them to the door. The quicker they get out of here, the faster I'll get Lola's response to my gift.

APPROXIMATELY AN HOUR LATER, the text I've been dying to get finally arrives.

Lola: *I love it! Thank you.*

Smiling like she told me she loves me, I reply:

Me: *You're welcome.*

The second best present I could ever be given arrives in my inbox two seconds after my phone whooshes, announcing my text has been sent.

Lola: *I miss you, Jacob.*

While smiling the biggest grin I've ever smiled, my fingers fly over the screen of my phone. They may not be the three little words I was seeking, but they're pretty fucking close.

Me: *I miss you too, C.T.*

My eyes float up from my phone when my dad asks, "Who has you grinning like the cat who ate the canary?"

I wait for him to sit in his favorite reading chair before replying, "A girl." I try my hardest not to grin, but I can't help but smile. I knew Lola would understand my gift the instant she opened it.

My dad balances his backside on the very edge of his chair. "Is it the same girl you mentioned a few months back? What was her name again...?"

"Lola." Even saying it for over a year hasn't dampened the sexiness of her name. "And, yes, she's the same girl."

"Sounds serious." The look on his face reveals he's moments away from giving me one of his infamous long lectures.

"Can we skip the safe sex lecture? If it hasn't sunk in by now, hearing it for the fiftieth time this year won't make any difference." I'm joking—not that he's aware of that.

"You should be thanking me. If I didn't give you the birds and the bees talk as often as I did, who knows how many women would have come forward, announcing you're their baby's daddy."

After giving me his *don't mess with me* look, he slumps into his chair before picking up his latest read. As he disappears into the world of fiction, I think about what he said. As much as it kills me to admit, he's right. His "talks" were drummed into me so often, any time I sampled a cookie jar, I always used protection. If I didn't wrap it, I didn't have it. Plain and simple. So, in some ways, I should thank him.

When I do precisely that, he grunts, acknowledging he heard me, but his gaze remains on his book...until I say, "Can I ask you something?"

That's the equivalent of an untapped goldmine to my dad. Talking only comes second to lecturing. Faster than I can snap my fingers, he slips a bookmark into place, closes his book, then drops it onto the coffee table. I regret my decision for a heart to heart when he wiggles his recliner until he's sitting across from me like a therapist would a patient.

"Okay. What did you want to ask?"

I've come this far, so I may as well continue. "What was your relationship like with Mom at the start?"

My question catches him unaware. He thought the focus would remain on me like it did when we chatted months ago.

"I know you don't remember much about your mom, but when she walked into the room, it was like the sun rising in the morning... but that doesn't mean she was a pushover. She was as strong as they come. She had to be for what she endured when she was a child." His voice falters at the end of his statement.

"Did you know right away that you loved her?"

The sadness in his eyes disappears when he nods. "From the instant I met her. Although she took a lot longer to realize it than I would have liked." He locks his eyes with mine; they're brimming with suspicion. "But you already know this, so why are you asking about it again?"

I only scratch my brow for half a second, but it tells him everything he needs to know. "She got to you, didn't she? And now you can't get her out of your head?"

"You have no idea." I take a few seconds to figure out the best way to explain my relationship with Lola. When I'm left with only more confusion, I go with straight-up honesty. "She's different from the other girls I've dated. Half the time, I want to strangle the sass straight out of her, whereas the other half, I want to wrap her in a cocoon to keep her safe and protected. She's the most stubborn, beautiful girl I've ever met, but I can't get enough of her—when she's not lumping me in the *friend's* zone."

"Is what she's giving you enough? Because if it is, take what you can get and enjoy it while it lasts. If it isn't, walk away. Not every love story is epic, Jacob. Some start slow; others rage out of control, and then there are the ones that dwindle over time. Every relationship is unique, so no one can dictate exactly what's right for one couple. What works for one may not work for another. Only you can decide what you can accept." My eyes float up from the ground when my dad places his hand on my bobbing knee. "Do you love her?"

I nod without pause for thought. I've loved Lola from the moment I laid my eyes on her.

"Then treasure every minute she's willing to give you, because not even the most perfect relationships are guaranteed a lifetime. My relationship with your mom is living proof of that."

CHAPTER THIRTY-FIVE

LOLA

Six months later...

Air rattles in my lungs before I free it into the world along with a handful of butterflies in my stomach. The atmosphere tonight is electrifying, but I can't control the nerves tap dancing inside me. I have no reason to be nervous—Jacob is undefeated—but without fail, at every fight, anxiety gets the better of me—although it's nothing compared to nearly getting hives when I opened Jacob's Christmas gift a little over six months ago.

Emily watched me like a freak when I opened the envelope Jacob asked her to give me. Her eagerness switched to confusion when a gold necklace fell out. The simplicity of the packaging matched the oval pendant attached to a single-strand necklace, but the thought Jacob put into his gift couldn't be denied. He had my pendant engraved with the initials *CT*. Although no one around me knew what it meant, I did and was extremely ecstatic with his gift. I hate the nicknames most couples use: *baby, sugar, sweetheart,* but I wear Jacob's pendant with pride because I love the nickname he gave me.

After putting on my necklace, I sent Jacob a text thanking him for the gift before spending the rest of the day with my family. I was disappointed Jacob wasn't a part of the festivities, but his essence was. It was him who suggested I order Noah's leather pants two sizes too small, so he got all the credit when Noah gagged upon opening his gift.

It was only later that night as I was heading to bed did I realize my pendant was only one half of my gift. Just before I entered my room, my mom handed me the envelope I had dumped in the trash earlier that day.

"There's a piece of paper inside. I didn't read it; I promise." My mom's high tone revealed the last half of her admission wasn't straight-up honorable.

Tucked neatly inside the envelope was a slip of paper thin enough to be hidden if you weren't snooping. It revealed that Jacob doesn't just know me, he also *gets* me.

*Merry Christmas, **C**ock **T**ease*
Saturday night 1o PM.
Jake the Giant vs. The Snake.
See you there.
Jacob xx

IT'S BEEN a little over six months since Christmas, but if memory serves, I'm reasonably sure I jumped into the air and shouted, "Finally!" at the top of my lungs. I nagged Jacob relentlessly for months to watch him fight, but he always refused my request. Now, I've been to every fight he's competed in.

This competition is different than what I saw on YouTube. For one, there's no cage; it's a standard boxing ring, but the main difference is that this fighting is done in secret. There are no promotional campaigns, no flyers printed, and only invited guests are allowed to watch the fights.

The lack of fanfare doesn't weaken anyone's enthusiasm. If anything, it makes it more palpable. The room is full of super-wealthy people who pay top dollar for the seats close to the action. A majority "own" fighters, and then there a handful who just enjoy the spectacle of a sport without rules.

When Jacob told me the fighters have "owners," I laughed. I thought he was joking. It didn't take me long to realize he was being serious. That was more because of the divide in the room than Jacob assuring me he wasn't.

Isaac is Jacob's owner. The original contract Jacob signed was only for twelve months, but with professional fighting off the table, he's continued their agreement the past six months. I don't know how long he plans to fight for Isaac. We've never discussed it. Actually, we don't discuss anything with the word "future" attached to it. We like to keep things simple by enjoying each other's company without looking two steps ahead all the time. We also don't live in each other's pockets. Jacob has his life, and I have mine. It might not be ideal for some, but our arrangement works well for us.

When I hear Rage Against the Machine's hit song "Killing in the Name" blaring over the speakers, I jump to my feet and holler. Even with the crowd screaming his name as he strides down the aisle, Jacob remains humble. He keeps his head down low and his headphones up loud as he shadows Isaac and Hank to the ring. When he slides through the ropes, his head lifts my way. I give him a seductive wink, loving that even in a packed room, he locates me like a missile locked on its target.

After boosting my wink with a cheeky grin, he makes his way to Hank, who is standing in the corner of the ring. He warmed up in the locker rooms, so this is just a final check Hank likes to do before each match. He's as pedantic about Jacob's safety in the ring as me.

Just as Jacob joins his opponent in the center of the ring, a deep voice at my side says, "Is this seat taken?"

With my heart in my throat, I shift my eyes to the highly recognizable voice. It's been over twelve months since I've heard it, but I'd never forget its smug, conceited pitch.

As suspected, Callum's brother Curtis is standing next to me. His arms are folded in front of his chest, and his lips are hard-lined. Before I can tell him the seat next to me is reserved for anyone but him, he slips into it. He slumps down low before spreading his knees to the width of his shoulders. To an outsider, his stance appears casual, but I'm not a stranger to the tension radiating out of him. He has that same egotistical aura he had every time he pushed Callum into acting like an asshole.

More than eager to get away from him, I stand before skirting past him. I don't make it two feet away before his hand darts out to seize my wrist. With a yank, he shoves me back into my seat before his lips get friendly with my ear. "Sit. *The fuck*. Down. The show is just getting started."

The threat in his words is the least of my problems. Since Jacob's eyes always stray to mine at the start of every match, he's noticed I have company. Unfortunately, the ref hasn't. When he blows his whistle, announcing the start of the fight, Jacob fails to notice the quick approach of his competitor.

Hank screams at him to protect his face, but it comes too late. Jacob's opponent strikes him hard against his left temple, momentarily diverting his attention from me.

"This is going even better than predicted." Curtis's laughter picks up when Jacob is hit for the second time, this time to his right jaw. The crack of his bone makes my stomach roll, but it also makes me jump into action.

After raising the hand Curtis isn't clutching in the air, I strike him hard across the face. My slap is so brutal, he needs both his hands to soothe his burning cheek. My palm is also on fire, but it doesn't slow me down. I scurry past the spectators, ignoring their hisses of annoyance when I block the view they paid thousands of dollars for. I'd apologize, but I don't have time for niceties. Curtis is on my tail, and his gaze is lethal.

When I step into the aisle between stadium seats, I pivot on my heels, then strengthen my stance. I stand heel to toe as Hank taught me before raising my balled hands to protect my face. Curtis finds my efforts to protect myself amusing. His chuckles are so loud, I hear them over the spectators cheering boisterously.

"Are you fucking kidding me...?"

His arrogant smirk is wiped off his face when my fist makes a whip-cracking noise as it strikes his nose. Pain zaps through my hand and rockets down my arm, but I remain strong, not letting on that I'm injured. Men like Curtis feed off others' fears, and I refuse to give him an ounce of power he doesn't deserve.

The redness dribbling out of Curtis's nose matches the anger on his cheeks. He's reached boiling point. "You fucking bitch!"

He rears back his hand, the fury in his eyes unnerving, but the hit I'm anticipating never comes. That might have more to do with the warning sounding through the crowd than Curtis suddenly learning morals.

"If you touch one hair on her head, I'll kill you."

Jacob is halfway down the aisle. Blood is coursing through his body so fast, veins are bulging all over his delicious sweat-slicked body. From what I can see past the wide span of his shoulders, his opponent is out cold in the middle of the ring.

I stop wondering if he just posted a new KO personal best when Curtis sneers, "You already had your shot, and look where that got you. Throwing in the towel."

I'm so shocked by Jacob's quick arrival, my mind is a little hazy. What are they talking about? Jacob has never thrown in the towel. He's undefeated.

Doubt flourishes in my gut when Jacob accuses Curtis of cheating. For a man with no morals, Curtis doesn't like being accused of unsportsmanlike conduct. He's up in Jacob's face in an instant. If Isaac didn't place himself between them, the spectators would get double their money tonight.

"Let it go, Jacob," Isaac warns Jacob before shifting his focus to Curtis. He doesn't say anything to him. He doesn't need to. His stern gaze is enough to have Curtis stepping back.

Although he's backing away, Curtis doesn't know how to keep his mouth shut. "Do you always let others fight your battles?"

It takes more than a glare for Isaac to hold Jacob back. It takes three men. "Name the time and the place, and I'll be more than happy to kick your ass," Jacob shouts over the men he's flinging off as if they're weightless.

"And lower myself to your standards? I'm the heavyweight champion in our region, yet you expect me to fight you in a second-rate match just so I can teach your dumbass a few more lessons?"

I can't hear what Jacob shouts next, but I'm reasonably sure he's seconds from murdering the men keeping him away from Curtis— even more so when Curtis's focus shifts to me. His gaze is highly demoralizing when he scans my frame. He takes in my fringed shorts and fitted shirt as if I'm standing before him naked before returning his eyes to my face. "Until next time."

He finalizes his cocky statement with a wink before galloping down the stairs. Even being held back by men his size, Jacob manages to grab the scruff of his shirt on his way by. "The only reason you won't agree to fight me is because you know as well as everyone else in this room that I'll beat you this time around, even if you cheat."

The drumming of the crowd's feet on the stadium floors shows they agree with Jacob's statement. If Curtis leaves now, he'll forever be seen as a coward.

Never one to back away from a fight, Curtis yanks himself out of Jacob's grasp before shifting on his feet to face Isaac. "I'll be in contact."

The crowd roars in victory as they do every time Jacob wins, but not an eye in the house leaves Curtis until he disappears through the tinted arena doors—not even mine.

"As much as I'd love for this to happen, you can't fight him, Jacob. You're banned from professional fighting, and he's contracted to *only* fight for them."

Jacob sidesteps Isaac's concern as quickly as he does his body. His focus is on one thing and one thing only: me. After his eyes scan every inch of my body and face, he raises my throbbing hand for a more thorough inspection. It's the one I used to punch Curtis.

"Your knuckles are swollen. We need to ice them."

Before I can agree or disagree, he curls his hand around my non-injured one before galloping down the stadium stairs. His strides are so clunky, I nearly miss what he murmurs to Isaac on the way past, "If you organize it, I'll fight exclusively for you for another twelve months."

When we enter the locker rooms at the back of the arena, Jacob lifts me to sit on the counter near the sink, then ambles to the other side of the room. He snags a handful of ice cubes out of a large chest before wrapping them in a blue dishcloth. He's so gentle when he places it on my swollen knuckles, if I hadn't felt the coolness of the ice, I wouldn't have realized he was touching me.

"It doesn't hurt... *much*."

Jacob doesn't take my comment playfully, like I did when he said it the night we met. The groove between his brows deepens as the vein in his neck works overtime.

I'm about to ask what has him all worked up when Hank's entry into the locker room steals the opportunity. "You did good, pretty lady."

"Thanks. I was taught by the best, but maybe next time mention how hitting hurts just as much as being hit. My hand is throbbing like a bitch."

Hank's hearty chuckle barrels around the room. He's the only one amused. Jacob's deep exhalation fans my already overheated cheeks with more warmth as his throat works hard to swallow. I've never seen him so high-strung.

"Let me take a look." After barging Jacob out of the way, Hank assesses my bruised knuckles as he does Jacob's at the end of every fight. "They'll be sore for a few days, but there's nothing to worry about. Everything is where it should be." He places the ice pack back onto my hand before raising his eyes to mine. "Might need to tape your hands at the beginning of every fight too."

Jacob's sigh isn't quiet this time around. "It's not funny, Hank. She could have gotten hurt."

A flare of agreement passes through Hank's eyes, but he plays it cool. "She's tougher than you give her credit for. She had him, and if she didn't, *we* would have."

His statement confirms what I've always suspected. Hank sees himself as the third wheel in whatever the hell Jacob and I have going on. I don't mind. I like Hank... his fighter isn't too bad either—when he isn't looking at me with sympathetic eyes.

While Hank packs away the mess they made earlier, Jacob devotes his attention back to me. I expect our conversation to center around my hand, so you can imagine my surprise when he asks, "How do you know The Constrictor?"

"Who?"

Hank jumps back into the conversation. "The guy you punched in the nose."

"Just now?"

Jacob gives me a look as if to ask, *how many guys have you punched in the nose?*

I give him a frisky wink before nudging my head to my pendant. "Not as many as I should have."

He smiles—*finally*.

I want to relish his grin for a few seconds longer, but the pleading look he's giving me rushes the process. "If you're talking about the douchebag out there," I jerk my chin to the doors we walked through ten minutes ago, "that was Curtis—Callum's brother."

Hank is confused by my reply, but Jacob knows exactly who I'm talking about.

While working his jaw side to side, he glances over his shoulder to lock his eyes with Hank. "Can you give us a minute?" Realizing Hank takes everything literally, he quickly adds on, "Or ten."

CHAPTER THIRTY-SIX

JACOB

Five months later...

"What's a guy got to do to get a beer around here?" Maggie's eyes missile to mine, prepping to rip me a new asshole until she spots my mischievous grin. "How the hell are you, Mags?"

I've gone from seeing Maggie once or twice a week at a minimum to only a handful of times the past six months. With Noah's band no longer performing at Mavericks, I have fewer reasons to visit. That and the fact Lola takes up a lot of my spare time—*thank fuck.*

"Alive, unlike you if you call me Mags again." After jogging around the bar to hug me, she guides me onto one of the many empty barstools. "It's been so long, Jacob. You need to visit more often. The only gossip I've heard lately is from Daisy, and you know what she's like...?" An unsophisticated eye roll ends her question. "Now come spill. I'm dying here."

Over the next hour, I update her on everything that has happened the past few months. How Rise Up hit the number one spot on the Billboard charts last weekend. The little blip Noah and Emily had. Jenni and Nick becoming parents, and how Noah's mom tried to force contact with him through the media.

Maggie sits and absorbs every little detail. She already knows most of it, but she's a good listener who'd never belittle someone for telling her gossip she already knows. Besides, she prefers hearing stories firsthand from the people involved instead of half-truths from those not in the know.

"And what about you, Jacob?" She peers up at me with her motherly eyes. "For the past hour, you updated me on everyone but yourself. What's happening in *your* life? Surely it's been just as exciting."

My lips twist as I struggle to come up with something. "There's not much to share. I'm still fighting." She huffs before motioning for me to continue. "I found out a couple of months ago, the only person who has defeated me is Callum's brother, Curtis."

Maggie's eyes widen as her mouth gapes open. "Seriously?"

"Yeah, don't worry, you weren't the only surprised. Lola had no clue he was a fighter. From what we can gather, he orchestrated our fight after he saw Lola and me together. That's why he cheated. He believed I had done his brother wrong. I'm still waiting for the opportunity to fix the injustice."

I take a swig of my beer, hoping it will hide the annoyance in my tone. I've been hounding Isaac relentlessly to arrange the fight with Curtis. He keeps saying he's working on it, but how long does it take? I get he has bureaucratic tape to cut through, but five months is a long time for revenge to fester. If I weren't still on probation for my first tussle with a Parker man, I'd look at other options. Alas, I'm stuck with a criminal record while the real criminal walks free.

I chug down my beer more freely, hating the fucked up way life works sometimes. It pisses me off that Lola isn't at fault here, yet she's left looking over her shoulder every time we go out. Thank fuck she is as strong as she is stubborn. A lesser woman would have crumbled by now.

Like she can hear my thoughts, Maggie asks, "And you and Lola? How're things?"

I smile at the apprehension in her tone. "We're good. Same as always..."

"Friends," we say at the same time.

I bump her with my shoulder. "You know how stubborn she is. If she doesn't want to do something, no one can force her to. That includes relationship statuses."

Grinning, Maggie nods. The pure joy on her face prompts me as to why I'm visiting a bar in the middle of the afternoon. After digging out the envelope Emily gave me earlier, I hand it to Maggie. She peers at it curiously before carefully prying it open. The more she scans the elegantly gilded document inside, the wider her pupils become.

"They're getting married, and I'm invited!" She slaps her hand over her mouth in silent apology to every patron in Mavericks. She just pierced their eardrums. Her remorse is a forgotten memory when she scans the rest of the invitation. "They're getting married next week—in Vegas!"

She sounds as shocked as I was when Emily told me her plans. "Yes, next weekend. Noah doesn't know – it's a secret. Emily wanted to give you your invitation herself, but since she has to plan a wedding in a week, I offered to deliver it. She wanted me to tell you they would be honored if you could attend, but they understand if it's too short of notice."

"I'll be there. I wouldn't miss it." My eyes track her when she races to the side of the bar. "Ollie, I have to finish early."

Ollie mumbles something back, but I don't catch anything he says.

Once she has her jacket on, Maggie returns to my side of the bar. "Tell Emily I graciously accept her invitation." With the giddy grin, she plants a kiss on my cheek before darting out of the bar like a woman on a mission. "I have a dress to buy!"

I'm still smirking over her excitement when "G'day, Jacob" sounds over my shoulder.

I swivel in my seat to face Flynn, lead singer of Wanting Wombats. "G'day, Flynn."

He laughs at my piss poor attempt at an Aussie accent before nudging his head to his bandmates sitting at the table that used to belong to Rise Up. "Wanna join us for a beer?"

"Sure."

FOR THE NEXT HOUR, I share beers with Flynn and his bandmates. It took me a while to catch on to their Australian lingo, but after Flynn explained a few key pointers, I caught on. *Sheila* is a girl; *having a root* is having sex, and a *ute* is a truck. So when the bassist said, "You should have seen the Sheila I was rooting in my ute last night," he meant to say, "You should have seen the girl I had sex with in my truck last night."

"What about that Sheila who used to work here? She was fine. Didn't you take her home one night?"

Flynn rubs his hands together at Paul's question. "Oh yeah, she was fine. Her rack still holds the number one spot in my spank bank."

I spit out the beer I just swigged. "You're the lead singer of a band, so why do you need a spank bank?"

"Don't judge, mate. If you saw this girl, you would add her to your spank bank as well. She was an easy eleven out of ten." When his eyes glaze over as if he's recalling her in his spank bank right now, I relocate my barstool. His bandmates laugh, nearly drowning out what he says next, "She has a little butterfly tattoo tucked away, so only the privileged get to see it. It's just down here." He yanks down the waistband of his jeans before pointing to his right hipbone.

I slam down the beer, almost cracking it in the process. I tell myself time and time again plenty of girls have butterfly tattoos on their hips, not just Lola, but nothing calms the storm brewing in my gut.

"What did you say her name was again?" I stare at Flynn, silently fucking praying he doesn't say Lola.

"I didn't, but her name matches her perfectly." Time stands still when the name I'd given anything not to hear rolls off his tongue. "Lola."

"When?"

Noticing the abrupt change in my composure, the hazy look into Flynn's eyes switches to unease. "It was a while ago, mate, maybe last year?"

With my heart close to tatters, I rocket out of my seat and storm toward the parking lot at the back of Mavs.

"Or the year before?" Flynn yells just as I burst through the wooden doors as fast as Maggie did an hour ago.

I punish my ignition with my key before taking out my frustration on my engine. My foot barely lifts from the floor of my car, meaning I arrive at Lola's apartment in record-breaking time. She still lives in Erkinsvale, but she moved into her own apartment a few months back. I thought her decision to move out of her parents' home was for privacy—neither of our cars are ideal for our steamy hookups—but now I'm wondering if that privacy was solely for me or are other men occupying her time when I'm not around?

After taking three flights of stairs two steps at a time, I bang furiously on her paint-peeling front door. My anger takes a step back when she opens the door with a beautiful smile on her face. "Hey, Jacob."

The lust detonating in her eyes frustrates me more than it comforts me. We had no plans to meet up today, so why is she pleased about my unannounced arrival? That's not the Lola I know. I risk having my nuts dissected with tweezers if I infringe on her "private" time, don't I?

I take two steps into her apartment before pivoting to face her. The hankering gleam in her eyes falters when I scratch my brow. "Is everything okay—?"

"Did you sleep with Flynn?"

CHAPTER THIRTY-SEVEN

LOLA

I take a step back, shocked. With how much time has passed, I completely forgot about the time I left Mavericks with Flynn. Although Jacob's anger is understandable, especially if he has the timelines confused, he has no right to question me. For months, I overheard play-by-play rundowns on the girls he "dated" when our friendship had a prolonged break, so if anyone has the right to be angry, it's me, not him.

"Did you sleep with Flynn?!" This time around, he asks his question so loud, half the population of Erkinsvale hears it.

It also makes my anger skyrocket. "You need to leave."

With my gut a twisted mess of confusion, I move back to my foyer to show him the way out. He's been here many times the past few months, so he knows the way, but I'm so close to snapping, I either show him out or kick him out forever.

When I nudge my head to the hallway outside my apartment, Jacob shakes his head. "No. Not this time. I'm sick of your stubbornness. For once, answer my fucking question. Did. You. Sleep. With. Flynn?"

Big, angry breaths separate his words, but it does little to quell my bubbling anger. "You have no right to question who I have or haven't slept with! We're not even a couple!"

He moves to stand in front of me, his strides heavy and angry. "We're not a couple?"

"No, Jacob, we're not." I bite the inside of my cheek, hating the quiver my words were delivered with. "We're friends, right? Friends who like to fuck each other. Isn't that what you told the guys after we broke up?"

My heart stops beating when hurt flashes through his eyes. My statement hurt him to hear as much as it pained me to say, but forever stubborn, I won't back down from my hostile stance.

"This is more than fucking, Lola. We've *always* been more than fucking."

His eyes beg me to agree with his statement, to admit I feel more for him than any other man I've ever known, but I can't. If I do that, one of us will get hurt. He thinks this is me being mean. It's not. This is me showing mercy.

Tears spring into my eyes when he murmurs, "If I leave, I'm done. I can't do this anymore." His blue eyes bounce between mine. "Is that what you want? Do you want me to leave?"

I want to tell him no. I want to beg him to stay, but I won't. I made promises to myself when I fled Callum's house covered in bruises. The main one: I'll never answer to any man ever again. Although some may say this is different, it isn't to me. Jacob is questioning me. He's believing gossip instead of seeking answers the right way, and he's doing it in a hostile, demoralizing way—much like Callum did before he assaulted me. Jacob would never hurt me, but that doesn't mean I don't need time to step back and evaluate things.

After several heart-clutching seconds, Jacob whispers, "Goodbye, Lola."

When he storms out the door, slamming it behind him, I slide down the wall to sit on the ground. Hot, salty tears are threatening to spill down my cheeks, but I fight with all my might to keep them at bay. That would be a lot easier to do if I had just told Jacob the truth about what happened that night.

Flynn is a great guy, but I wanted to strangle him when we left Mavericks only for him to take me to Bronte's Peak. I hadn't been back there since the night I met Jacob. The lot was overflowing with cars, which wasn't surprising since it was a Saturday night.

Flynn and I were about to get "friendly" when my phone rang. When I glanced down at my open handbag, Jacob's smiling face was lighting up the screen of my phone. I reached for my phone before I remembered he had stood me up, so I let his call go to voicemail.

A few seconds later, my phone dinged with a text. I tried my hardest to keep my focus on Flynn, who was placing a trail of kisses from the band of my midriff top to my jeans, but my curiosity got the better of me. When my eyes flicked down to my phone, I discovered the text was from Jacob. It said he was at Mavericks, waiting for me. I missed him by minutes.

Although Jacob and I had a mutual understanding about our "friendship," guilt still engulfed me. I was only occupying my time with Flynn because I was angry. Neither Flynn or myself deserved that low level of respect.

I was already having second thoughts, but when Flynn popped open the button of my jeans, exposing the butterfly tattoo on my right hip, I knew in an instant our night was over. Every single time Jacob and I had fooled around, he kissed my butterfly tattoo. He was the first person to do it, and for some stupid reason, I wanted him to be the last.

After demanding that Flynn stop, I confessed I was at Mavericks to meet someone else, and that I only left with him because I was hurt about being stood up. It was the most awkward conversation I've ever had in my life, but Flynn handled my honesty better than expected. He acted like a true gentleman by driving me back to Mavericks.

"If it doesn't work out with that bloke, give me a call. I wouldn't mind getting to know you a little better," he told me before he reversed out of the lot and drove away.

When I spotted Jacob's car in the lot, I did consider going inside to see him, but with the lines of our friendship severely blurred, I went home to think instead. It's typical, though, isn't it? The one time I didn't do anything wrong is the one time I get blamed for it.

I stop reminiscing when I hear my cell phone ringing on the kitchen counter. After scampering off the floor, I dash for it, hoping it is Jacob wanting to apologize for questioning me. Disappointment smacks into me when I see it is a call from Emily.

"Hello." I hide the disappointment in my tone with a friendly greeting.

"Hey...are you okay?"

I roll my eyes, hating that my efforts were fruitless. "I'm all right, what's up?"

I'm the one who grows suspicious when Emily takes in several small breaths in a row. She only does that when she's nervous or about to cry. I find out it's the former when she rambles, "Noah and I are getting married next weekend. He doesn't know—it's a secret. We're getting married in Vegas. Jacob paid for your flights and accommodations because he knows how badly I want you to be there."

"Hold on, what?" I ask when she stops to suck in much-needed air.

"I know you think we're too young, but we don't agree. I love him, and he loves me, and this is something we want to do, so I want your support."

She said a similar thing when they announced their engagement the morning after Christmas last year. I nearly had a coronary. She was only eighteen... Well, technically nineteen, but that wasn't the point. She had plenty of years to figure out what she wanted to do with her life, so she shouldn't tie herself down so quickly. When I told her that, she shot daggers at me before she stormed into her room. Mom thought I reacted to her news too harshly. I didn't agree. I was merely looking out for my little sis.

"Why are you rushing this, Em?"

"I love him—"

"It's not that simple. Life isn't a fairytale. It's messy and yuck—"

"And more times than not, the good outweighs the bad. When you love somebody, you love them wholeheartedly. You give yourself to them and *only* them. Noah is that person for me. I want to share his last name; I want to be the mother of his children, and I want to spend every day of my life loving him how he deserves to be loved. When you know, you know. It's *that* simple."

My chest rises and falls three times as I contemplate what she said. Is love really that simple? Emily and Noah dove into their relationship headfirst, while everyone around them watched with caution, but that doesn't mean they didn't discover greatness. Noah loves Emily—I know this beyond the shadow of a doubt—and she loves him, so maybe love is that simple?

With my heart as murky as my stomach, I say nine little words I never thought I'd say: "What time do you need me at the airport?"

CHAPTER THIRTY-EIGHT

JACOB

"What the hell are you doing in Los Angeles, Jacob?" Cormack dumps a heap of paperwork onto a makeshift desk in the studio Rise Up has been working out of the past six months to welcome me with a handshake.

While he does that, I try to think of a legitimate reason as to why I've arrived in LA in the middle of the day. "Just visiting."

What? I've never been any good at thinking on the spot.

"Where is everyone?" The recording booth is noticeably empty, considering Rise Up is mere seconds from greatness.

Cormack slaps my back, his excitement uncontained. "I gave the boys the day off before their tour starts. Last I heard, Slater, Marcus, and Nick were at the hotel. I haven't heard from Noah today. Would you like a ride to their hotel? I'm about to head that way."

"Sure, that'll be great." After gathering my bag off the floor, I follow Cormack to a shiny black BMW convertible. It's a nifty ride that leaves no doubt to his wealth. I don't think this make is even on the market yet.

Noticing my prolonged gawk, Cormack chuckles under his breath. "Business is good."

"Clearly."

When he slides into the driver seat, I follow suit. I'm halfway through latching my belt when he asks, "Is everything alright? You seem a bit quiet."

I jerk up my chin. "Yeah, I'm good. Just trying to work out how I'll untangle myself from this sardine tin once we arrive at the hotel."

Cormack laughs, but his suspicion remains high. I haven't felt myself since I left Lola's apartment two days ago. Even Dad noticed a change in my personality. He simply suggested: "Perhaps it's time to let her go."

It hurt to hear, but I'm beginning to wonder if he's right. I don't want to be Lola's friend; I want to be her *everything*, but that's not something she's willing to give me. I know she cares about me, and I understand her last relationship has made her apprehensive about trusting again, but we can't keep running on the same hamster wheel we've been spinning the past two years. I want her to be my girl and *only* my girl, but if she's not willing to give that to me, maybe I need to move on?

This weekend apart will do us more good than harm. We don't spend every waking moment together like other couples do, but for the past month, we've seen each other daily. But space is good. Sometimes space helps...unless you're being smacked with a bad bout of jealousy.

I trust Lola. From what I've heard the past year, I'm reasonably sure that even during our six months' separation, she wasn't sleeping around, but all it takes is for one seed of doubt to be planted, and before you know it, you're infested with weeds of distrust. That's what happened two days ago. I let jealousy get the better of me.

Lola's tattoo is a symbol of her strength. She got it after Callum assaulted her. It represents her metamorphosis, the re-growing of the wings Callum tried to pluck. I love her tattoo because it shows a side of her no one else but me sees. She's perfect yet fragile. Flynn saw that side of her, and in all honesty, I fuckin' hate it.

Don't misconstrue, I also hate the way people misinterpret Lola's warrior attitude as nothing but spitfire sassiness. But I don't need any competition. I'm already facing an uphill battle. I don't need more issues.

My eyes float up from my phone when Cormack pulls into the entrance of an impressively large hotel. "If you need anything, let me know."

I thank the concierge for taking my bag with a head bob before turning to Cormack. "Thanks. See you around?"

Nodding, he chuckles at my departure from his car. It's as awkward as a woman squeezing into Spandex for a blind date. Legs and arms are going in every direction. As much as it'd be nice to have a sports car, I'll never own one. They're too uncomfortable for guys my size.

Once Cormack's taillights blur into a sea of traffic, I enter the hotel Rise Up is slumming at. Obviously, their success is rolling in. This place is way too fancy for my polo shirt, cargo shorts, and Vans shoes combination. I feel underdressed just entering their lobby.

I don't know why when the first person I spot is Slater. He's both shirtless and shoeless. "Jakeyboy, how the fuck are you?" He throws his arms around my shoulders before tugging me into his tattooed chest. "I would've picked you up from the airport, but Emily didn't know what time you were landing."

"It's all good. I found my way."

As I shadow Slater to the floor the band is occupying—*yes, you heard me right, they have the entire story of a hotel to themselves*—I take in the opulent surroundings. This hotel is massive. The chandeliers hanging from the raked ceilings are the size of my living room back home, and all the finishes are done in gold. With how many snooty people are in one spot, I wouldn't be surprised to discover the gold is real. I feel like I stepped into a real-life palace.

When we enter their apartment-sized hotel room, Marcus greets me with a handshake, and Nick jerks up his chin in silent greeting.

"Where's Noah?" His bandmates are great guys, but even when

they're not on stage, the absence of their lead singer is highly noticeable.

"Being a soft cock." Slater dumps my bag on one of three white leather sofas before moving to a full-size bar in the corner of the room. "He went to visit Emily. Left us a note."

Marcus hands me the note Slater is referring to.

Morning, Fuckers,
Gone to visit my girl.
Be back sometime tomorrow.
Noah

AFTER SNATCHING the note from my hand, Slater replaces it with a crystal glass full of brown liquid. "Doesn't mean we can't have his bachelor party on his behalf." He clinks his glass against mine. "Bottoms up."

I hesitate. I'm not much of a hard liquor drinker, but what have I got to lose? Everything I've ever wanted is slipping from my grasp, so why not get rip-roaring drunk with friends in a strange city?

What's the worst that could happen?

THE NEXT MORNING, I wake up to my phone hollering and my head thumping. I want to say that's the worst of it. Unfortunately, it isn't. I feel like I've swallowed a dozen razor blades, and my mouth is as dry as the Sahara.

As I scrub sleep from my eyes, my eyes trail over the room. Slater is sleeping upright on a chair; he has a pretty blonde draped across his bare thighs, mercifully covering his cock from my view. I'm sprawled on the loveseat—thankfully solo—and Nick and Marcus are nowhere to be seen.

When my phone hollers again, I swipe my sweaty finger across the screen, silencing its ear-piercing screams. It's not ringing. My alarm is going off. For some stupid fucking reason, I chose to fly home at six in the morning. For what purpose? None, other than I'm an idiot who didn't want to miss the training session Lola and I attend every Tuesday at Hank's gym. I booked my flights before our argument, and with it being so close to peak holiday season, I wasn't able to change them—*not that I would have.*

As Slater would say, "I'm a soft cock."

Gingerly, I snag my cargo shorts off the floor and head to the bathroom, my steps shaky. If the taxi the concierge scheduled last night arrives on time, I have five minutes to get my ass downstairs or risk missing my flight.

My eyes bulge out of my head when I accidentally bump into a large-breasted lady on my way into the bathroom. She's wearing nothing but a sheer pair of panties. By sheer, I mean they leave *nothing* to the imagination.

"Morning, Jacob." After planting a kiss to the edge of my mouth, she staggers into the living room to pass out on the chair I just woke up on.

Who the fuck is she, and how does she know my name?

Although I'd love nothing more than a few minutes to work through my confusion, I don't have time. It's 5:05 AM. I don't even have time to scrape the roadkill off my tongue, let alone work out why a practically naked girl knows my name.

After throwing on my pants and some random shirt I find on the ground, I grab my duffel bag off the floor then bolt to the hotel entrance, where I slide into my waiting taxi. Morning traffic is light, meaning I make it to the gate of my flight by the skin of my teeth.

"Sorry."

The flight attendant either misses my apology, or she doesn't care for excuses. She snatches my ticket out of my hand before gesturing for me to enter the gangway. "You're the last to board."

As I flop into my seat, my phone dings. Once again, it isn't a message. It's Facebook notifying me that Noah tagged me in six photos. With my lips pursed, I slide my index finger across the screen of my phone. I'm just about to log into my Facebook app when I hear someone cough above me.

Lifting my gaze, I'm met with the same narrowed pair of eyes that were glaring at me minutes ago. "Please turn off your phone. We're about to depart." She refuses to leave my side until my cell is switched off and stored in my pocket.

"Thank you." Even though she continues her checks around the cabin, her eyes remained planted on me. If I so much as move for my phone, she'll be on my ass like white on rice.

The entire flight home, I rack my brain, trying to recall any events that occurred last night.

SIX HOURS OF PONDERING, and I'm still fucking clueless. It's nothing but a complete blur.

As I stroll down the departure gate of my flight, I switch on my phone. I can't see the flight attendant, but I'm certain her eyes are still on me as I dial my voicemail to check the two messages I received during my flight. She kept a close watch on me all trip. Usually, I'd savor the attention, but today it just feels creepy. There's only one girl's attention I want. That person doesn't wear wings on the breast of her jacket; she wears them on her hip.

My race to baggage claim slows when a chirpy voice sounds down the line. "Hey, Jacob, it's Nat. Where did you run off to this morning? Call me."

Who the fuck is Nat? And how the fuck did she get my number?

My questions are left unanswered when my second message plays. "Jacob, it's Ryan. Call me back. It's urgent." His voice is rattled, like he's close to crying. There's only been one time I've heard him like this. It was when Noah's brother Chris killed himself...

Oh fuck.

With my heart in my throat, I scroll through my contacts for Ryan's number. My hands are shaking so much, I scroll past the R's three times before I realize why I can't find Ryan's name. I've never had a reason to use it, so I never stored his number in my phone.

As my fingers rake through my hair, I try to think of another way I can get his number. It showed up as private on my cell, so that won't work. I don't see it being listed, so that's off the table as well, but there's got to be a way. I just have to find it.

Think, Jacob, think.

Five seconds later, a light bulb switches on in my head. Ryan wrote his cell number on the business card he gave me when I was arrested. He said if Callum tried to contact me, I should call him.

Ignoring the tremors making the floor beneath my feet shudder, I yank my wallet out of my pocket to dig through the business cards stored there. A sigh spills from my lips when I locate Ryan's tattered card a few seconds later. While bolting to the airport's short-term parking lot, I dial his number. He answers on the very first ring.

"Ryan Carter."

"Ryan, it's Jacob. Is Lola okay?" The fear in my voice is undeniable. I'm beyond petrified that Callum has hurt her again.

"Lola is fine."

My sprint slows to a jog. My heart is still fitfully beating, but knowing Lola is uninjured is a relief.

My gratitude doesn't linger for long. "It's Noah. He isn't good."

I start running all over again.

CHAPTER THIRTY-NINE

LOLA

With a huff, I glance at my alarm clock for the tenth time the past hour. I've barely slept a wink the past three days. Insomnia drives me nuts in general, but this latest case could have been avoided if I'd just listen to one of the many pleas my heart has been issuing since Jacob stormed out of my apartment.

Alas, Jacob doesn't call me a hellion for no reason. My brain could be getting sucked out by a zombie, but I'd still deny that we're in an acropolis because I don't believe in zombies. That's how stubborn I am.

Rolling over, I shift my view from faded painted walls to a water-stained roof. My apartment is anything but glamorous, but it's mine. I saved enough of my wages the past two years to put down a reasonable deposit on my own little place. It's nothing flashy, but it's a start, and you've got to start somewhere, right?

When my head lolls to the side, my brain screams at me: *Don't do it, Lola. You'll only get hurt,* but with my heart as rebellious as its smarter counterpart, I don't listen.

Lifting my pillow, I mash it into my face. I'm not trying to suffocate myself—much to the dismay of every local in this town—I'm breathing in Jacob's aftershave. We had a handful of nighttime sleep-overs the past three months, so his Hugo Boss aftershave is embedded in the pillowcase. Even changing my sheets didn't fix the injustice. I can smell him on every surface of my apartment. On my sofa. In my bed.

On my skin.

This kills me to admit, but I miss him more than I thought possible. I miss his laugh, his smell, and the way he looks at me like I'm clever, even when I'm being stupid. He taught me how to play poker here after he set up the two-seater dining table I brought for us to eat at, and he fixed the busted pipe under my sink before showing me a much more effective way to get wet in the bathroom. This apartment was supposed to be my humble abode, but so much of the space reflects Jacob. He even has his silly vinyl records stacked up in the corner of my room. He says they're some of his most valued possessions, yet here they are, dumped on my bedroom floor.

Ugh! Maybe I should just call him and tell him what happened with Flynn? That doesn't mean I forgive him for questioning me, but it might help me get some sleep...and perhaps help us move past this little glitch. I don't like this. I hate relying on anyone, but it also sucks not being anyone's crutch.

Before I can talk myself out of it, I snatch my cell phone off the bedside table. My plan to right the wrongs I made flies out the window when I realize it's only five AM. I can't call him at this time, no matter how desperate I am to hear his voice.

After dropping my cell on my table, I wiggle down the mattress until the duvet is covering every inch of me. Now matters are worse. Jacob's scent is stronger down here. It's so rich, if I close my eyes, I can imagine the grin he gives me every morning when I wake up to discover him watching me. It's that stupid lopsided grin he does just before he causes trouble. It's super cute, nearly as handsome as him.

Groaning at the lovesick idiot I'm becoming, I throw off the bedding and make my way to my small, outdated kitchen. Coffee has always been my savior, and today won't be any different.

Once I have a strong cup of brew in my hands, I flop onto the springless chair in my living room. A ghost of a smile cracks onto my lips. I joke that my sofa is springless, but in reality, its springs worked perfectly fine before Jacob and I broke them. We also broke my bed— three times.

Enjoy this, because I doubt it will happen again anytime soon, but my first impressions of Jacob were wrong. He knows how to fuck. Not once have I left unsatisfied.

There, I said it, I was wrong...*mostly*.

Just because he fucks well doesn't mean he doesn't want to make love. He just does whatever makes me happy. Fucking makes me happy.

This, though, the dreary TV shows on at this time of the morning... they're nothing but a mood killer. No wonder birthrates are on the decline. Who wants to stay up watching this crap while feeding a baby who didn't quit crying all night long? Not me.

After turning off the TV, I scurry into my room to grab my phone. Facebook is full of people pretending to have a perfect life, but it's a good diversion for boredom.

Like a perfectly timed skit, the first image that pops up on my wall is Jenni breastfeeding baby Jasper. She looks tired, but I can admit she also looks happy. She's smiling and giving the peace sign to the camera. I like her photo before I continue scrolling. I scan through multiple posts from "friends" who were devastated that yesterday was Monday. Most of my real-life friends went to college before getting desk jobs they all hate. I've never understood how that's considered living. If you hate what you do every day, why continue doing it? My bartender job isn't flashy, but I enjoy it, and I'd rather be underpaid than turn up to a job I hate every day.

As I'm about to put down my phone, Facebook notifies me that there are new posts in my feed. When I click the link, it takes me to some photos Noah tagged Jacob in. The first couple of images look innocent, but that becomes null and void when I open the entire album. Jacob is tucking dollar bills into a stripper's panties. That can be expected; he was at a bachelor party, but it's the pictures where he isn't front and center that are the most concerning.

In the background of one photo, a woman with long blonde hair is sitting on his lap. I could assume he's getting a lap dance, but the more I scroll, the more apparent it becomes that isn't the case. The same girl pops up in multiple photos taken throughout the night. If the timestamp is anything to go by, it was a good eight hours.

In the very last image, there are no heads, but I recognize the lower half of Jacob's body. He loves his cargo shorts, no matter how much I despise them. The same girl who was sitting in his lap earlier is crouched between his legs. She's in the process of lowering his zipper. She has a look on her face, one I know all too well. It's the look all women get when they realize Jacob's cock is as big as the rest of him.

The grip on my phone tightens as a long growl grunts from my lips. Here I am moping in my apartment like a loser who can't get a date, when he's out doing anything or *anyone* he wants.

With anger strangling my senses, I type Jacob's name into the search bar at the top of my Facebook feed. I'm acting like a child, but euphoria dashes through me when I click the block button on his profile. Just like changing your status from "in a relationship" to "it's complicated" sparks the rumor mill, unfriending someone is the equivalent of giving them the one-finger salute in public.

I sit cross-legged on my bed for the next several minutes, trying in vain to reel in my anger. I want to hurt someone, but the person deserving of my wrath is in Los Angeles. With the early hour in mind and more adrenaline than I know what to do with, I dart out of my apartment. I'm so frustrated, I don't even take a second to pat myself on the back for getting ready in under ten minutes.

With traffic light, it only takes me forty-five minutes to get where I'm going. My anger didn't reduce in the slightest, though. I maybe even more angry now than I was earlier. Not even the poor rusty hinges on Hank's Gym door survive my rage. They buckle when I throw open the door before stomping to the bag hanging mid-space.

"Good morning, pretty lady, what are you doing here so early?"

I ditch my handbag, snag a pair of gloves off the rack, then spin to face Hank. "I really need to punch something, figured what better place to do that than at a boxing gym?"

Hank's brows furrow as he scans my face. Once he finishes his vigorous assessment, he jerks his chin to the ring. "You don't need to work the bag. You need to hit something real, so how about we put your frustration to good use?"

After tying my gloves, he dons his own pair.

"What are you doing?"

"You want to box, so we're going to box." He uses his teeth to tie his gloves before holding apart the ropes for me. When I hesitate, he smiles. "Don't worry; I won't hit you for real."

I climb through the ropes before cocking my hip. "I'm not worried about me. You, on the other hand..." My arched brow talks on my behalf.

Hank's loud laugh rumbles right through me. "Bring it on." He motions with his hands for me to move toward him.

I take on the fighting stance I've perfected over the past year and a half before raising my hands to protect my face. A proud smile stretches across Hank's face a mere second before his fist sails past my head. I bobbed down in just enough time to miss his left hook.

"Good. Now back on your toes."

For the first few strikes, I hesitate. Hank isn't wearing the protective gear he usually does when we box, so I'm worried I'll hurt him.

It doesn't take me long to realize the error of my ways. He confidently blocks Jacob's hits, much less my puny ones. With that in mind, I put more effort into our battle. More times than not, Hank sweeps his hand in front of himself, making me completely miss my mark. For the occasional one that connects, they either land on his glove-covered fist or his torso. I'm aiming for his head, so I've got nothing to brag about, although the gleam in Hank's eyes says otherwise. He's proud of me—and my anger is finally starting to dissipate.

By the time an hour has ticked by, I'm exhausted, and my lungs are burning. I lean my arms on top of my head before sucking in big, jagged breaths. It takes several tedious minutes to get my heart rate back within safe levels.

Hank wipes away a trail of sweat running down his face with a white towel before tossing one to me. "Do you feel better?"

While glancing into his nearly black eyes, I nod.

"Do you wanna talk about it?"

My head bob turns into a shake. I'm just now getting my anger under control, so I don't want to bring it to the surface again. I also can't breathe, much less speak.

"Alright. You know where I am if you need me. Until then, hit the showers. You stink."

He noogies my head as he always does to Jacob before climbing out of the ring and making his way to his office. On my way to the locker rooms, I spot him through the crack in his office door. He's not sorting paperwork like you'd expect any business owner to do when things are quiet. He's folding blankets.

Upon noticing my curious glance, he musters up his best fake smile before closing his office door, barely blocking out the makeshift cot in the corner of his already cramped space.

LATER THAT AFTERNOON, when back in my apartment, I can't stop thinking about Hank. Although he had everything packed up by the time I got out of the shower, what I saw can't be denied. He's living out of his office.

Is Jacob aware he uses his business premises as a home base? If so, why hasn't he offered him an alternative solution? Jacob isn't rolling in money, but the proceeds he gets fighting for Isaac would surely provide something more suitable than a concrete floor, wouldn't it? And what about the money Isaac pays Hank to train Jacob, where's that...?

Like a lightning strike brightening a dark sky, reality dawns. I've never paid a cent to use Hank's gym—not one. I show up with Jacob and use his facilities without paying him a dime. How many other people do that as well?

Guilt makes itself known in my gut. I've been using Hank for months when he's never been anything but kind to me.

Snagging my cell phone off the coffee table, I log into my banking app. "$143.24," I groan with a huff. A hundred dollars won't cover over a year's worth of gym membership, but it's a start.

Just as I'm about to set down my phone, it rings, startling me. It's Jacob. I consider letting his call go to voicemail, but I'm curious if he's aware Hank is sleeping in his gym, so I answer it instead.

"Hello, Jacob."

CHAPTER FORTY

JACOB

I'd take a moment to assess the anger in Lola's tone if I had the chance. Regrettably, the last item on my agenda is starting World War III. Things aren't good for Noah. By not good, I mean I have no clue how he is. I've yet to get an update. Emily was only granted visitation twenty minutes ago, and we've been pacing the glossy tiled floors of the emergency department for hours. Some say no news is good news. I'm not that person. I hate not knowing what's going on. That's why I'm frantically updating everyone on Noah's accident. I know what it's like to be in the dark, so I won't subject anyone else to it.

With that in mind, I remember the purpose of my call. "Ah...hey, Lola. It's Jacob." *Jesus, I sound like an idiot with half a brain. My number has been in her phone for years, so who would she think was calling?* "Noah was in an accident. He's in the Intensive Care Unit at Parkwood University Hospital."

"What? Is he okay?" Nothing but unbridled panic now reflects in her tone.

My shoulders inch toward my ears. "I don't know; I haven't seen him. Em is with him now."

My eyes stray to the door Emily walked through twenty minutes ago at the same time Lola offers up her sympathies. I'm about to tell her she has nothing to be sorry for, but Emily's pale face steals my words. She's stumbling out the double doors of the ICU, her face as white as a ghost.

"I have to go." My voice turns gravelly and thick when I see the shock and distress on Emily's face. "I'll call you back as soon as I have more information."

After slipping my phone in my pocket, I move to Emily's side. With every step I take, I scan her grief-stricken face for signs on Noah's condition. "Is he okay? Is he awake?"

Her throat works hard to swallow before she shakes her head. "He's on life support." She swallows another three times before taking a wary step forward.

"Em...?"

Before my question can leave my mouth, her eyes roll into the back of her head as her knees buckle. I catch her a mere second before she hits the light gray tiles we've paced nonstop the past four hours.

"Em..." I shake her shoulders, attempting to wake her. "Emily!"

When she doesn't respond, I gather her in my arms before sprinting back to the emergency department I darted through like a maniac when I first arrived. "Help. I need help!"

A nurse with kind brown eyes cranks her neck my way. When she spots Emily flopped in my arms, she gestures for me to follow her. "What happened?"

I set Emily down on the bed in the emergency triage room before shrugging. "I don't know; she just collapsed."

The nurse completes a set of observations on Emily before passing her stats on to a male physician. He checks Emily's pulse, flicks a light in her eyes, and lowers the waistband on her jeans to push on her stomach.

His somewhat carefree demeanor is nipped in the bud when his eyes lift to me. "How far along is she?"

"Far along what?" I'm not acting daft. I have no clue what he's asking.

My jaw drops when he replies, "Pregnant. How many weeks is she?"

"I don't know... I didn't know she was pregnant."

I'm not lying. Noah never said a word to me, which is shocking. I didn't think we kept anything from each other.

"She's dehydrated, so we'll put her on a drip, but please note, visits to the ER can be avoided with adequate nutrition. She needs to eat and drink regularly."

Still too stunned to speak, I accept the doctor's disdain with a dip of my chin. Although Emily's diet isn't my responsibility, it will be until Noah wakes. I promised him I'd always look out for her when he freaked about her not answering her phone her first night at college. I'm a man who keeps his promises.

"SHE'LL MOST likely sleep for a few more hours. The first trimester is very tiring." The nurse who aided me an hour ago finishes checking Emily's vitals before her eyes drift to me. "Why don't you go grab something to eat and come back in around an hour? We'll have a better idea on how things are going by then."

The last thing I want to do is leave Emily's side, but I'm also dying to get an update on Noah. All Emily told me before she collapsed was that he was in a coma. I've not heard a thing since.

"Can I borrow that?" I nudge my head to the pen in the nurse's uniform pocket. When she hands it to me, I jot down my number on a scrap of paper. "If Emily wakes before I'm back, please call me." After standing, I hand back her pen and my number. "Even if she says not to, call me."

Although the nurse agrees to my request, I'm still torn about leaving. Noah is in a coma, and his girl is passed out on a hospital bed. Today couldn't get any more shit for me. After a final squeeze to

Emily's hand, I bolt back to the ICU. It's lucky I'm fit. All the running I've done today while hungover would put an average man on his ass.

I've barely blasted through the double swinging doors when Ryan spans the distance between us. "Where the hell did you go? One minute you were on your phone; the next minute you were gone."

His anger takes a back seat when I reply, "Emily fainted; I just left her in the ER."

"Is she okay?"

"Yeah, she's... ah." I nearly say "pregnant" until I realize it isn't my place to say. If Noah is aware and keeping it secret, it's for a reason. "Have you seen Noah?"

Ryan shakes his head. "No, they said only immediate family are allowed to see him."

"Immediate family?"

When Ryan nods, I turn on my heels and stride to the ICU doors to hit the intercom button. Ryan shadows me but remains quiet. Not long later, a gray-haired nurse pushes open the door. She has a clipboard in her hands and two pencils holding together her messy bun.

"I'm here to see Noah Taylor."

The nurse checks a list of names on her clipboard before raising her eyes to me. "Your name?"

"Chris Taylor, Noah's brother."

I hear Ryan's Adam's apple bob up and down, but not even the badge on his hip has him stepping in to recant my statement. After checking her list for the second time, the nurse steps to the side, unblocking the doorway from her plump frame. "Okay, come in."

I glance back at Ryan, shocked my ruse worked. He smiles before giving me the thumbs up, knowing I would have worn a dress and pretended to be Noah's mother if it guaranteed I'd see him.

The nurse makes me wash my hands before guiding me to the bedside of a man I don't recognize. When I read the nameplate above the bed, my fists clench into tight balls. Now I understand why Ryan dragged Emily away from Noah at the accident scene. He has significant head injuries that make him barely recognizable.

A bandage covers a majority of his head and one of his eyes. A ventilator tube inserted into his mouth and his chest is rising and falling in rhythm with the machine on the right side of his bed. His left leg is covered in plaster and held up in a brace, and his rocker clothing has been replaced with a light blue hospital gown.

"How is he?"

The nurse gives me a sympathetic smirk. "We stopped the internal bleeding by removing part of his spleen, but he had a cerebral edema to his brain. We drained the hematoma, but he's not out of the woods just yet. The bleed to his brain caused it to swell. Although we released the pressure, we won't know the extent of the damage until we conduct further tests."

"When will they be done?"

She takes a moment to deliberate by shrugging. "We can conduct tests while he's in a coma, but we won't know the full extent of his injuries until he wakes." She rubs my arm in a comforting manner. "Talk to him; you'd be surprised what coma patients hear."

I swallow harshly before jerking up my chin. After running her hand down my arm for the second time, she moves toward the nurses' station in the middle of the room. As I walk to Noah's beside, my heart beats in a similar rhythm as the machines keeping him alive. It's an annoying, *thud, thud, thud* I'd rather hear without the beep of a life support machine.

With words eluding me, I curl my fingers around his hand instead. Just as my index finger circles his wrist, something sharp jabs it.

What the hell?

When I flip his hand, I notice many scratches and grazes on his wrist, but I don't see anything that would cause a jabbing sensation. With my curiosity high, I run my fingertips over his cuts. I'm not meaning to hurt him, but something is off. My lips quirk when I feel something sharp nick my skin for the second time.

"Excuse me." A nurse walking by stops what she's doing to peer at me. "Can you feel this?"

When she stops next to me, I run her fingers over Noah's wrist in the same manner I just did. I can tell the exact moment she feels what I did when her brows scrunch.

"Doctor Matthew, can you please come here?"

When an elderly male doctor arrives in Noah's cubicle, the nurse does the same routine to him as I did to her.

"Hmm, interesting."

I watch the doctor in silence when he moves around the cubicle, gathering equipment from little nooks throughout the sterile smelling space. Once he has everything in order, he places a blue dressing sheet over Noah's arm, then slices open his wrist with a scalpel.

"What the fuck! Why aren't you taking him to surgery?"

My stomach rolls when he stuffs tweezers into the wound before digging around. Certain I'm seconds from passing out, I concentrate on a speck on the wall in front of me while fighting to keep the contents of my stomach in their rightful spot.

A few seconds later, the doctor lifts a large shard of thin glass into the air. "I got it!"

After dumping the offending material on a stainless steel tray at the side, he sews stitches into Noah's wrist. The seven butterfly stitches make it seem like his operation was child's play, but I'm still shocked.

"Why did you do that here?"

Dr. Matthew's eyes stray to mine. "He wouldn't have survived another operation. He barely made it through the first one."

"He's stronger than you think."

He finishes rolling a white bandage around Noah's stitches before standing. "I'm sorry if I seem harsh, but I've never been one to sugarcoat things. Do you want me to speak the truth or give you a well-rehearsed line?"

"The truth." *I hate being lied to.*

"Okay. Then here it is." His pause is more worrying than

comforting. "Noah's chances of surviving the next twenty-four hours are sitting at five percent. He has *significant* head injuries and may have sustained permanent brain damage." Dr. Matthew's tone is stern, but it also shows his genuine concern.

"He'll prove you wrong."

He squeezes my shoulder, either thinking I'm an optimist or an idiot. "I hope he does—because he's in for one hell of a ride."

While they pack away the medical equipment they used, I move to Noah's bedside to remind him of the promise he made to me four years ago.

"Remember the pain you went through when Chris left? Don't do that to me, Noah. I won't let you leave me like they left you. You have to fight; you have to fight to live. Emily would want you to live." I squeeze his hand in mine when his eyes rapidly move under his eyelids. "Promise me you'll fight. Promise me, and I'll promise that you won't go through this alone. I'll be there for you every day. I'll fight alongside you. You will survive this, Noah. It'll never stop hurting, but you will survive this."

We will survive this.

I sit with Noah for another ten minutes before my phone buzzes in my pocket. I almost let it go to voicemail before I remember I gave the nurse my number. As I slide my phone out, my call goes to voicemail. I'm about to check my messages when the nurse who showed me in nudges her head to a sign advising cell phones are banned in the ICU. It's just above the sign that states visitation is limited to fifteen minutes.

"I'll be back, alright?"

Noah can't reply, but I'm certain he knows I'm watching over him. I did the same thing when his brothers died, and I'll continue doing it until he's recovered.

As I exit the ICU, I dial my voicemail. While it walks me through the process, I cup the speaker of my phone so I can answer Ryan's wordless questions.

"He's..." I struggle to find an appropriate word, "...fighting." I nudge my head to the door I just walked through. "The nurse who let me in just left for lunch, so as far as the others are aware, Chris hasn't visited Noah today."

"Thanks, Jake." He slaps my shoulder before ramming his finger into the ICU buzzer on repeat.

"You might want to hide that." I drop my eyes to the badge on his hip. "And that." My eyes drift to his gun holster poking out of his jacket.

Ryan stuffs his badge into the breast pocket of his jacket and adjusts his gun holster a mere second before a nurse arrives to answer his call. When he successfully pulls the wool over her eyes, I return my attention to my phone.

My first message is from Lola. "Hey...umm... I just wanted to say I'm here if you need me—for anything. Just call me. Okay? Umm... bye."

I've never heard her so nervous before. It honestly unsettles me as much as seeing Noah holed up in the ICU. I'm about to return her call when my next message arrives. It's from yesterday.

"Hey, Jacob, it's Flynn." He pauses like he's unsure what to say. "I wanted to talk to you about what happened the other day. The...ah...Lola incident. When you get a chance, give me a call... or pop into Mavericks. Whatever's easiest. Yeah, well, until then..." He recites his number before hanging up.

Now I'm not just panicked out of my mind, I'm pissed. Between waking up to a topless woman knowing my name and seeing Noah in the ICU, my day has been a clusterfuck of emotions. I'm tired, anxious, and now jealous as fuck. To say I'm holding on by a very thin thread is an understatement—a major one.

With my mind not up for more meddling, I shut down my phone, slide it into my pocket, and make my way back to the emergency department. As much as I'd love to know exactly what happened between Lola and Flynn, I've got more pressing matters to deal with right now.

CHAPTER FORTY-ONE

LOLA

My knees clang together when I enter Noah's hospital room on the heels of my mom. Visiting hours were only invoked today because Noah's record label transferred his care to Ravenshoe Private Hospital.

I'm not a fan of hospitals in general, but Noah's badly battered face is upping the ante. His injuries are horrifying. Surviving a head-on collision with a semi is already remarkable, much less all the prodding he's endured the past seventy-two hours. He has machine tubing coming out of him in all directions, and the portions of his face I can see give no indication to the man hiding beneath the layers of bandages.

"I'm going to sit over there," I say to anyone listening.

When no one voices an opinion, I make a beeline for a chair in the far corner of the room. It's close enough to Noah's bedside he knows I'm here, but far enough away, I'm not in anyone's way. His room is full to the brim with those nearest and dearest to him. His bandmates and their significant others sit on the left of his bed; Jacob and Emily are on his right, and there's a man I've never met before floating at the back.

The mood in the room is so gloomy and sad. It almost seems as if I'm attending a funeral. Noah might be seriously injured, but he's alive. The people in this room need to remember that.

Hoping to lighten the mood, I make my way to Emily. Jacob watches me approach under lowered lashes, but he doesn't say anything. That's not unusual. Not even my offer of assistance three days ago made him reach out to me. Under different circumstances, I'd be pissed, but this isn't anything close to ordinary. I thought I had all my personalities worked out, but even I don't know how to act in this situation.

Once I reach my sister's side, I bump her with my hip. "You never thanked me, you know."

Emily lifts her watering eyes to mine. "For?"

I glare at her, silently warning her to keep her tears at bay. If she cries, I'll cry, and then I'll have to kill every person in this room just to salvage my "bitchy" reputation. There's only one person in this room who's seen me cry, and I plan to keep it that way.

Confident Emily has her teary eyes under control, I say, "The night Jacob dropped me home from Mavericks, I told Noah the bathroom was on the left."

Emily's furrowed brows reveal she heard my confession, but she remains as quiet as a church mouse. Perhaps she's confused? I'll try and settle it. "The instant I saw him, I knew he was perfect for you, so I gave fate a little push."

I don't believe in destiny or every other crock-of-shit love remedies people try to palm off to excuse them from moving in together after three weeks and marrying within six months, but Emily does. She always says she and Noah were destined to be together, so why isn't she putting that same faith in believing he'll do everything in his power to stay with her? Besides, surrounding Noah with positivity would have to be more beneficial than acting like he's one step from his grave—surely!

My *empowering the world with positivity* rant ends when a heartbreaking sob rips through Emily's lips. When she sways like a leaf on a hot summer's day, Jacob grabs the tops of her arms, steading her unsteady movements. He talks to her in hushed whispers, and I realize they're closer than I thought.

After he wipes away the tears sitting high on Emily's cheeks, Jacob's eyes stray to mine. They're brimming with anger. "What?" I whisper, unable to comprehend what I did wrong. I was trying to embolden Emily with optimism, not make him angry at me—*again*.

When I scan the room, seeking support, I realize Jacob isn't the only one glaring at me. I've attracted the narrowed eyes of many. Disdainful looks are nothing new to me, but in a small, stuffy hospital room, it's more than I can bear.

"Coffee, anyone?"

I only see my mom's nod before dashing to the vending machine in the hall outside Noah's room. My attempts to lighten the mood seem to have had the opposite effect. One by one, Noah's guests filter out, all glaring at me on the way by, but none of them are brave enough to say anything. That's one of the good things about being seen as a bitch. People are too scared to approach me. It's a lonely life keeping everyone at arm's length, but it does save a lot of heartache.

I stop searching for change in my purse when a pair of polished black shoes enter my peripheral vision. As my eyes float up from the floor, they drift past tailored pants, a rounded belly that would make Father Christmas proud, and a cropped peppered beard before landing on a pair of gentle blue eyes.

"I'm assuming you're Lola?"

I cock my hip, my sassiness returning. "What gives it away? The prolonged glares? Or the hushed whispers of scorned women?" My chipper tone hides the hurt I feel for being constantly ridiculed. If only I could fix the pained gleam in my eyes.

"Hushed whispers? Damn, I'm missing out." The stranger glances over my shoulder like he's seeking the horde of women who bicker about me every chance they get. When he doesn't locate anyone but us, he returns his sparkling eyes to mine. "They seemed to have left, although I'm sure they'll talk about you for at least another hour."

"Only an hour? Sheesh, I was aiming for three." While he snickers, I feed quarters into the hot drink dispenser. "I didn't mean to upset anyone. I just wanted to lighten the mood."

"I know."

Who knew two little words could have so much impact? I don't know this man, but I certainly needed his reassurance.

I begin to wonder if I have the situation all wrong when the stranger asks, "Did you want to grab a *real* cup of coffee? The gunk in the dispenser is nasty, but I've heard the barista whips up a good brew in the cafeteria."

"Just a coffee? Nothing more sinister...?"

His lips curl in the corners from my questioning look. "What's more sinister than coffee at four in the afternoon?"

"I can think of a few things." When I push off the wall and head down the corridor, my new companion follows me. He remains quiet, but I can feel the shudders of his laughter. "You're not the type I usually date, but you seem harmless enough, so what the hell, let's do coffee."

After jabbing the elevator button, I shift to face my new best friend—*my only friend.* "You seem to have me at an advantage. You know all about me, but I don't even know your name." His face is familiar, like I've seen him before, but for the life of me, I can't work out where.

"Yes, I do have the advantage, don't I?" After gesturing for me to enter the idling elevator car before him, he holds out his hand in offering. "Thomas, my friends call me Tom."

"Nice to meet you, Tom." I accept his handshake. "Or should I call you Thomas?"

The elevator car shakes from Tom's hearty chuckle. It's so robust, my body shudders right along with his. "You can call me Tom." When our car reaches the lobby, he gestures for me to exit the elevator first. "Ladies before gentlemen."

I let his comment slide since he was most likely born in an era where men were expected to act like gentlemen.

Once we receive our order from the barista, we take a seat in an empty booth at the back of the packed cafeteria. I add cream and sugar to my coffee. Tom drinks his as is.

"No sugar or cream? Yuck."

Tom chuckles. "I don't need to add sugar because I'm sweet enough as it is."

Clumps of sugar plop into my mug when I whack the shit out of the sugar dispenser. "If my earlier performance is anything to go by, I should switch my order to straight sugar."

Tom laughs so hard, he has to dab his eyes with a napkin. He's spurting happy tears. "I like you, Lola."

I nearly reply, *I'm glad someone does,* but I keep my mouth shut. Today isn't about me. It's not even about Jacob. It's about Noah and Emily and supporting them through an ordeal I hope will be over soon.

For the next several minutes, Tom and I sit in silence, enjoying our coffee. It's weird that I find comfort in something I generally find confusing. Silence and I have never been close, but Tom makes it not so daunting.

When I set down my empty mug, Tom's gaze seeks mine. "Did you want another?"

I shake my head. "No, I better not. I'm barely sleeping as it is, so adding caffeine won't help."

"You're not sleeping?" When I shake my head again, he adds on, "Anything you want to talk about?"

"No." My one word sounds like an entire sentence since it was delivered with a long, harsh breath. "I'm good. Fine. Just chipper." Loathing my dejected tone, I shift the focus away from me and my mood-killer temper. "How do you know Noah?"

The worry in Tom's eyes remains, but nothing can hold back his smile. "He's like a son to me. I've known him since he was this high." He splays his hand across his chest.

"So, you know my sister, Emily?"

"You're Emily's sister?" The longer his eyes roam over my face, the more his eyes bug. "I missed the similarities at the start, but there's no denying them now. Your identical nose and the eyes should have given away your relation, but the contrast in your skin tone and hair coloring threw me off the scent."

When he nudges his head to the milky white skin on my wrist, I cringe. I don't hate that Emily has gorgeous olive skin while mine is a little bland—I'm noticing the time. It's nearly 5 PM, which means I have under an hour before my shift at Pete's. Although it would be nice not to have to work during situations like this, unfortunately, bills don't take a back seat for a crisis. I still have a mortgage and a car payment to make at the end of the month.

After sliding out of the booth, I offer Tom my hand to shake. "It was a pleasure meeting you, but I have to go. I have to be at work in an hour."

"The pleasure was all mine." Instead of accepting my handshake, he pulls me in for a firm, much-needed hug. "I'll see you soon. Okay?"

When he scoots back to absorb my nonverbal confirmation, recognition slaps me hard in the face. I'm staring at an older version of Jacob.

CHAPTER FORTY-TWO

LOLA

Eight weeks later...

"Excuse me, are you finished with that?" I point to the *Ravenshoe News* newspaper a gentleman just set down.

"This?" When I nod, he slants the newspaper my way, but before I can grasp it, he pulls it out of my reach. "What are you willing to give me for it?"

"The three dollars it's worth?"

I stop digging through my purse for loose change when the gentleman counter bids, "I'd rather have your number."

He's cute... if you like your men in a business suit, but the last thing I need is more complications, meaning the only guy I'm interested in is BOB: my battery-operated boyfriend.

"I'm sorry, but I'm married."

When his eyes drop down to my bare ring finger, I make my voice extra-nasally. "My rings are getting resized. I only got married last week. You should have seen the wedding. O.M.G—it was *fab..u...lous—*"

"Congratulations." He dumps his newspaper on the counter before skedaddling out of the café.

"Sucker," I mumble under my breath while flipping to the entertainment section I saw him flick past earlier. It has a small article about Noah hidden amongst a ton of advertisements. From what I read over the man's shoulder, it's an extremely inaccurate editorial on his current whereabouts.

"Rise Up was noticeably absent from the O'Reilly Brothers concert tour due to their lead singer Noah Taylor's current admittance at the Hope Hills Rehabilitation Center for drug and alcohol counseling," I read from the paper.

Why in the world are they reporting Noah is in a rehab center for drug and alcohol issues? It doesn't make any sense. He's been in a coma for weeks now. Christmas, New Years, and even Emily's twentieth birthday went by without any signs of him waking up—*or word from Jacob.* Noah's bruises have healed, and they're hoping to remove the bolts from his leg later this month, but he's still a very sick man. Rehab would be a walk in the park compared to what he's endured the past almost two months.

Annoyed at the paper's inability to separate fact from fiction, I search the credentials of the journalist at the bottom of the story in *Ravenshoe News* before dialing her number. A friendly female voice answers a few seconds later. "*Ravenshoe News*, this is Tracy Peters."

"Hi, my name is...oh, I don't want to mention my name." I'm tempted to punch myself in the throat for how scratchy my voice is. "The story you published in *Ravenshoe News* this morning about Noah Taylor—"

"I'm glad you enjoyed my story, but I'm swamped, so I don't have time to answer more questions from deranged fans of Rise Up."

My mouth falls open when she hangs up on me.

Gritting my teeth, I redial the number.

"*Ravenshoe News*—"

"Hang up on me again, and a deranged fan will be the least of your problems." My voice is a threatening snarl, and it gains me the attention of a few pairs of eyes in the café. "I didn't *enjoy* the story you published—because it's nothing but lies."

"Look, I appreciate that die-hard fans like yourself get upset when they learn the stars they idolize aren't perfect, but I stand by my story."

My teeth grit. "I'm not a die-hard fan. I know Noah—*personally.* He's not in rehab!"

"Noah's management team informed us that he is in rehab, so why would I believe anything that comes out of the mouth of a random groupie?"

My nostrils flare as my cheeks heat. "I'd rather be a groupie than an imbecile who claims a man is in drug rehabilitation when he's fighting for his life in an intensive care unit!"

It's nearly impossible to disconnect our call the old-fashioned way. I'd rather smash my phone on the ground. I would if I could afford to replace it. Alas, broke people don't have the luxury of ruining things on a whim because they're frustrated.

When I let out a long and frustrated growl, numerous pairs of eyes turn to face me. "What?!" A little old lady with big, sympathetic eyes peers at me, quelling the rage tearing me in two. "I'm sorry."

With my eyes close to bursting, I snatch my order from the barista's hands before hightailing it out of the cafe. The past eight weeks have been the worst weeks of my life. I've been to visit Noah a handful of times, but any time I enter the room, Jacob makes an excuse to leave. Tom assures me he's just being courteous, so I don't feel uncomfortable, but I'm not convinced. He's avoiding me like I'm not the one who had risqué photos splashed all over Facebook for the world to see.

Ugh! I'm still angry as hell about those photos. I haven't slept with anyone but Jacob since the night we met. We never agreed to be exclusive, but why would I seek solace from another man when Jacob was giving me everything I needed?

Don't get me wrong; during our six-month gap, I came close. Hearing about Jacob's "dates" had me dusting off moves I hadn't used in months, but it never went further than innocent flirting. I forgot how annoying some men are. The tacky one-liners, the false promises, I had heard it all before—except from Jacob. He convinced me he was cut from a different cloth. How stupid was I?

The unease I felt every time I visited Noah is the reason I've cut my visits back the past five weeks. Emily barely acknowledges my presence; she's too busy staring at Noah, praying he'll wake up, and everyone else hates me, so why bother? My only saving grace is Hank.

I still attend my boxing class with him every Tuesday afternoon, except now he's my sole coach. I also hang out with him on the days I'm not working. People probably think it's pathetic that I'd rather hang out in a smelly rundown gym than with people my own age, but don't be quick to jump to conclusions. Hank is a great guy. His life is tough, but not once does he let negativity tear him down. A few people I know could learn a lesson or two from him—myself included.

"How's my pretty lady today?" Hank greets me with a big smile when I enter his gym. "Still not sleeping, I see."

I roll my eyes. I could have a mountain load of concealer on to cover my bags, but Hank would still notice them. "I'm good. You?"

His smile picks up when I hand him the donuts and coffee I purchased at the café for him. Since he refuses payment for services rendered, I found another way to pay my dues. Coffee isn't much, but it's better than nothing.

"Great now." A moan seeps from his lips when he takes a large bite of a sugar-coated donut. I can't help but giggle over his enthusiasm. Who knew something so cheap could create so much happiness?

"There's the sound I've been missing." When I peer at him in shock, he nudges his head to my mouth. "I haven't heard you laugh in ages. I've missed it."

My heart melts a little, but I fully comprehend what he's saying. I haven't heard Emily's giggle or Jacob's chuckle in weeks. You don't realize how much you miss certain things until they aren't around anymore.

"Shall I start without you?"

Hank stops shoveling a second donut into his mouth to nod.

AFTER A MUSCLE-TIGHTENING WORKOUT, and a super long shower, I pad into Hank's office. "Do you want to come visit Noah with me today?"

Hank and Noah grew close after Jacob introduced them a little over a year ago. Although I've assured him many times he's more than welcome to visit him, he always refuses.

"Not today. I've got...*stuff to do.*"

I dump the towel I'm drying my hair with on Hank's desk before plopping my ass on his big leather chair. "Why don't you visit him?"

His dark eyes pop up from the paperwork he's scrutinizing. He considers my question for a few minutes before setting down the papers and sauntering to my side of his desk. "Do you know why I started this gym?"

Keeping my gaze arrested on his, I shake my head. He's very fit, so I've always assumed he was a gym junkie back in his heyday.

"From the time he was a little whippersnapper, my son Derrick was a huge boxing fan. He watched reruns of Muhammad Ali's fights on repeat, convinced they were the secret sauce he needed to become the next heavyweight champion of the world." He waves his hand around his gym. We're the only two people here. "I opened this gym to prove no dreams were impossible to reach if you're willing to put in the work."

"Did he?"

"Yes." The pride in his eyes forces a smile onto my face. "I'm not biased when I say he had pure, unrivaled talent—much like Jacob. He climbed the rankings so quick, his dream was this close to becoming a reality." He holds his thumb and index finger an inch apart. "Then, poof, it was all stripped away from him."

"What happened?"

It takes him a few seconds to continue his story, and when he does, it shreds my heart into pieces. "After a State Championship bout, Derrick was gunned down by his competitor as he left the arena. He tried to hold on, but his injuries were too critical." He peers up at the ceiling while rapidly blinking. "On the doctor's advice, his mother switched off his life support machine a week later. She believed she was doing the right thing, but I wanted to give him more than seven days to prove how strong he was. As you can imagine, that's a tough thing for even the strongest of marriages to endure."

He returns his eyes to me when I nod. "A couple of months after Derrick's death, I moved in here." I hate his story, but I love his honesty. "I tried to keep his dream alive, but as the years moved on, they faded into the distance. I was in the process of shutting down this place when I stumbled upon Jacob." The pain in his eyes switches to humor as his lips furl. "He had that same goofy look on his face Derrick always had at the start of every fight, but he also had the magic in his eyes, the gleam that revealed he could be something great if he was willing to put in the hard yards." He shakes his head as if he's still in shock. "I don't know why I approached him. To this day, I'm still wondering if I did the right thing."

"You did. He'd be lost without this..." I wave my hand around his gym as he did earlier. "And you."

My eyes bounce between his as I struggle to hold in the moisture teeming in them. I lose the chance when Hank says, "Now that I've shared, maybe you'll be willing to do the same? What happened between Jacob and you?"

CHAPTER FORTY-THREE

JACOB

"That'll be $18.95."

As I hand the café attendant a twenty, my gaze strays to the TV program behind her shoulder. I've barely looked at my phone the past eight weeks, let alone any other electronic device. I'm not much of a social media fanatic as it is, but my dislike has grown tenfold since Noah's admission. Not because I don't want to read the crap gossip reporters pump out multiple times a day, but because the first time I logged onto Facebook, I automatically veered straight to Lola's page—a page I could no longer see since she had unfriended and blocked me.

I don't know about you, but as far as I'm concerned, that a massive *fuck you, we're done* message for the entire world to see. I'm aware of Lola's coping mechanism—when she's scared, she runs—so my first thought was to reach out to her, but every time I tried, something popped up. Noah's first lot of brain scans came back inconclusive, him being sued for failure to fulfill his contract with Summit Records, his birthday, Christmas, and a whole lot of other shit that has me so close to the edge, I'm literally holding on by a thread.

With how loose my grip on reality is, I can't add any more to my plate. Call me a coward, but since there's only so much I can handle at once, I stuck my head in the sand in regards to all aspects of my relationship. Just the hurt look Lola gives me every time she enters Noah's room has me on the verge of breaking. I can't add more.

Me losing my marbles won't help anyone. It won't help Lola; it won't help Noah, and it most definitely won't help Emily. She hasn't nosedived into depression like Noah did when his brothers died, but I can't guarantee that wouldn't have been the case if I wasn't at her side the past eight weeks. She's not strong like Lola. She's only half as brave as my girl is—*was*.

I run a shaky hand over my head, pretending the world hasn't fallen out from beneath my feet. I'd give anything for a redo of the past two months. I wouldn't do anything the same—not a single fucking thing. I'd stop Noah from getting in that fucking cab; then I'd handle my disagreement with Lola in a more respectable manner— and I wouldn't let jealousy stop me from talking to her for weeks on end.

Even without knowing what happened between her and Flynn, I miss her more than words will ever explain—enough to have me reaching for my phone for the tenth time this morning. It takes a few seconds to fire up since I turn it off while in Noah's room, but when it does, it explodes with Google alert after Google alert I set for Noah. They all follow a similar tune:

Noah Taylor, lead singer of Rise Up, in tragic accident.

When I click on a link, it takes me to a live broadcast of a popular morning news program. My breath hitches when the reporter's location registers as familiar. She's standing at the front of a hospital—a hospital that looks remarkably similar to the one Noah is a patient at.

Ignoring the barista's attempt to hand me my order, I move to the main window of the café. It faces the main street. I can barely see the reporters standing shoulder to shoulder on the entrance stairs of Ravenshoe Private Hospital because over a dozen news vans are blocking my view. Security personnel have them contained for now, but I don't see that lasting long. The paps are a hungry bunch.

As I bolt back to Noah's room, the breakfast I was fetching for Emily and me is long forgotten. Emily's hungry gaze notices my empty hands within a nanosecond of me entering Noah's suite, but my quick snatch of the remote from Noah's bed shifts her focus. "It's all over the media."

"What is?"

When I switch on the TV hanging above Noah's bed, we catch the last half of the live broadcast.

"Noah Taylor, lead singer of Rise Up, was reportedly involved in a serious traffic accident six weeks ago. Initial reports indicated that Rise Up failed to fulfill their contractual agreement with Summit Entertainment because Taylor was admitted to Hills Hope Rehabilitation Center for a mandatory drug and alcohol program. We've since learned Taylor's transport was struck by a semi-trailer, killing taxi driver Ben Ebbett. Rise Up's publicist, Delilah Winterbottom, confirmed Taylor is in serious but stable condition. We'll keep you updated on his progress as we receive it. Back to you, Kylie."

When the segment switches back to the morning show hosts, I turn off the TV before gesturing for Emily to join me in the corridor. We're barely halfway out of Noah's room when Emily's curiosity gets the better of her. "Why would initial reports claim Noah was in rehab? What benefit would anyone get pretending he has a drug and alcohol problem? It doesn't make any sense."

"I don't know what benefit they'd get, but I'm reasonably sure I know who did this." When Emily peers at me with wide, confused eyes, I do my best to settle it. "Delilah has been calling nonstop. Her messages all focused on one thing: did I know why Noah had a marriage license issued in his name?"

I dig my phone out of my pocket before opening up my internet app. After typing Noah's name into the search bar, I hand my phone to Emily. "Every media source in the country is running the story of

Noah's accident. Who's to say eight weeks ago, they weren't prepared to expose his plans to wed?"

Emily shrugs, unconvinced. "I kept details of our wedding on the down-low."

"Marriage licenses are public record. It wouldn't take an intern long to discover your plans, much less a publicist hellbent on keeping her star's status as single."

Emily stomps down her foot like she's about to have a tantrum. "You're right. She was ropeable when Noah declared he was in love on MTV, so she'd do everything in her power to bury any stories on his plan to wed. But this...making Noah look like a drug addict. That's lower than low. We can't let her do this, Jake. We need to stop her."

"I think I know how." The anger lining her cheeks fades when I ask, "Will you be okay if I leave you with Noah for a couple of hours?"

"Yes, I guess—"

I cut off her confirmation by planting a kiss on her cheek. I hate leaving Noah, but this can't wait. "I'll be back in an hour. If anything happens, call me right away!" I shout while sprinting for the parking lot.

I'm not going to lie; my body kicks up a stink about my fast pace. My fitness has slithered down the drain the past eight weeks.

After throwing open my car door, I slip into the driver's seat. My fingers tap my steering wheel as effectively as my heart pounds my ribcage when my first turn of the keys has my engine roaring to life. With how long my car has been sitting unused, I'm shocked the battery has any charge.

My luck appears to have run out when the parking attendant advises me the amount required for me to exit the secure lot.

"How much?"

"One thousand, nine hundred, and sixty dollars," he repeats, his voice growing squeakier with every syllable he speaks.

"How the fuck is it so high?"

"The parking rate is thirty-five dollars a day. You've been parked here for eight weeks."

He gives me a look as if to say *you do the math.*

I do. It doesn't work out well for me.

After biting out a curse word, I hand the attendant my credit card. I'll most likely be hit with an overdraft fee, but I'll worry about that later.

I make the ten-mile trip from the hospital to my childhood home in record-breaking time. My speed was nearly as fast as my dad's when he gallops down the front stairs. "Is Noah okay?"

Guilt makes itself known with my gut. I haven't been home since the day Noah was transferred to Ravenshoe—not even for Christmas Day—so my unexpected arrival probably startled him half to death.

"He's fine, but I need that contract you stored for him in your safe."

Nodding, my dad follows me to the safe bolted to the floor in his office. He enters the combination—my mother's birthday—before handing me the document, which was right next to the contract I signed to be Isaac's fighter nearly two years ago.

"What's going on? Anything I can help with?"

"You know how you always said to read every line of a contract before signing it?" I pause so he can nod. "I don't apply that rule just to contracts I sign. I do it for others as well..." My words trail off when I find what I'm looking for. "And it's about to pay off."

I slap my father's cheeks before planting a sloppy peck to the edge of his mouth. "Thanks, Dad! You're a fucking lifesaver!"

He loses the chance to reprimand me for swearing when I tear out of his driveway as fast as I entered it.

"I'M SORRY, Mr. Walters, neither Cormack or Delilah are answering."

"Can you try Cormack's cell again? Tell him Jacob is waiting for him, and I'm not leaving until I see him." I point to a chair butted up against her desk. "I'll wait for him right there."

Destiny Records' head receptionist's throat works hard to swallow before she redials Cormack's number for the fourth time the past ten minutes.

An hour passes before Cormack *finally* strolls into the office. His low-hanging shoulders have me hesitant to approach him, but the bitch smirking at me from behind his shoulder quells any chance of me walking away quietly. Delilah is on his heels, looking as snarky as ever.

Peta, Cormack's receptionist, rushes to his side to announce he has a pesky visitor, but I beat her to the punch. That's not hard considering a man of my size only needs to stand to gain the attention of every person in a room.

"Jacob, what are you doing here?"

I slant my head to the side so I can lock my eyes on Delilah. "Maybe you should ask her that question?"

"What now?" Cormack mutters before shifting on his feet to face Delilah. She tries to act innocent, but it's a woeful waste of time. No one with eyes of the devil can pretend to be saintly. "Let's take this somewhere else."

Cormack waves his hand to a boardroom at the side of the foyer. When we enter, I move to the far side of the table. I don't want anything blocking my view when Delilah discovers what I have up my sleeve for her.

After sitting opposite me, Cormack locks his blue eyes with mine. "What can we help you with?"

"Fire her—*immediately*." My eyes stray to Delilah. "Then, if you're lucky, Rise Up will remain the star act of your record label."

Spit shoots out of Delilah's mouth like venom when she snarls, "Rise Up is contractually bound to Destiny Records, and nothing you or that silly little hick Noah wanted to marry say will change that."

"Is that right?" When Delilah slumps in her chair, believing she has the advantage, I lay out my winning hand. "The contract Noah signed is null and void."

I push the contract to their side of the desk. It's open to the section I was seeking earlier. A missed signature might not seem like much, but it's the equivalent of a fatal error on a legally binding document.

I can tell the exact moment Cormack spots what I'm referring to. He hisses out a curse word as his fingers rake through his hair. "What do you want?"

"Fire Delilah, or I'll encourage Emily—who happens to be Noah's power of attorney—to sign the country's current number one selling band to another label."

I anticipate for Cormack to react negatively to my demand, so you can imagine my surprise when he simply smiles before shifting his gaze to Delilah. "I'm sorry, Dee, but I have to let you go."

She shoots out of her chair like her ass is on fire. "Why are you letting this ape dictate what you do? You're the managing director of this company, yet you're allowing an imbecile bully you into firing me."

Delilah's face reddens with anger when Cormack mutters, "Be sure to have your desk cleared out by the end of the day."

"You're a..." Look up every swear word you've ever heard, then you'll have an idea of what Delilah just said. "This isn't the end! I'm taking this further."

After snatching her coat from her chair, she storms out of the office. She rambles the entire way, startling more than a dozen employees at Destiny Records.

Once her rant dulls to a hum, Cormack slumps low in his chair before making a tipi with his index fingers and thumbs. "How long have you known about the missing signature?"

A victorious grin stretches across my face. "Since the day Noah signed the contract."

"Then why didn't you say something? We could have used that when he was being sued!"

"I never got a chance. Isaac interrupted our conversation by offering to pay the amount Summit Hill was requesting. Although it wasn't ideal, I was confident Rise Up's record sales would easily cover their debt, so I held off until I needed it. Today I needed it."

Cormack smirks. "If only you had told me an hour ago, then I wouldn't have wasted my precious time searching for a legitimate way to fire her." He leans forward until his elbows are resting on the table. "I bumped into Delilah having a go at Emily—that's why I couldn't be reached. Emily assured me she's fine, but I think she's still a little rattled. You should probably go check to make sure she's okay."

When I stand, he slides Noah's contract back to my side of the desk. "What happens now?"

"That's up to Noah." I stuff the contract in the breast pocket of my jacket. "But I know him. If you do right by him, he'll have no reason to seek alternative representation."

Cormack isn't a bad guy; he just hired the wrong woman to represent Rise Up. For what reason, I don't know, but I'm glad it's over.

I wait for Cormack to nod before exiting the boardroom. After returning the contract to my dad's safe, I head back to the hospital. For the first time in weeks, my pulse is thrumming with excitement instead of fear. I can't wait to tell Noah and Emily about how I slayed a dragon without breaking a sweat.

Just as I enter Noah's hospital room, I'm blinded by a flash of light. After squinting to adjust my vision, I spot a man with a camera barging past Emily. When he elbows the little curve in her stomach, I see red.

"What the fuck are you doing in here?" I grab him by the scruff of his shirt so I can yank him into the hallway.

He fights me all the way. "Get off me; I'm just doing my job."

When he snaps another two pictures of Noah lying lifeless on his hospital bed, I snatch the camera out of his hand before searching for the SD card. Once it's in my hot little hand, I throw his camera to the ground then shatter it with my foot. I don't know if it has an internal memory, so I can't risk him having images on there.

As I hand Emily the SD card, the paparazzi venomously snarls, "You should turn off the life support. He'd be worth more dead than alive."

Rage fills me. It's hot, black, and ugly. Those are the *exact* words Noah's mom said when I called to tell her about Noah's accident.

"You fucking piece of shit!" In a blur of fury, I charge for him. I pole drive into him so hard, his head cracks the glass of the room opposite Noah's before he hits the floor like a bag of shit. Recklessly, and without pause for consideration, I rain my fists down on his face. I beat the living hell out of him, not stopping until two security officers drag me off him, and even then, an occasional fist hits its mark.

"You're arresting the wrong person. Jacob didn't do anything wrong. He's the one you should be arresting."

When I follow the direction of Emily's finger point, blood scorches my veins. The stupid fuck I just assaulted is smirking at me, like elbowing a pregnant woman who's attempting to protect her fiancé is funny.

I'll show him how funny it is.

After shrugging out of the security officers' hold, I dive for the unnamed man again. Two of his front teeth scatter across the floor a mere second before it feels like someone sets my eyelids on fire.

"Fuck!" I drop to my knees, my hands darting up to rub my eyes. The harder I scrub, the more they burn. It feels like someone poured gasoline over my head before tossing a match at me.

When someone wraps their arms around my shoulders, I yank away from them. I can't see anything through my swollen eyes, so I have no clue who is approaching me and for what reason.

"It's me." Emily's tone is as silky as the water she pours over my eyes after raising my head via my chin. "They hit you with pepper spray. This should help the burn." After dumping a bottle of water over my eyes, two round circles cover them. I can't be certain since I can't see two feet in front of me, but I'm reasonably sure they're the cucumber slices she picks off her sandwiches every day. She hates cucumber with a passion.

Once the burn lessens, so does the fury in my veins. "I'm sorry, Em—"

"Don't you dare apologize. You did *nothing* wrong." She stops to suck in a quick breath before advising me she'll be back.

Even though I can't see, my hearing works just fine. "You need to help him. He didn't do anything wrong. He was defending Noah."

"I don't know what I can do. It's not just the paparazzi pressing charges; the security officers are lining up as well." I hear a noise, like someone scrubbing stubble on their chin. "I'll do everything I can, but he needs a good lawyer."

I blink through the blur in front of me when someone helps me from the ground before circling cuffs around my wrists. I'm not one hundred percent certain, but I'm reasonably sure the blob of blue in front of me is Ryan.

My suspicions are confirmed when he says, "You have the right to remain silent. Anything you say can and will be used you against you in a court of law..."

CHAPTER FORTY-FOUR

LOLA

I slide a beer across the bar to Bob, one of Pete's regulars, before digging my ringing cell phone out of my pocket. Although Pete has a stern no phones at work policy, he gave me a free pass after I informed him about Noah's accident. He's adamant I can only use it in emergency situations, which I'm fine with. No one calls me anymore, so that's all it would be used for.

"Hello." My voice is apprehensive since I didn't recognize the number flashing across the screen.

I exhale my nerves with a big breath when my caller asks, "How's my pretty lady?"

"I'm good, Hank. You?" With my phone held to my ear by my shoulder, I refill the empty peanut containers on the bar. "Miss me already? I only left you at lunchtime."

"I always miss having a pretty lady around, but that's a story for another day."

Smiling, I ring up Tallas' tab before devoting my focus back to Hank. "I offered to hook you up. You keep denying my requests." I hand Tallas his change before pulling another beer for Bob. By keeping busy, I don't feel as guilty about breaking Pete's rules. "Have you changed your mind?"

"Do pigs fly?"

I shrug. "I don't know. Do they?"

A small stretch of silence passes between us. It's nothing new for us. We can go an hour without talking, and it never feels awkward.

What Hank says next, though, it's as awkward as it comes. "I know you say things are over between you and Jacob, but I know you still care about him, so I thought I oughta tell you what's going on."

"Okay..." I wait for him to fill in the gaps.

Mercifully, he doesn't leave me hanging for long. "Jacob has been arrested for assault and battery again."

"Is his original probation over?"

Hank sighs. "I don't know; he's cutting it close."

"Fuck." I have no better response. If he's convicted of assault while on probation, he won't skip jail this time. That's not a probability; it's a given.

"Where did they take him?"

"Ravenshoe PD. Meet you there?"

"Yep!"

After disconnecting my call, I race toward Pete's office. He grants my request to leave without a five-page explanation. It probably helps that I didn't elaborate that I'm going to the police station instead of the hospital like he assumes.

When I pull into an empty space at the front of the police station, I spot Hank waiting for me on the front steps. He's as uneasy about our visit as me; he just does a better job of hiding his emotions. I'm a jittering bag of nerves.

As we enter the lobby, I scan the area. There are dozens of men and women in blue, but I'm not looking for a uniform. I'm seeking a familiar blue suit.

I find it a few seconds later. "Ryan!"

He inches back from the interrogation room to crank his neck my way. When he realizes it's me, apprehension washes over his face. If that didn't occur more times than I can count the past few months, it would bother me more than it does.

"I'm doing everything I can, but it's out of my hands this time." Ryan's low tone sinks my heart into my gut.

"Can we see him?"

My heart slides straight past my stomach to collide with my feet when he shakes his head. "He's in the process of being charged with three counts of battery."

"Three counts?" When Ryan nods, I ask, "Is his original probation period over?"

His nod turns into a shake. "He had one week left. That's why it's out of my hands. It's higher than me."

My tongue darts out to replenish my lips with moisture, but no amount of wetness makes my next question any easier to ask. "Will he go to jail?"

Tears burn my eyes when Ryan replies, "Most likely."

"Is there anything we can do?" This question comes from Hank.

Ryan shakes his head again. "If he didn't have his original conviction, we would have had a better shot of keeping him out of jail, but with that hanging over his head..." An uneasy shrug finalizes his reply. "I'm sorry. I wish I had better news; I just don't."

His gaze flicks between Hank and me for many heart-thrashing seconds before he pivots on his heels and walks away.

Just the thought of Jacob going to jail makes me sick to my stomach. I can't let this happen to him. If he weren't protecting me, he would have never been on probation...

I stop reflecting when a brilliant idea pops into my head. After telling Hank to wait for me outside, I dash to the desk clerk, praying she'll have answers to the questions I have.

She's not overly smart, and she's somewhat deaf, but she slathers my idea with so much sugary goodness, I'm on the verge of becoming diabetic by the time I join Hank outside.

"I need your help, but you can't tell anyone what we're about to do."

Hank's nearly black eyes stare deeply into mine. "Is it illegal?"

I grimace. "Quite possibly?"

He twists his lips. "Okay, then. Let's do this. What have I got to lose?"

MY THIGHS QUIVER with every stair I climb at the house I used to call home. It's different than I remember. Darker and more lifeless. There are more weeds in the planters I put under the windowsill than flowers, and the screen door has more holes than an eighteen-hole golf course.

I'm about to knock when the creak of old wood under my feet announces my arrival before I can. "Look what the cat dragged in." Callum strolls down the long hallway of his childhood home, his eyes darting between Hank and me. "And to what do I owe the pleasure?"

Pretending he didn't just swipe his index finger under his nose like all drugs addicts do to ensure they get every last morsel of powder they're sniffing, I ask, "Can we come in?"

After a short period of contemplation, Callum jerks up his chin. "He looks harmless enough."

He shouldn't underestimate Hank. I've seen him take down men twice his size.

When we enter the living room at the front of Callum's house, he zooms around to clean up the mess of beer cans and pizza boxes covering nearly every surface. Although his home is a dump, nothing can distract me from seeing the three lines of white powder on his glass coffee table.

"I thought you were clean?"

Callum shrugs like it isn't a big deal he's using again. "Thought if I were clean, you'd come home, but that never happened, did it?"

After pushing the debris from his sofa onto the floor, he gestures for me and Hank to sit.

"I'd rather stand."

"Of course you would, because you'd never do anything I ask without first whining." After tossing a moldy pizza box into his unlit fireplace, sending ash floating across the room, he turns his massively dilated eyes to me. "Is there a reason for your visit? Or did you just come here to fuck with my head all over again?"

I nearly rebut, but Hank's jacket brushing my wrist when he puts himself between Callum and me reminds me that my trip down memory lane isn't about me. It's not even about Callum. It's for Jacob.

"I want you to amend the statement you issued to Ravenshoe PD two years ago." My voice is surprisingly firm for how hard my heart is raging. "I want it changed to say you hit Jacob first."

Callum cocks his brow as a grin inches his cheeks high. "And why the fuck would I do that?"

"Because if you don't, I'll have you charged with attempted murder. You choked me with the intent to kill me. That's more than a standard assault charge. "

Hank's eyes rocket to mine at the same time Callum laughs. "That was years ago. You don't have a leg to stand on."

"There's no statute of limitation for attempted murder, which means I can proceed with charges at *any* time. The photos the detective took of my neck and wrist are damning enough, let alone the official statements from Maggie and me. You'll go away for a very long time if you don't follow my demands."

Callum's smirk doubles. He's not convinced. I'm sure I can get him over the fence.

"I wonder how many years the DA will add to your sentence when the arresting officers tell him about the white powder you have all over your house." I nudge my head to the cocaine lines on his coffee table. "I'm sure that's not the only coke you have stashed here."

I yank my phone out of my pocket and dial two numbers: nine and one. My finger hovers over the one when Callum swipes his hands through the air. "Hold on, just wait a minute. Give me some time to consider your suggestion." When he skittishly peers at the silver chest that used to hold his mother's ashes, I realize my assumption that's he's hiding drugs is accurate. "I can't just have Jacob un-arrested. It doesn't work that way."

"I didn't ask you to do that. All you need to say is that you swung at him first. If it's self-defense, Jacob's original probation period could be shortened."

Callum throws his hands in the air. "Why does it matter? He only has a week left."

"It matters, Callum. Not just to Jacob, but to me as well. I made a mistake not having you prosecuted. I should have told them what you did just so Jacob wouldn't have to live with a conviction hanging over his head for the rest of his life."

Callum hears something in my confession I didn't mean to expose. "You love him." He drags his fingers through his hair before tugging the ends into spikes. "I can't believe this. You're bringing *this* here! Into *my* fucking home to save *him*." He thrusts his hand to his front door like Jacob is standing behind it. "What the fuck does he have that I don't have? Is it money? A big dick? What?!"

When Hank attempts to pull me behind him, I sidestep him. What I'm about to say should have been said years ago. I'm not willing to hold it back for a second longer. "That isn't what this is about. It's about justice and doing the right thing. Jacob didn't assault you for no reason, Callum. He did it because he cares about me like you once did—"

"*Still* do," Callum corrects.

With a shake of my head, I fold my arms in front of my chest. "That isn't true. If you cared about me, you wouldn't have hurt me."

"I was high! I didn't know what the fuck I was doing."

"That time, but what about the first time you shoved me, and the second and third? What about the time you beat me until I was barely recognizable? What were your excuses then?"

Sparks of the boy I once knew flash through his eyes when they glisten with tears. "I made a mistake, one I've regretted every day since."

"But not enough to do the right thing." I throw a palm in his face, brushing off his supposed regret. "I'm over this. You don't care about anyone but yourself, so why should I give a shit if you get locked up for years?"

After hitting the one on my phone, I press it against my ear. Callum is too spaced out on drugs to realize I didn't hit the call connect button. "Alright, alright! Fuck, Lola. I'll do it. I'll say I swung at him first."

CHAPTER FORTY-FIVE

JACOB

Three days after being released on bail, I'm nervously tapping my foot in the court chambers with another dozen delinquents waiting for their turn before the judge. I've rehearsed my plea nonstop the past two hours, praying a sob story will make the judge lenient on me. From what I'm hearing, even pleading guilty won't stop me from spending time behind bars this time around. I fucked up, but come on, after the hard few months I've had, tell me you wouldn't have reacted the same way?

My eyes float up from the floor when Michael, Jenni's dad, rushes my way. He only agreed to represent me after Jenni reached out to him. Things have been tense with them since Jasper's birth. I don't know what caused their rift, but I'm glad it didn't stop Jenni from seeking his assistance. Michael is a brilliant lawyer, and from what Ryan said during my incarceration at Ravenshoe PD, I need the best lawyer money can buy.

"You're one lucky son of a bitch."

After yanking me to my feet like his belly isn't the size of Santa's, he straightens the knot in my tie, then gestures for me to enter the courtroom door we're standing next to. I do a double-take when we enter. The judge is already seated at the podium, and he bears an uncanny resemblance to famous actor Morgan Freeman. If I weren't seconds from spending the next three-plus years in jail, I'd snap his picture to show Emily. Alas, freaky resemblances will have to wait until my livelihood isn't on the line.

Michael gestures for me to sit in the pew behind the defense's table before requesting permission to approach the bench. When his request is granted, he hands the judge a single piece of paper. They discuss the particulars of my case, but I can't hear a word they're speaking.

Once they've finished their chat, the judge gestures for me to move forward. My nerves are so rattled, my legs shake with every step I take. Here it is; I'm about to be handed my fate.

Please, God, don't take me away from Lola for years. We've already endured our share of unfair separations.

I'd give anything to have just an hour alone with Lola. To see her smile, smell her skin. To feel her pulse flutter under my fingers when we kiss, but since I didn't want to burden her with my stupidity, she's unaware I'm facing sentencing today. Excluding Emily, Michael, and Ryan, no one knows. I didn't even tell my dad. I don't know why. He is who I get my strength from. I just didn't want to see his disappointment. It's bad enough seeing it in Lola's eyes. I don't want to see it in his too.

My eyes drop from the ceiling when the judge says, "After speaking with your lawyer, I've reduced the four-year sentence I had planned to serve you to six months' probation with five hundred hours of community service." I stare at him in astonishment, certain I heard him wrong. "Along with your community service, you'll be required to attend mandatory counseling for anger management."

I remain quiet, muted by shock. Ryan said I had no chance of escaping incarceration, so how the fuck did I only get six months' probation?

When the judge smacks down his gavel, Michael's feet lift an inch off the ground. His celebration shifts to a more respectable one when the judge's bushy brow arches high. "Thank you, Judge, thank you. That's a very fair verdict."

After banding his arm around my shoulders, he guides me outside. The cool afternoon is heavenly to my overheated skin, but I'm still stunned.

"How did you do that?" Emily said he was a good lawyer, but she failed to mention he performed magic tricks.

"I don't deserve all the credit." Modesty will never be his strong point. He only needs to fan out some feathers, and he'd have the peacock look down pat. "The judge overturned your original conviction, which means you didn't have a prior conviction on your criminal record. A standard sentence for a first-time offender is probation and, if you're unlucky, community service."

"My original conviction got overturned?"

Michael chuckles at the bewilderment in my tone. "Yes—"

"How?"

"The DA was handed compounding evidence. The judge had no choice but to overturn your previous conviction." He whacks me in the chest with the manila folder he's holding. "Why do you look so worried? You should be celebrating."

"I'm happy. I'm just... shocked."

"Shocked works. Shocked is still living. I can handle shocked." After exhaling so harshly, he ruffles my hair, he nudges his head to the doors he just forced me through. "How about we get this wrapped up so you can be shocked anywhere but here? I've got golf to play."

When I roll my eyes, he slaps my shoulder. "If you dis golf, I'll be tempted to lose the evidence that just saved your ass. I don't have much to look forward to these days other than chasing that little white ball around acres of rolled turf."

"Not even your grandson?"

The distress my face has been holding the past ten minutes leaps onto Michael's. "Grandson? What grandson?"

My silence says more than my words ever could, and it jumps

Michael into action. Within twenty minutes, I'm sitting in my car with my probation documentation on my passenger seat and the business card for my new therapist in my wallet. I'm also harboring a shit-ton of grief. I didn't realize Michael was unaware Jenni gave birth months ago.

On my way back to the hospital, I dig my cell phone out of my pocket to power it up. Within seconds of turning on, it indicates I've received a text message.

Lola: *Good luck today xx*

This is the first text I've received from her in over eight weeks, but it isn't the reason for my gaped jaw. How did she know what was going on today? As I said earlier, neither Emily nor I told anyone about my second brush with the law.

Like a flash of lightning in the sky, it dawns on me. Lola was one of a small handful of people who knew about my first conviction.

Does that mean...?

Did she...?

Am I still in with a chance?

A car behind me honks when I complete an illegal U-turn to direct my car away from the hospital. It's nearly two PM on a Tuesday, meaning the answers I'm seeking are in the opposite direction of the way I was traveling.

MY STOMACH LURCHES when I enter Hank's gym, then it leaps when a giggle I'd never forget sounds through my ears. "You'll get used to it. From what I've been told, the funky smell grows on you—let's hope they mean figuratively."

After dropping a sweaty towel on the bench next to us, Lola slings her glove-covered hands around my neck. "I'm glad you're not behind bars. We were getting worried when we didn't hear anything."

When she pulls back, it's the fight of my life to let her go. I wouldn't if I hadn't seen Hank jogging toward us from the corner of my eye. "Jacob!" He replaces Lola's arms with his own. "It's been so long since I've seen you." After pulling back, he pokes his index finger into my stomach. "If you stay away too much longer, you'll get pudgy on the inside."

He's joking, but it doesn't stop my spine from straightening when Lola's hooded gaze floats my way. When she smiles, my heart races. I know that smile. I know it very well. She still digs me.

Once Hank unties her gloves, she smiles before sauntering toward the locker rooms. "It was nice seeing you, Jacob."

She's engulfed by steam before I can assure her the pleasure was all mine. I stare at the empty entrance for several heart-thrashing seconds before shifting on my feet to face Hank. "How's she doing?" She looks tired, but she's still as gorgeous as ever.

"She's good." Hank's smile fades into a frown. "Why didn't you tell me what her ex did to her?"

"She told you about that?" The disbelief in my tone makes my words come out louder than intended. I'm not angry. I'm more shocked than anything. Lola was adamant she didn't want anyone to know what happened to her, so I'm surprised she was upfront with Hank. Don't get me wrong, she isn't a liar, but she's a pro at sidestepping interrogations.

"Not in so many words, but yeah, she told me, but why didn't you? I was mad for weeks after your arrest. If you'd told me what had happened, I would have understood. I'm not a complete asshole."

Recalling the words Maggie said to me years ago, I notch up my shoulder. "It wasn't my story to tell."

I never understood what Maggie meant that night, but I have more comprehension now. When Callum assaulted Lola, he didn't just make Lola lose her faith in him; she lost it in everyone. Trust takes years to build, seconds to break, and a lifetime to repair. I should have remembered that when rumors circulated that Lola was back with Callum. She doesn't trust him because she doesn't trust anyone—*not even me.*

With my shoulders hanging lower than they were seconds ago, my eyes drift to the locker room. I can feel Hank's gaze burning a hole in the side of my head, but nothing can take away from the movie rolling through my head. Lola and I had so much fun in that shower stall. I taught her how to protect herself mere minutes before she taught me she already knew how. That's why her shell is so hard. She protects herself by keeping everyone away—*everyone except me.* Not a single fight I've won the past two years was more victorious than breaking through Lola's shell. It was my hardest-fought battle, and I'm not even halfway through it yet.

Spotting my forlorn look, Hank nudges me toward the locker room. "Go talk to her, Jake."

"I can't."

If I endure the hurt look in her eyes one more time, I might snap like I did three days ago when I knocked out the paparazzi's teeth. I don't know who the fuck that man was, but I'm reasonably sure he wasn't me. I don't react in violence. I'm the easy-going, *never let anything bother me* guy. I just... snapped.

Hank moves to stand in front of me with the same determined look he had every time I argued I wasn't ready for my first fight. His gloves are on and ready to pummel some sense into me. "Why not?"

I scratch my brow while sighing. "It's complicated—"

"Complicated, my ass. You two are just too stubborn for your own good!" He gets right up in my face like a drill sergeant screaming orders at a private. "Go and talk to her, or I'll ride your ass so hard, you won't sit for a week."

He pushes me until I'm standing in front of the women's locker room entrance. I'm double his weight, so I could easily push him off if I wanted to, but maybe he's right? Perhaps we should talk. Silence hasn't gotten me anywhere fast, so perhaps it's time to try something new.

The nerves jittering in my stomach are audible in my voice when I ask Lola, "Is it safe to come in?"

Hank chuckles at my corniness. He can laugh. He hasn't experienced the wrath of an angry Lola.

My zipper bites my cock when Lola replies, "It's not like you haven't seen it all before, Jacob."

My eyes bug out of my head when I enter. Lola is standing in front of a row of mirrors. She has a tiny towel wrapped around her curvy body. That's it—just a towel. A. *Tiny*. Towel.

Pretending I'm not seconds from coming like a virgin dipping his hand into a cookie jar for the first time, I pace closer to her. I try to keep my eyes on her face. I horrifically fail. I've spent hours upon hours studying every delicious inch of her body, yet I've still got so much left to discover. Her body is pure dynamite. There's no better word to describe it. Tight, compact, and so explosive, it'll impact more than your heart when she explodes.

Noticing my not-so-inconspicuous gawk, Lola stops brushing her hair to gaze at me in the mirror. "How long has it been?" She shakes like someone just walked over her grave. "Actually, I don't want to know."

Her uneasy expression reminds me why I'm here. "Did you get my original conviction overturned?"

She cranks her back to peer at me, her mouth as open as her eyes. "It got overturned?" When I nod, she spins, spans the distance between us, then leaps into my arms. "Holy shit, I didn't think it would get overturned!"

Her beautiful scent is enough to have my cock raring to life, much less the heat of her body plastered to mine. Relishing having her in my arms again, I hold her close before inhaling her scent. She smells fresh and pure, a smell a woman as seductive as her shouldn't be able to pull off.

When she wiggles, requesting to be set down, I comply—reluctantly. Her request for space comes to light when her eyes drop to the crotch of my pants. "You need to watch where you point that thing. I don't recall signing up for pole vaulting classes."

I'm hard enough to drill the soap scum off the tiles surrounding us without a jackhammer. "Sorry." I adjust my cock so it's not pitching a tent. Now it's just peeking out the top of pants like a creeper about to get freaky in the bushes outside. "I'll wait for you outside. I can't control this..." I nudge my head down. "...with you looking like *that*."

Lola proves why she's deserving of her nickname when she giggles.

Fuck, I've missed her laugh, but nowhere near as much as I've missed her.

CHAPTER FORTY-SIX

LOLA

When Jacob bolts out of the locker room, uneasy excitement trickles into my veins. My ego is stoked I can still spark a reaction out of him, but I'm also apprehensive. Not even the best battery operated boyfriend can compete with the real thing, and when you've felt the best of the best rubbing against your stomach, it will take more than a multi-combination vibrator to forget it.

Fake it until you make it, Lola, I chant to myself.

After getting dressed and prepping my face for no particular reason, I exit the locker room. Although Jacob said he'd wait for me outside, I'm still shocked to see him leaning against the interior wall of the gym. I'm not a person who gets ready in two minutes, so I figured he'd have better ways to occupy his time than waiting around for me.

"Hey?" Don't ask why my greeting sounded like a question. I don't know why I'm a ditz with half a brain when I'm with Jacob, so how could I possibly give you an explanation for the insanity?

"Hey." Jacob drags his eyes down my body before returning them to my face. "Clothes aren't helping."

When he adjusts his crotch, the tension bristling between us floats away. He's not a metaphor. He's Jacob, the man who knows me better than anyone.

"Where's Hank?" His office light is off, and he's nowhere in sight.

"He had to head home. He asked if we could lock up for him once we're done." Missing the alarmed expression on my face, Jacob nudges his head to the front door. "Do you have time to talk?"

"Umm..." I drop my eyes to my watch. "Yeah. I'm not due at work for another two hours."

While following Jacob outside, I scan the premises. Hank has to be here because he has nowhere else to go. I find him hiding in the alleyway of the gym, watching Jacob and me like a hawk. When he raises his index finger to his lips, requesting I keep quiet, I nod. Relief crosses his features. I don't know why. I only agreed to keep his secret because Jacob has enough on his plate right now. Once the groove between his brows smooths, I won't hesitate to tell him precisely what I think about Hank's living conditions.

After slipping the key under the mat, Jacob curls his hand around mine before guiding me to his car. His chivalry isn't unusual, but holding his hand in public is foreign. Excluding Bronte's Peak, we've never done PDA. Expensive misdemeanor fines would make even the most affectionate couple cautious.

"Don't," Jacob murmurs under his breath when he opens my door for me.

"I wasn't going to say anything." I was, but I'm not now.

Jacob's cheeky grin remains on his face for the ten minutes of our trip, then it bounces to mine when he pulls into the parking lot at the back of Mavericks. I haven't been to Mavs in years, but it will always feel like home to me.

Although Jacob doesn't open my door for me, he continues to hold my hand as we make our way to the bar. It's the same as it's always been, just a couple of years older. With Maggie nowhere in sight, Jacob places an order for two beers from a beautiful blonde behind the counter. For how often she bats her eyelashes at him, anyone would swear he ordered her for dessert. Her flirting pisses me off. He's holding my hand, for fuck's sake, yet she still goes there. *Someone call up the old biddies. There's a new harlot in town.*

The envy turning me green slides away when Jacob doesn't flirt back with her. He's too busy peering at me beneath lowered lashes to pay her any attention, and I'm not the only one noticing. When the hostess slams down our beers hard enough to froth the tops, I give her a snarky wink.

Take that, bitch. Not even your fake titties could persuade him to take a second look.

I sip on my beer, smiling like a smug bitch as Jacob guides us to a booth at the back of the bar. I'm still not a fan of beer, but if I don't drink something, nothing will douse the victorious fire raring in my gut.

After slipping into the seat across from me, Jacob's eyes float across his old stomping ground. "Being back here nearly makes me forget everything going on."

Because his comment is more rhetorical, I don't say anything. I put the silence to good use by roaming my eyes over his face. Dark rings circle his eyes, and the scruff on his chin is the thickest I've ever seen it, but he's still gorgeous. I just wish I could see what's going on in that head of his. He dropped everything to support Noah like he has many times in his short almost twenty-four years. That's a massive burden to be placed on anyone's shoulders, even if they're as strong as Jacob's.

I slant my head to the side when an accented voice says, "There's the final piece of the puzzle I've been seeking the past two months."

Flynn is standing next to our table. He has a beer in his hand and a broad grin etched on his handsome face, although I don't see it lasting with how many daggers Jacob is shooting his way. He's glaring at him. I don't mean a friendly, *hey mate, how's it going?* glare. He's staring like he's seconds from digging his intestines out via his back entrance.

Either oblivious to Jacob's anger or blindly brave, Flynn locks his eyes with me. "It was Jacob, wasn't it? The one you ran off for?" His tone is neither angry or upset. He's more curious than anything.

One of Jacob's daggers misses its mark when I timidly nod. I'm not agreeing with Flynn to save his life. I just hate lying.

"I knew it." The neck of Flynn's beer bottle can't hide his mammoth grin. "Then I guess I should leave you love birds to talk." His eye drift to Jacob. "Nice seeing you again, mate."

When Jacob jerks up his chin, Flynn moseys to his bandmates sitting at the table Rise Up once commanded. Although Jacob's anger isn't as volatile as when Flynn interrupted us, his angry scowl remains. His gaze is enough to set my skin on fire, and not in a bad way. I'm heating up everywhere, which equally frustrates and excites me.

"I didn't sleep with Flynn." Huffing, I fold my arms under my chest. "But you have no right to question me, Jacob. Not after what you had splashed all over the internet."

His scowl is replaced with confusion. "You didn't sleep with Flynn?"

Typical male, only hearing what he wants to hear.

"No, I didn't."

My heart skips a beat when a massive grin raises his cheeks high. I haven't seen him smile like this in months, and as much as it pains me to admit, I've missed it so much.

When my tongue darts out to replenish my lips, the sexual tension brewing between us turns blistering. It's as hot and heavy as the pulse in my pussy from his smile.

"Don't even think about it." I give him a stern finger point. "You've got a lot of explaining to do before you'll ever get into my panties again."

Groaning, he adjusts his crotch. "Please don't say panties again. I'm wound up so fucking tight right now, I might explode." He sounds like he's in pain. "I found out weeks ago that blue balls do exist. I thought it was just a manufactured line guys use to get into a girl's cookie jar, but it isn't. It's a real medical issue."

When I giggle, he glares at me. "I'm deadly serious."

I laugh even louder. It's not a ladylike laugh. I chuckle so hard, tears stream down my face, and I'm hit with an urgent need to pee. "God save the lady who has to handle that eruption. I hope she's confident—"

"Confident enough to know I'd never want anyone but her."

My spine snaps straight as my eyes rocket to Jacob. He's staring straight at me, ensuring that even if I missed the innuendo in his tone, I can't miss the honesty in his eyes.

The hope in his eyes fades away when I slump low in my chair. There's nothing more I'd like to do than climb onto his lap and take out my sexual frustration on him, but I'm still hurt about the pictures I saw months ago. Why can he question me about Flynn, but not expect to face his own interrogation when he gets "friendly" with a random blonde at a bachelor party? That's not fair. We never agreed to be exclusive, but what's good for one is good for the other.

Trying to push our conversation back onto mutual ground, I ask, "What happened in court today?"

I'm dying to discover what happened with Jacob and the blonde in the photos, but now is not the time to ask him. He's juggling too many things at the moment. If I add another prickly subject matter, who's to say he won't drop everything? I want to pretend I don't know the man sitting across from me, but I do. I know him well enough to say he's only holding on by a thread. That's why I refuse to cut it. I don't mind being seen as his predator, but I never want to be seen as his destroyer.

"I got six months' probation and community service. My community service will be served at Hopeton House. It's a youth home for kids who have nowhere else to go." He glances past my shoulder, staring at nothing in particular. "The only negative is they scheduled me to be at the house twenty-four hours a day, Monday through Friday, starting this week, which means I have to break my promise to Noah."

"I'm sure he'll understand." He's been there for Noah more than anyone ever expected, so I'm confident in my declaration. "If not, I'll be sure to kick his ass when he wakes."

Jacob laughs, taking my comment as I had intended: playfully.

After taking a swig of his beer, he returns his eyes to mine. I'm glad they're not as pained as they were when we arrived. "How did you get the conviction overturned?"

"Who said it was me?"

He cocks his brow, calling out my deceit without words.

I shrug like it wasn't a big deal. "I threatened to press charges against Callum if he didn't change his statement. Although he wasn't pleased I showed up uninvited, he did as requested."

Jacob lets out a low growl. "Please tell me you didn't go to his house alone?"

"I didn't..." He releases a sharp breath that's quickly redrawn when I add on, "I took Hank with me."

CHAPTER FORTY-SEVEN

JACOB

Shock is the first thing that hits me from Lola's confession, closely followed by relief. Hank is harmless... until you piss him off. I found out just how tough he is in the days following my arrest. He didn't hold back in the ring, meaning I was sporting more than just bruised knuckles. Because I understood his anger, I took it in stride. My arrests didn't just flush my dreams down the toilet; they killed Hank's as well. I plan to make it up to him. I just haven't worked out how yet.

I'm drawn from my thoughts when Lola says, "I'm sorry, Jacob, but I have to go. I'm due at work in an hour, and I've still got to get back to Erkinsvale."

Nodding, I slip out of my seat. "I should head out too. Em is most likely panicked out of her mind that I've been gone so long."

If it were any other person but Lola standing across from me, the possessiveness in my tone would have caused conflict. Mercifully, Lola is as confident as she is beautiful. She knows I'm not supporting Emily because I want to get into her panties. It's because not everyone is as strong as her.

We make our trip back to Hank's Gym in silence. It isn't

awkward, more that Lola needs a few minutes to figure out what she wants to say. I understand the cause of her long deliberation when my car pulling in beside her Jeep coincides with her lips landing on my mouth. It's the briefest peck, but the accompanying words are enough to coerce the most suicidal man off the ledge. "I miss you, Jacob."

I lose the chance to tell her I miss her too when she bolts out of my car, jumps into her Jeep, then races out of the parking lot like a woman on a mission. I hate the missed opportunity, but nothing can wipe the smile off my face. Today has been a good day. I escaped a jail sentence, found out Lola didn't sleep with Flynn, and she admitted she misses me. Some may say the last one isn't a victory, but they obviously don't know Lola. Just her admitting she misses me is huge—nearly as big as those other three little words I'd give my left nut to hear come out of her mouth.

***

WHEN I STRUT BACK into Noah's hospital room—*yeah, I'm strutting like a peacock*—I notice Emily is on a call. Not wanting to interrupt her, I prop my shoulder on the doorframe to wait. It's only when she asks her caller if Lola has seen me do I announce my arrival with a cough. Her eyes snap to mine so fast, I'm certain she's now dizzy.

She tells her caller she has to go before racing across the room to throw herself into my arms. "You're back!" The vanilla cloud that engulfs me pops a reckless, yet hopeful idea into my head.

After tugging Emily closer to my body, I move to stand next to Noah's bed. "Come on, Noah, don't act like you don't want to get out of that bed and kick my ass." If anything will get a rise out of Noah, it will be me using Emily as bait. "I have your girl in my arms, and you're not going to do anything about it?"

Not recognizing my ploy to stimulate a response from Noah, Emily slaps me across the chest. "Don't be an ass, Jacob."

With my mind still hazy from my unexpected afternoon, a chuckle rumbles in my chest. One, Emily can't scowl no matter how hard she tries, and two, she hits like a girl. She and Lola couldn't be more opposite if they tried. Lola would put me on my ass for laughing at her, but Emily's slap was like a fly colliding with my chest.

My laughter is nipped in the bud when I realize my ploy worked. Noah's fist is clenched. It isn't as tight as the one he shook at me when I let gaping holes in the defensive line back in our football days, but it's still a fist all the same.

"I knew you wouldn't be able to help yourself." After setting Emily on her feet, I curl my hand around his fist. It firms even more. "Come on, wake up and kick my ass." *Then I won't need to break my promise.* "You know I wasn't just hugging her. My crotch also got friendly with her thigh. What can I say? I'm a horny dog, and her leg was mighty enticing."

My eyes rocket to Emily when Noah's hand I'm not clutching lifts from the bed. "Get a nurse."

While she does that, I move Noah's hand away from the ventilator. His eyes are closed, but there's no doubt he's seconds from yanking out the tube responsible for his breathing the past two months.

My eyes lift when Emily's return to the room is closely followed by a plump nurse. "Help him."

"We can't remove the ventilator tube before conducting a set of complex tests. If we remove it too soon, his lungs may collapse."

She flicks the top of a syringe filled with murky liquid before emptying it into the IV line in Noah's wrist. Not long later, Noah stops fighting against my hold. Although I'm shocked beyond belief at his strength, guilt is hammering me. The last time I held him down like this was when he tried to hurt himself after Chris's funeral. He smashed the mirror in this seedy motel he went to drown his miseries in. Even though the shards of glass scattered around his feet never got near his wrists, I knew him well enough to know the thought was there.

Once Noah settles enough I'm not worried about him hurting himself, I raise my eyes to the nurse completing a set of observations on him. "Why can't you take it out? He obviously doesn't want it in there."

"When patients have been on a ventilator as long as Noah has, they need to be weaned off it. If we just remove it, there's a possibility his lungs could collapse. We'll start the process of weaning now. If he handles that, we'll fully remove it within a few days."

THEY REMOVED Noah's tube four days later. Although his heart rate initially climbed, he maintained the oxygen levels the doctors were aiming for. It was a day of firsts for both of us. A couple of hours after his tube was removed, I attended my first anger management class. Let me just say, it isn't my cup of tea.

Then, the very next morning, I have to leave again—longer this time. My probation officer is adamant I either do community service as stated or become a prisoner of the state for the same period of time. Although I hate breaking the promise I made to Noah, it'd be ten times worse if I didn't have the option to return every weekend.

"I'll come back and visit every weekend, I promise." I wrap Emily up in a tight embrace. "If anything happens, call me straight away."

"I will, I promise."

She wipes away the tears sitting high on her cheeks before watching me say goodbye to Noah. It's even harder than I predicted. I'm confident Emily has everything under control. It just sucks realizing that not all promises can be kept. I can only hope Lola is right, and that Noah will understand when he wakes.

After messing up Noah's hair—I know how much he hates it—I spin on my heels and dart out of the room without so much of a backward glance. If I look back, I may never leave. I rush away like Lola did, knowing there's a right time and place for everything. Right now isn't our time, but she'll be my forever. I'll make sure of it.

When my elevator arrives at the lobby, I think I'm out of the danger zone.

I'm an idiot.

Just as I step into the sterile-smelling space, I spot a face I never expected to see. Noah's mom is at the reception desk. She dressed up for the occasion with silky slacks and a shirt that costs more than a medical receptionist can afford.

I stomp her way, certain she's only visiting for one reason: she wants money. "What are you doing here?"

Maree's evil eyes lift to mine. "I want to visit my son, but supposedly there's no one named Noah Taylor at this hospital."

Maree stops glaring at the receptionist like she's gum stuck under a bus seat when I drag her to the side of the desk. I'm not an aggressive person, so my clutch on her arm would usually cause me to feel guilty, but after witnessing the way she treated Noah at Michael's funeral, she lost any right to be treated like a lady. The person standing before me is nothing but a vindictive, conniving, two-faced monster.

"Why are you really here? Did you run out of money—*again*?"

Her eyes narrow into thin slits. "That's no concern of yours."

"No concern of mine? You had no issues taking my money previously, so what's changed?"

I put money in her account every month for the past year in the hope it would keep her claws out of Noah. I only canceled the deposit arrangement after Noah informed me she had signed a nondisclosure agreement.

"It's just dawned on you that your bottomless money pit dried up, hasn't it—?"

"Is he dead?"

I nearly shake my head, until the excitement in her tone slams into me. She's not upset at the prospect her only son may be dead. She's hopeful.

What the fuck?

She thrashes against me, trying to remove herself from my firm grip. "Let me go. I have to call a lawyer." Her smirk reveals she's even more psychotic than I thought.

When she slips out of my grip, she hobbles toward the hospital exit, her brisk departure thwarted by more than the high heels on her shoes. It's also from me shouting, "Even in his death, you won't get a cent."

She flashes me an evil grin over her shoulder. "Like hell I won't."

Her attitude is way too superior for my liking. I better knock her down a peg or two. "Noah had his will drawn up not long before his accident. He made Emily his power of attorney and had it notarized that you were *not* to get one penny from his estate in the event of his death."

"He'd never be so barbaric. I'm his mother!"

"Who's undeserving of the title." Needing distance before I say or do something I regret, I dart past Maree and break through the double glass doors of Ravenshoe Private Hospital. "Enjoy living in the gutter, where you belong."

CHAPTER FORTY-EIGHT

LOLA

My brisk pace slows when I hear someone call my name. I pause entering Hank's Gym to peer back at the person accosting me early on a Monday morning. My palms slick with sweat when I realize it's Curtis—Callum's brother. I haven't seen him since I socked him in the nose nearly a year ago.

When he stops at my side, he slants his head before planting his infamous evil grin on his face. "So this is where you learned your famous right hook from, hey? It's been so long, I was beginning to wonder if that night was a figment of my imagination."

"I can hit you again, if you like? Then you can be assured it wasn't a dream."

Curtis shakes his head. "Always riled up."

"Always an asshole."

My comment was only for my ears, but from the way his eyes narrow, I'm certain he heard it. When the tint on the window next to my shoulder darkens, I realize we have company. Hank won't step in unless necessary, but I'd rather keep him out of a fight he doesn't belong in any more than Jacob does.

"What do you want, Curtis?"

He steps closer to me, bringing the shadow inside Hanks gym closer as well. "I don't want anything. I just noticed you walking by and thought I should say hello. I haven't seen you around. Kinda missed ya."

When he trails the back of his hand down my cheek, my nerves set on edge. He's not a sweet, *missed you* type of guy. He's a menace who'd rather have his dates quaking in fear than ecstasy.

Just as rusty hinges creaking open sounds through my ears, Curtis winks before sauntering to his truck parked in the middle of the empty lot. The anxiety wreaking havoc with my stomach doubles when I notice he isn't traveling alone. Callum is sitting in the passenger seat. It's clear his brush with the law didn't scare him into coming clean. His already svelte frame is missing even more pounds.

Once the taillights of Curtis' truck blur into the distance, Hank joins me on the sidewalk. "Everything okay?"

"Yeah, I think so."

I want to give a more confident reply, but I can't shake the feeling that Curtis is up to something. Hank's gym is tucked at the back of a shopping complex. There's no way he spotted me because he was driving past. He went out of his away to approach me.

I shift on my feet to face Hank. "Will you reconsider my offer?" When Hank huffs before entering the gym, I chase him down. "Just think about it. You need a place to stay; I need a roommate. It's a win-win for both of us..."

My words trail off when I'm subjected to his narrowed gaze. "A fifty-seven-year-old man doesn't sleep on the couch of a twenty-three-year-old woman without rumors circulating. What would people think?"

"You'd be the envy of every old geezer in town."

Hank tries to maintain his stern expression. He should never give up his day job. Acting is not his forte. "I'm gracious for the offer, but I'm fine how I am." His thankful eyes bounce between mine before he pulls out the rug from beneath my feet. "Now, get your ass into the ring and give me thirty burpees."

"Thirty?!" I must have heard him wrong. I hate burpees, and Hank knows this.

"Argue with me again, and I'll bump it up to a hundred."

I'm in the ring before half his threat leaves his mouth. Hank doesn't care what bits you have between your legs. If you go against *anything* he says, you'll pay.

AFTER A GRUELING WORKOUT that included a record number of burpees, I take one of the world's longest baths. The hot water soothes my overworked muscles, but I won't sit unaided for a week. It's safe to say I've learned my lesson. I'll never be sassy to Hank again.

As I make my way out of the bathroom, my cell phone scuffles across the kitchen counter. A smirk curls my lips when I see Jacob's grinning face on the screen. We've texted back and forth the past few days, but this is the first time he's called me in months. After swiping my finger across the screen, I press my cell to my ear.

"Good afternoon, Jacob." *Jesus, whose voice is that?* I sound like I'm applying for a position as a sex phone operator.

"Hey, Lola, how are you?"

The apprehension in his voice spikes my heart rate. "I'm good. You?"

"Umm, yeah, I'm good... Ah... Are you busy Saturday morning?"

My brows furrow. "No...why?"

He coughs to clear the nerves from his throat. "I was wondering if you could meet me somewhere?"

"Somewhere...?" I leave my question open for him to answer how he sees fit.

He doesn't follow the script like I'm hoping. "It'll be better if I tell you in person."

"Okay. Where?"

He recites an address for a property in Ravenshoe before requesting I meet him there at nine AM Saturday.

"Should I bring anything?"

I hear him swallow before, "Just an open mind."

My suspicion grows when he forces out a quick "goodbye" before disconnecting our call.

***

WHEN I ARRIVE bright and early Saturday morning, I double-check the address written down. I must have mixed up the digits because there's nothing but a bank of office buildings in front of me.

After ensuring the address in my GPS matches the one I scribbled down, I pull into an empty spot at the front to call Jacob. Just as I'm about to hit the call button, I realize my navigation skills are as good as they've always been. Jacob is standing in the foyer of the building. He's wearing his standard cargo pants and a polo shirt, but his Vans have been replaced with shoes only men over the age of sixty should wear, when on a yacht, far away from anyone who could possibly see them in such hideous shoes.

I'm still laughing at my funny inner monologue as I glide down the hedged sidewalk. When Jacob notices me approaching, his throat works hard to swallow.

"Hey. You okay?" Although they're the words that come out of my mouth, my voice makes it more sound like: *Why the hell am I meeting you at an office building?*

"Lola." Jacob adds a head bob to his greeting, but eye contact seems to be a thing of the past as far as he's concerned. No matter how often I seek his gaze, I never get it. His eyes shoot in any direction I'm not standing.

Realizing I'll get more of an idea about our meeting from my surroundings than the man who dragged my backside out of bed at ass-crack o'clock, I follow his fleeting gaze around the modest, yet dated space. There's a wooden staircase to my right, a small hallway table to my left covered with various pamphlets, and half a dozen doors line the corridor.

When I read the plaque on the first door, my furious gaze snaps to Jacob. "Why the hell are we at the offices of a bunch of counselors? You know what I think about this type of industry." The way I spit out "industry" leaves no doubt to my anger. I hate therapists—with a passion!

My fury builds when my question is interrupted by a squeamish voice at the end of the hall. "Come on in, Jacob." Realizing Jacob isn't alone, the intruder strides down the hall. His approach is so quick, I'm not even halfway out the door before he grips my elbow. "You must be Lola. It's a pleasure to meet you."

An awkward-looking man with a wonky eye and a lopsided grin thrusts out the hand not gripping my elbow. I accept his greeting, although it's the fight of my life not to squeeze his hand to the point of death. If it were Jacob's nuts, I wouldn't hold back.

"I'd say the pleasure is all mine, but right now, I'm not so sure it is."

Jacob snickers at my sassy remark. His smile doesn't linger for long. One sideways glance, and he's choking on his spit. He knows I'm planning to kill him, and when I do, it'll be a prolonged and excruciating death.

"Interesting." The unknown man's eyes tumble when he strives to figure me out by only glancing into my eyes like they're windows to my soul. "How about we discuss your concerns a little further in my office?"

Don't misconstrue; he's not offering me a free counseling session. He's telling me that's what we're doing. Although I could break away from his hold when he begins to guide me toward his office, I'm too busy working out the many ways I'm going to kill Jacob to put up a protest.

Many options are filtering through my sadistic head, but the same one continues playing on repeat, so I think I'll stick with it. I'll drain the blood out of his body via the vein that feeds his magnificent cock. My torture must occur with us both naked; that way, any time Jacob gets hard, he'll take another step closer to death.

It'll teach him what I failed to years ago: being attracted to me never ends well.

OVER THE NEXT HOUR, I sit in on Jacob's anger management class. I don't speak a word the entire time. His counselor explained that he requested my presence today because he believes I'm partly to blame for Jacob's aggression issues. When he said that, I was seconds from implementing my quest for revenge. I would have if Jacob's face wasn't registering as much shock as mine. He was just as numbed by his therapist's assumption as I was. Doesn't mean I'll go lightly on him, though. The instant we exit this building, he's a dead man walking.

At the end of our session, and after declining the counselor's offer for a private consultation, I storm to my car. I'm so angry, steam is billowing out of my ears.

"Lola!" Not even my long, furious strides stop Jacob from catching up with me. "I didn't know that was his plan today. He just demanded I bring in my significant other. If I didn't comply with his request, I wouldn't have fulfilled my half of our agreement."

I whip around so fast, my hair slaps my face. "*Significant other,* Jacob? Since when did a booty call become a *significant other?*"

His face reddens with anger, but it's got nothing on the fury boiling in my veins. "You're not a booty call. Not to me."

"Then what do you call this?" I motion my hand between us, "A fucked-up friendship?"

"It's us. It's the way we are." His eyes plead with me to hear the words he can't speak. When that fails to happen, he spells it out for me. "Why can't you see it? Why don't you understand I'd do anything for you because I love you, Lola? I'll love you even after the sun dies." He steps closer to me, his eyes bouncing between mine. "I'll love you even after taking my last breath, and I'll love you even if you *never* love me back."

I freeze, shocked. I'm not just stunned by his declaration of love. I'm surprised my first thought was relief. I shouldn't be relieved he loves me. I should be angry. This wasn't the plan. We weren't supposed to fall in love.

Do I care about him? Yes, I do.

Do I love him? Yes. More than I care to admit.

Will I ever tell him that? No, I won't.

Why? Because I'm still fuming over the photos I saw of him on Facebook. I opened my heart to the possibility of loving again, and look what happened. It got trampled on all over again.

Jacob glides his finger down my face. His touch is soft, like he's afraid I'll vanish. "Say something—anything. I just told you I loved you, so the least you could do is give me some words back. You don't have to tell me you love me, but I need something, Lola."

I try to think of a way to explain what I'm feeling without adding to the burden he's already carrying. When seconds shift into minutes without a single idea breaking through the fog in my head, I go down a route I never wanted to travel. "Can I borrow your phone?"

His brows scrunch in confusion, but what he said earlier is true. He'd do anything for me. When he hands me his cell, it asks me for a security code.

"0923."

My gaze shoots up to Jacob's. That's my birthday. I was born on the twenty-third of September. God—this is worse than I realized. He's just as far gone as me.

Snubbing the crazy thump of my heart, I press the PIN into the phone, then locate his Facebook app. Once I have his feed opened, I scroll to the photos he was tagged in before handing his phone back to him. The longer he stares down at his phone, the wider his eyes become. I can tell when he reaches the last photo because he bites out a curse word before locking his remorse-filled eyes to mine.

He tries to talk, but I beat him to the task. "Now tell me again how much you love me."

CHAPTER FORTY-NINE

JACOB

Lola doesn't give me a chance to respond to her comment. She just slips into her car, starts the ignition, then takes off down the street. I do love her. I love her with all my heart, but now I understand why she looks at me like she does.

When she handed me my phone, the first photos showed me tucking dollar bills into a stripper's panties. I was embarrassed, but tell me one bachelor party that hasn't featured strippers? It was only once I continued scrolling did I realize what her anger centered around. The topless woman I bumped into the morning after Noah's party starred in several photos with me.

The most risqué thing she did was sit in my lap, but the last photo was by far the worst. She was kneeling between my splayed thighs, lowering the zipper on my pants.

Even seeing evidence of my betrayal firsthand hasn't freed the buried memories in my head. I thought my haziness was because I haven't had time to sit down and evaluate what happened that night, but this proves that isn't the case.

I fucked up. I can't put it any more simply than that. And for what? A woman who isn't half the woman Lola is. If everyone weren't relying on me, I'd bury myself in a hole in the middle of New Mexico. Unfortunately, not even death would guarantee me an hour of peace.

MY STRIDES into Noah's room slow when I overhear a conversation in the bathroom. Both voices are female, but I only recognize one of them. Emily.

"When did Noah last see you, Emily?"

I hear Emily sniffle before she replies, "The day of his accident."

A toilet seat dropping into place overtakes my pulse shrilling in my ears.

"Can you explain to me what happened that day?"

"Yeah... umm...I was rushing to tell Noah... to tell him something important when the traffic became bumper-to-bumper. A police officer said there was an accident and that I had to go another route. When I put my car in reverse, my intuition begged me to stay, so instead of doing as the officer requested, I ran toward the crash scene."

I float closer to the bathroom, interested in the rest of Emily's confession. She's never told me this story.

"A detective who knows Noah was standing behind the police barrier. When he recognized me, he walked over to me, and that's when I spotted the guitar I had bought Noah for his birthday on the roadside. It was shattered beyond repair." She chokes back a sob. "But it was nothing compared to how badly Noah's body was damaged. He was just left of the accident scene... There were half a dozen EMTs working on him."

A lady with shoulder-length blonde hair bobs down in front of Emily. "Was Noah unconscious by then?"

Emily shakes her head. "No, he said my name when I kneeled down beside him."

"Then what happened?" the stranger probes.

"Noah started convulsing." Emily twists a tissue tightly around her fingers. "That's when I was dragged away from him by his detective friend."

"Okay. That helps. Thank you for sharing." The blonde squeezes Emily's knee before standing. "I think the circumstances that pushed Noah into his comatose state are the reason he reacts negatively any time I mention you during our sessions."

A sob tears from Emily's throat. It sounds like it came from a woman who just had her heart cracked into a million pieces. It's the noise I expect Lola to make if she ever gives in to the hurt I see in her eyes.

"I'm not saying Noah doesn't love you, Emily. He's fighting to come back to *you*. We just need to work out how we can do that in a positive way."

When the unknown woman spins around without warning, I get busted standing in the doorway like a creeper. With my mind shut down, I blurt out the first thing that pops my head. "Is everything okay? You? The baby?"

Emily looks five seconds from killing me as she grinds out, "We're fine. *Both* of us."

When the lady wearing a white doctor's coat drops her gaze to the barely visible bump in Emily's midsection, I mouth a silent apology. I've never been good at thinking on the spot.

***

"I'M SORRY, Em, you know what I'm like when I'm nervous. I speak out of my ass."

Emily rolls her eyes as she continues down the corridor. We're going to the cafeteria for lunch. It's the least I can do after breaking news of her pregnancy before she was ready. "It's fine; don't worry about it. I doubt I can keep my secret much longer. My belly is too round."

"You could blame it on donuts?"

When she laughs, some of the guilt on my shoulders eases.

"Speaking of airless holes, how was your anger management class this morning? Do you still think your counselor is a few nuts short of a fruitcake?"

My thoughts immediately drift to Lola, but I try to keep the mood carefree. "A few nuts short? He's got enough for two cakes."

Emily laughs again. It's nice to hear with how tired she looks. I thought my time away would only be tough on me. If the bags under her eyes are anything to go by, I was way off the mark.

After grabbing the cafeteria special, we take a seat at one of the many empty tables. This is the first time we've sat and eaten since Noah's accident. I doubt either of us would have left Noah's side if the lady in charge of his physical therapy hadn't banned us from his room during this session. She wants to test out a new technique that she doesn't believe she can do with Emily and me in the room.

I prepare my stomach for the slosh on my plate that's supposed to be sweet and sour chicken before shoveling a forkful in my mouth. I gag. It's worse than predicted. I've never tasted something so disgusting, and Lola and I have sampled some crazy food the past two years.

"Who was the lady in the bathroom with you?" I ask through the bile racing up my throat.

Emily pulls a face before explaining that Dr. Miller is a specialist Noah's record label brought in to help with Noah's recovery. She works exclusively with coma patients, and although her techniques are unheard of, they're believed to be effective. She sounds like a whack job to me, but whatever floats your boat.

I stop checking my phone to see if Lola has returned any of the calls I made en route to the hospital when Emily gags. "How are you eating that? It's disgusting!"

I freeze with my fork sitting a mere inch from my mouth when she pushes her plate away from her. I arch a brow, reminding her what the doctor warned during her brief admission at the ER months ago. Slops might not be tasty, but it's better than nothing.

My brows lower when she rolls her eyes before popping a chunk of the bread roll that came with our orange broth into her mouth. "Better?"

"Much."

Now can you work your magic on your sister?

AFTER SPENDING my weekend with Noah, Emily, and Dr. Miller, I walk into the Hopeton House for my second week of community service. Dr. Miller has an... *interesting* personality. She seems a little standoffish, but after watching the effort she puts into her sessions with Noah, I began to wonder if she's misunderstood. A lot of women are misunderstood these days, but none more so than Lola.

It took hours of voicemail groveling and over two dozen text messages before Lola returned my contact. It was only a brief, one-line message, but the fact she replied at all gave me a glimmer of hope that I haven't completely fucked things up with her.

I'll make things right with her; I've just got to sort out my messed up life first.

THE NEXT TWO weeks follow along a similar path. I do community service at Hopeton House Monday to Friday, then Friday night to Monday morning, I stay at the hospital with Emily and Noah. Dr. Miller—or Rachel, as she has asked me to call her—has become a close acquaintance the past two weeks. She's conservative but a good listener. She often lends me an ear when I need to gripe about my anger management classes. I wouldn't mind taking them if I had an issue with anger, but since I don't, they're a pain in my ass— nearly as painful as the lumpy recliner I'm sleeping in.

As I shuffle from my right ass cheek to my left, I notice Emily slipping out of Noah's bed. She's slept at his side since the day he was transferred. I can't see it being comfortable. His bed is larger than the one he had at Parkwood, but it's still a twin. I guess that's why she's walking awkwardly? She's barely lifting her feet as she makes her way to the bathroom.

My eyelids are in the process of closing when a startled "No!" comes out of the bathroom.

My muscles groan in disgust when I head to the bathroom to check on Emily. "You okay?"

Nothing but silence greets me.

I rattle the door handle to check if it's locked. It is.

"Em?"

I'm seconds from busting down the door to make sure she hasn't passed out when she murmurs, "Just a minute."

When she throws open the bathroom door, I take a step back. Her face is as white as a ghost, and she appears seconds from crying. Before I can ask her what's wrong, she barges past me and races into the hallway.

I follow after her. "What's wrong?"

Her lips twitch, but not a word falls from her mouth. I peer into her watering eyes as I strive to figure out what would make her this upset. It isn't Noah. He's still in a coma, but he's doing better every day. I was talking to Lola last night, and I know she's fine, so other than that, I'm stumped. Unless...

"Is it the baby?"

She uses her sleeve as if it's a tissue before nodding. "I'm bleeding."

My heart plummets into my stomach. I don't know anything about pregnancy, but I'm reasonably sure you're not supposed to bleed when you're pregnant.

When a pained sob rips through Emily's body, I tug her to my chest. "It's okay; it'll be okay." I run my hand down her hair as my brain struggles to work out what to do. "What can I do? Tell me what to do, and I'll do it."

"Whatever you do, don't tell Noah. Dr. Miller is adamant he can hear us, so I don't want him to know I lost our baby."

Her response kills me for two reasons. One, I hate keeping secrets, but more than that, the thought of her miscarrying now, this far into her pregnancy, is devastating. "Are you sure you've lost it? Maybe this is just a part of pregnancy, and the baby is okay?"

Emily stiffens. When I glance over my shoulder, I discover the cause for her frozen state. Dr. Miller is standing just behind me. I can't guarantee she didn't hear us, but the worried expression on her face is questioning.

Emily waits until she's out of earshot before raising her eyes to mine. "I don't know what's going on. I've never done this before."

"Could you ask someone? What about Jenni? She only had Jasper a couple of months ago."

She shakes her head. "I don't want *anyone* to know. Noah deserves to know before anyone else."

Although I agree with her, she needs to speak to someone...

My thoughts trail off when my brain finally switches off sleep mode. Emily stares at me in shocked silence when I yank my cell phone out of my pocket and type "pregnancy doctors" in the search bar. I scroll down the list of candidates until I find one that offers emergency appointments.

When I tap the number and raise my phone to my ear, Emily freaks. "You can't tell anyone."

Before I can assure her I'll never share her secret, a chirpy female voice answers my call. "Dr. Morgan's office."

"Hello, I need to make an urgent appointment, please. My friend is..." I stop, remembering I have no clue how far Emily is. I cup my phone before dropping my eyes to Emily. "How many weeks are you?"

She shrugs. "I don't know. I think four or five months?"

I devote my attention back to my phone. "My friend is four to five months pregnant, and she started bleeding today."

"Oh, dear. Let me see what appointments we have." A keyboard being stroked sounds down the line before, "Will 2 PM work? I'll need payment upfront."

"That's fine." I dig my wallet out of my pocket before giving my credit card details over the phone.

"Wonderful. You're all set. Ask your friend to drink lots of water before arriving. The doctor may do an ultrasound to check on things, so the fuller her bladder is, the better."

"Okay, thank you. Bye." I shove my credit card back into my wallet before returning my focus to Emily. She's peering up at me with big, wide eyes. "Dr. Morgan, a local obstetrician, scheduled you for an emergency appointment at 2 PM today. It's been paid; you just need to show up. The reception said to drink lots of fluids before you arrive, something about needing to have a full bladder or something?"

"Okay." She sounds both relieved and panicked. "What about Noah? I don't want to leave him."

"I'll stay with him." When she hesitates, I sweeten the deal. "You'll never forgive yourself if there was something you could have done to save your baby and didn't. Noah is fine. I won't leave his side."

"Okay." Fresh tears glisten in her eyes.

I wipe them away before they can fall, then nudge my head to Noah's room. "Come on, let's see how his session is going, then I'll call a cab to take you to your appointment."

"I... umm... have to... umm... get lady *things*."

My cheeks heat. "Okay. I'd offer to get them for you, but I wouldn't have the faintest clue what to get."

"I'd never ask you to do that. I just..." Her words drop as quickly as her eyes. She's staring at something below her waist. Something bright red and utterly terrifying. A massive trail of blood is gushing down her leg. "Oh, god."

"It's okay. You'll be okay." I usher her into the bathroom, like hiding from the truth will stop it from happening. "I'll be back in a few minutes, okay?"

I wait for her to nod before darting out of the room panicked. I don't know what the fuck I'm supposed to do in these situations, but I'm hopeful the pharmacist in the hospital lobby will have more clue than me. I sprint down there as fast as my quivering legs will take me, blurt out my needs, and buy one of everything the female pharmacist suggests before bolting back to Noah's room.

Something inside of me cracks when Emily opens the bathroom door far enough I can see the amount of blood that seeped into her pants during my five minute trip to the pharmacy. She's bleeding —a lot.

Knowing I'm seconds from detonating, I move into the hall to pace. I drag my fingers through my hair before clenching and unclenching my fists. I've never wanted to punch something as badly as I do now.

When will the pain stop?

Hasn't Noah been through enough?

When Dr. Miller joins me in the corridor, I stop violently tugging on my hair. "Is everything okay?"

"I'm...ah...it's... ah..."

With words eluding me, I raise my finger, requesting a minute. If I speak, my voice will crack, then the emotions I'm trying to strangle are at risk of being freed. Dr. Miller uneasily smiles before returning to Noah's room.

Several minutes later, after I've regained a small sense of composure, I stride back into Noah's room. With Emily still in the shower, it's just Noah, Dr. Miller, and me.

"I know something that will cheer you up." Dr. Miller motions for me to join her next to Noah's bedside. When I do, she lowers her eyes to Noah. "Isn't Emily beautiful, Noah?"

I glare at her like she's insane. No wonder she was ridiculed during medical school. She needs a straitjacket, not a doctor's coat.

I take back every bad thing I've ever said about her when Noah's lips tug into a smirk. It isn't his usual broad grin, but it's a smile nonetheless. The only thing that could make it better was if a thick, bushy beard didn't hide it.

My heart quickens when a brilliant idea slams into me. "I'll be back."

After kissing Dr. Miller's cheek in glee, I race back down to the pharmacist. She's alarmed when I ask to be pointed in the direction of shaving cream and razors. She can look at me as if I'm batshit crazy as long as I get what I need. I want Emily to see Noah's full smile, not one hidden by scruffy facial hair.

I take a mental note to start using the stairs when my return to Noah's room arrives with a bout of breathlessness. I'm so unfit, Hank's concerns about me becoming pudgy might be more factual than in jest.

My fast pace slows when I notice Emily next to Noah's bedside. Her dark locks are saturated and hanging loosely down her back, and her face still bears evidence of tears. She looks so defeated, beard or not, she needs to see Noah's smile.

After curling my hand around her in support, my eyes drift to Dr. Miller. "Show Emily what you showed me."

Dr. Miller's smile competes with mine when she whispers, "Isn't Emily beautiful, Noah?"

The look on Emily's face when she sees Noah smile is priceless. The gloomy cloud hovering above her head dissipates in an instant, replaced with one that reveals she's fighting just as bravely as Noah.

"He's smiling?" She raises her watering eyes to mine. "He's smiling, Jacob."

"He is. He's smiling about you."

"During our twice-daily sessions the past two weeks, I've been striving to replace Noah's last memory of you with a happy, less confrontational one." Dr. Miller joins us on the other side of Noah's bed. "I've been asking him questions about your relationship before sharing stories about my own marriage. I'm still a little unsure what's going on in that head of his, but I'm happy with his progress."

"Me too. That's amazing." Emily gazes lovingly at Noah. "He's coming back. The old Noah is coming back."

"This might help him." I move to the bedside table to grab the razor and shaving cream I purchased. "Do you want the pleasure, or shall I do it?" While waggling my brows, I wiggle the goodies in my hand.

With the biggest smile I've seen the past almost three months, Emily replies, "I'll do it."

When I empty Noah's water jug, Dr. Miller makes an excuse to leave. She's a stickler for protocol, so she'd never use a piece of hospital equipment for anything other than its intended use.

After checking the coast is clear, Emily dips her hands into the water jug, then scrubs them over the scruff on Noah's jaw. Once she has a good amount of foam, her focus shifts to the razor. I probably shouldn't grimace with every stroke she makes, but I didn't think this through. She has a very sharp razor right near Noah's jugular.

"Stop staring; you're making me nervous."

"Don't worry about me; watch what you're doing!"

She thrusts the disposable razor my way. "Do you want to do it?"

I shake my head, mortified she'd even ask.

"Then shut up!" My chuckle nearly drowns out what she says next, "I've done this before, you know."

When my brows shoot up my face, as if to say, *do tell*, she murmurs, "After my surprise birthday party, Noah let me shave him at the hotel." She smiles like she's recalling a fond memory.

I can only hope it isn't the only one she has today.

LATER THAT AFTERNOON, after Emily reluctantly left for the appointment I scheduled earlier, and I've finished sending Lola a text, Dr. Miller arrives for another physio session with Noah. She's quieter today than she's been the past two weeks, and her ring finger is missing the diamond solitaire ring she spins a minimum of a three dozen times every thirty minutes.

She has many obsessive-compulsive behaviors, such us, spinning her engagement ring any time she mentions her husband, using antibacterial solution like it's lotion, and tucking her hair behind her ear when you stare at her too long. I may now stare at her for prolonged periods just to freak her out.

What? I'm bored. Nothing is entertaining about sitting in a hospital room all day.

Once her session with Noah is over, my curiosity gets the better of me. "Why aren't you wearing your wedding ring today?"

She talks fondly of her husband, so I'm somewhat surprised she's no longer wearing them.

"I thought it was time to remove them." Her face pales when her attempt to spin her missing engagement ring around her finger is thwarted by an empty hand. "My husband died last year. He had thyroid cancer. We tried every treatment recommended by his doctors, but nothing worked. I became his nurse in the last few months. The pain of watching the man I love fade into a man I no longer recognized was harder than I ever anticipated. Noah is my first patient since his death."

Tears well in her eyes when she shifts them back to Noah. "I forgot how hard this was. I thought it wouldn't bother me as much because the person in a coma was a stranger." Tears splash down her cheeks when she shakes her head. "I was wrong. This is just as painful. I may not know Noah, but I understand his pain." She grips Noah's hand before lowering her lips to his ear. "Be the man Emily wants you to be. Fight for her; make yourself the man she has always wanted."

When I draw her to my chest, her tears soak my shirt. Unfortunately, her devastation doesn't lower the volume of her next confession. "I'm so sorry about the baby. No one should lose a child. Not even one who isn't born yet—"

Dr. Miller's second sentence is interrupted by Noah's heart rate triggering an alarm, a horn blaring down the corridor to advise there's a code blue in Room 34. As Dr. Miller races to hit a big red button above Noah's bed, I move to his bedside. His eyes are rapidly moving under his eyelids, and his fists are clenched.

"We didn't tell you because we didn't want to hinder your recovery." When my confession coincides with Noah's heart rate monitor announcing he's flatlining, my anger gets the better of me. "You said he could hear us, so why the fuck would you say that?! This is your fault. If he dies, it's on your shoulders."

My angry outburst startles Dr. Miller so much, she mouths a silent apology before running out of the room. I feel terrible for what I said, but my focus has to remain on Noah. I told Emily he'd be fine. This isn't fine.

"Hold on; help is coming. I need you to fight, Noah. You have to fight."

As nurses frantically gather supplies, Emily arrives out of nowhere to grab Noah's other hand. I've barely gotten over the shock of her sudden arrival when a doctor in scrubs yanks on my shoulder. "Move back."

When I step back, she drops down Noah's bed so it lies flat before she requests for Emily to move so they can wheel a defibrillator close to Noah's bed. I jump into action before she can voice the denial I see in her eyes.

"Noah!" She thrashes and kicks against my hold when I drag her away from him. "Please, Noah, fight!"

"Charge. Fully charged. Stand back. Clear!"

When they zap Noah with the defibrillator, I close my eyes. The image of his back bending as he's zapped with a massive bolt of electricity is too much for me to bear. This is bullshit. He just started living again, so why the fuck is his life being cut so short? He deserves more than two years of happiness after the many years of grief he endured.

"Still no cardiac output."

"Charge again."

This shock is enough to buckle Emily's knees. I barely catch her before she tumbles to the floor. After pulling her close to my chest, I beg and beg and beg for Noah to be given another chance, for God not to be so fucking cruel. I even promise never to do anything remotely illegal again if I can just hear the faintest beep on Noah's heart monitor.

Twenty seconds later, when I'm on the brink of cracking, the beep I've been praying for pulsates through my ears.

It's followed by another.

And another.

And another until I feel confident enough to open my eyes.

I see a face I wasn't expecting to see. It isn't the weeping face of Emily. It's Noah's doctor, Dr. Fitzpatrick. He looks as bewildered as me.

"What happened?"

He shrugs. "I have no clue. Patients usually go into cardiac arrest before they're comatose, not after." He lowers his eyes to Emily. "I'll have a cardiac specialist come check on him. He'll assess if the lack of oxygen caused any damage to his brain, but I doubt that has occurred. Going into sudden arrest here significantly lowered the chances of his brain being without oxygen long enough to cause permanent damage."

"Okay. Thank you."

Nodding, Dr. Fitzpatrick makes his way back to Noah's bedside.

"He just scared the fucking shit out of me."

Emily tightens her grip around my waist before murmuring, "Me too."

CHAPTER FIFTY

JACOB

I spot Lola the instant she enters the room. It wouldn't have mattered how crowded it is, I'd locate her no matter what. She's too breathtaking to miss. I called her after Noah went into cardiac arrest, and she promised she'd come straight to the hospital. Although that was forty minutes ago, the trip from Erkinsvale to Ravenshoe is a bitch at this time of the day. Commuter traffic is at its peak, and don't get me started on the increase in tourists since news of Noah's hospital admission was broadcast across the country. Fans line the sidewalks of the hospital as far as the eye can see.

I stalk Lola from a distance when she makes her way to Emily. Seeing them side by side reveals how similar they look but how differently they're treated. Emily's gazes are full of admiration and respect. Lola's are not. I'd do something about it, but I lose the chance when she catches me watching her.

With a smile bright enough to illuminate hell, she saunters my way. The swing of her hips gains the attention of my cock, but the fire in her eyes utterly seizes it. I've still got a chance—I'm certain of it.

Her sexy scent engulfs me when she bands her arms around my shoulders to give me a quick hug. Pretending we don't have the eyes of a dozen people gawking at us, I draw her into my chest. Her breaths heat my neck when she laughs about her feet leaving the ground. "Miss me?"

"More than you'll ever know."

Before she can respond, a voice breaks through my pulse thumping through my ears. "What, no love for me?"

My brows furrow when Lola climbs down to hug my father like he's a long-time friend. "Don't be jealous, Tom. There's plenty of Lola to go around."

Lola notices my confusion, but instead of elevating it, she winks before prancing to her mom, who's sitting on the reclining chair next to Noah's bed. Once she's out of earshot, I devote all my attention to my dad. "How the hell do you know Lola?"

His eyes sparkle with respect as his lips curve high. "I met her a few weeks ago. I like that girl, Jacob."

He walks over to offer an introduction to Lola's mom, missing my mumbled, "You're not the only one."

WITH NOAH'S room bursting at the seam with visitors, I don't get the chance to talk to Lola before she announces she has to return to work. Our hug goodbye gains us another prolonged gawk, but only one man is brave enough to bring it up when Lola slips into the elevator at the end of the corridor.

"What's the deal with you two?"

I wait for the elevator doors to snap shut before dragging my eyes to Slater. I'm prepared to shrug, genuinely unsure how to explain our relationship, but he sees something in my eyes before I can.

"Oh, man, you're screwed. Out of all the women in the world, you had to fall for that one."

My nostrils flare as anger bubbles in my veins. "What the fuck does that mean?"

When I step up to him, so we're standing chest to chest, he

holds his hands in the air, signaling for me to stand down. "Jesus, Jakeyboy, calm down. I meant she'll keep you on your toes." My growl rumbles through both our chests. "In a good way, man. *Fuck*." He chuckles. Idiot. I'm five seconds from ripping his nuts off, and he's laughing. "You've got it bad. Does she feel the same way?"

"I have no fucking clue. She's barely spoken a word to me since *you* fucked everything up."

He balks. "Me? What the fuck did I do?"

I backhand him in the chest. "Did you have to put up *every* photo of the bachelor party on Facebook? You couldn't have kept some private?"

He shrugs like it's not a big deal. "I don't know how that shit works. I just hit the button thingy, and *voomp*, every photo on my phone was available for the world to see." He makes a face, as if he too is facing backlash from his stupidity. "Why does it matter, anyway? Is your dick getting served to you on a stick?"

"Yeah, something like that."

When he laughs so loudly, everyone in the room's eyes snap to us, I usher him outside. The last thing I want is for my dad to hear about the rumors that may be circulating about me.

"It was a bachelor party, man; strippers are a requirement."

"Not when your girl sees another removing your pants."

Slater's pupils dilate as he swallows bleakly. "Are you talking about Nat?"

"I don't remember her name, but if she's the blonde in the photos with me, then yeah, I'm talking about Nat."

He stomps from foot to foot like he just won the lotto. "You didn't sleep with Nat. You didn't even touch her."

"I didn't?"

"Nah. You pissed her off by calling her Lola all night; then when she wanted to sample your sausage, you shut her down like she had the clap. That lost you *any* chance of tapping her ass. You missed out, man; she sucks like a fucking Hoover."

My heart beats triple time. "I didn't do anything with her? *Nothing* at all?"

"She hung off you like a leech, but you didn't touch her."

"Are you sure?" I triple double-check.

He marks an X on his chest. "Cross my heart and hope to die, you didn't touch her."

I take off down the hall so fast, my shoes fail to gain traction the first hundred feet. My heart thrashes against my ribs as efficiently as I jab the elevator button. When it displays the car is still in the lobby, I throw open the emergency exit stairwell to begin my sixteen-floor descent.

With adrenaline fueling my pace, I make it to the lobby in record-setting time. I'm panting hard; my lungs are burning from a lack of oxygen, and my body is covered with a fine layer of sweat, but I made it.

When a quick scan of my surroundings fails to find Lola, I dart for the multistory parking garage outside, praying she hasn't left yet. My prayers are answered when I find Lola jabbing her keys into the driver's side door of her Jeep. "Lola!"

She pivots around to face me; panic is all over her face. She thinks I'm chasing her down for Noah. I'm not. I'm here for one thing and one thing only: her.

"Is everythi—"

Her words are cut off by me grabbing the back of her head to pull her delicious mouth to mine. She stiffens for a second before her lips part at the request of my lashing tongue. I kiss her with everything I have, a blinding embrace of tongue, lips, and hands.

I'm not the only one getting carried away. Lola is so swept away by our embrace, after curling her legs around my waist, she grinds down on my stiffened shaft, not the least bit worried that we're being indecent in public—*again*.

When I crowd her against her car, she moans into my mouth. The millimeter of air between us is too much. I need her closer. Firmer. Beneath me. It's been months since I've had sex, but abstinence isn't the reason I'm seconds from blowing my load in my pants. It's her. Lola. The woman whose killer legs stole the land from beneath my feet before her picture-perfect face utterly annihilated me.

I pull away from Lola's tasty mouth when I hear someone chuckling. Turning toward the noise, I spot Slater sitting on his motorbike with his tattooed arms folded in front of his chest. He gives a quick nod, pleased he killed my mojo before he kicks over his bike and darts for the exit.

Once the rumble of his Harley becomes a hum, I return my attention to Lola. Her eyes are brimming with so much lust, it's the fight of my life not to reacquaint our lips. I would have if I hadn't promised to keep illegal activities on the down-low only two hours ago.

Kissing isn't illegal...unless you're kissing a girl with lips as sinful as Lola's.

CHAPTER FIFTY-ONE

LOLA

"Can I get fries with that shake?"

I continue for the cash register, ignoring Bill's fifth attempt to flirt with me today. "If I hear that pathetic pickup line one more time today, I'll charge you double."

"Or I could take him outside and teach him some manners."

With my heart pumping out a funky tune, my eyes rocket to the person defending me. I know that voice. I know it very well.

My intuition is proven spot on when my eyes land on Jacob. His elbows are propped onto the bar, and he's shooting daggers at Bill. His hunched position has the cuffs on his shirt riding high on his thick biceps, exposing to Bill and his half a dozen friends that he'll have no issues delivering the threat he just served.

Although his pledge of protection floods my nether regions with wetness, Bill is harmless. "That won't be necessary; will it, Bill?"

When I hand Bill his change, he shakes his head before scampering back to the table he occupies a minimum three times a week. His footing is so unsteady, half the beer I just pulled for him lands on the floor. Mercifully, the peanut shells coating the battered wood mop up the mess on my behalf.

Once Bill's friends join him, I shift my focus to Jacob. "What are you doing here?"

It's been two weeks since we last kissed, so I pull his lips to mine by the scruff of his shirt. We kiss like drunken cheers aren't floating around us, only stopping when Jacob murmurs two words I thought I'd never hear. "Noah's awake."

I inch back, my mouth tingling in both euphoria and annoyance. Excited by his confession. Annoyed his mouth is no longer on mine. "Really?"

He nibbles my lips, my chin, and my ear before murmuring, "Yes."

With a squeal, I throw a tea towel in his face before hightailing it to Pete's office. "Your car or mine?"

"Mine," Jacob replies a mere second before I burst into Pete's domain.

HALFWAY TO RAVENSHOE, my gaze shifts from the bright blue sky to Jacob. Since excitement has been clutching my throat the past thirty-five minutes, none of the millions of questions flooding my head has had a chance to be asked until now. "When did he wake up?"

After grasping my hand in his, Jacob pulls it over until it's resting on his thigh. "Before dawn."

Now his hand-holding makes sense. He thinks if he has at least one of them contained, he'll suffer fewer injuries.

Un-fucking-likely.

It's near midday, so why am I only finding out now?

When I ask Jacob that, he says, "I wanted to tell you in person, then some shit went down with Noah, and I couldn't get away as quickly as I would have liked." He thrusts the hand originally wrapped around his steering wheel toward the bumper to bumper traffic in front of us. "Then this." His remorse-filled eyes stray to mine. "Sorry. I should have just called."

"No." I wave off his worry like it's a fly. "I like that you told me in person. It made it more special. Like I'm privileged or something."

"You *are* privileged, Lola. Especially to me."

I roll my eyes. I know people hate me, and I'm fine with that. I just somehow fooled Jacob into believing I'm a nice person. I'm sure his opinion would change if he ever discovers the thoughts I've had about him since he sexually tortured me against my car two weeks ago. Yes, it was torture, because I've suffered nothing but hours of distress since that afternoon.

You'd think discovering that Jacob didn't touch the stripper in the photos he was tagged in would arrive with a heap of relief. It did, but it was quickly overtaken by sexual frustration. First, Slater interrupted our hot and heavy make-out session, then Tom.

Getting down and dirty in a busy parking lot is risqué enough. I don't need it witnessed by a man I've grown to admire the past few months. Tom isn't a drinker, but that hasn't stopped him from popping into Pete's for a ginger ale every Thursday afternoon. He updated me on Noah's condition without once pointing out the fact he knew I wasn't visiting Noah because disappointment can be articulated without words. Usually, criticism doesn't bother me, but it's been harder to handle the past three months. Noah's coma made me soft... and perhaps the man beside me.

Jacob and I have maintained regular contact the past two weeks, but it's only been via text messages and phone calls. I'm scheduled at Pete's every weekend, and Jacob's weekdays are tied up doing community service. Although I don't work twenty-four hours a day, I know the promise he made to Noah at the start of his admission, so I'd never make him choose between his best friend and me—I hate losing.

If you had told me two weeks ago our phone conversation would be more heated than some face-to-face interactions we've had, I would have laughed. Now I'm calling myself an idiot for not adding electronics into the mix earlier. The amount of teasing...*my god.* I'm coiled so tightly, just sitting across from Jacob has my orgasm teetering. I remember the dirty words he whispered, and how his breathing hitched when I followed his instructions to a T.

God—being this dirty should almost be saintly.

When Jacob notices me squirming in my seat, he rakes his eyes down my body, slowing at the parts that make the dampness between my legs undeniable. "You alright?"

The lack of crinkles in his crotch reveals he knows what has me squirming, but he's playing the game how he's been taught. He was trained by the best—AKA me.

"I'm fine. You?"

Now his pants have crinkles, more from the material bunching around his crotch than anything. That probably has something to do with the seductive purr my question was delivered with. I said he was taught by the best, not that I didn't have the skills needed to return his tease.

"I'll be good... *soon.*" As his teeth rake his lower lip, his eyes drift back to the road.

I want to say a lack of eye contact cools my turbines, but that would be a lie. Ravenshoe Private Hospital peeking out over the horizon, though, that's a quick reminder we're not traveling to Bronte's Peak to become reacquainted.

After finding a parking space at the top of the garage, barging through thousands of fans who recognize him from Rise Up's early days, then wrangling past a handful of reporters offering a ridiculous amount of money to sneak a camera onto Noah's floor, Jacob guides me into Noah's room. The scene we walk into this time is a stark contrast to two weeks ago. Emily's cheeks are rosy; her hair is knotted... and she's moaning instead of sobbing.

"I was about to tell you to get a room, then I realized you're already in one."

Jacob's voice is full of jest, but Emily still dies a thousand deaths of embarrassment. It could have been worse. At least they're clothed this time around. They weren't when I walked into Emily's room without knocking last Christmas.

"I thought dry humping ended in high school?"

Jacob's fingers sizzle against mine, appreciating how my burn complemented his. After bumping Emily with my hip, loving how her cheeks inflame even more, I lock my eyes with Noah. "Way to scare the shit out of us, asshole."

Call me naïve, but I don't expect him to reply to my taunt. He just woke up from a coma, so he shouldn't be talking, should he? So imagine my surprise when he mocks, "Sorry about that, *princess.*"

Aware of my absolute hatred of nicknames, he calls me one at every given chance. *Princess, baby, darling, honey*—you name it, he's called me it at one stage the past two years. They make me want to vomit in my mouth. There are only two names I'll tolerate: Noah's pet name for Emily—who wouldn't want to be called Beautiful all the time?—and the name nickname Jacob gave me. He shortened it to CT, but I know what it stands for, and I friggin' love it!

I'm drawn from my thoughts when Noah asks Emily, "Does Lola know?"

"Does Lola know what?"

When neither Emily or Noah give me any indication as to what they're talking about, I shift on my feet to face Jacob. He freezes, utterly terrified. "Jacob...?"

Before I can read a single confession streaming from his eyes, Emily blubbers out, "I'm pregnant."

I jackknife back so quickly, I almost lose my footing. I thought her belly looked more rounded when Noah had a heart attack two weeks ago, but I brushed it off as a consequence of living off vending-machine food. I never considered that a baby caused the extra pounds on her svelte frame.

"How far are you?"

When I walk past Jacob, I punch him in the arm. He lets out an *oomph* before his scrumptious chuckle fills the uncomfortable silence plaguing the room. I can't believe he kept this from me. I'm not angry, but I am taking note that I still have a lot to learn about this man.

My foot suspends midstride when Emily replies, "Twenty-three weeks."

"Twenty three weeks?! You're twenty-three weeks pregnant!"

Mistaking my shocked tone as anger, she attempts to calm me down. "You're the first person we've told. No one else knows."

"You can't sugarcoat shit, Em. At the end of the day, it's still shit." Confident I've got her right where I want her, I gallop the last three steps between us, throw my arms around her shoulders, then squeal, "Congratulations!"

She stiffens, certain I was going to react badly. I won't lie; that was my first thought, but after everything they've been through, that would have been the worst thing to do. Young or not, they deserve this. Furthermore, I'll be the coolest aunt in the world. I don't have to demand they abide by their curfews or change into more respectable clothing. I can spoil them rotten and not suffer a single consequence. It's quite brilliant, really.

"Group hug!" Before Emily or I can react, Jacob wraps us up in a firm hug. "Too bad you're stuck in bed, Noah; you're missing out. Sisters..." A growl that makes me wish we were alone finalizes his tease.

Fortunately for both Noah and Jacob, Noah's bandmates and members of his inner circle arrive before Noah can issue any of the threats he's shooting Jacob's way. They're as stunned as I was about how well Noah seems considering the circumstances. Just looking at him, you'd have no idea he spent the last three months in a coma.

My mom cries happy tears when Emily informs her she's pregnant. Tom's reaction is more subdued. He glares at Noah with his mouth hanging open and his head shaking. When Noah and Jacob laugh as if they're the only ones privy to the punch line, my confusion has Jacob's lips getting friendly with my ear.

"I'll tell you later... when you're in bed... panting from sexual exhaustion."

This—this is what I was referencing earlier. I thought I'd teach

Jacob all the moves before setting him free in the wild to defend himself. I had no clue he'd use all *my* best tricks on me.

After squeezing my ass firmly enough to assure not even BOB will scratch the surface of my horniness, Jacob saves Noah from a much too late *birds and the bees* talk from Tom.

———

A COUPLE of hours pass before the party-like atmosphere in Noah's room is ended by an attractive blonde with a stern face. She reminds Noah's guests that although he's awake, he still has a long road to recovery. That kills the mood even more than Jacob asking Noah if he could raid his condom stash since he clearly doesn't know how to use them.

Don't get me wrong, everyone laughed at Jacob's comment, I just hated that only two sets of eyes floated my way when they did. There were over twenty people in Noah's room at that stage, yet only ten percent peered my way. Those aren't good odds.

After hugging Emily and Noah farewell, I tell Jacob I'll wait for him in the corridor. Because he's more popular than me, it takes him triple the time to say goodbye. He mainly bids farewell with man hugs and shoulder slaps, but an occasional cheek kiss or two are thrown in as well.

My pulse spikes when the lady who kicked us out says goodbye with a peck on the lips. They must know each other because their exchange lasts a good five minutes longer than everyone else's, and even with the boost in time, she seems disappointed that he's leaving, which is weird considering she told us to go.

My confusion is set aside when Jacob stops in front of me. "Ready?"

When the sexy purr of his words has my knees joining, I push off the wall and head to the elevator bank. "Is the ocean salty?"

CHAPTER FIFTY-TWO

JACOB

As my car careens down the ramp of the multistory parking garage, my hand glides up Lola's thigh. I'm reasonably sure I'm seconds from being castrated, but I can't help but tease her. I love how her eyes gloss over when my hands are on her.

She was named Cock Tease for how relentlessly she teased back when my face was still carrying baby fat, so when I realized I had the upper hand in our relationship, I thought a bit of revenge was in order. Don't misinterpret; I'd never recommended going against a woman as fierce as Lola without first knowing all your facts. It only dawned on me an hour after she left two weeks ago that I had the advantage.

How did I stumble upon this wisdom, you ask? Our kiss.

I kissed her before revealing I didn't have any relations with Nat, yet she didn't pull away. She encouraged our embrace. That in itself proves she cares for me.

When Lola's squirming grows to the point of looking like she has ants in her pants, my eyes stray from the road to her. Biggest mistake I've ever made. She's no longer watching the scenery zoom past the window. She's watching me with hungry, *I'm going to devour you without coming up for air* eyes.

The desire in her hooded gaze has my dick stiffening so quickly, the lead in my zipper is now tattooed on my dick. I'd give anything to have her lips on me. On *any* part of me. My lips. My neck. *My dick.*

Sensing my silent bidding, her eyes drop to my crotch. The heat I feel a mere inch from my pinkie intensifies when she takes in the effect she has on my body. She only needs to breathe in my direction, and I'm as hard as stone.

I plant my foot on the accelerator, hoping to finish our thirty-mile trip as fast as possible. Lola doesn't have the same level of patience. "Fuck it."

After throwing off her seatbelt, she crawls over the console, slides down my zipper, then frees my dick from my pants with a *boing*. My grip on the steering wheel tightens when her velvety tongue teasingly circles the rim of my cock.

"Not now, Lola. Please. Fuck. I can't take it."

Incapable of withstanding her teasing a second longer, I guide her head downward at the same time I jerk my hips upward. An indescribable grunt seeps from my lips when a couple of inches of my cock rams into her mouth. It's silky and wet and could only be better if it were her pussy.

Her heated breaths make condensation bead on the crest of my dick when she murmurs, "Someone's impatient."

Impatient is too innocent for the wicked thoughts streaming through my head. She's been a tease the entire time I've known her, but I'm wound up too fucking tight to take her torment tonight. After months of abstinence and two weeks of sexting that could have me thrown in jail if my phone ends up in the wrong hands, I'm more than ready to have my wet dreams turned to reality.

Lola's head collides with my door when I yank my steering to the left without warning. I was so determined to get her lips exactly where I want them, I didn't notice the double-trailer semi heading straight for us. It roars past us with a honk, rattling my windows as effectively as Lola is rattling my composure. A second later, we would have been toast.

Adrenaline races through my veins. It isn't our near-accident that has my heart hammering; it's Lola's lips sinking down my shaft. She's taking me in slowly, one glorious inch at a time. This will make me sound like an ass, but I'd rather be honest. Before Lola, I had never been deep throated. Some of my dates got a few inches from the base. Others straight up refused to try. Lola gets an A for effort. She can't quite take all of me, but she gives it her very best shot every single time. And thankfully, she has no gag reflex.

Air whistles between my teeth when the crown of my cock hits the back of her throat. She doesn't gag, but the sexy-ass moan she releases has my balls constricting. There's nothing hotter than a girl who enjoys giving head.

I almost beg for her lips to stay wrapped around my cock when she guides her head back up, but I don't need to. After a quick lick to replenish them with moisture, she glides them back down just as eagerly.

"Fuck yeah, baby, just like that."

When she attempts to protest my term of endearment, I rock my hips, stuffing her gripe into her throat with my cock. She bobs up and down on repeat, her lips descending more with each suck. In no time at all, she's taking more of me than any woman before her.

"I knew you'd do it. There's nothing you can't do when you put your mind to it."

As her mouth sucks at me like her pussy does, her tongue pays dedicated attention to my knob. She laps up my pre-cum before it has the chance to spill while keeping the tip well lathered for her multiple descents.

When she fists my cock so she can work the sections her mouth is failing to reach, keeping my eyes on the road is a fucking hard feat. The purrs ripping from her mouth match the rumble of my engine, and she's working my cock like she was born to do it.

The harder she sucks, the faster my car flies down the highway.

My heavy compression on the accelerator has us traveling at a speed well above the designated limit, but I can't help it. The image of her sucking my cock is pure fucking heaven. It has every muscle in my body pulling taut, prepping for release. My balls tuck in close to my body as my shaft grows heavy with need. I'm going to blow, and I'm going to do it in Lola's mouth.

Just as my car zooms past our exit, my thighs flex, my lips part, and hot, salty cum erupts from my cock, spurting into Lola's already overstuffed mouth. She moans a noise I've only heard a handful of times the past two years as she battles to swallow the spawn pumping out of me in thick, hot bursts. It's a sexy, needy purr that keeps my cock as hard as it was before I came.

After ensuring every drop of cum is taken care of, her attention shifts to nibbling on my ear. Like my night could get any better, it skyrockets to a never-before-reached level when she whispers in my ear, "Fuck, I missed you."

LOLA ROLLS over until her chin is resting on my chest. "I'll never regret the day I showed you that trick with your tongue."

I arch my brow, pretending I'm not loving her tousled hair and makeup-free face. It's rare to see her like this, carefree and natural, so I relish it as much as I can. "You taught me?"

She slaps my bicep as her eyes narrow into thin slits. After nipping at her kiss-swollen lips, I scoot down her body, dragging my lips over her generous breasts, down her washboard flat stomach before coming to a stop at the sexiest fucking pussy I've ever seen. "Want me to show it to you again?"

I'm two seconds from slicing my tongue through the heat capable of destroying me when she shakes her head. "I can't believe I'm going to say this." She grimaces like she's about to tell me we're related. "But I need time to recover."

My cock deflates like someone letting air out of a balloon when her hop off the bed causes pain to flash through her eyes. With her eyes on anything but me, she slips on my shirt before scrambling into the bathroom.

I'm on her heels two seconds later. "Did I hurt you?" I sound like a wimp, but I don't give a fucking shit. Months of sexual frustration meant things got a little rowdy, but I'll never forgive myself if I hurt her. I love her. I'm not supposed to hurt her.

The weight on my chest eases when she pivots around to face me. She's biting her bottom lip, and her eyes are sparked with lust. When she shakes her head, I inwardly sigh, relieved as fuck. She's tough, but she's also a tiny little thing, and I'm... not so tiny.

"Don't look so worried, Jacob. It's not a bad pain."

After placing a squirt of toothpaste on her toothbrush, she begins brushing her teeth. She makes even the most mundane tasks sexy. I doubt even scrubbing the toilet would look boring if she were doing it.

"Don't even think about it."

She spits foam into the cracked vanity sink before peering at me in the mirror. I eye her curiously, unsure what her statement means. After cocking her hip, her eyes drop to my crotch. When I follow their descent, a chuckle vibrates in my chest. My dick clearly enjoys the visual of her brushing her teeth. I'm hard like I haven't already come twice tonight.

"If you're expecting him to calm down, you've run out of genie wishes. You only have to breathe, and the beat of my heart lowers twelve inches."

I expect her to call me a pig or to leave me hanging in a bathroom too small for a man my size to get a good grip, so you can imagine my surprise when my comment awards me a minty-fresh version of Lola for the next thirty minutes.

***

"WHO WAS THAT LADY TODAY? The one in Noah's room?"

Lola joins me on the couch in her tiny living room to devour the Chinese we just had delivered to replenish the shitload of nutrients we lost the past few hours.

"Which one?" I talk around the forkful of fried rice in my mouth, too hungry to remember my manners. I'm beyond starving. I haven't eaten since last night, but with Lola being hungry for something other than food, I had more urgent matters to attend to before my hungry tummy.

"The blonde." Her brows stitch as she stares into space. "The one who kissed you goodbye."

I'm about to reply that no one with blonde hair kissed me— Jenni's is more strawberry blonde than platinum—but recalling Rachel's unexpected peck on my way out stops me. "Do you mean Rachel? About this tall." I hold my hand to my pecs. "Smells like wildflowers and antibacterial soap?"

My throat works hard to swallow when Lola glares at me with steam billowing from her ears. Faster than I can snap my fingers, the vibe in the room goes from playful to me being concerned I'm about to get my dick cut off.

"What?" Her glare is telling me I've fucked up, but I have no clue what I did.

Lola folds her arms under her perfect tits. "You know what she smells like?"

"Yeah, but only because it takes an hour to get her smell out of Noah's room when she leaves."

My confession doesn't alleviate the redness on her face in the slightest. If anything, it increases it. "She visits often, does she?"

"Well, yeah." I shrug like she's not seconds from castrating me. "It's kind of a requirement of her job... since she's Noah's therapist."

As quickly as Lola's anger arrived, it fades. "She's Noah's therapist?"

I jerk up my chin. "The record company brought her in to work with him while he was in the coma. She specializes in that type of rehabilitation. Why, who did you think she was?"

"No one." She takes a bite as if nothing happened. "She just seems a little... *friendly* for a hospital worker."

"I guess you could say that. We've talked a lot the past few weeks."

When her eyes slit, reality finally dawns. The woman who'd swear until she was blue in the face that she doesn't get jealous is jealous.

It's about fucking time!

"You're jealous." Excitement jingles on my vocal cords. I've been waiting for this day for over two years, so you can be assured I'm going to milk it for all it's worth.

"I am not."

She snatches up the remote from the coffee table to switch on the TV, wordlessly announcing our conversation is over. I'm not as willing to back down. After snatching the remote out of her hand, I turn the TV back off. "You are so."

Her eyes rocket to mine. They're slit and brimming with anger. "I don't get jealous, Jacob. Never have. Never will."

When she adjusts her position so she's sitting cross-legged, my shirt rides up high on her thigh. I know what she's doing. She's distracting me as only she can. I'm not strong enough to deny her silent pleas for me to forget our conversation, so I tug her onto my lap instead.

Her not putting up a protest already tells me everything I need to know, but the nervous delivery of her next set of words seals it without a doubt. "I've never been jealous before."

The last word in her sentence is the final nail in her coffin. "Before" implies back then, not now.

When she peers up at me with big, confused eyes, it's the fight of my life not to smile. She looks like a lamb who's about to be released into a pen of hungry wolves.

That's shocking because there's only one lamb in this relationship. It isn't Lola.

LOLA and I spend the next two days in our own little cocoon. It's nice having a normal existence again. I called Emily and Noah a handful of times, but from what I heard, they're also relishing the privacy. We're only rejoining the real world today because Lola has to return to work. Once again, her mortgage repayment will be deducted out of her account on the seventh no matter how sexually sated she is.

After dropping her off at Pete's for an eight-hour shift, I head to the hospital to visit Noah and Emily. I'm just about to enter his room when a warning sounds over my shoulder. "I'd suggest knocking before entering."

When I spin around, I'm met with the smiling face of Rachel. She's standing at the nurse's station doing paperwork.

"I didn't see you knock once the past two months, so what changed?"

She grimaces. "Discovering a patient's inability to walk doesn't hinder other parts of their body is a great reminder about using your manners."

I laugh. "Oh, really? Do tell."

She slaps my chest before slinging her arms around my neck. "Where have you been? I missed our chats."

"I was with Lola, my—" I suddenly stop talking, unsure how to address Lola. She's always been my girl, but I don't think I should give her the title of girlfriend without first asking her. I like my nuts where they are, thank you very much.

"Lola?" Rachel coughs before rearranging the paperwork in front of her. "It doesn't matter where you were. You're back now, and that's all that matters. However, I still wouldn't recommend entering without knocking."

She giggles. It's a nice thing to hear. I wasn't sure I would hear it again after how I reacted to Noah going into cardiac arrest. Once he was stabilized, I went to Rachel's office to apologize for what I said.

She didn't know we were keeping the baby a secret from Noah, so how was she supposed to know he wasn't aware?

During my highly uncomfortable attempt to apologize, Rachel disclosed why she reacted so badly. Only a month before her husband passed away, she suffered a miscarriage. She was sixteen weeks along. She was still grieving the loss of a child when her husband died, so her erratic behavior was easily excusable. Mine wasn't. I still feel like an ass.

I guess that's why I don't immediately shoot down her offer for an early dinner. Lola won't leave Pete's until close, so I've got plenty of hours to kill. "Sure. Why not? As long as it isn't at the hospital cafeteria. I still have nightmares about that place."

Rachel laughs, assuming I'm joking. I'm not. "I'll work something out. See you in a bit?"

I jerk up my chin before entering Noah's room, not bothering to knock. If I hadn't stopped to chat, I'm reasonably sure I'd be washing my eyes out with soap right now. The bathroom lock slipping into place echoes at the same time Noah waggles his brows.

"Perfect timing."

Chuckling, I pace to stand next to his bed. "Two days not enough to get it out of your system?"

I'm teasing. Lola and I barely got dressed the past forty-eight hours, and I'm still craving another hit. Fuck—I'm hard just thinking about the way she kissed me goodbye in Pete's lot. She was as reluctant to part as me.

Noah's wide eyes stray to the bathroom door. "I'll never get enough of her."

I try to keep things lighthearted. "She'll come out eventually. It could be two minutes; it could be twenty. That's the beauty of these things we call women. You'll never figure them out."

When Noah's gaze flicks to mine, the torment in them hits me for a six. He still believes the nightmares he had in the coma are real. "I swear to you, she was at your side the entire time. She didn't go anywhere. She's *not* going anywhere."

"It still feels so real." He stops when he chokes on his words. He's not the only one getting misty-eyed. I haven't seen him like this since his brothers died. He's truly grieving, except the person he's grieving is alive and well. "I thought I had lost her, Jake." He returns his eyes to the bathroom door. "I thought she was dead."

"It wasn't real. It was just a dream."

"That's not what in here is telling me." He taps his temple with his index finger. "Or here." He drops his hand to his heart.

I scratch my brow while stepping closer to him. He was quick to shut down my offer of counseling when Chris killed himself, but maybe Rachel is right: perhaps most of his recovery from here on out should focus on his mental wellbeing instead of physical health.

Before I can beg him to tell Rachel what's going on, a door creaking open breaks the silence teeming between us. Noah scrubs his hand down his face before forcing his lips upward. As Emily makes her way across the room, his eyes drift to mine. He doesn't say anything, but I don't need words to hear his pleas. He hasn't told Emily what he told me the morning he woke, and he wants me to keep it a secret. As long as he isn't asking me to keep secrets from Lola, I'm okay with that. I don't like it, but I can do it.

Relief crosses his features when I nod. I don't know why he's surprised. I'll always have his back. I thought he knew that.

"Hey, Jacob." Emily curls her tiny arms around my shoulders. "Where have you been the past two days?"

"A real man never kisses and tells." I waggle my eyebrows. "So you better get yourself a real man. The stories he's been sharing..." I yank on the collar of my shirt, loving that Lola's claims that Emily blushes on cue are accurate.

CHAPTER FIFTY-THREE

LOLA

As I hobble into the break-room at the back of Pete's, I reflect on the past forty-eight hours. I'm surprised I can walk. I'm probably bowlegged, but it's more than worth it. Not only did I get rid of all my pent-up sexual frustration, but Jacob and I also talked like we've never talked before. Our subjects were diverse, ranging from our favorite foods to who the front runner is in the upcoming election.

We even discussed what Jacob was planning to do with his life now that Noah is awake. He dropped everything to be at Noah's side, and he doesn't have a single regret. I hope Noah realizes how lucky he is. There aren't many people who can say they have a friend as reliable as Jacob. If you have one, hold on to them for dear life because you may never find another.

During our many chats, I informed Jacob about Hank's living situation. He was as blindsided by my revelation as I was when I stumbled upon it. Although Hank featured in a majority of our conversations, we've yet to work out how we can help him get back on his feet. We have a few ideas; we just need to solidify them a little more.

It's been a great weekend. The only thing that would have made it better was if I hadn't let my curiosity get the better of me. I wasn't jealous. I was just curious as to who Rachel is. Jacob hadn't mentioned her during our lengthy sexting the prior two weeks, so I was somewhat surprised—and perhaps a little peeved—when she kissed him goodbye. That's not jealousy. It's just...

Whatever. It's not important. Jacob is adamant they're only friends, so I've got nothing to worry about. I just wish the swishing feeling in my stomach would stop every time her name is mentioned. It's nauseating how twisted up she's made me, but it's nothing compared to the somersaults my stomach does when the prospect of a future with Jacob pops into my head.

I'd be lying if I said the feelings I've developed for him aren't scaring the shit out of me. I'm petrified. I tried not to fall in love with him, but he's just too easy to love. I have no clue where we go from here, but I'm confident I'll enjoy it. If Noah's accident taught me anything, it is to cherish every moment. You're not guaranteed a lifetime. You're not even guaranteed a safe journey, but you could die lonely if you don't realize not everyone is your enemy.

My sloth-like pace into the break-room slows when a familiar voice trickles through my ears. "An entire weekend without seeing my pretty lady made me worried enough to come and check on her, and what do I find? Her staring into space with a goofy look on her face."

When I turn toward the voice, I'm met with Hank's smiling face. He's standing at the end of the bar, wearing a thick coat and the grin of a man much younger than his fifty-seven years.

"Did you miss me?" I saunter toward him, my earlier concerns about a broken pussy a forgotten memory.

"I wouldn't necessarily say 'miss.' More like I couldn't figure out why a nagging voice wasn't yapping in my ear every five minutes. It's been peaceful."

"Peaceful enough you had to track me down?"

Hank chuckles before holding his hands out in defeat. "I got used to having you around. Kill me." His expression takes on a serious note. "Where did you disappear to, anyway?"

I freeze as guilt makes itself known in my gut. I completely forgot to tell him Noah is awake. "Noah woke up Saturday morning."

Thankfully Hank is precisely the man you'd expect him to be. "That's great news. How is he? Are there any side effects?"

I shake my head. "Not as far as the specialist can tell. It's as if he woke up from a nap."

"That's one long-ass nap."

I laugh. "Yeah, it is."

After squeezing my hand, he makes his way to the exit. "Now that I've seen you're okay with my own two eyes, I better get a wiggle on."

"Can I get you a beer or something first?" I feel incredibly guilty he came all the way to Erkinsvale to check on me, so the least I can do if offer him a drink.

"Nah, I'm good. I just wanted to make sure you were okay." He takes another three steps before spinning around to face me. "Will I see you tomorrow?"

Smiling, I nod. "I wouldn't miss it for the world."

With a smile as big as mine, he breaks through the back entrance of Pete's. I check the coast is clear before slipping my phone out of my pocket. Although Noah is now awake, old habits die hard—especially when it comes to this man.

Me: *Hank's gym tomorrow?*

Jacob's reply has me making a mental note to sign up for yoga classes.

Jacob: *Are you going to wear those little pink gym shorts you usually work out in?*

My smile competes with the moon.

Me: *Maybe...*

Jacob: *Then I'll be there.*

I do a jig on the spot while my fingers fly over the screen of my phone.

Me: *See you bright and early tomorrow morning.*

Jacob: *I look forward to it.*

For the rest of my shift, I smile like the cat who swallowed the canary. It's been three months since Jacob and I worked out together, and for some stupid reason, I'm looking forward to the pain. I guess it's the equivalent of bedding a man with a cock as large as Jacob's. The gain will always exceed the pain.

WHEN I HOP into bed later that night, I'm prepared for another night of tossing and turning, but to my surprise, I instantly fall asleep. It's a peaceful sleep... until my phone starts hollering.

"Hello." The huskiness in my voice has nothing to do with just waking up, and everything to do with being disturbed. I could have slept the day away without an ounce of guilt.

"Shall I come over and *personally* wake you?" The sexual innuendo in Jacob's tone has my pussy pulsating, but I've got an hour of vigorous activities to tackle before we can slip back between the sheets.

When my eyes lock on my alarm clock, I nearly fall over backward. It's a little after noon. "Fuck!"

"I was going to suggest we do that after we work out, but if you want me to come there now, I can."

"Shut up, Jacob."

His deep chuckle sounds down the line.

"I'll be there in thirty minutes."

I dump my cell on my bed before rummaging through my drawers for the gym shorts Jacob requested last night. I search my drawers, my closet, and my laundry basket before I finally locate them stuffed in the back of my underwear drawer. They're short enough to be classed as panties, but still, did they have to be in the last place I checked?

After changing my clothes, I throw on my gym shoes then scurry for the door. I'm halfway out when I catch sight of myself in the mirror in my entryway. I nearly left the house without an ounce of makeup on.

What the hell is this man doing to me?

After applying foundation, mascara, eyeliner, and lip gloss at a record-setting pace, I bolt out of my apartment. Twenty minutes later, I saunter into Hank's gym like I don't suspect I triggered a speed camera on the way. I'm just praying a speeding ticket is the only fine I get.

The farther I go into Hank's Gym, the more confused I become. The usually deserted space is at full capacity. There are boys of all ages using the outdated equipment, and there's a line for those waiting. If I hadn't spotted Hank in the middle of the fraying boxing ring, I would have believed I was in the wrong place.

"About time you showed up."

I shift on my feet to face Jacob, who is tying the laces of a boy I'd guess to be no more than five or six. "There you go, Matty. Go tell Rick I'll be there in a minute."

Matty thanks Jacob for his assistance with a toothless grin before charging toward a boy standing ringside. Because I'm struggling to work out what parallel universe I'm in, I don't notice Jacob sneaking up on me until his arms wrap around me and his lips are on my temple. He's not cuddling me how he cuddles Emily. He's hugging me from behind—having my back like he does Noah's.

"Who are all these boys?"

"They're from Hopeton House. I'm hoping that teaching them how to fight will show them the discipline needed to be a fighter. Their rough start means they need to know how to protect themselves, but Hank will teach them how to respect the craft so they won't use it unless needed."

My heart rate doubles when I scan the room. A handful of the older boys would be mid- to late teens, but the one Jacob was helping is only a baby. It tugs at my heartstrings that he doesn't have a home to live in.

"Matty is the youngest. He's five." Jacobs points to the little boy waiting to box a bag bigger than him. "Then their ages increase until we reach Drake, who's seventeen." He gestures his head to a blond boy sparring with Hank in the ring. "And this is Chloe."

When his eyes drop, I follow the direction of his gaze. There's a little girl with gorgeous curly hair peering up at me. "Excuse me." She tugs on my shorts. "I need to go to the bathroom *really* bad."

My eyes dart to Jacob when she crosses her legs like she's seconds from bursting. With a cheeky grin and a cocky waggle of his brows, he backs away with his hands held out in front of himself.

"Jacob!" My eyes soundlessly beg for him to come back. I don't do kids, especially not ones about to pee on the floor. "Please come back."

Chloe tugs on my shorts for the second time. "I'm *really* busting."

Realizing the skirt she's wearing is most likely the only one she arrived with, I usher her toward the women's locker rooms. "Quick."

When I curl my hand around hers, I send a private prayer to God, praying she's toilet trained. If she isn't, Jacob will have more than one messy situation to clean this afternoon.

CHAPTER FIFTY-FOUR

JACOB

Lola is adamant she doesn't have a maternal bone in her body, but after seeing her interact with the kids of Hopeton House, I'm not so inclined to agree. She shot daggers at me after she returned from the bathroom with Chloe, but she's smiled more times than she's scowled the past two hours. That might have something to do with all the attention she got from the teen boys. She thought they were eager for her boxing tips. In reality, they were gawking at the scandalous amount of skin she's showing.

I would have warned her the gym was going to be brimming with minors if I knew that when I requested she wear my favorite shorts. I only came up with the idea of teaching them how to fight last night after talking to my dad. Although I don't appreciate the horny eyes on Lola all day, she's a guarantee they'll return next week. They're not the only ones who'll suffer hours of grueling drills if she's here for their visual stimulation. I'll be standing right next to them.

I just hope she'll still be here after I tell her what happened last night. . .

After spending a couple of hours with Noah and Emily, Rachel arrives at their room to collect me for our date. Noah smiles like a smug prick when Emily's eyes seek anything but Rachel's gaze. She's mortified.

Just as eager to suffocate the tension hanging thickly in the air, Rachel tilts my way. "Are you ready?"

When I jerk up my chin, Emily's eyes snap to us in an instant. I thought the tension was thick before, but it has nothing on the glare Emily gives us. Certain her stare centers around food, I ask if she'd like me to bring something back for her.

She just stares at me, unblinking and unmoving.

"Food, Em, do you want me to bring back some food?"

When I wave my hand in front of her face, her trance ends. She shakes her head, but her curious eyes remain glued on Rachel and me as we make our way to the door. On the way to Petretti's, Rachel shares the story of her walking in on them in her physical therapy room.

"I swear, I only left them for ten minutes."

"Ten minutes is way too long to leave Noah alone with Emily. I've been caught unaware many times the past two years."

She laughs before walking through the door I'm holding open for her. My stomach grumbles when we follow our waiter to our table. It's in the far back corner of the restaurant, an intimate, secluded setting that adds to the authentic ambiance of the space.

After the waitress takes our order, Rachel requests a bottle of wine be brought to the table for sampling. As the waitress skedaddles away, my phone buzzes with a text message from Lola, asking if I want to go to the gym tomorrow. I cringe. Not because I don't want to spend time with Lola, but because I know Hank will hammer the shit out of me the instant I return to his gym.

Any reservations I'm having evaporate when Lola says she might wear the hot pink shorts she worked out in before Noah's accident. I'll suffer a month in hell just for the chance of seeing her in her teeny tiny shorts.

"Did your mother not teach you manners, Jacob?"

When my eyes pop up from the screen of my phone, I notice Rachel is glaring at me, unimpressed that I'm more interested in my *phone than a real-life conversation. After murmuring a quick apology, I hit send on my text, then put my phone away, returning Rachel's eyes to their standard width.*

They widen even more when I ask, "Did I not tell you my mom passed?" I sound shocked. Rightfully so. After everything we've talked about, I'm surprised my mom's death never came up.

"No, you didn't. I'm so sorry."

"It's fine. It was a long time ago."

We're saved from more awkwardness when the waitress returns with the bottle of wine. Rachel samples it like a real connoisseur. She sniffs it, swirls it around her glass, then takes a delicate sip that's spat back into her glass after swishing it around her mouth. I laugh. I had no clue she was so girly.

"There'd be less hassle if you drank beer."

The waitress smirks at my comment. Rachel doesn't. She grimaces before advising the waitress the fruity essence of the wine would match the palate she's aiming for tonight.

Although our evening got off to a slightly rocky start, the rest sails by without a single hiccup. We chat back and forth and share an array of delicious Italian food. It's so delicious, I order one of each item on the menu for Noah and Emily. I'm not trying to be flashy; I just have no clue what Emily can eat since she's pregnant, and I don't want to upset Rachel by asking her if she knows.

With a bag full of food on my hip, I walk Rachel to her car at the back of the hospital.

"You do know the saying 'eating for two' isn't real?"

Rachel giggles when I shrug. If the pureed food they fed Noah in a tube the past three months is anything like the gunk they serve in the cafeteria, he'll be dying for real food as much as he wishes he could go home.

"This is me." She waves her hand over a mini convertible coupe.

"It's safe to say I won't be driving anywhere with you in the near future. Your car is a matchbox." Rachel's smile is replaced with a

frown, but I can't dwell on that. The food I spent a fortune on is going to be cold. "Thanks for dinner; it was a lot of fun."

"It was; I had a wonderful time."

When she leans in for a hug, I do my best to return her embrace with the one arm I have access to. It's an awkward hug that grows thornier when Rachel's lips brush against mine. I've handled my share of friendly goodbye pecks, so I'd be prepared for that, but that isn't what Rachel is doing. Friends don't swipe their tongues along other friends' lips.

I yank back so quickly, I nearly lose my footing. When Rachel peers at me with wide, rejected eyes, I mumble, "I have a girlfriend."

Her hand shoots up to her chest for a mere second before she dives into her car. With her hands as erratic as my heart, it takes her several attempts to get her seatbelt latched into place. Once she has it fitted, she rockets out of her spot, narrowly missing another motorist.

I'm so surprised by what happened, I go straight home, forgetting about the food I purchased for Noah and Emily. It goes cold in the passenger seat of my car as I rack my brain about how I gave Rachel false signals...

I'm pulled from reminiscing when Hank joins me at the side of the ring. "They're a good bunch of kids, Jacob."

I pull apart the ropes to help him out before murmuring, "Yeah, they are."

When I signed on to do community service at Hopeton House, I was pissed. Because they forced me to break the promise I made to Noah, I went in with a filthy attitude and the intention to do my time and leave without a single attachment.

I was an idiot.

The kids at Hopeton House have very similar stories to Noah. There's just one difference: Noah was fortunate enough to be offered a ride home one rainy afternoon. The residents at Hopeton House weren't as lucky. They have no one on their side—except me. My community service officially ended on Friday, but I refuse to turn my back on them like so many before me have. I'll have their back like I do Lola, Noah, and Hank's. It's why I was born so big—so there's plenty of me to go around.

AFTER CLEANING up the mess the kids made, I head into Hank's office. He and Lola have been hiding out in there the past hour. I have no clue what they're doing, but if the paperwork they're shuffling around is anything to go by, I'd rather not know.

Who am I kidding? If it involves Lola in any way, I'm interested.

"What are you two up to?"

Hank snatches up the papers they're looking at as Lola spins around to block them from my view with her generous rack. "Nothing interesting. Just trying to balance the books."

"Do you want me to take a look at them for you?"

Hank shoos away my offer with a wave of his hand, unaware I graduated business school with honors only twelve months ago. I am used to strangers thinking I'm all brawn and no brains, but I'm shocked Hank would believe that. He knows there's more to fighting than just brute strength.

"My offer stands if you change your mind." I grab my gym bag off the ground before connecting my eyes with Lola's. "Your place or mine?"

My dick twitches when she purrs, "Mine. I don't want to give Tom a heart attack."

After telling Hank I'll see him tomorrow, I guide Lola to her Jeep. Since we arrived in separate cars, we travel to Erkinsvale separately. I try to put the alone time to good use. It does me no good. No matter how hard I deliberate, my brain can't find a plausible way to explain what happened last night without hurting Lola.

Technically, I didn't do anything wrong—Rachel kissed me, but I didn't kiss her back—but I agree with my dad. By not telling Lola what happened, I'm establishing our relationship on a rocky foundation. Although we've had this weird on and off thing the past two years, the dynamic of our relationship has shifted the past two weeks. I'll never be overly confident with any assumptions I make about Lola, but I'm reasonably sure the one step forward, three steps back routine we've been dancing since we met is now ancient history. She's my girl—well, she will be when I ask her.

When I pull into the lot of Lola's apartment complex, I spot her waiting for me on the front stairs. The eagerness on her face makes what I'm about to do ten times harder. I swear, I'm on the verge of coronary failure.

Please God, don't take her away from me just as I've finally won her over.

My heavy stomps to Lola's third-floor apartment are audible over the goth music her neighbors are playing. That's shocking considering it's loud enough for three towns over to hear. After jabbing her key into the lock, Lola swings her front door open before gesturing for me to enter. I'm not surprised by her chivalry. I'm reasonably sure I'm the only one wearing a skirt right now.

She waits for me to dump my bag under the entranceway table and spin around before arching her brow. "What's going on, Jacob? I haven't seen you this quiet since... *never*. Usually, we don't make it up the stairwell without your lips on me, but tonight you're acting like I have cooties."

"I know you don't have cooties. If you did, I would have caught them by now."

I grimace when she doesn't take my comment as I intended. I thought a little bit of playfulness would dampen the tension, but all it did was add another log to the fire.

Realizing delaying the inevitable will only make matters worse, I pull off the Band-Aid with one swift yank. "I need to tell you something." Panic flares through her eyes when I scratch my brow. "And I'm reasonably sure you won't like what I have to say."

CHAPTER FIFTY-FIVE

LOLA

Three and a half months later…
Noah and Emily's Wedding.

I fold my arms in front of my chest with a huff, annoyed the pesky security officer made me hand in my phone at the start of the service. If he hadn't confiscated my phone, I would have made a fortune selling the photo of Noah scowling at Jacob when he interrupted the wedding ceremony to tell Emily he was still available. I swear Noah is seconds from having a heart attack—*again*. I don't know why he wasn't prepared for Jacob to do something like this. Every guest at his wedding knows how much Jacob loves teasing him. Wedding day or not, nothing will change that.

Speaking of weddings, Jacob and Noah did a spectacular job planning today's event. Everything is perfect; they just missed one thing: me. When Emily announced she was engaged late last year, I didn't take her news as well as I could have, but I've been nothing but supportive the past six months. And how did my loyalty get rewarded? It didn't. I couldn't even get a lousy invitation to be part of the bridal party. I just got lumped in the regular section with the ordinary people like Rachel.

She's sitting three spots over from me, wearing a pale blue dress and white stilettos. This is the first time I've seen her since the day Noah woke up. When Jacob told me she kissed him, I was furious. I knew there was something more between them than he let on. Jacob was adamant he didn't kiss her back, and although violence is usually my go-to when I feel deceived, the honesty in his eyes shelved my retaliation. He could have kept what happened from me. The fact he didn't shaved weeks off the sentence I had planned to serve him.

Now things are running smoothly. I wouldn't say our relationship is perfect, but we're getting pretty darn close—even with him being a little corny at times. After calming my anger the only way he knew how, Jacob asked me to be his girlfriend. I shouldn't have laughed, but you didn't hear the way he asked. It sounded as if we were in middle school, but I'm not an idiot. Jacob is a catch, and I was more than eager to keep him to my greedy self. He was surprised when I agreed, but my acceptance was awarded in a way I never saw coming. That night still rates as one of the hottest sex moments we've had. Just thinking about it gets me all hot and bothered.

Noticing my unladylike squirms, Jacob locks his eyes with mine. When I give him a flirty wink, I'm rewarded with his cheeky grin. He watches me with affectionate eyes for the next several minutes before the officiant breaks our connection by requesting the rings.

Once the ceremony is over, the bridal party and their guests head to a large reception tent erected on the grounds of Noah and Emily's cabin. Because Jacob is Noah's best man, he's required to do the formalities of the wedding, which means we're seated at separate tables. I'm at the family table, whereas Jacob is sitting with the bridal party.

Suspicion runs rife in my veins when Slater taps Jacob's shoulder opposite of the direction he's seated. When Jacob cranks his neck to see who is accosting him, Slater dumps a massive nip of whiskey in his weak whiskey and Coke concoction.

As Slater slides his flask back into his suit jacket, he busts my watchful eye. My lips curl into a grin when he presses his index finger to his mouth, requesting I keep quiet. Nodding, I return my glass of wine to the waiter's tray. One of us has to drive home, and with Slater's plan unearthed, I guess that person is me.

I'm a little excited about how this will pan out. I've not seen a drunk Jacob before, so I'm curious to see how he handles his liquor.

If the heated looks he gives me as he downs his spiked drink is anything to go by, this could end up very interesting indeed.

***

"*YOU'RE* JACOB'S GIRLFRIEND?"

I finish ordering a soda water with a twist of lemon from the bartender before pivoting to face the voice. With Noah's bandmates' crazy antics drying my throat from laughing so much, I'm in desperate need of a bit of moisture.

When my eyes land on Rachel, I hold out my hand in offering. I won't lie; it's not an easy task—even more so with how slit her eyes are. "Yes, I am. Hi, I'm Lola."

She begrudgingly accepts my gesture, but not without using it to further her disdain with a firm grip. "Funny, he never mentioned he had a girlfriend."

I wait for her to finish absorbing my tight black mini dress and gravity-defying heels before replying, "That's understandable. Back then, I wasn't his girlfriend. We just fucked—*repeatedly*."

My eyes stray to the right when the bartender sets down my order. The ego Rachel tried to squash gets a second wind when I notice the napkin tucked underneath has a number scrawled across it. That's the fourth number I collected today, and I'm not even putting out feelers.

Although grateful for the bartender's interest, I snag my drink off the bar top, leaving the napkin behind. There's only one devilish blue-eyed man I'm interested in taking home today. The bartender isn't him.

As I twirl back around, I realize Rachel is still next to me. I thought my comment would have scared her off. Perhaps she isn't as timid as the rumors suggest.

It dawns on me that she's entirely misunderstood when I realize who's holding her attention. She's not formulating a witty comeback or working out a way to insult me without words. Her focus isn't even on me. She's eyeing Jacob from across the room, her stare awfully wanton for someone who only wants to be friends.

Sensing my bubbling anger, Jacob peers my way. His brows furl when he notices I'm standing next to Rachel. Although I hate that I'm jealous, my heart warms when he mouths, *"You okay?"*

He could have toyed with my jealousy, worked it to his advantage, but instead, he'd rather comfort me than make me more upset. If that doesn't prove I made the right decision when I accepted his ride all those years ago, nothing will.

I grin to ease the worried groove in his forehead before sauntering his way. His eyes swing like the pendulum on a grandfather's clock when they take in the sway of my hips. He's mesmerized in under a second, entranced by a body he knows nearly as intimately as his own.

"Everything okay?"

I balance on my tippy toes to plant a kiss on the edge of his mouth. "Everything's fine."

My pussy tingles when he bands his thick arm around my midsection and tugs me back until his dick nuzzles my ass cheeks. He's not hard, but he doesn't need to be for my body to pay attention. "You're not getting jealous again, are you?"

If I believed he'd remember any of this in the morning, I'd protect my dignity by denying his claims, but since the whiskey seeping out of his pores is enough to get me drunk, I keep my mouth shut. I am jealous. I'll just never let him know that.

"Are you ready to head out?"

I nod. If he's a *fall over while drunk* type of man, I'll never get him off the floor.

"Okay, I'll be back in a minute."

He presses his lips to my temple before stumbling toward Emily. I grin when he wraps her up in a big bear hug. My giddiness doesn't linger for long when he adds to his farewell by planting a sloppy peck on her mouth. I know what he's doing—he's riling Noah up as he always does—but it still sucks to see his lips on any woman who isn't me.

Jealousy hits me full force when Rachel joins Jacob and Emily at the side of the reception tent. If she's hoping Jacob will say goodbye to her in the manner he just did Emily, she has another thing coming. I don't share. Never have. Never will.

With jealousy heating my steps, I make it to Jacob's side in record-breaking time. The most adorable smile I've ever seen in my life stretches across his face when I throw myself into his arms. Even with him more intoxicated than he's ever been, I'm not afraid he'll drop me. He'd never hurt me. Not in a million years.

As he spins us away from Emily and Rachel, he nibbles on my lips as he drops his eyes to mine. "I thought you didn't get jealous?"

"Shut up and kiss me."

His chuckle vibrates my mouth before he does as instructed. Like every kiss we've shared, things soon become heated. Needing privacy, Jacob heads outside. Considering how much alcohol he's unknowingly consumed, I'm impressed at how quickly he moves. Before I know it, I'm pinned to his car by his hips, and his mouth is savaging mine. It's the best goddamn twenty minutes of my life.

Only once he has me on the brink of an orgasm does he pull back, and even then, mayhem ensues. It isn't the impressive moves of his mouth making me giddy but the words he speaks.

"I love you, C.T."

My heart thrashes against my ribs as I whisper words I never thought I'd say, "I love you too."

I've known for a while that I love him, but I've been too scared to say it back. Knowing he'll have nothing but photos to remember tonight freed me from worry. Don't get me wrong, I want him to know, I just need to keep some cards to myself. Over the past three months, he's had me backflipping on many rules I swore I'd never break. This one is the biggest, so I need to keep it in my arsenal for a little longer.

I don't think Jacob heard my declaration of love. He doesn't respond as I anticipated. He merely taps my nose before jogging around to hop into the passenger seat of his car.

Shrugging, I slide into the driver seat. A majority of our trip home is silent, and I'm beginning to wonder if Jacob is asleep. It's only when his hand slips onto my thigh do I realize he is. Whatever is going on with him, it has him heated up—everywhere.

"You okay?"

I hope he isn't going to be sick. We're in his car, but I'd rather not spend my night cleaning vomit from the carpet.

"Never better," he responds just as we arrive at my apartment building.

Climbing three flights of stairs with a heavily intoxicated Jacob is an interesting experience, but it proves my theory that he's a happy drunk. He often steals kisses and tells me he loves me during the torturously long trip from the car to my front door.

Once we finally stumble inside, he kicks off his shoes before tackling his belt. "Home sweet home."

Only months ago, I would have been pissed at him declaring my humble abode as his, but tonight it has a nice ring to it. His ass is indented in my couch; you can't get more moved in than that. He's practically been living with me the past three months anyway. He hasn't decided what he wants to do career-wise yet, but he saved enough pennies the past two years fighting to supplement his income until he figures out what he wants to do.

I hope he continues his current arrangement. Most of his days are spent with Hank, helping him train a dozen boys and one girl from

Hopeton House. When he isn't there, he's here with me. Noah endorses the new inductees' fighting scholarships. When he heard about Jacob's plan to take them under his wing, he paid their gym memberships in cash for the next three years, thus not only helping disadvantaged kids but Hank as well. It's a win-win for all involved.

When Jacob staggers toward our room, I head into the kitchen to grab a glass of water and a bottle of Advil. By the time I trace the steps he took a mere minute ago, he's crashed on our bed. Although I'm glad he made it to the bed before passing out, I would have preferred for him not to hog the whole thing.

After removing my makeup, and having a steaming hot shower, I join him in bed. I've barely slipped between the sheet when his hands shoots out to drag me to his side. My insides do a stupid flippy thing when he murmurs, "That's better."

You could park a truck between us when we go to bed, but by the time I wake, every single morning, I'm smothered by him.

Any chance of instantly falling asleep flies out the window when his cock braces my backside. Unlike earlier, this time around, he's as hard as stone.

Ignoring the screamed demands of the hellion in my ear, I roll onto my opposite hip, so I can nuzzle into his chest. Halfway around, my breath hitches. His eyes are open, staring straight at me. Even being drunk can't hide the admiration in them.

When he glides his index finger down my right cheek, every fine hair on my body prickles. The shift of air between us is almost palpable. When he adjusts his position to perch himself above me, his hair falls into his face. He's overdue for a trim, but nothing can take away from the sheer brilliance of his handsome face as he stares down at me with needy, hungry eyes.

Desire tightens my core when he rocks his hips forward. The crown of his thick cock rubs along my panties, inspiring a breathless moan to part my lips. Hearing the need in my voice, he yanks my sleeping shirt over my head before sliding my panties down my thighs. His warm breaths pebble my skin with goosebumps when he places feather-like kisses from my neck to my collarbone before coming to a stop at my aching-with-desire breasts. Unlike the many times we've slept together, his pace is slow and more controlled.

After rolling his tongue around my nipple, he draws it into his mouth. A grunted moan tears from my throat when he guides me toward climax by using nothing but his talented mouth. I've never orgasmed just from having my nipples stimulated, but if my shuddering thighs are anything to go by, Jacob is about to achieve the unachievable.

I have no idea what the fuck is going on. Usually, I'd be begging for him to increase his pace, but now I'm relishing every gentle suck and tweak. I've never been coiled so tight, even with him going at a slow, tender pace.

Any further thoughts on my newfound weirdness halt when a familiar tingle brews low in my gut. As every nerve in my body sparks, my breathing levels, and a low, shuddering moan escapes my parted lips. He did it. He brought me to climax by only fondling my breasts, and the simplicity doesn't dampen it in the slightest. It's the most intense orgasm I've ever had. I feel like I'm drunk, even without touching a drop of alcohol, and my entire body is shaking.

After guiding me down from my awe-inspiring climax with gentle nibbles and teasing teeth grazes, he slithers his hand down to cup my pussy. Air whistles between his teeth when he feels how wet I am. I'm more than ready for the next phase of our night, and clearly so is he when he snags a condom from my bedside table to roll it down his magnificent cock. Even seeing him do the same mundane task hundreds of times the past two years doesn't weaken my interest. I'm still astounded—by both him and his cock.

He nestles his cock between the folds of my pussy before raising his eyes to mine. My heart beats double. Something in his eyes has changed. The cheeky spark that regularly fires in them is still present, but something stronger, more tangible is lighting them tonight.

"Ready?"

With my mind still in a lust cloud, words are eluding me, so I nod instead. I take in the first five inches of his cock without hesitating, but the slow sheath of his last few inches has my eyes fluttering closed. It is impossible to act impassively when you're this full, and don't even get me started on when his crown hits my cervix. Most girls run for the hills when pain sparks through their wombs. I'm not most girls. I love that he can fill me like no one else can. I can't take all of him—*unfortunately*—but what I can feels so fucking good.

Realizing he's reached a point where he can't go any further, he slowly withdraws before re-entering me at the same painstakingly slow pace. When he does the same thing another four times, I wrap my legs around his waist, then dig my heels into his glorious ass, urging him to go faster.

He scoops his arm around my back to raise my hips from the bed so he can take me deeper, but he denies my request to go faster with a shake of his head. "Not tonight, Lola. I'm not fucking you tonight."

You'd think his words would have my bitchy claws spiked, but surprisingly, they don't. Don't ask me why, because even I'm confused by my reaction.

Confident he'd never leave me hanging, I loosen my grip around his hips before sealing my lips over his. Our kiss is as slow as the pace he's fucking me, but it takes nothing away from our exchange. I'm the fullest I've ever been—and I'm not just talking about my pussy.

He rocks into me on repeat, his pace quick enough for my second climax to build, but slow to ensure me he isn't fucking me. I'm shocked. I never knew you could achieve such mind-spiraling emotions while fucking at a leisurely pace. I've always been a girl who likes to fuck—the harder, the better—but now I'm wondering what I missed out on by not slowing things down. There's such a raw, carnal feeling associated with... with... *making love.*

My pupils dilate to the size of saucers. *Oh my god. Is that what Jacob is doing? Is he making love to me?*

When I seek confirmation from his eyes, desire rockets through my body. His eyes tell me everything I need to know. He's making love to me. If his slow, perfect strokes aren't enough evidence, the devoted look in his eyes is a sure-fire sign.

My entire body quakes, not only gobsmacked that I'm making love and enjoying it, but because of the core-shattering climax hitting me without warning. My pussy ripples around Jacob's cock as a low, shallow moan simpers from my lips. I claw at his back as I struggle to find my way out of an earth-shattering orgasm. It's a long, terrifying two minutes.

"What the hell was that?" I mumble when I've returned from hysteria.

Jacob smiles a full-toothed grin. "It's called making love, and I'm planning to do that to you for several more hours tonight, so you better hold on tight, C.T, because things are about to get rowdy."

THE NEXT MORNING, nearly comatose from sexual exhaustion, I pretend I can't feel Jacob's heated gaze roaming over my body. I'm still recouping from the inconceivable number of orgasms that ripped through me last night, so I need more sleep. At least an hour or fifty. Then I'll need just as long to comprehend how making love can invoke such awe-inspiring feeling.

I'm stunned—ecstatic—but still stunned.

Jacob doesn't buy my poor acting skills. "Stop faking it."

I have no clue how he knows, but he can tell when I'm awake even before I've opened my eyes. "Shh."

I roll over to burrow my thumping head into his chest. Bad move. He's still shirtless, meaning my eyes can't help but pop open to drink in the visually satisfying image of his naked torso. His body is a masterpiece that deserves more than a double take.

After drinking him in like an alcoholic chugging down a can of beer, I lift my eyes to his face. I groan at his bright smile. I have no clue why he's so chipper this early in the morning. He should have a hangover—a massive one.

"Say it again."

I cock my brow, confused. "Shh," I repeat, assuming that's what he means.

It isn't. "Not that." The smile on his face switches to a serious smirk. "Say what you said last night." He scoots down until we're eye to eye. "The words you whispered when we were leaving Noah and Emily's wedding."

My eyes open wide as a brutal grunt steals every drop of moisture from my mouth.

He remembered.

CHAPTER FIFTY-SIX

JACOB

Twelve months later...

"You do it like this." I lower three of Maddie's chubby fingers, leaving her index and middle finger poking up. "Peace, man."

She blows a sloppy raspberry. Spit sails into the air, but I know the real reason for her joy; she appreciates my efforts to show her the peace sign.

"You're teaching her the wrong finger."

My eyes float up in just enough time to witness Slater get a nasty stink-eye from Emily. Her gaze is so hot, the marshmallow fondue on the cupcakes she's replenishing almost melts. With her gaze devoted solely to Slater, I tuck away Maddie's index finger before directing her hand toward Slater.

"That one is just for Uncle Slater... "

My words trail off when Noah's abrupt entrance into the family room of his cabin has him stumbling onto me showing his one-year-old daughter how to flip the bird. He curses under his breath before handing Emily the napkins he's now clutching for dear life.

"You'll save Unky Jake, won't you?"

Maddie blows another raspberry—all over my cheek this time around.

"Give her to me before you ruin her for eternity."

Lola steals Maddie off my lap before I can protest that she's more of a bad influence than me. She must have sewn the outfit she gifted Maddie today because I've never seen stripper outfits at Baby Gap. Today is Maddie's first birthday. She was born the day after Noah and Emily's wedding, or, as I prefer to call it, the day following Lola's admission of love.

Twelve months have flown by since then, but I still recall the petrified look on Lola's face when I requested she repeat what she said. She was the most scared I'd ever seen her, but that didn't stop her from pretending she never said anything. Mercifully, I knew she was full of shit. No amount of alcohol would make me forget hearing those three little words for the first time. They were the reason I spent half my night ensuring she knew how deeply they impacted me. We didn't fuck that night. We made love. And we have a good dozen or more times since then.

Did she repeat those three little words? Yes, she did... after I sexually tortured them out of her. Now I have the pleasure of hearing them once, sometimes even twice a day. It never gets old.

It's been a hectic, crazy twelve months. Today is the first time all the old gang has gathered in one room since Maddie was born. A few months after Maddie's birth, Noah and his bandmates went on tour. Not long after that, I started fighting again.

I thought my fighting dreams were destroyed after being put on probation for assaulting Callum, but Lola and Hank found a loophole in the system, so once my probation was over for attacking the cameraman who tried to get photos of Noah in a coma, I was allowed to fight again.

Climbing back up the ladder has been a long process, but every fight I win puts me another step closer to securing a rematch against The Constrictor. Although Lola knows the real reason I want to be on the top rung, she still supports me. She always watches me train, and sometimes she's my sparring partner in the ring. We bounce off each other. I use her as motivation to fuel my revenge, and she uses the tricks I taught her in the self-defense class she runs at Hank's Gym for battered woman.

When she first started, Lola, Hank, and I made up more than half her class, but as the months went on, and word got out that a woman was teaching the classes, the numbers soared. If they continue to grow at the rate they have the past six months, she'll need to look at hiring another instructor.

Lola's non-profit business adventure isn't the only one going gangbusters the past twelve months. Hank's gym is kicking ass as well. His clientele are so diverse, there's no chance his doors will close anytime soon. He's putting the profits to good use. He has his own little house in Ravenshoe and is often included in family events like today—although I'm sure he wishes he wasn't when he notices my hand getting a little friendly with Lola's ass.

He still thinks Lola is my weak spot, but he's also aware my wish to succeed in the cage doesn't solely revolve around revenge. Lola still works at Pete's bar, her self-defense class is run out of her own pocket, and we still live in her run-down apartment in the middle of the 'burbs. Being the champion in my field will give me the means to spoil her like she deserves.

I could give her the world now if I had kept the money Noah sneakily placed in my bank account every month. It took me longer than I care to admit to figure out why the nest egg I built fighting with Isaac had grown larger than I expected. The reason was only discovered when Lola noticed the synchronized deposits at the same time on the same day every month. It was 3:43 PM on the seventh—the exact day and time Noah slid into the backseat of my dad's car, shivering like he was trekking through snow without boots.

Although I appreciate he was looking out for me, I immediately had a check drawn up in his name. Noah worked for everything he has earned, and I wanted to do the same. When he refused to take back the check, I told him I'd give it to his mother. He snatched it out of my hand so fast, it almost ripped in two.

When Lola, Emily, and Maddie go into the kitchen to get Maddie a drink, Noah joins me at the side of the room. "Were you teaching my daughter the finger?"

"No. I'd never do such a thing."

He chuckles while rolling his eyes. After ensuring the coast is still clear, he leans in close to my side. "Did you get it?"

I run my hand over my pocket to ensure the ring box I'd placed in there earlier is still present before nodding.

"Are you crapping your pants?"

When I nod once again, Noah laughs. "What's the worst she can say—?"

"No?" I interrupt. *God, I really fucking hope she doesn't say no.*

Noah cocks a brow. "And where will that leave you?"

I look at him with a confused, almost constipated look on my face.

Spotting my turmoil, he strives to ease it. "Exactly where you are now."

That's easy for him to say. He got the lovey-dovey sister. I fell in love with the more stubborn, bossier, and opinionated version of his wife. Does that mean I wish Lola were more like Emily? Definitely not. One of the main things I love about her is that she doesn't take crap from anyone. She knows she won't please everyone, so she lives her life the way she wants. It doesn't make her selfish or a bitch; it makes her smart. The world we live in is ruthless, so Lola's ways of dealing with things are perfect.

"People will either love you or hate you. As long as you get an even number of people in each column, your life will turn out okay."

I couldn't agree with her more, and I'm so fucking grateful I'm in the column of people who love her. Thankfully, she loves me back.

LATER THAT EVENING, back in our apartment, Lola cocks her hip before thrusting the pants I left in the middle of the floor my way. "Do you have to leave your pants on the floor? My apartment is tiny. Two more steps, and you would have reached the laundry hamper."

I continue flipping through the television channels, pretending I'm not on the verge of coronary failure. From the corner of my eye, I peer at her through lowered lashes. My inability to respond to her question nearly has her eyelids touching. I silently stalk her, praying she'll respond how she usually does. When she screws up her nose like a rabbit, I know she's close.

Come on, Lola, throw a tantrum.

My silent prayers get answered when she hooks my pants across the room. "I'm not your slave. Put *your* pants in the hamper."

Halfway across the living room, a black ring box darts out of my pocket. It drops to the floor in slow motion, capturing Lola's attention before she storms out of the room in a huff.

She twirls back around, her hand shooting up to her chest. I play it cool, even though I'm anything but. After glancing my way to see if I've noticed the ring—*I pretend I haven't*—she cautiously bends down to pick it up. My heart beating is the only audible noise when she slowly cranks it open. When the lid pops up, she takes in a sharp breath while I move into place.

"Don't freak out." I kneel in front of her, making her shocked gaze stray from the diamond solitaire ring in the box to me. "I know you don't do hearts and flowers, but I've loved you from the moment I saw you. I want you to be my wife and the mother of my children, even more than I want you to have my last name." I gather her other hand in mine. I'm so jittery with nerves, I need two hands to hold her dainty one. "If you accept this proposal, I promise this will be the last romantic gesture I'll ever do for the rest of our life."

Hope clutches my insides when she smirks. It's not the smile I was aiming for, but it's better than a flat out, "No!"

"I'm not asking you to marry me today; I'm just asking you to marry me *one day*." I remove the ring box from her deathly tight grip.

"Will you please do me the honor of becoming my wife, next week, next month, next year or within the next decade?"

The silence in the room is near deafening as I wait for her to reply. She's said many times that she has no intention of getting married, but I want her to be my wife. I want her to have my last name, and I want my ring on her finger, declaring to the world she's taken.

"I love you, Lola." My declaration nearly has me missing the slightest bob of her head. "Yes?"

"Yes," she repeats as tears spring into her eyes.

I stare at her with bewilderment, certain I heard her wrong. She just said yes, didn't she?

Laughing at my shocked expression, she lowers herself to her knees before slapping my cheeks with her hands. "Yes, Jacob. Yes!"

I'm so overwhelmed with excitement, I wrap my arms around her before she's prepared. We hit the floor with a thud, but Lola doesn't mind. She giggles before requesting I roll because she can't breathe. When I do as asked, the glimmer of a one-carat diamond catches my eye.

The ring! I'm supposed to put the ring on her finger.

After gathering the ring box in my hand, I clumsily remove the creation my dad helped me choose last week, then raise my eyes to Lola's. Her smile competes with the moon when I slip the ring on her finger.

It glistens as brightly as the tears in her eyes when she murmurs, "It's beautiful. Classic yet refined." — *Much like its owner.* — "I love it, Jacob."

When she straddles my lap to show me just how much, I make love to my soon-to-be wife.

CHAPTER FIFTY-SEVEN

LOLA

Six months later...

The day Jacob has been waiting for is finally here. His rematch with The Constrictor will be held tonight in Hopeton. The winner, whom I have no doubt will be Jacob, will be crowned national champion in our region. That will give him an instant green light to fight in the professional league. Jacob is giving it his all to win. His workout regimen the past year has been brutal. He's the fittest I've ever seen him. There's not an ounce of fat on his body. Believe me, I've checked every inch of him—more than once.

"Are you sure you can't cancel your class today to come to the arena with Hank and me?" Jacob asks as he paces into our kitchen.

I shake my head. "No, sorry, I can't. Those ladies rely on me. I can't just cancel on them."

He jerks up his chin in understanding, but his eyes still show the disappointment he'll never express. He knows how much the ladies in my class mean to me because he saw firsthand my reaction when I volunteered with him at Hopeton House one weekend. At the start, I was confused as to why children were living in a home if they had parents, then I realized most of the children's mothers lived on the streets, and over half were victims of domestic violence.

With memories of Jacob and Hank teaching me how to defend myself filtering through my mind, I offered Chloe's mom a private lesson. I was shocked when she turned up the following weekend with two women in tow. Since then, the number of attendees has climbed tenfold. I don't make any money teaching them what Jacob and Hank taught me, but the reward I get seeing their confidence soar is plenty of compensation for my time.

"I'll be there as soon as my class is over. That'll be good a good hour or two before the first bell."

Jacob kisses my temple, revealing he's pleased with my negotiation. He's not surprised, just pleased. I've matured a lot the past few years. It's hard not to when you surround yourself with people like Jacob and Hank every day. They kind of rub off on you. Does that mean I no longer have a resting bitch face? Hell no! But Jacob loves me for who I am, so he puts up with all my prickly personalities.

Jacob stops guzzling orange juice straight out of the carton. "Just don't be late. You know how much Hank hates tardiness."

After rolling my eyes, I bridge the distance between us. "I was late once." I hold my index finger in the air to amplify my reply. "And you've never let me live it down."

When I balance on my tippy toes to give him a chaste peck on his juice-flavored mouth, he talks over my lips. "Have you decided on a date yet?"

He chuckles when my teeth get friendly with his lower lip. He's asked this exact friggin' question every day for the past six months. Although my ego loves his eagerness, I'm five seconds from killing him.

My brow cocks when a brilliant idea pops into my head. "Actually, I have." I let him stew a little before saying, "When you become the heavyweight champion of the world, I'll become your wife that same week."

"Deal."

The swiftness of his reply knocks the wind from my lungs. My eyes bounce between him when he holds his hand out for me to shake on our agreement. My head is screaming at me to renegotiate, but my heart makes me reach out for his hand without a single objection.

Confident he has me right where he wants me, Jacob waggles his brows. "You do realize, when I win this fight tonight, I can contend for the heavyweight championship in less than six months?"

My eyes bulge. "What? Are you serious?"

"I've never been more serious in my life." He slaps my backside before strutting into our bedroom. Yes, I said strut. "You better get planning, baby, because in six months' time, you're going to be my wife."

His tone alone reveals he'll train even harder now. He's not leaving that cage without the championship belt, and considering I never back out of a deal, in six months, I'll most likely be his wife. A part of me is petrified, but the other half—the sentimental mucky side —is a tad bit excited.

"ARE you sure you don't want me to clear away the mats?"

My eyes stray to Lydia, Chloe's mom. "It's fine. It'll only take a minute; then I'm out of here."

We've just finished our final defense class for today. It was my biggest yet, with thirty women in attendance. Lydia has become a close confidant of mine the past year, so she helped me run today's class with the hope of taking over the reins of a class or two in the next few weeks. Things have been tough for Lydia, but ever since Maggie offered her a job at Mavericks, things have picked up. She and Chloe no longer live at Hopeton House, and with Michael's help, she's hoping to soon regain sole custody of Chloe.

"See you next week."

Lydia waits for me to nod before heading for the exit of Hank's gym. After rolling up the mats and placing them back on the shelf, I scan the area. Hank's gym has changed so much the past twelve months. The old, rusty equipment has been updated with sleek new machines, and a new set of ropes and a new mat make the boxing ring look brand new. Even the showers in the locker rooms have been retiled.

Although cosmetics have given Hank's gym a slick new look, it still holds the funky smell that makes everyone's stomach lurch when they enter. Jacob isn't convinced, but I'm certain the scent is a combination of hidden gym socks stuffed at the back of the lockers and sweat. Hank swears it's the smell of hard work and determination. Whatever it is, it's gross, and even years later, my stomach still protests when I walk through the large glass door.

I crank my neck when the bell above Hank's gym jangles. "What did you forget this time?"

The mirth in my tone is pushed aside when the face I'm expecting to see isn't there. Lydia isn't standing in the entranceway of Hank's gym. Callum is.

My heart beats furiously when he fixes the lock into place. After flipping the sign to advise the gym is now closed, he pivots on his feet to face me. "Hello, Lola."

His brittle tone makes butterflies bunch in my stomach. Although unnerved, I'm confident I have what's needed to take him down. If he attempts anything remotely intimidating, he'll be on his ass faster than I can snap my fingers.

Callum's eyes drift from my clenched fists to my face, taking in my gym shorts and crop top on the way. When our eyes collide, I strengthen my stance. He doesn't need to voice his disdain about my outfit for me to hear it. His slit gaze and ticking jaw tell me everything I need to know.

"Violence won't be necessary... Or I might need to use this."

My heart sinks into my gut when he drags his index finger along his nose. His drug use is nothing new; rumors have circulated for months that he's back on the wagon. It's the gun in his hand that has my heart stuttering.

He may be double my weight, but I still had the ability to take him down. I can't say the same about his gun.

"Why don't you come give your boyfriend a kiss?"

Keeping my eyes firmly planted on the gun, I shake my head. His hand is trembling so badly, I'm afraid he might accidentally shoot me. "I'm good here."

Unhappy with my response, he storms my way. Air hisses between my teeth when he fists my hair so roughly, he yanks many strands from my scalp. That's not the worst of it. With my hands needed to save my hair, my mouth is defenseless to his infiltration. He seals his lips over mine in under a second before he slides his tongue along them. My stomach threatens to spill from the disgusting stench of his breath. It's worse than any roadkill I've smelled.

When several attempts to poke his tongue between my hard-lined lips fail, he inches back before dropping his bloodshot eyes to mine. They're utterly soulless, like peering into a bottomless dark pit.

He stabs the barrel of his gun into my right ribcage, demanding my utmost devotion. "Where's your phone?"

Too breathless to speak, my eyes stray to my bag sitting open on the gym floor. Noticing the direction of my gaze, he frees my hair from his grip to stalk to my bag. Knowing this is my only chance to escape, I sprint for the exit as fast as my quivering legs can take me.

Just as I reach the front door, gunfire rattles throughout Hank's gym. A squeal emits from my lips as I freeze like a statue. There's a bullet stuck in the drywall a mere inch from my head. I'm only alive because Callum has a bad aim. Next time, I may not be so lucky.

I signal with my arms that I'm surrendering before turning back around. This time, Callum doesn't try to hide his gun. He keeps it pointed at my head, as angry now as he was when I refused his kiss. When he nudges his head to the bench he's standing next to, I hesitantly pace toward him. Being the sole hostage of a madman isn't ideal, but when it's your only option, you must run with it.

Every step I make is done with a shudder; I just don't know if I'm shaking in fear or from the massive surge of adrenaline racing through my veins. After sitting on the bench, I raise my eyes to Callum. I'm quick enough to see the butt of his gun careening toward my temple, but not quick enough to stop it from knocking me out.

CHAPTER FIFTY-EIGHT

JACOB

I push my cell phone close to my ear when Lola's voicemail answers my call. "Hey, Lola, it's me. Where are you? You're not sleeping again, are you?"

I try to downplay my worry with a chuckle, but the knot in my stomach can't be denied. Lola's last class usually finishes by three PM, so I'm somewhat surprised she hasn't arrived at the arena yet. When I teased her this morning about being late, I was just playing. She was only late the day I bombarded her with the kids from Hopeton House, but since she doesn't have many flaws, I tease her repeatedly about the few she does have.

When I lower my phone from my ear, Hank stops taping my knuckles. "She's still not answering?"

"No." The concern in Hank's voice echoes in mine. Even with us arriving hours before everyone else, Lola usually hangs with us, so I'm not the only one noticing her absence. "Can you check the arena? Maybe she's already in her seat? Noah and the boys are here, so maybe she went straight to them?"

Nodding, Hank cuts the tape before pushing it down until it sits flush. "I'll take care of this while you get your head in the game. Now is not the time for your mind to wander. Curtis may be an asshole, but he was trained by the best. If you walk into the cage distracted, you won't walk back out."

Hank waits for me to jerk up my chin before exiting the locker room. I jump to my feet to prep my muscles for the fight I've been trying to secure for years. There's no way I'm walking out of that cage without a victory. The time has come to teach Curtis a lesson, and I look forward to teaching him the hard way. Then, once I'm crowned Heavyweight Champion of the World, I'll make Lola my wife. That's my prime motivation—making Lola solely mine. I don't want the fame or the glory. I just want her.

When we made our deal this morning, part of me thought she knew how long the process would take. She's such an integral part of my team, people refer to her as my manager, so she knows how the schedule works. She just doesn't want to admit she wants to be my wife sooner than she originally planned. I don't mind. I convinced her time and time again the past three and a half years that she wants me more than she realizes, so I have no qualms doing it again.

My head slings to the side when Noah enters the locker room on Hank's heels. "You ready for this?"

"Sure am."

My cockiness slumps when Hank answers my curious gaze with a shake of his head. My eyes drift to the clock hanging on the wall. It's nearly eight PM. Even if traffic was bumper-to-bumper the whole way here, Lola should have been here hours ago.

Upon noticing my concerned face, Noah asks, "What's up?"

"Lola hasn't turned up yet," I answer. "Have you seen her?"

He shakes his head. "I assumed she was with you."

Worry churns my stomach. "Can you call Em to see if she's heard from her?"

While yanking his phone out of his pocket, Noah nods.

Emily wished me luck tonight but said she couldn't watch me fight. I assured her it's a professional sport with rules and shit, but she still looked sick with worry that I'd get hurt, so she and Jenni are preparing Mavericks for my celebration party, where I intend to repay Slater for spiking my drink at Noah and Emily's wedding.

I watch Noah carefully when he stores his phone back in his pocket. "Em hasn't heard from her."

"Fuck, then where could she be?"

Noah shrugs, unsure what he could say to calm me down. He freaks if he can't reach Emily, so he knows all too well what I'm going through.

Hank slaps my shoulder. "She'll be here soon, but until then, you need to get your head in the game." His tone firms when he says, "This is why you shouldn't have gotten yourself a weak spot."

"Don't go acting like she isn't your weak spot too, Hank." He loves Lola as if she's his daughter.

"She is, but I'm not the one about to go into a fight with my head shoved up my ass."

Noah coughs, hiding his chuckle. When I give him a nasty stink-eye, he holds his hands in front of his body while retreating from the locker room by walking backward. "If she turns up, I'll send you a message."

FOR THE NEXT THIRTY MINUTES, I continue my warm-up routine with my eyes locked on my phone. I pray for it to ring or buzz with a text, but nothing but silence surrounds me.

Just as I finalize a set of reps with Hank, it finally rings. I dive for it so fast, I nearly barrel Hank over. He excuses my bad manners without a word when he sees the name flashing across the screen of my phone. It's Lola.

"Jesus, Lola, you scared the fucking shit out of me—"

I stop talking when a voice I don't immediately recognize interrupts, "That's the point. We want you scared."

The pulse thrumming in my neck is audible in my words. "Who is this? Where's Lola?"

Hank balances on his tippy toes so he can press his ear against my phone. He stops trying to eavesdrop when I lower my phone to turn on the speaker.

"She's here with me, though she can't talk right now."

When he sniffs after laughing, it dawns on me who it is. "Callum." Hank's fretful eyes snap to mine. "If you fuckin' touch her, I'll kill you."

"I won't touch a hair on her head if you do as instructed."

He's lying. I don't know how I know that. I just do.

"How can we trust Lola is with you? You could have just stolen her phone."

A ruffling sound is closely followed by my phone receiving a picture message. When I click on the image, my heart drops into my stomach. Lola has a gag in her mouth. Her eyes are open wide but woozy. That might have something to do with the large bump on her forehead.

Anger floods my veins, turning my blood potent. I will kill him this time.

I nearly throw up when Hank points to something in the corner of the picture. There's a gun pointed at Lola's head.

Fuck!

With words eluding me, Hank takes over the negotiations. "What do you want?"

"Jacob needs to throw the fight. Not in the first round. It has to look legitimate."

"And then?"

"Then I walk away and leave her as is." I wait, knowing there's more. I'm right. "But... if he fails to impress the crowd, I'll blow her brains out."

"I'll do it." My voice is stricken with fear. "Let her go; I'll keep my word, I promise, but you need to let her go."

"No can do. She won't leave my sight until the fight is over. Once it's done—*right*—I'll text you her location."

When he disconnects our call, I run a shaky hand over my head. I want to kill him, or second-best, his brother who's waiting for me out in the cage, but if I do that, he'll hurt Lola. I can't let that happen, so as much as this kills me, I'll throw the fight. I'd do anything to save Lola. Anything at all.

My hand falls from my head when a fight promoter pops his head into the locker room. "It's time to go."

While sucking in a long, ragged breath, I follow him out of the room. Hank shadows closely behind me, removing my phone from my hand and replacing it with a pair of gloves. When the promotor stops just outside the arena to wait for me to be introduced, I'm too impatient to wait. I make a beeline for the cage, my heart pumping in tune with the music booming around me. Curtis is in the cage, awaiting my arrival. Even the officials knew he wasn't the drawcard for our act. The fans are here for me, not a man unworthy of their praise.

When I enter the cage, Curtis lifts his gaze to me. He has a condescending smirk etched on his mouth, convinced he has the world at his feet. He does—for now. Once Lola is safe, all bets are off.

The crowd boos at my unusual bad sportsmanship when I refuse to tap gloves with Curtis. I'll make it up to them later, but right now, right here, nothing but Lola is on my mind.

When the referee announces the start of the fight, I slam Curtis with a brutal left and right combination. Callum said the crowd had to get a show. I'm keeping my end of the bargain, dispelling my anger over seeing a gun pointed at Lola's head.

Curtis stumbles back, his glare more worried than cocky. When the first round comes to an end, and Curtis is sporting a black eye and a split lip, he stares me down across the cage with nothing but hate in his narrowed gaze. While returning his glare, I plan my next attack. Before I have all my stones lined up, he makes a throat-slitting gesture, harnessing any desires of a beatdown. I swore years ago to protect Lola any way I could. I plan to keep my promise.

I protect my face as much as I can during the second round, but I grant Curtis unlimited access to my body. He instills punch after punch after punch until we're dragged apart by the referee. The third round follows a similar routine... until I become distracted by Hank moving away from Noah in the front row. Curtis uses my distraction to his advantage. He strikes my left temple hard, sending me to the ground with a sickening thud.

When I stand, my vision blurs, and my stomach lurches.

"Do you want to tap out?" The referee holds my gloves in his hands as he coerces my eyes to him. "You with me?"

"I'm good."

My brain rattles in my head when I shake it to clear the fog inside. The referee watches me cautiously when I make my way to Curtis with my hands held high to protect my face. He pummels me the entire round, hitting me with a grueling combination of swings, kicks, and tumbles. He works me over real good, but it's got nothing on the mess crippling my heart.

Just before the bell rings, announcing the end of the third round, Curtis whispers, "Next round," instructing it's time for me to throw the fight.

When I stumble to the edge of the cage, Hank doesn't mop up the blood streaming down my cheeks, he just points to something on my phone. "She's at the gym."

Through the blood obscuring my vision, I take in the photo Callum sent me with more diligence. I don't see what Hank's showing me until he taps the screen twice, zooming in on the smallest portion of a Hank's Gym logo in the background.

"Finish him." Hank's voice is a dangerous snarl. "Then go get our girl. Noah is waiting out front."

My first thoughts are to leave now, but if I leave Curtis conscious, there's a chance he'll alert Callum of our arrival before we get there. I can't let that happen. I have to take him down first.

I'll try not to enjoy it too much.

I return my eyes to Hank. "If he wakes up, don't let him leave this cage."

"I won't; I promise," he immediately replies.

As soon as the bell dings, signaling the start of the fourth round, I charge for Curtis. When my fist makes a sickening crunch with his left cheek, shock morphs onto his face a mere second before he plummets onto the mat. I'm on him in a second, punishing him as I plan to punish his brother.

The crowd leaps to their feet, nearly drowning out Curtis's snarl, "She's dead."

If he's hoping his threat will hinder my onslaught on his face, he's shit out of luck. I hit him with everything I've got, only stopping when his eyes roll into the back of his head, and the ref is dragging me away from him. He's down for the count, and I'm out of the ring.

I sprint past the spectators screaming my name before darting by the ones still looking for their seats, unaware the fight is over. I run and run and run until I dive through the cracked open door of Noah's truck. "Go, go, go!"

Noah plants his foot to the floor, rocketing us out of the parking lot with squealing tires and a plume of smoke. I've never seen him drive so fast before. He weaves in and out of traffic, pushing his truck to its absolute limit, helping us arrive in Ravenshoe in under fifteen minutes. Adrenaline from the fight is still coursing through my veins —thank fuck—otherwise, I might have crumbled in fear by now. Just the thought of Lola being hurt utterly guts me.

When Noah's truck mounts the curb at the front of Hank's Gym, I throw open my door, clamber out, then sprint for the entrance. I stop frozen halfway in when gunfire booms through the silence of the night. It's followed by a scream I know all too well.

With my heart in my throat, I continue my mission. I beg on repeat for Lola to be safe, for her not to be hurt by the gunfire, but when I scan the gym floor, I'm afraid my worst fear has come true. There's a body lying on the ground Lola and I wrestle on multiple times a week. It's not moving.

CHAPTER FIFTY-NINE

LOLA

An hour earlier...

I blink my eyes, clearing my blurred vision. I can't see two feet in front of me, but it doesn't take me long to realize I'm at Hank's gym. The smell is undeniable.

Just as my vision clears enough to see blobs of color, a voice that forever haunts my dreams trickles into my ears. "She's here with me, though she can't talk right now."

As my memories roll back, I take in my surrounding through blurry eyes. The hardness under my thighs reveals I'm still on the wooden bench Callum demanded I sit on, but the lack of natural light means the low-hanging sun has been replaced with an inky black sky.

I must have been knocked out for a while as it was a little before three when Lydia left. Callum took advantage of the time. My hands are bound in front of my body, and he removed anything that could be used as a weapon to the other side of the room. I could commend him on his smarts if I didn't hate him so much.

When Callum notices I'm half-lucid, he taps his gun on his lips, demanding I remain quiet before devoting his attention back to my phone attached to his ear. "I won't touch a hair on her head if you do as instructed."

My pupils widen when he lowers his gun to my temple before snapping a photo of me with my phone. After a whoosh sounds through my ears, he squashes my phone back to his ear. "Jacob needs to throw the fight. Not in the first round. It has to look legitimate."

I silently pray for Jacob not to believe a word he says. He's not like Jacob. He can't be trusted.

"Then I walk away and leave her as is." He makes a *pop* noise with his mouth when he pretends to shoot me. If the smile on his face is anything to go by, he's been fantasizing about doing precisely that for months. "But if he fails to impress the crowd, I'll blow her brains out."

His smirk reveals he intends to follow through on his threat no matter the outcome of the fight. If proof of life wasn't needed to get Jacob to agree to his plans, I'm confident I wouldn't still be breathing right now. That's how unrepentant Callum's eyes are.

"Once it's done *right*, I'll text you her location."

He just made a huge mistake. I didn't know Jacob was unaware of my location until now, so I'm more than willing to fix that. I scream with all my might, getting out "Ha—" before Callum silences my screams by pinching the skin between my brows with his gun before disconnecting his call. He stares down at me, his hate unmissable.

"You just went and got your boyfriend killed. If he doesn't turn up for his fight, he won't make it out of the stadium. There's big money riding on him losing tonight, and the men who put it on him aren't as nice as me."

When I suck in a sharp breath, the gag in my mouth lodges in the back of my throat. I cough, panicked I'm moments from asphyxiation. My teary response amuses Callum. He watches my struggles with a ghost of a smile cracked on his lips, loving that I'm walking myself to my grave.

My lungs burn in fear when my flaring nostrils fail to suck in the air needed to keep them functioning. I've never lacked confidence, but I'm reasonably sure I'm in the midst of a panic attack. No matter how hard my nostrils suck, I can't get enough air. I feel like I'm suffocating, like I'm literally seconds from death.

Just before I fully tiptoe into hysteria, my savior finally arrives. It isn't who I'm hoping. Callum tugs the gag out of my mouth a mere second before I give in to the darkness encroaching me. Although my first thoughts should center around replenishing my lungs with oxygen, my head takes on a different plight.

"Please let me go." He could have let me die, but he didn't. That means somewhere in the bottomless pit in his eyes is the boy I once knew. "Please, Callum. I won't tell anyone what happened. We'll pretend as if today never existed."

When I place my hands over his to enhance my pledge, the light above our heads sends rainbow hues dancing across my face. They're from the light capturing the diamond engagement ring on my finger.

Callum's calm, cool composure cracks before my eyes when he unearths the real reason for the extra gleam in my eyes. He's the most unhinged I've ever seen him, even more reckless than he was the day he choked me.

"Is that a..." He taps his gun against his temple, like he can't force the words "engagement ring" out of his mouth. I realize that's the case when he roars, "I thought you didn't want to get married?!"

"I didn't."

Even a stranger wouldn't miss the words I didn't express. I never wanted to get married, until I met Jacob. He makes me crave things I never knew I wanted.

"I love—"

Before all the words can leave my lips, the butt of Callum's gun skims across my temple for the second time.

I DON'T KNOW how much time passes before I'm awoken by someone yanking me to a standing position. Once I'm on my feet, Callum plasters himself to my back before his gun digs in my temple. Although I can't see him, I know it is him. Nothing can replicate the scent of a deranged man.

The reason for Callum's startled response comes to light when my eyes float up from my shoes. Ryan is entering the gym via the door I left open during my attempt to flee. He has his gun drawn, and he's peering down the sight.

"Drop your weapon."

Callum drags me closer to the mats Jacob and I have wrestled on many times the past two years. "Put down your gun, or I'll fuckin' shoot her." He digs his gun into my ribs so severely, tears fill my eyes. In the silence, I hear him inch back the trigger, preparing to shoot me. "This is your last warning. I'll do it. I'll kill her."

"Then I'll kill you. Is that what you want, Callum? Do you want to leave the legacy of a murderer?"

With his eyes locked on me but his gun focused on Callum, Ryan bobs his head to my shoes. I'm certain he's trying to signal something to me, but with my brain fritzed, it takes me longer to work out than I care to admit.

When he steps forward with a big stomp, I finally understand. He's encouraging me to use the skills I've been teaching the past twelve months—to defend myself against my attacker.

Five seconds after I sneakily nod, Ryan yells, "Now!"

I stomp down on Callum's foot with all my might before ramming my elbow in his ribs. After throwing my head back so it collides with his nose, I sprint toward Ryan as fast as my quivering legs can move. A gun being dislodged rattles me for all of two seconds, but I keep running. I'd rather be shot trying to flee than die a coward.

When I crash into Ryan with an *oomph*, a tormented scream shreds through my ears. It isn't coming from the man Ryan just gunned down. It's from a man who made me realize I'm worthy of the greatest battle—as is he.

"Lola!"

As Ryan spins me away from Callum's lifeless body slumped on the floor, Jacob's grief-stricken face presents. Moisture is glistening in his eyes, and his face is as white as a ghost. When our eyes collide, he falls to his knees, sending three little tears trickling down his face.

"Jacob..."

I race to him, crashing into him so fiercely, we topple to the floor as hard as my belief I'd never love again was knocked out of the park.

"I love you, Jacob. I love you; I love you; I love you."

Today made me realize I don't tell him nearly enough how much I love him. So, from now on, every time the thought pops into my head, I'm going to say it out loud.

I loved him back then.

I love him now.

And I'll love him forever.

EPILOGUE
JACOB

Six months later...

Noah and Emily sprint down the aisle, their steps as fast as my heart is racing. "I told you we wouldn't miss it." Noah slings his arms around my shoulders. "Although a little more notice would have been nice."

"I had to get her down the aisle before she changed her mind."

Lola may now tell me multiple times a day that she loves me, but that doesn't mean she'd skip down the aisle without first putting up a protest.

"You look very dashing, Jacob." Emily replaces Noah's arms with her own. "Even if you're sporting a black eye in your wedding photos."

I waggle my brows, more than happy to have the photos retouched in exchange for holding Lola to the bet we made six months ago. Last night, I became the Heavyweight Champion of the

World. Today, I'm about to become Lola's husband. Can you guess which title I like the most?

Having the fight held in Vegas presented a perfect opportunity to get Lola down the aisle. I had planned to get married straight after being awarded the title, but Noah begged me to wait. He was performing in San Francisco at the same time my fight was being broadcast around the world. He hated missing my match, but the thought of missing my wedding was cutting him raw.

"I want to stand by your side like you have my entire life," he said last night when I called to tell him my plans.

The past six months have been some of the toughest in my life. Noah was at my side the entire time, as was my wife-to-be, so I couldn't deny his request.

Because the discharge of his weapon resulted in a death, Ryan was investigated by the Internal Affairs Department. He was cleared of all charges on the day Curtis's hearing began. Curtis faced charges for conspiracy to commit false imprisonment, kidnapping, and attempted murder. He was refused bail, and last month was found guilty by a jury of his peers. We won't know his sentence until later this week.

To say I'm incredibly proud of how Lola handled everything would be an understatement. She's been incredible. She testified for the DA, not once stumbling when Curtis glared at her in warning, before expanding her self-defense classes to include ways to disarm armed assailants. The past six months have been tough, but they proved what I've always known: there's no one stronger than the woman I'm about to marry.

When the celebrant joins us at the end of the aisle, Noah waggles his brows. "You ready?"

"I was born ready."

My eyes get a little misty when Slater, Marcus, Nick, and their partners mosey down the aisle to take a seat in the second row of pews. Noticing my shocked response, Noah slaps my shoulder. "You didn't think I'd let you get married without your family and friends in attendance, did you?"

Before I can answer him, my dad and a lady with ocean blue eyes walks down the aisle. She looks familiar, but I can't place her face. After greeting me with a hug and a whispered, "I'm proud of you, son," my dad guides his date to the front row. By the time Maggie, Ollie, Hank, and Lola's mom, Patrice, join the celebration, the little chapel we're getting married in is almost bursting at the seams.

While an Elvis impersonator serenades us with "Love Me Tender," I catch the first glimpse of Lola. She's rounding the corner on the arm of her dad, her eyes as wide and as glossy as mine. When her eyes clash with Hank in the front row, she motions for him to join her. He peers at me in shock, unsure what to do. I shrug before gesturing for him to do as Lola is requesting. He does, although hesitantly.

Once he joins Lola at the end of the aisle, she spins him around before looping her arm around his elbow. The smile on Hank's face when he realizes she wants him to walk her down the aisle along with her dad is priceless. He'll never admit it, but tears are welling in his eyes.

As they make their way down the aisle, I drink in my soon-to-be wife. She's wearing a smoking-hot white lace fitted mini dress that shows off her killer legs. Her hair is tousled, appearing as if we've just had a romp in the bedroom—it was in the backseat of a limo, but close enough—and her makeup is dark and smoky. She's fuckin' gorgeous, and she makes my dick twitch.

When I adjust myself, her smile makes the world fade away. It's just her and me, a cock tease and the man who'll never grow tired of her sexy goading.

Hank slaps my shoulder when they reach the end of the aisle, while Lola's dad places her hand in mine. When her eyes lift to mine, her teeth rake her red-painted lips. "Are you sure this is what you want, Jacob?"

The seductive sexiness of her question reveals my furrowed brows aren't required, but I can't hold back my worry. If she backs out now, I'll never recover.

My panic subsides when she murmurs, "I can't give you anything more than my friendship." That's the exact phrase she said to me over four years ago when she was still trying to deny her feelings for me.

With a smirk that gets her all hot and bothered, I say, "It's better than not having you in my life at all."

The gleam I saw in Lola's eyes mere minutes before we arrived at Bronte's Peak shines bright as she saucily winks. "Then let's be friends."

If the last four years are any indication of how she treats her friends, I'm going to be the best fucking friend she's ever had.

The end!

Part three in the Perception Series is Nick's book: <u>Taming Nick</u>

DON'T ASSUME *you already know his story. The peeks you got in Noah and Emily's book was only the beginning.*

Facebook: facebook.com/authorshandi

Instagram: instagram.com/authorshandi

Email: authorshandi@gmail.com

Reader's Group: bit.ly/ShandiBookBabes

Website: authorshandi.com

Newsletter: https://www.subscribepage.com/AuthorShandi

If you enjoyed this book - please leave a review.

ACKNOWLEDGMENTS

Once again, we have the acknowledgment page. I hate this part. Don't get me wrong, I'm forever grateful. I love my readers, family and friends more than words can express, but like everything in life, ensuring they know that is difficult. I'm not stubborn like Lola. I'm just... *stubborn*.

I guess I'll just keep it simple. Thank you! Thank you reading. Thank you for reviewing. And thank you for being you!

Much love,

Shandi xx

"At the end of the day, it isn't about how many breaths we take, but how many moments take our breath away." — Isaac, Enigma of Life.

ALSO BY SHANDI BOYES

Perception Series

Saving Noah (Noah & Emily)

Fighting Jacob (Jacob & Lola)

Taming Nick (Nick & Jenni)

Redeeming Slater (Slater and Kylie)

Saving Emily (Noah & Emily - Novella)

Wrapped Up with Rise Up (Perception Novella - should be read after the
Bound Series)

Enigma

Enigma (Isaac & Isabelle #1)

Unraveling an Enigma (Isaac & Isabelle #2)

Enigma The Mystery Unmasked (Isaac & Isabelle #3)

Enigma: The Final Chapter (Isaac & Isabelle #4)

Beneath The Secrets (Hugo & Ava #1)

Beneath The Sheets (Hugo & Ava #2)

Spy Thy Neighbor (Hunter & Paige)

The Opposite Effect (Brax & Clara)

I Married a Mob Boss (Rico & Blaire)

Second Shot (Hawke & Gemma)

The Way We Are (Ryan & Savannah #1)

The Way We Were (Ryan & Savannah #2)

Sugar and Spice (Cormack & Harlow)

Lady In Waiting (Regan & Alex #1)

Man in Queue (Regan & Alex #2)

Couple on Hold (Regan & Alex #3)

Enigma: The Wedding (Isaac and Isabelle)

Silent Vigilante (Brandon and Melody #1)

Hushed Guardian (Brandon & Melody #2)

Quiet Protector (Brandon & Melody #3)

Enigma: An Isaac Retelling

Twisted Lies (Jae & JR)

Bound Series

Chains (Marcus & Cleo #1)

Links (Marcus & Cleo #2)

Bound (Marcus & Cleo #3)

Restrain (Marcus & Cleo #4)

The Misfits (Dexter & Megan)

Russian Mob Chronicles

Nikolai: A Mafia Prince Romance (Nikolai & Justine #1)

Nikolai: Taking Back What's Mine (Nikolai & Justine #2)

Nikolai: What's Left of Me (Nikolai & Justine #3)

Nikolai: Mine to Protect (Nikolai & Justine #4)

Asher: My Russian Revenge (Asher & Zariah)

Nikolai: Through the Devil's Eyes (Nikolai & Justine #5)

Trey (Trey & K)

K: A Trey Sequel

The Italian Cartel

Dimitri

Roxanne

Reign

Mafia Ties (Novella)

Maddox

Demi

Rocco

Clover

Smith

RomCom Standalones

Just Playin' (Elvis & Willow)

Ain't Happenin' (Lorenzo & Skylar)

The Drop Zone (Colby & Jamie)

Very Unlikely (Brand New Couple)

False Start (Cash & McKayla)

Short Stories

Christmas Trio (Wesley, Andrew & Mallory -- short story)

Falling For A Stranger (Short Story)

One Night Only

Hotshot Boss (Octavia & Jack)

Hotshot Neighbour (Jess & Caleb)

The Bobrov Bratva

Wicked Intentions (Katie & Ghost)

Sinful Intentions (Alek & Ana)

Devious Intentions (Yev & ??)